Heroes in
Sworn Protector

JANIE CROUCH

B.J. DANIELS

TYLER ANNE SNELL

MILLS & BOON

First Published in Great Britain 2021
By Mills & Boon, an imprint of HarperCollins*Publishers,* Ltd
1 London Bridge Street, London, SE1 9GF

www.harpercollins.co.uk

HarperCollins*Publishers*
1st Floor, Watermarque Building,
Ringsend Road, Dublin 4, Ireland

HEROES IN HOT PURSUIT: SWORN PROTECTOR
© 2021 Harlequin Books S.A.

Protector's Instinct © 2017 Janie Crouch
Cardwell Christmas Crime Scene © 2016 Barbara Heinlein
Private Bodyguard © 2016 Tyler Anne Snell

ISBN: 978-0-263-30279-0

MIX
Paper from
responsible sources
FSC C007454

This book is produced from independently certified FSC™ paper to ensure responsible forest management.

For more information visit: www.harpercollins.co.uk/green

Printed and Bound in Spain using 100% Renewable electricity at CPI Black Print, Barcelona

PROTECTOR'S INSTINCT

JANIE CROUCH

This book is dedicated to Girl Tyler. It's wondrous to have a friend who can walk with me through this craziness known as—duh, duh, duh—writer's life. Thanks for all the talks, encouragement, TMI shares and getting messages to me from editors when I'm out of the country. And ALL CAPS. And All the Words. Boldly go, babe.

Chapter One

You're a liar. And everyone is going to know.

Caroline Gill glanced at the text on the phone, then promptly shut it down and put it away. She had ignored similar texts for the last four days, hoping they would stop. Someone obviously had the wrong number.

Caroline may be a lot of things, but a liar wasn't one of them. Life was too short to live surrounded by lies.

She'd learned that the hard way eighteen months ago.

She made a mental note to call the phone company or look into how to block texts on her phone after her shift tonight.

Because she definitely didn't have time to do it right now. She had a real crisis to deal with. As the ambulance pulled to a stop, Caroline jumped out of the passenger side and surveyed the utter chaos around her.

As she looked around the wreckage, she took a deep breath, trying to ascertain what she needed to do first. The thick morning fog that had blown in from the coast of Corpus Christi made everything more difficult to deal with—especially a deadly crash.

As a paramedic she dealt with accidents and injured people on a daily basis. Thankfully she didn't experience a situation as bad as this often: at least seven cars in a deadly pileup.

She turned back to her partner, who was just getting out of the ambulance. "Kimmie, radio Dispatch. We need help. Mass casualty. Let them know."

Kimmie did so immediately as Caroline further studied the situation before her. The fog had been a big factor in what caused this multicar pileup on State Highway 358. But a bigger factor looked to be like some idiot who had been driving the wrong way down the crowded street.

"Help me."

Caroline heard the weak voice coming from a truck a few yards away, just one of many. Some were sobbing, some begging for help, some basically screaming. Absolute chaos in a situation where no one could see more than two or three feet in front of them.

Caroline blocked out the voices—she had to, despite their volume or the words or sounds they made. She had learned a long time ago as a paramedic that the loudest people weren't always the ones who needed the most help.

Caroline pulled on gloves as Kimmie came running around from the driver's seat of the ambulance they'd arrived in together. "Dispatch is sending who they can. There's multiple calls because of this fog."

Caroline pulled out her triage kit, including the tags of four different colors inside. "We're going to have to tag everyone until help gets here. Thirty-second evaluations, okay? Green for minor injuries. Yellow for non-life-threatening. Red for life-threatening. And black…"

Caroline faded out. They both knew what black meant. Dead or so near to dead the victim couldn't be helped now.

Kimmie looked a little overwhelmed. Caroline's partner was relatively new and this was probably her first mass casualty situation. "Kimmie, you can do this. You've done it in training. Don't spend more than thirty seconds with each person and make sure the tag is the first thing seen when more help arrives."

They split up and began the always difficult job of choosing who would be treated first when more help arrived. Everyone was hurt. Everyone was scared. Everyone wanted to be the first ones treated. But they couldn't all be.

Caroline sprinted to the first victim, who unfortunately didn't take long to be evaluated. He was lying on the pavement covered in blood. He obviously hadn't been wearing his seat belt and the force of the impact had thrown him through the windshield. Caroline quickly searched for a pulse, felt none, so removed her hands before trying once more, hoping she was wrong. A lot of blood loss didn't always equate to death.

But in this case it did. "Damn it," she muttered under her breath before pulling out a black tag and placing it near the man's head. This would discourage other first responders from stopping for him until the other more critical cases could be taken care of.

She ran to the man screaming at the top of his lungs next. His car was the one facing the wrong direction. She braced herself for what she would find because of the sheer volume of the man's yells. But instead of finding some gaping wound or bones protruding in a hideous injury, she found a man, probably in his late twenties, holding his hand where it looked like his pinkie was dislocated.

"Thank God," he said as soon as she got close enough. "What took you soo-long?"

If the words slurring together didn't give her enough of a clue of his drunken state, the stench of alcohol that immediately accosted her senses did.

"Sir, are you injured besides your finger?"

"My finger is *broken*, not injured." He held it up as

proof. "And the window of my car is smashed and the door won't open. I need you to fix that right away."

What did he think this was, AAA? Caroline didn't have time for this jackass who—coupled with the fog—had probably been the cause of this entire situation.

"Sir, I need to know if you have any more injuries. There will be someone here soon who can help you get the door open."

The man just narrowed his eyes and let out a string of obscenities. "Don't you leave me here, you bitch."

Caroline could hear the cries of other people, including at least one child. She vaguely wondered if she smashed her elbow in this guy's face if it would look like something that just happened in the wreck. But she forced herself not to.

She handed him a yellow card. "Sir, give this to the next EMT or firefighter who comes your way, okay?"

The man immediately scoffed and threw it on the ground. "Don't you dare leave me. All these people were driving on the wrong side of the road." He grabbed her arm through the window. "I'll have your job if you leave me."

She grabbed his other, uninjured, pinkie, bending it back, knowing the pressure would cause him to release her arm. It was one of the self-defense moves she'd learned in the multiple classes she'd taken over the last year and a half.

No man would use his strength against her and make her a victim ever again.

"Unless you want me to break your other pinkie," she said to the drunk guy, "I suggest you let me go. Besides, you're going to be too busy sitting in jail to have my job."

The man released her and went back to yelling his obscenities at the top of his lungs. Caroline picked up the yellow tag and removed the adhesive cover on the back, sticking it to the outside of the car. Hopefully the guy wouldn't mess with it. She quickly moved on to the next car.

"Please help me." A mother was sobbing in the driver's seat, blood dripping from her face. A young girl and a baby sat in the back seat. The little girl was crying also.

"Ma'am, I'm here. It's okay," Caroline said, taking in the situation. The woman was pinned inside her vehicle where the front end had been crushed when it had been rear-ended into a safety railing. Her legs were trapped.

"My kids." The mom was hysterical, unable to see or help her children in the back. "Why is Nicole crying? Are they hurt? Is the baby okay?"

Caroline used her flashlight to shine into the car as she talked to the woman. "Hey, what's your name?" she asked the mom as she pulled on the door handle, but it wouldn't budge. The woman's legs were definitely pinned. The firefighters would have to get her out of here.

"Jackie."

Caroline couldn't tell what state Jackie's legs would be in, but for right now she was a yellow card. Needed help, but wasn't life-threatening. But the woman was still sobbing.

"Jackie, I'm going to check the kids now. But I need you to stop crying, okay? And hold this." She gave the woman the yellow tag. "This lets the firefighters know what to do."

She could see Jackie try to get herself under control. "My kids. Please, my kids."

Caroline touched her on the shoulder through the window that had been broken. "I'm checking right now."

She moved to the back door and opened it. A little girl in the back, about three years old, was sobbing, obviously terrified.

"Jackie, what's your daughter's name?"

"Nicole."

"Hey, Nicole," Caroline crooned. "You doing okay, sweetie?" The fog floating around the car and her mother's cries were frightening the girl. Caroline touched her gently on the cheek and she settled a little bit.

"I want Mama," the little girl said, hiccuping through her tears.

"I know you do. It will be just a few minutes, okay? Does anything hurt, sweetheart?" The girl seemed to be fine, but it was difficult to tell.

"No. I want Mama."

"I'm here, sweetie." Jackie was pulling herself together now that she could talk to her daughter. Nicole calmed down more as her mother did. "Is David okay?"

"Can you hold this for me, hon?" Caroline handed little Nicole a green tag. Someone else would check her out more thoroughly, but for right now, the girl didn't seem to need more medical attention. "Nicole seems fine, Jackie. I'm going to check on baby David now."

Baby David hadn't made a sound the whole time. Caroline's heart caught in her chest as she ran around the car to his side.

The baby, not older than six months, lay silently in his rear-facing car seat as Caroline pried open the door. As she reached over to check the baby's pulse, she could hear Jackie's ragged, terrified breathing.

She couldn't see any blood or noticeable injuries, but he didn't move at all at her touch. Caroline sent up a silent prayer that the child was alive. With babies, everything was tricky, since they were unable to communicate.

She found his pulse at the exact moment little David opened his eyes. He studied Caroline intently before taking his thumb and jamming it in his mouth, sucking on it.

"He's okay, Jackie. He's sucking his thumb." She reached over David and squeezed Jackie's shoulder. "I can't say for certain that he is injury free, but he's alive and he's alert." Caroline laid a yellow tag on baby David. He probably could be green-tagged, but with a baby she'd rather be safe than sorry. Someone would still need to check him more thoroughly.

"Jackie, you saved your kids' lives by having them properly restrained in their car seats. You did great. I have to check on others, so I need you to keep it together. Help will be back again soon."

Caroline didn't wait to hear any response. She rushed to the next victim. By the time other sirens approached a few minutes later, she had evaluated many victims.

Two were dead. At least two with severe injuries. A half dozen more with minor injuries that would require attention.

And a drunken jackass, still yelling, with a dislocated pinkie.

That first dead guy she'd come across had a couple of children's dolls in the back seat of his car. Somebody's dad was never coming home again. Yet a drunk driver who'd never even known he was driving the wrong way down a highway was going to be just fine.

Sometimes the world just wasn't fair. Caroline knew that much better than most by what had happened to her nearly two years ago.

This just reaffirmed it.

It was going to be a long, hard day.

TWELVE HOURS LATER, shift finished, having showered and changed at the hospital, Caroline made it home.

Except, it wasn't exactly home, was it?

It was the fourth place she'd lived in eighteen months, the place she'd moved into six weeks ago, but it wasn't *home*.

How could you call a place home when every time

someone knocked on your front door it sent you into a panic?

Caroline stood in her driveway, looking up at her town house's entrance, duffel bag swung over her shoulder, unable to go any farther. It had been the longest, professionally worst day she'd had in a long time. Her body was exhausted from the physical exertion of moving patients, administering CPR and going to one call after another today because of the fog. Her emotions were exhausted as the death toll had risen each hour.

By all means, she should go inside her house, fall into bed and be asleep before her head hit the pillow. Despite the deaths that couldn't be avoided, Caroline and the other paramedics had done good work. Had helped make sure the death count hadn't risen any further than it had. She should rest now. She deserved it.

But she couldn't seem to force her legs to move any closer to her empty house.

She knew she could call one of the officers over from the Corpus Christi Police Department to come walk through her town house for her. They would understand, and someone would come immediately.

Although not the person she really wanted—really *needed*—to be here. He wasn't part of the police force any longer. Zane Wales had hung up his white hat—literally and figuratively—the day they'd found Caroline raped and nearly beaten to death in her own home. The last victim of a serial rapist.

Caroline looked at her town house again, still unable to force herself to walk any closer.

What would Dr. Parker say? Caroline had been uncomfortable talking to a psychiatrist here in Corpus Christi, so her friend Sherry had convinced her to speak—just once—to the Omega Sector psychiatrist over the phone.

That "just once" had then turned into talking to Dr. Parker every couple of weeks.

If Caroline called Grace Parker right now—and she had no doubt Grace would take the call—would Grace tell Caroline there was nothing to fear? To just put one foot in front of the other?

No, she would tell Caroline that only Caroline could determine what would be the best thing to do. That pushing herself too far did more damage than it did good.

Her phone buzzed in her hand and she looked down to read the text.

How do you look in the mirror knowing your lies?

She rolled her eyes. Another one? This was getting out of hand. Caroline wasn't big on smartphones in general, so she didn't do a lot with hers. But she had to see if there was a way to block these texts.

The text was almost enough to distract her from her fear of entering the house. She took a step forward, then stopped, wiping her hand across her face.

She couldn't go in right now.

The thought frustrated her, but she let it go. It was okay. She would go to the Silver Eagle, a bar in town, and relax for a little while. A lot of the law enforcement and EMT gang hung out there. She could have a drink or a bite to eat or just chat. Get someone to show her how to block the annoying texts. When she was done, maybe she'd be more ready to face the big scary front door.

Once the decision was made, she didn't second-guess her choice, just jogged back to her truck, throwing her duffel in the passenger seat beside her. The ride to the bar didn't take long and she knew she'd made the right decision when she pulled into the lot.

Kimmie's little VW Beetle was parked here and almost every spot was full. Caroline would chat and unwind for an hour or two. She would face her town house when she was ready.

It had been a bad day. This would hopefully make it better.

She grabbed her purse, got out of the truck and made her way inside. The familiar smell of beer and fried food assailed her, as did the country music pouring at a perfect volume from the speakers. She smiled at Kimmie, who waved for Caroline to come join the people at her table.

Maybe being here wouldn't make her fears back at the town house just disappear, but nothing could make this day worse.

She glanced over at the bar as she walked toward Kimmie and almost stumbled as she found her gaze trapped by the brown eyes of Zane Wales. Compelling her, drawing her in, as always. She forced herself to look away from him.

Her day definitely just got worse.

Chapter Two

Zane Wales didn't come into the Silver Eagle very often. A lot of law enforcement guys hung out there, and generally Zane didn't need a reminder of what he no longer did for a living.

But today had been a long, weird day and Zane had found himself here an hour ago, rather than going straight back to his house on the outskirts of Corpus Christi. Just for a beer, a bite to eat. Hoping maybe none of the detective force would even be here.

They were *all* here.

If he could back out without any of them seeing him, he would've. But Captain Harris, along with Wade Ammons and Raymond Stone, both detectives Zane had worked with when he'd been on the force, waved him over to the bar where they sat as soon as they saw him.

Zane liked all three of the men—he really did. He chatted with them for a while before Wade and Raymond saw some ladies who interested them and said their goodbyes.

"How's the private aircraft charter business treating you?" Captain Harris asked as he took a sip of his beer.

Zane chewed a bite of the burger he'd ordered. "Today was different than most. A little crazy."

"How so?"

"Fog was causing problems up and down the interstate,

so I got called for an emergency organ donation delivery. A heart. Flew it into Houston."

The entire flight had been tense—a very real deadline looming in front of them. Zane hadn't been sure if the deadline was because of the patient waiting for the heart or if the heart itself was only viable for so long. The two-person organ donation team flying with him hadn't said. They'd just told him the deadline.

Zane had gotten them there. Not much time to spare, but enough. He hoped the surgery had been successful.

"Yeah, fog was hell around here for us too this morning. Multicar pileup with a drunk driver. Half dozen other accidents that took up all our resources. Hell, even Wade and Raymond were out helping today."

That would've meant Caroline had a hard day. Not that he could do anything about that. Moreover, not that she would *want* him to do anything about that.

"Must have been a mess if you had to pull in Wade and Raymond."

"Sounds like your day was equally exciting. Heart transplant. Important stuff. I'll bet you miss that on a daily basis when you're carting around cargo or rich people from place to place."

"Don't start, Tim." Zane already knew what was coming. A conversation they'd had more than once in the seventeen months and six days since Zane had quit the department.

"Son, I've known you since you were in elementary school. I had no hesitation at all about hiring you straight out of college or promoting you to detective, even after the trouble you got into in your younger years."

Evidently the man wouldn't be deterred. Zane raised his beer slightly in salute. "I know. And I appreciate it. High school was tough after Dad died."

"You can't tell me that running your air charter business means as much to you as chasing down criminals did."

Captain Harris was right; Zane couldn't say that with any sort of honesty. He enjoyed his business, loved to fly, loved working for himself, but it didn't challenge him the way working for the force had. Didn't challenge him nearly as much mentally or physically.

But Zane had lost his edge. Lost what had made him a good cop the day Caroline was attacked.

"I don't have it anymore, Tim. Don't have what it takes."

Captain Harris scoffed. "Don't have what, exactly? You're still in just as good a shape. I know you have a permit for that concealed Glock you're carrying."

Zane didn't ask how the older man knew that. But he was right. Zane had never stopped carrying the gun, even after he'd quit the force. He just now had a different permit for it.

"I'll bet you have just as much practice on it and have aim just as precise as you did when you worked for me."

Zane shrugged one shoulder as he took a sip of his beer. "Just because I can hit what I'm aiming for doesn't mean I'm good as a law enforcement officer, Cap."

"Just because someone you care about got hurt doesn't mean you're not one," the captain shot back.

Caroline had been so much more than *hurt*.

"The rapist was right under my nose the whole time." Zane pushed his plate away, no longer interested in his last bites of food. "I shook the man's hand multiple times."

"Dr. Trumpold fooled us all," the captain reminded him. "Including that Omega Sector agent who came here to help us."

Zane just shrugged. "Jon Hatton did everything he could." But in this case, being part of an elite law enforcement agency like Omega hadn't been enough, either.

"And," the captain continued, "if I recall correctly, if you hadn't followed your instincts and gone after Hatton and Sherry Mitchell, Trumpold would've killed them both. That it was *your* bullet that put a stop to him."

Yes, Zane had stopped Trumpold. And hadn't lost a bit of sleep when he'd died in prison a year ago.

But that still didn't change one simple fact: Caroline Gill had opened the door to a rapist because she'd thought the knock on her door was Zane. Because Zane was supposed to be with her that night.

But he'd changed his mind at the last minute, wanting for once to have the upper hand in their tumultuous relationship. Stayed away as part of the head games the two of them played with each other all the time.

He would regret that decision for the rest of his life.

"If it had happened to someone else, you wouldn't blame them, Zane," Captain Harris continued. "Why are you holding yourself to a different standard?"

"It's not about standards. It's about my instincts. I can't trust mine anymore. And I won't put anybody else at risk."

"Zane, you need to—"

Harris stopped talking as the door to the bar opened and they both—engrained law enforcement instincts kicking in—looked toward it.

Caroline.

Zane hadn't seen her in a few months. They'd run into each other at a restaurant, a totally awkward exchange where they'd both been on dates, and their dates had both known Zane and Caroline used to be together. They'd said uncomfortable hellos and then spent the rest of the night trying not to notice each other.

Now Zane stared at her from where he sat, as always almost physically incapable of *not* looking at her. Taking in her long brown hair, pulled back in a braid like it so often was. The curve of her trim body filling out the jeans and fitted sweater she wore. His body responded, as it always had, wholly aware of her anytime she was around, in a completely carnal way.

What sort of pervert did that make him? Looking at Caroline—a rape survivor—with blatant sexuality all but coursing through him?

Just reinforced his decision to get out of law enforcement altogether. His instincts weren't to be trusted.

He knew the exact second she saw him, the slight hesitation in her step, but her gaze didn't falter. She didn't smile at him, but then again, he didn't expect her to.

Of course, he had to admit, even before the attack she hadn't always smiled at him. That was how their relationship had been: fire or ice. Never anything in between.

A friend called out to Caroline and she broke eye contact with him and headed in the caller's direction. Zane felt oddly bereft without the connection with Caroline.

He should've never come here in the first place.

He was about to ask for and pay the bill when Wade and Raymond came back over to sit with him and Captain Harris again. Raymond ordered them all another round before Zane could stop him.

"What happened to your lady friends?" Captain Harris asked.

"Married," Wade and Raymond both said at the same time, crestfallen.

"I might go talk to Kimmie." Raymond took a sip of the beer the bartender handed him.

Wade rolled his eyes. "Hasn't she shut you down enough times already?"

"Yeah, but she looks happier now. Especially since Caroline's here." Both men looked over at Zane as if they'd said something wrong.

"I wasn't going to hit on Caroline, man," Raymond was quick to announce.

He damn well better not.

Of course, Zane had no say over who Caroline dated. Although she better not go out with a horndog like Raymond Stone.

Zane shrugged. "Caroline can go out with whoever she wants." He forced his jaw not to lock up as he said it and carefully kept his fists unclenched. "Does she come in here a lot?"

Damn it. Zane wished he could cut off his own tongue. Why was he asking about her? But no one seemed to make anything of his interest.

"Not as much as we would like," Wade said. "I know Kimmie, her partner, invites her all the time."

"Kimmie's her partner? How long?"

"Awhile now," Captain Harris answered this time. "I talked it over with the hospital staff and we thought Kimmie would be a good professional fit for Caroline."

"What sort of professional fit?" Maybe Kimmie had some sort of specialized training Caroline didn't have. But she looked awfully young for that to be the case.

Harris fidgeted just a little in his seat before looking away.

"What?" Zane asked. "Did Caroline need help? This Kimmie have training or something Caroline doesn't?"

Captain Harris shook his head. "No. Kimmie was pretty much brand-new. Anything she's learned outside schooling, Caroline has taught her."

That didn't surprise Zane. Caroline was stellar at her job as a paramedic. Could spot potential problems or injuries others would miss. Kept her head in a crisis. Had a way about her that kept people calm.

"So what was it about Kimmie that was a good fit for Caroline?"

Wade and Raymond glanced over at the captain, who was looking away. Then it hit Zane.

"Oh, Kimmie's a *woman*. That's why she was a good fit for Caroline. I guess nobody could blame her for asking for a female partner."

Now all three men refused to look at Zane.

Not all his detective skills had left him. "But she didn't ask for a female partner, did she? You just assigned her one."

Captain Harris pointed toward where Caroline and Kimmie sat, obviously easy and friendly with each other. "I've known Caro since she was born. Her parents are some of my best friends. So I did what I thought was right for her. She and Kimmie are a good team. It wasn't the wrong choice."

But it hadn't been *Caroline's* choice. And he would bet she hadn't liked it, no matter how chummy she and her new partner looked now. If Zane had been there, he would definitely have spoken up, at least told Captain Harris to talk to Caroline about it.

But he hadn't been there, had he? Zane grimaced.

"I'm glad they get along," he muttered.

He saw Caroline glance over at them before quickly looking away and taking a casual sip of the beer the waitress had brought. She was just as aware of him as he was of her, although he doubted her awareness of him stemmed from attraction. Disgust at best, possibly even hatred.

So they both ignored each other, which everyone in the entire bar seemed completely aware of.

"I'm glad Caroline is finally going on a vacation," Wade said, trying to break some of the obvious tension. "She deserves it."

That was good news. "Where is she going?" Corpus Christi was a beach town and she'd always loved it. Did she still after what had happened? She used to live near the beach but had moved after the attack. Nobody in their right mind blamed her after someone had broken through her front door and viciously attacked her. Zane didn't know if she still even liked the beach at all.

Wade looked like he didn't want to answer. "How hard a question is it, Wade?" he asked the younger man, smiling. "A cruise? Tropical island? The mountains?"

Oh, hell, maybe she was going with another man. Maybe that was what Wade didn't want to answer.

"Who is she going with?" Zane could feel his jaw clench but couldn't seem to stop it.

He knew he had absolutely no right to be upset if she was going with another man somewhere. It was good—healthy—for Caroline to have other relationships. Someone important enough for her to move on with, to go on vacation with.

That was why he'd stayed out of her life for so long, right? So she would have a chance to move on, to put the past—including him and his part in her nightmare—behind her?

But damned if his hands didn't clench into fists as he waited for Wade's answer. As he prepared himself to hear the news that she really had moved on. That he had officially missed his chance.

"Just say it, Wade."

"She's not going with anybody, Zane. That's her whole deal. She said she wants time to be alone. Get away from the frantic pace for a week."

Zane refused to acknowledge the relief that poured through him at the knowledge Caroline hadn't found a man she was comfortable enough to vacation with.

He turned to Wade, rolling his eyes. "Why are you jerking my chain? I don't blame her for wanting peace and quiet. I guess that means she's not going to visit her family in Dallas. It's never peaceful around them."

Wade shrugged. "Nah, she's going hiking at Big Bend. She'll get plenty of quiet there."

Zane set the glass of beer that was halfway to his mouth back down on the bar. "She's going hiking in Big Bend Ranch State Park?" One of the largest parks in Texas, covering over three hundred square miles. Breathtaking views, multiple types of terrain. A hiker's dream.

Wade nodded. "Yeah."

"Alone?"

"Yeah, but she's been planning it for months. She's got a GPS that will let the park rangers know where she is at all times and has a course all planned out. She's super excited about it."

Wade continued to talk about how prepared Caroline was, how thrilled, but Zane tuned him out. He stood up. "Excuse me."

He turned and strode toward Caroline's table with definite purpose. There was no way in hell she was going on a weeklong camping trip by herself. Obviously none of her colleagues or friends were willing to tell her how stupid an idea this was.

Zane had no such problem.

Chapter Three

Her body was aware of Zane. She'd been conscious of him the entire time they'd been here, ignoring each other while totally mindful of each other's every move. They'd always been like that. Whether they'd been about to kill each other or fall into each other's arms, they'd always been *attuned* to one another.

She was attuned to him now. Aware of how damn virile and sexy he was. Not working for the Corpus Christi Police Department hadn't turned him soft or dimmed the edge of danger that had always surrounded him.

It drew her, just like it always had.

Damn him. Because the only thing that matched her passion for Zane Wales was her fury toward him. She'd like him to come over so she could slap him across his perfectly chiseled cheek.

And as if he could hear her and was going to call her bluff, he stood up and began walking toward her table.

"Holy cow, who is that?" Kimmie asked. "The guy that was talking to Captain Harris."

Caroline didn't say anything. But Kimmie's friend Bridget, sitting across from them in the booth, spun her head to the side so she could get a look at the eye candy.

"Ohhh." Bridget's eyes flew to Caroline. "That's Zane Wales. He's Caroline's."

Kimmie's face swung around to look at Caroline, shock evident in the wide circles of her eyes. "What?"

Caroline shook her head, her own eyes rolling at Bridget's remark. "He's not *mine*."

"Are you sure about that?" Kimmie looked back at Zane. "He sure is looking at you like he's coming for you."

"We used to date back in the day. It's been over for a long time." Zane had made sure of that.

Although she had to admit, it did look like he was coming directly to their table. But it most certainly would not be to talk to her. He'd gone out of his way to avoid her for the past eighteen months.

But five seconds later he stood right in front of their table, looking ridiculously sexy in his jeans and dark blue, long-sleeved collared shirt with sleeves he'd rolled up halfway to the elbow. November in Corpus Christi wasn't cold enough for a jacket.

He wasn't wearing his hat—that damned white cowboy hat he'd worn all the time. He was a Texan through and through and wearing it had been as natural to him as breathing.

He'd taken it off when he'd quit the force and she hadn't seen him in it since. Not that she'd seen him much at all.

He didn't need the hat. He wasn't hiding anything but thick, gorgeous hair underneath it. But Caroline missed him in it. Missed what its presence had stood for.

"Hey, Zane," Bridget purred. Caroline resisted the urge to slap her. Barely.

"Hey, ladies."

Caroline didn't know why Zane was at their table, but on the off chance it was to ask Bridget or Kimmie out, she couldn't stick around and watch.

"Excuse me." Caroline started to stand. "I've got to get going, you guys."

"Actually, I'm here to talk to you, if you don't mind," Zane said. He was looking directly at her now, closer than he'd been in nearly two years. She slid back into her seat, unable to draw her eyes away from his.

"Um, Bridget and I have to use the restroom anyway," Kimmie said, standing and grabbing the other woman's arm before she could protest.

Zane nodded at them as they left, then slid into the booth across from Caroline.

"Hi."

Of all the things she'd been expecting tonight, Zane coming over to chat with her hadn't been one of the possibilities. He'd withdrawn from her so completely over the past months that a conversation hadn't even been on her radar.

"What are you doing here?"

As far as greetings, it wasn't concise or friendly, but hell, nothing about Zane made her feel concise or friendly.

"I had some errands to run in town and thought I would grab a bite to eat."

He deliberately wasn't answering the question he knew she was asking. "Yeah, it looked like you were pretty close to done when I arrived."

He nodded and eased himself a little farther back in the booth, raising one arm up along the edge and knocking his knuckles gently along the column behind him. Damn the man and his comfortably sexy pose.

And damn sexy wrists exposed by his rolled-up sleeves. How could she have such a reaction from *wrists*, for heaven's sake?

"I wanted to talk to you," he finally said.

Her eyes flew to his face at that, in time for her to see his gaze slide over to his fingers that were still tapping against the column.

So whatever it was he wanted to say, he wasn't exactly comfortable with it.

"Spill it, Wales. Just say what you came to say." She honestly had no idea what it was. Her heart fluttered slightly in her chest that maybe he wanted to apologize for being so distant. For pulling away from her when she'd needed him. For keeping himself away.

Not that she'd forgive him and just let it go. Too much time and pain had occurred. But at least it would be a start.

His arm came down from the back of the booth and he leaned forward, placing his weight on both elbows. She couldn't break her gaze from his brown eyes even if she wanted to.

"Caro…"

Now she almost closed her eyes. How long had it been since she'd heard him call her by her pet name? The name he'd called her when they were alone. The name he'd called her when they were making love.

Unbidden, she felt herself leaning closer, desperate for his next words. It didn't have to be an apology; she knew the attack had cost him almost as much as it had cost her, although in a different way. Just some sort of acknowledgment that something had to change.

He cleared his throat, then continued. "You can't go on that hiking trip. Alone? That's absolutely stupid."

It took her a second to process his words. To realize what she'd hoped to hear from him wasn't anywhere near what was coming out of his mouth.

The pain reeled through her and stole her breath. Zane wasn't here to tell her they should be together; he was here to tell her she was stupid. She wrapped her arms around her middle, almost afraid she would fly apart if she didn't.

She looked away from him now, not even able to look

him in the eye. She was an idiot. Why would she think anything had changed?

"Did you hear me, Caroline? I really don't think this solo hiking trip is a good idea."

Did she hear him?

Did she hear him?

Fury crashed over her like a tidal wave, obviating the pain. It was all she could do to stay in her seat.

"Do I hear you, Zane?"

He had the good grace to look alarmed at her quiet, even tone. At least he still knew her well enough to know when she was about to blow a gasket.

"Caro…"

"Oh, no, you don't. Don't you dare call me that." The anger felt good, washed away the slicing pain of being wrong about him again. "You don't get to call me anything with any affection ever again."

Her words hurt him, she could tell, before he shut down all trace of emotion on his features. Good. She was glad she had hurt him. Glad she still could.

"Fine," he said. "I don't have to call you any friendly name to tell you that going hiking by yourself in the middle of the wilderness is just plain stupid."

Caroline looked over at the waitress who was walking by. "I need the check, please."

"I need mine too," Zane muttered.

The woman looked back and forth between them, a little concerned, before nodding. "Sure. I'll be right back."

"Where I choose to take my vacation is none of your concern, Zane."

"It is when no one is willing to tell you how risky and stupid it is."

Her eyes narrowed. "Really? How much do you know about my plans, exactly?"

"I know you're going hiking alone in Big Bend. That's enough."

Caroline clenched her fists by her legs and forced herself to breathe in through her mouth and out through her nose. She would not get in a screaming match with Zane Wales in the middle of a bar.

Unable to look at him without giving him the full force of her opinion—loudly—she surveyed the bar. Just about everyone was watching them, waiting for the fireworks. It wouldn't be the first time they'd provided a colorful show. But it had been a long time.

"You don't know anything about my plans, Wales. You don't know anything about my life. Remember?"

"You say that like me getting out of your life wasn't the best thing for you."

She just stared at him. "Seriously?"

"And regardless, this plan of yours—" he said the phrase with such derision her eyes narrowed and she felt her temper rising to a boiling point "—is ridiculous. You can't do it."

Oh. No. He. Didn't.

The waitress brought them both their checks and Caroline counted it one of her greatest accomplishments that she didn't say anything at all. She just got out a twenty-dollar bill, threw it down on the table and stood, not caring that she was tipping the waitress almost as much as the bill itself.

She felt every eye on her as she turned and walked out the door. She didn't care and definitely wasn't afraid to go back to her house now. She was too damn pissed.

She made it to her truck before she heard him.

"You can't seriously be going on this trip."

She didn't turn around. "You know what, Zane? You don't know anything about it."

"I know it's dangerous."

Now that they didn't have an audience, she didn't even try to keep her volume in check. "No, you're making a snap judgment that it's dangerous because you don't know all the facts."

"Then tell me all the facts."

Now she turned around. "I'm not stupid. And believe me, I have no desire to put myself at risk. I have taken precautions to make myself as safe as possible."

What was more, she needed this. Had talked extensively to Grace Parker about this time by herself. The psychiatrist had agreed that, with the right precautions for her personal safety, it was a good idea.

She would've told Zane all of this already if he'd been around. If he'd been a part of her life. But he hadn't been. So by damn, he did not get to have a say in her decisions.

"You know what? Just forget it." She spun back toward her truck.

"Hey, I'm not done talking to you."

"I don't give a damn if you're done with me or not. Have you thought of that? Maybe I'm done with *you* this time."

He strode directly to her. "What do you mean, this time?"

His nearness didn't bother her. Zane's nearness had never bothered her. This entire shouting match—so much like old times—was so freeing in a lot of ways.

"You bailed on me eighteen months ago, Zane. You don't get to have a say in anything I do anymore."

His volume rose with hers. "I didn't *bail* on you. I knew me being around you would be a constant reminder of the worst day of your entire life. So I tried to do the noble thing and get out of your way."

"Noble?" She all but spat the word, poking him in the

chest. "You were too much of a coward to fight for us, so you ran."

"This discussion is not about the last year and a half. This discussion is about your asinine plan to go hiking for a week by yourself."

"Why do you think you get to have a say in what I do, Zane?"

She got right up in his face and shouted the words.

God, it felt so good to yell. To have someone yell back. To not have someone treat her with kid gloves like she was going to break any minute.

"You don't, Zane," she continued, poking him in the chest with her finger again as she said it.

His eyes flared as he wrapped his hand around her finger against his chest.

And then, before either of them realized what was happening, he yanked her to him and kissed her.

Caroline had been kissed since the rape. She'd even had sex with a couple guys since. But they hadn't been Zane. Hadn't been who, deep inside, she truly wanted.

And it sure as hell hadn't been a kiss like this.

Zane's lips were like coming home. His arms banded around her waist and hers slid up his chest and around his neck.

That hair. Thick and brown. She thought of how many times she'd flicked off his hat and ran her fingers all the way through it as he kissed her. Exactly like she was doing now.

He devoured her mouth and she couldn't get enough of it, pulling him closer with fists full of his hair, moaning as his fingers bit into her hips in his urgency to get her closer.

He backed her up until she was against her truck, then grabbed her by the hips and hoisted her up to the engine's hood. Now she could wrap both her arms and her legs around him.

Passion simmered through her blood as his lips nipped down her jaw to her neck. Not gentle, not timid. Just Zane. Fierce and passionate, the way lovemaking had always been for them. She moaned as one of his hands came up and fisted into her hair, holding her so he had better access to what he wanted.

Her.

And she couldn't get enough of it.

Dimly she was aware that they were still in the parking lot of the Silver Eagle. That any minute her colleagues, law enforcement officers who generally tended to frown on sex in public places, were going to make their way out.

This needed to be taken back to her place. Or his. Or a hotel room.

Stat.

"Zane, we've got to stop."

She sighed at another one of his nipping kisses, at the feel of him pulling her closer. She'd missed this so much.

But damn it, she didn't want to get arrested.

"Zane, stop."

She gripped some of his hair and gave it a tug.

She could tell the exact moment he came back to his senses. His hands dropped from her hair and he all but jumped back from her body.

But it wasn't until she saw his face that she understood. He was ashen. Distraught.

"Zane—" She reached for him, but he moved farther back.

"Oh, my God. Caroline, I'm so sorry. I don't know what came over me, I—"

She jumped down from the hood of her truck, desperate to wipe the distressed look off his face. Zane hadn't done anything wrong. He'd done everything right and she wanted more.

But at that moment Wade yelled from the open door of the bar. "Hey, Captain sent me out here to make sure the two of you hadn't killed each other."

Caroline rolled her eyes and turned toward Wade, waving her arm at him over the hood of her truck. "We're fine. Leave us alone and you guys mind your own business."

Wade's chuckle rang out in the still night air as he went back inside.

"So I wasn't saying, 'No, let's stop. I don't want to do this.' I was saying, 'Let's move this party someplace a little more...'" She turned back to Zane, her biggest smile in place.

But Zane was gone. She heard his truck start on the other side of the parking lot before his tires squealed as he sped onto the street.

Chapter Four

Zane woke from the nightmare, heart pounding, sweat covering his entire body despite the cool air coming through the screened windows of his bedroom.

He'd dreamed about the night Caroline had been attacked by Paul Trumpold a year and a half ago. It had been a while since he'd dreamed about it. Although it was no surprise that he'd had it again after what had happened in the parking lot of the Silver Eagle two nights ago.

He probably would've had the dream last night if he'd slept a wink.

The dream—really more of a memory—always started the same way: Zane sitting at his desk at the CCPD headquarters, even though it was late at night, doing some work, avoiding doing what he really wanted to do, which was accept Caroline's invitation to go over to her house when he got off work. He hadn't wanted to give her the upper hand in their relationship. Wanted to keep her a little off balance like she so often kept him. Wanted to let her know, for once, what it felt like to wonder what would happen next. She did it to him without even thinking. He wanted her to know—wanted *himself* to know—that he could do it to her.

It all seemed so ridiculous now.

The uniformed cop—a young kid, Zane couldn't even remember his name—who'd wanted to give Zane a heads-up before he got the official call had run up to Zane's desk, knowing Zane was lead detective in the case. The cop had been out of breath when he told Zane the serial rapist had struck again.

Zane always remembered that moment in his dream and in his life. Because that had been the last time he'd ever been okay. The last time his world had been whole.

He'd been pissed that the rapist had struck again before they could catch him, but his world had still had a foundation.

He could never stop the next moment in his dream any more than he could in real life: when the cop gave him the address of the rapist's latest victim.

Caroline's address.

He'd written down the first two numbers as the cop had said it out loud before he'd realized where it was, then had dropped everything and run as fast as he could to his car, driving way past the limitations of safety to get to Caroline's house.

Praying the entire time that there had been some mistake. That the address was wrong. That the kid cop, in all his excitement to be helpful, had gotten the numbers wrong or something.

The numbers hadn't been wrong.

The ambulance at Caroline's house had thrown him. He'd seen an ambulance there before, one Caroline had driven. Hell, she'd even driven an ambulance to his house to meet him for a quickie once.

But she hadn't driven this one. This time the ambulance had been *for* her.

The dream sometimes changed from there. He always had to cross her yard to get to the door of her house. Sometimes as he ran across the yard in his dream the ground swallowed him like quicksand, slowing him from reaching the door. Sometimes there were thousands of people all over the yard and he couldn't get through no matter how hard he tried.

Sometimes he ran as fast as he could, but the door kept getting farther and farther away.

But no matter what happened, the rapist—Dr. Trumpold—always just stood there laughing at Zane. And when Zane would finally fight his way to the door, the man would turn and whisper, "You know why she opened the door for me? Because she thought it was you knocking. Thanks for the help." Then he would disappear.

And in his place would be Caroline. Lying on the floor of her own foyer, beaten until she was unconscious. Clothes ripped off her small body. Being treated by her own EMT colleagues, handling her with care even though she was long past feeling any pain at that point.

Zane had just stared, watching his entire world lying broken at his feet. He hadn't been able to move, hadn't been able to say a thing, even if there had been something that could've been said or done.

In real life Zane had ridden in the ambulance with Caroline, had stayed by her side in the hospital until she'd finally woken up forty-eight hours later and helped them catch the rapist.

But in his dream he was always stuck there in the doorway of her house, looking down at Caroline's broken, battered body. Knowing she would never be okay again, that *they* would never be okay again.

And in the worst of the nightmares she would open her eyes from where she lay on the floor—although he knew that would've been impossible, since the blows from the rapist had caused both her eyes to be swollen completely shut—and echo her rapist's earlier comment, in an oddly conversational voice.

Where were you, Zane? I thought it was you knocking at the door.

And he would never have an answer.

He got out of bed now, knowing he wouldn't get any more sleep. Hell, he'd be lucky if he got any sleep any night this week after what had happened in the parking lot of the Silver Eagle.

He'd flown at least one flight each of the last fifteen days straight, so he should be glad he had nothing scheduled for today, but now he wished he could get back up in the air. After the nightmare, today wasn't a good day to be grounded. Zane wanted to be up in his Cessna.

Flying had been the only thing that had come even a little close to filling the hole in his life since he left the department. Like Captain Harris suggested, flying wasn't enough to completely eliminate the void, but it at least did something.

Zane wished he had another organ donor trip. That had been exciting. The deadline, the pressure, knowing someone was counting on you to get the job done.

That had been what his life had been like every day when he'd been a detective on the force.

Life when he'd had Caroline in it.

That wasn't any easier to think about than not being on the force any longer. Especially after what had happened in the Silver Eagle parking lot.

What in heaven's name had come over him? How could he have possibly treated Caroline like that?

They'd been fighting just like old times. Yelling at each other.

Then she'd poked him in the chest with that tiny finger of hers, just like she had so many times in the past. And in the past it had almost always ended with them on top of each other.

He had moved out of muscle memory more than anything else. Covered her finger with his hand like he had so many times before, moving in for a kiss.

Basic instinct, a primal need for Caroline, had taken over from there. He'd been so caught up in the kiss, knew she had been too. Had felt her hands in his hair, felt her legs pull him closer when he'd set her up on the hood of her truck. It had been so long; they'd been desperate for each other.

But then she'd told him to stop and his first instinct, the only one he'd been able to hear at all, had been to keep kissing her. Keep kissing that throat. That neck. Those lips.

Then when she should've slapped him, she'd simply tugged at his hair and told him to stop again.

And finally reason had returned.

He scrubbed a hand over his face now, despair tugging at him. He'd been holding her in place, unwilling to let her go.

Caroline, a rape victim.

He had to give her credit; she hadn't seemed panicked. She hadn't cried or punched him or run screaming back into the Silver Eagle. When he'd jumped back, she'd started to say something to him.

He could think of a number of things she'd had a right to say to him. And none of them were pretty. So when Wade had yelled whatever he had to say—Zane totally hadn't been listening—he'd gotten away from Caroline.

Because once again, as had been true for the past eighteen months, the greatest thing Zane could do for Caroline was to keep away from her. He'd made as quick an exit as he could manage.

She'd be in the middle of Big Bend State Park now, on her hike. He still didn't like it. But she'd been right in one argument: what say did he have in her life?

None. Which was the best possible thing for her.

But the thought of her hiking alone still stuck in his craw. Maybe if he had kept his temper, used reason to discuss it with Caroline, he could've changed her mind.

But who was he kidding? *Reason* had never had anything to do with their relationship. Passion, fighting, yelling, heat. All those had. But never reason.

She'd driven him crazy from the moment they'd met in high school when her family relocated from Dallas. In both the best and worst of ways.

God, how he'd missed her the last year and a half. Missed the woman who had always stood toe-to-toe with him and refused to back down.

But now all he could picture was her broken body lying in the hospital bed eighteen months ago. Crying when she didn't know he could see her.

She'd never be able to go toe-to-toe with anyone again.

Not that Zane hadn't been willing to change everything about their relationship to fit her needs. Over those first few months, he'd tried. Went out of his way to be gentle, easy, light with Caroline. It had been weird, so different than what had always transpired between them. But for Caroline he'd been willing to do it. To do anything.

But it had all just seemed to make her upset. Sad, even.

Every time he'd let her win an argument, every time she'd poked him in the chest with that little finger and he'd just pulled her in for a hug, it had just made her more sad.

Finally, Zane realized that being around him at all made her sad. So he'd given her the only thing he'd had left to give: his absence. He'd quit the department, moved to the outskirts of town, made it so they never ran into each other.

And it had absolutely gutted him. His entire life became empty.

But for his Caro he'd been willing to pay that price.

And after his behavior two nights ago, obviously he needed to continue keeping himself away from her. The thought that he could've hurt her, scared her, brought back memories of her attack ripped a hole in him.

He started the day doing paperwork—owning your own charter flight company was perhaps the only business in the world that created more paperwork than law enforcement—but soon found he needed the release of some sort of physical activity. He decided yard work was in order. If his mother came by and saw the bushes and grass looking the way they did now, he would never hear the end of it.

And at least the hard, physical work of cutting and trimming allowed him to force the thoughts of kissing a stunning brunette—and how very good it had been before turning so bad—to the back of his mind.

He was going to have to see her in a couple of weeks from now for Jon Hatton and Sherry Mitchell's wedding in Colorado, since Caroline was one of Sherry's best friends and in the wedding. But Zane would be damn sure to keep his distance.

He'd kept his distance for nearly two years. He'd keep on doing it now.

When his phone rang, Zane wiped the sweat from his head before removing his glove and grabbing the device. Speak of the devil; it was Jon Hatton.

Zane hit the receive button. "Hey, Jon, I was just thinking about you."

There was a short pause. "Well, I hope you weren't in the shower, because that would be weird."

Zane laughed. "No, just tackling some yard work that has been a particular pain in the ass."

Zane had met the Omega Sector agent here in Corpus Christi when the local police had needed help with the serial rapist case. He and Jon had solved the case, but too late for Caroline.

Jon had tried multiple times to get Zane back into law enforcement since Zane had quit, even talking to him about working for Omega Sector, but Zane hadn't budged. Although he had helped Jon with a couple of cases that had brought the man back to Texas.

"If you're calling to get me to help you pick out china patterns, I'm afraid I'm going to have to decline."

"As scary as that thought is, no, I'm not calling with anything about the wedding. We've got a problem, Zane."

Zane knew the other man well enough to know that if Jon was calling him with "a problem" it was something serious.

"What's going on?"

"Can you get to your email right now?" Jon asked.

"Let me go inside." Zane grabbed the nearest dish towel from the kitchen and wiped as much sweat and dirt off his face and arms as he could before heading into his office.

"All right, I'm at my computer."

"I'm sending a picture of a Damien Freihof."

"I've never heard of him."

"He went to jail five years ago because he was about to blow up a bank full of people in Phoenix."

"Okay." Zane had no idea what this had to do with him.

"He escaped last year. Nearly killed Brandon Han and his fiancée, Andrea."

Zane knew Brandon; the man had helped figure out who the rapist was. But he didn't know about this Freihof guy or that he almost killed Brandon.

"That time—" it would've been right after Caroline's rape "—it's pretty fuzzy for me, Jon."

"Sure, man, I understand and don't expect you to know any of this."

"Okay."

"Freihof went to ground after he attacked Brandon and Andrea. He was injured in his own explosion. He resurfaced last week."

Zane still had no idea what this had to do with him. "Okay."

"I just sent you a picture of him."

Zane opened his email. "Okay, I got it." He studied the mug shot of Damien Freihof from five years ago. "I don't recognize him at all."

"I'm sending you another picture."

The second picture was a totally different man, roughly the same height and build but different jaw, eyes, hair.

"Okay, who's that?"

"That is also Damien Freihof."

"Damn." Zane whistled through his teeth. "He's good."

"Yeah, he is." Jon's tone held grudging respect. "Good enough to beat all our facial scanning software and to avoid the statewide warrant for his arrest."

"Do you think he's moved on to Texas?" If he had, it wasn't like Zane could do anything about it.

"Two days ago, Freihof masterminded a pretty elaborate plan. A bomb that killed one of our junior agents and put another agent in a coma. Looks like Freihof wants to make Omega Sector pay for putting him in prison. Plus, he nearly killed a mother and her toddler daughter in the process."

Zane's expletive wasn't pretty. "Sounds like this bastard doesn't care about collateral damage."

"Exactly. He wants as much collateral damage as possible. We've already been given that message. He's coming after people with ties to Omega. He's trying to hurt civilians we care about in order to split Omega's focus. I'm sending you one more picture."

The picture Zane received was of some sort of wall with a staggering amount of information on it: newspaper clippings, photos, drawings, police reports, Google search printouts, fingerprints.

"What the hell is that?" Zane couldn't make any sense of it at all.

"That's the wall of clues Freihof left for us. A very complicated puzzle that points out Freihof's next intended victims."

"How the hell were you able to make any sense of it?"

"It took us a long time, believe me." Jon paused for a second. "It looks like you and Caroline are on his intended victims' list, Zane."

"What?"

"There were very specific clues referring to you by name on the wall of clues. We think he might be coming after you soon, if he's not there already."

Zane's expletive this time was even uglier. "Caroline's off on her own."

"What?"

"She's on some damfool hiking trip in Big Bend State Park. Alone. Do you think this Freihof character might be aware of this?"

"Honestly, Jon, the man is a genius. I wouldn't put anything past him."

"Thanks for the heads-up, Jon. I've got to go. I'll keep you posted." Zane disconnected the call and was running for his bedroom, grabbing his go-bag. He would call Captain Harris on the way to the airport and get him to contact the park rangers at Big Bend and find out Caroline's exact GPS location.

He would file his flight plan and be in the air in less than an hour. He'd be with Caroline in under two. A madman genius had gotten to her once. There was no way in hell he was letting another.

So much for keeping his distance.

Chapter Five

Over the last few months, Caroline had been learning to trust her instincts again. Her instincts had told her a few months ago that this trip to Big Bend would be a healing one for her.

Now, nearing the end of day two, all alone with no one around for miles, she could honestly say she was damn happy she had followed her instincts.

She hadn't done it recklessly or without proper thought. She had planned. She'd considered. And finally, she'd just decided to take the chance.

Sort of like how she'd learned to do everything else in her life. She knew that bad things could still happen; people intent on harming others would always be around. Caroline did her best to prepare herself never to be a victim again, including multiple self-defense classes and hours of strengthening her body in the gym. She'd trained her mind to be more aware of what was going on around her so things didn't catch her off guard.

But ultimately after all the preparations, she had to choose to just do it. To just do that thing that was a little bit risky.

To trust that she could handle it.

It wasn't easy. And ironically, if Zane hadn't come along at the Silver Eagle a couple of nights ago and told her she shouldn't do it, Caroline might have chickened out. But that had been the final push she needed.

"So suck it, Zane Wales!" she yelled at the top of her voice, since no one could hear her anyway.

She loved being out here in the open. Loved that there was a one hundred percent guarantee that no one would knock on her door—the one sound that threw her into a panic every time she heard it.

Why? Because there were no doors out here. Caroline grinned.

The door-knocking thing was something she and Dr. Parker had been working through. Grace warned her that it may always be a trigger, and if so, Caroline would have to learn to live with it.

She was proud of the progress she'd made. Proud of how far she'd come. Proud of her certainty that no man, no matter how big or strong, would ever be able to get the drop on her again. She may not win a fight, but she knew she wouldn't be the only person hurt at the end of it.

She just wished she could convince everyone else of that. Of her growth. She wished she could get people to treat her the way they had before the attack.

As much as she liked Kimmie as her partner, Caroline would've had no problem working with a man day after day. But Chief Harris—one of her parents' best friends and someone she'd known her whole life—hadn't asked her. He'd had clout with the Emergency Medical Service director and had just done what he thought was best.

Her parents and brother still couldn't talk about what happened to her. They had wanted to hire a full-time bodyguard for her. When she'd brought up fairly basic questions—with what money? Why would she need a bodyguard when her rapist had died in prison?—they hadn't had a good answer. So no bodyguard. But they still didn't treat her the way they had before the attack. Everything they said to her or did around her now was always tinted with some sort of combination of protectiveness, worry and pity, depending on the activity.

She hadn't told them about this trip at all. It just would've put them over the edge. She'd sworn Captain Harris—Uncle Tim—to secrecy too.

But she missed Zane most of all. She missed her friend, her lover, the person she spent hours arguing with about every topic under the sun. Of all the things she'd lost in the attack, the one she regretted the most was Zane.

Like everyone else, he hadn't known how to deal with what had been done to her. Hadn't known how to treat her. It had been even worse for Zane because he'd been the lead detective on the case and hadn't realized who the rapist was.

But hell, Caroline had worked with Dr. Trumpold for months and hadn't known it was him. They'd all been duped.

She'd needed gentleness for the first few months as her body had healed from the attack. But then she'd needed her life to get back to normal. Nobody seemed to understand that. Zane definitely hadn't understood it.

Their relationship had always been so tumultuous, almost emotionally violent. It was just how both of them were wired: live hard, fight hard, love hard. But when Caroline had been ready to get back to the fighting and the yelling and, yes, the lovemaking, Zane had already programmed himself to be something else. Something she didn't recognize. Didn't want.

And he'd quit the force. She'd been unable to fathom that. When she'd gone to his house, ready to fight him about it—honestly looking forward to the screaming match and whatever would come after it—he'd refused to engage. At all.

He'd offered iced tea and told her they should maybe talk later when they were both calm.

She could fully admit that she hadn't handled the situation well. That she'd told him she didn't want to be around him like that. That she didn't even recognize him. Didn't *want* to recognize him. To stay away from her until he could figure out who they were.

She didn't think he'd take it to mean she didn't want to ever be around him at all. But that had been the last time they'd been close to each other. Until a couple of days ago at the Silver Eagle.

She'd been such a fool thinking he'd seen the light, first when he came to talk to her and then when he'd kissed her. Zane Wales wasn't ever going to see the light when it came to her. So she wasn't going to pine for him any longer.

Instead, she was going to celebrate being out here by herself. Celebrate the development of another coping strategy. Celebrate being alive.

Trumpold had been escalating, and based on what Sherry and Jon had told her, he'd definitely planned to move on to killing.

Caroline knew, deep in her bones, she was lucky to be alive. That Trumpold hadn't been able to decide whether to kill her or not.

She was alive. She looked around at the stark landscape of the Big Bend. She loved it here. Loved the open, loved the vast skies, loved being alone in the late-afternoon sun.

She turned, annoyed at the sound of a plane flying relatively low overhead. A small plane, probably a flyby for tourists. Caroline just went back to gathering what she needed to build a small fire tonight for coffee and to warm up some of the food she'd hiked in with her. She also needed to check in with the park rangers. She did that every eight to twelve hours out of courtesy for her colleagues back in Corpus Christi. They'd get the report too and not worry.

She was tempted to tell them all to just bug off and leave her alone, but she couldn't. These were people who loved her. She wished they wouldn't smother her with that love, but she couldn't fault them for it.

The plane came back by again and Caroline rolled her eyes. Big Bend was beautiful, but there wasn't enough to see for a double flyby. Then she realized the plane was landing not even half a mile from where she was camped.

Caroline grabbed her radio. She believed strongly in her independence, but she believed more strongly in not being stupid.

"Ranger station, this is Caroline Gill." She gave them her GPS coordinates. "I've just heard a plane land about a half mile south of me. Small aircraft."

"Yeah, we received a call from a Captain Timothy Harris in Corpus Christi."

"Captain Harris, yeah, I know him. Is there some sort of emergency?" She couldn't think of any reason Captain Harris would be on his way or have someone on their way if it wasn't an emergency.

"No, no emergency. He was clear about that. He was letting us know that a detective from his precinct was coming in via small aircraft. He said you wouldn't mind. Or that you probably would, but you'd get over it."

Damn it, Captain Harris was sending a babysitter. She wondered if her parents had gotten word of this trip. She wouldn't put it past them to browbeat Uncle Tim into sending someone to watch over her.

Well, whoever it was, she was sending them right back home.

She continued organizing her little camp, refusing to let

anything get in the way of the peace she had found over the past two days. One of the things she'd worked very hard on with Dr. Parker was accepting what she had control over and what she didn't. Certain circumstances she had no regulation over. But how she responded to them was up to her.

She left her little camp and made her way the few hundred yards to the jagged edge of one of the cliffs Big Bend was known for with a stunning view of the Rio Grande river. She could feel her babysitter's eyes on her as he or she got off the plane and walked toward her, but she didn't pay any attention. Instead, she continued to stare out at the river as the sun began to dip in the sky.

Finally, she knew she couldn't avoid it any longer and turned back around.

And found Zane standing about twenty yards behind her. She froze.

"What are you doing here?" she stammered. Captain Harris had sent Zane to babysit her?

And what's more, Zane had actually agreed?

"I didn't mean to startle you. The ranger station was supposed to let you know I was coming." He took a few steps toward her.

"They did. I mean, they said Harris had called and told them someone was coming out here and to let me know. But I didn't know it would be you. What are you doing here?" she couldn't help but ask again.

"Right now? Enjoying the beautiful view."

Caroline turned back out toward the river. "Yeah, amazing, isn't it? The sun has set on the river this way for thousands and thousands of years. Makes you feel part of something much bigger than yourself."

Zane didn't say anything, simply absorbed. They stood in silence watching the sun drop farther, casting a purple hue throughout the entire area. Caroline just took it in with him. She had to admit, there was no one else in the world she'd rather share this moment with than Zane. She closed her eyes and felt the warmth of the setting sun on her face.

When she opened them again, she found him studying her.

"What?"

"Nothing. You look good. Peaceful, capable. Being here, at this place, obviously agrees with you. I was wrong to tell you not to come."

"You got that straight. I still don't know why you're here."

"I needed to make sure you were all right."

He stuffed his hands in his jeans pockets just like he always did when he wasn't telling the full truth. She'd never told him she knew that tell because she'd never wanted to give up the upper hand.

"You know I've been checking in with the rangers every few hours. You could've just asked them. I'm sure some of the CCPD have, including Captain Harris."

He shrugged. "I needed to see it with my own eyes."

He still wasn't telling her everything, but she trusted him enough to know that if there was some true emergency he would've already hustled her off to the plane and gotten her out of here.

A thought struck her. "My parents didn't call you and make you come, did they?"

He chuckled. "No. I just wanted to see you for myself."

Her eyes narrowed. "You flew a long way just to look at me, Wales. You might want to consider taking a picture. It would be a lot cheaper."

"A picture of you, here, in this light couldn't possibly do this moment justice."

Damn it if the man didn't still know how to make her insides go gooey.

"Are you here to try to get me to leave?"

Zane looked around, taking in the vastness surrounding them. "No. I don't think there's any place else you ought to be than here right now. Like I said, it obviously agrees with you."

She shook her head and began walking back toward her little camp. She still didn't know exactly why Zane had come. He would tell her when he was ready. And honestly, as long as he wasn't here to try to make her leave her hike early, she didn't care. She didn't mind having him around. She'd never minded having him around.

"I can take care of myself, you know," she said without turning back to him.

"I'm beginning to see that more clearly," she heard him mutter.

Good. He should've seen it long before now.

Chapter Six

Zane didn't want to tell her his true purpose for coming.

He could admit he had been so wrong when he'd told her she shouldn't do this trip. He'd been arrogant and judgmental. She'd been right to get angry at him.

God, she looked so beautiful out here. At ease. Strong. Capable. With a Glock G22 in a holster at her hip.

Damn, if that wasn't just the sexiest thing ever. Like she'd been transported through time from the Wild West. A rancher's wife, ready to do whatever was needed to make her way securely through this wilderness.

"You know how to use that Glock you're carrying?"

She didn't even turn around. "Don't try to piss me off on purpose, Wales. You know I wouldn't be wearing it if I didn't know how to use it. I told you I wasn't coming out here unprepared."

Zane had no doubt what she said was the truth. If some sort of animal—four legged or otherwise—threatened her, she would be prepared to protect herself.

Of course, she wasn't exactly prepared for a terrorist, one of Omega Sector's Ten Most Wanted, who might have set his sights on her. How did anyone prepare for that?

She looked so relaxed and peaceful he didn't want to tell her about Damien Freihof. Just because their names had come up on some psychopath's wall of clues didn't mean an attack was imminent. Zane would eventually have to tell her about the conversation with Jon Hatton, but not right now. Not when there obviously wasn't any danger out here.

Not when Caroline looked so peaceful.

He hadn't been lying when he'd said he just wanted to see her, to be with her. Hell, he'd wanted that for the last year and a half.

They talked about the weather, and how her hike had been so far. But at her small camp area she finally turned to him. "Okay, you obviously don't want to tell me the reason why you're here. And I'm assuming if someone was hurt at home, or if I was needed, we wouldn't be sitting around here chitchatting like a couple of old ladies."

Zane laughed out loud. Lord, how he'd missed her sharp tongue. "Nope, nothing like that."

"It's not Jon and Sherry, is it? Nothing's happened with the wedding?"

He stiffened at the mention of Jon's name, afraid she'd ask for more specifics about him. "No, the wedding crazy is still in full gear as far as I know."

"Good. Because I'm rocking the bridesmaid dress Sherry picked out. She let us each choose our own style as long as it was the teal color she wanted. I got a halter style."

He had no idea what halter style meant but was glad to see her so excited about it. "Wedding is still a go, so your dress is safe."

She studied him for a long while.

"Well, it's getting dark, Zane. Have you seen whatever you need to see—that I'm alive and not throwing myself off the cliff, I presume—and you're leaving? Or are you going to stay?"

"Can I stay?" He did his best not to think too much about the question and what it meant for either of them. Right now he just wanted to be with her.

She shifted her weight onto one hip and stirred her fire with a stick. "It's a big park, Zane. I don't think I can stop you from camping here. Although I do think you're supposed to have a permit."

"You know what I mean."

"Do you have your go-bag?"

"Yep, plus a sleeping bag and MREs in the plane."

"Did you grab them for this trip or do you always have them in there?"

He knew she was still trying to ascertain exactly why he was here. "They're always in the plane. Although the go-bag is fresh."

"Meals Ready to Eat aren't very tasty."

Zane shrugged. "Some of them aren't too bad. And they're better than going hungry."

She smiled. "That's true. Maybe if you're lucky, I'll give you some of my food. Real stuff."

They hiked to his plane and got out his belongings. He showed her around the small prop plane.

"Do you like it? I never knew that flying was more than just a hobby for you before you started your business."

They had gone up a few times together over the years. Zane's grandfather had taught him how to fly in high school, and he'd gotten his pilot's license not long after he'd gotten his driver's license. Of course, Caroline's parents had categorically refused to let their only daughter up in a plane with a teenage pilot while she was in high school.

When she'd turned eighteen, she'd stopped asking their permission.

"I remember how your dad lit into me after that one time for taking you up." Zane got what he needed out and handed his sleeping bag to her. "You didn't tell me that you hadn't asked."

"I was eighteen, I didn't need their consent."

"Yeah, well, evidently your dad didn't know that."

That had been one of the last times Zane had flown with her, although not because of her father's threats to kill him. They'd both gone away to separate colleges, dating other people, but never seriously. When they'd both come back to Corpus Christi, things had gotten much more serious between them.

But that wasn't what he wanted to be thinking about right now.

"Anyway, my granddad left me the plane three years ago. And Jacob Scott was retiring from his air charter business, so I just took over. Worked out for everyone."

They started back toward the camp.

"Yeah, I'm glad that worked out," she murmured.

Her tone was sad, but he didn't push it. He didn't want to fight with her. Didn't want to do anything that would spoil this time and place with her.

DAWN THE NEXT morning broke just as gorgeous over the Rio Grande as sunset had left it the night before. And despite sleeping outside with no pillow, Zane woke feeling better than he had in a long time.

Eighteen months, nine days to be exact. The day Caroline had been attacked.

They'd spent the entire evening joking and fighting and arguing ridiculous points with one another about every topic from the Texas Rangers to the Rangers hockey team. Even when they were yelling the mood was easy between them. An underscore of happiness derived just from being with each other.

She didn't seem upset about how he'd treated her at the Silver Eagle. And, if it didn't upset her, then he knew he just needed to let it go.

He still hadn't told her about Jon Hatton's call. Honestly, there hadn't been any need to. Zane didn't want to ruin her trip for no reason.

But neither was he going to leave her here alone.

"So what's your plan, Wales?" Caroline asked as they shared breakfast consisting of oatmeal and dried fruit and some coffee she'd made over the fire. "You flew a long way just to camp out under the stars. I'm pretty sure we have those back in Corpus Christi."

Zane would've flown twice as far, hell, *more*, to have gotten the hours he'd had with Caroline. Hours where his presence didn't bother her. Where she was comfortable, confident.

"How would you feel about me paring down my gear and coming with you for a couple of days?"

Her eyes narrowed as if she was trying to figure him out. If she pushed now, he would have to tell her the truth about Damien Freihof. He'd have to tell her soon anyway.

"You got water in your plane?"

"Yeah. And a purifying bottle. It doesn't work quickly, but it will get out anything that will make you sick." It was standard equipment in his plane's emergency kit as well as some protein bars and the MREs.

Not to mention the Glock and extra ammunition he'd brought. The weapon was always nearby.

Of course, as he'd noticed yesterday, Caroline wasn't without her own weaponry.

"Okay, we might have to hunt a little small game to supplement our food if you decide to hang out more than a couple days, but I'm good if you are. Let's get camp packed up and ready to go."

And that was it. Just like old times, Caroline and her no-nonsense manner.

She broke camp as he went back to the Cessna and reloaded his go-bag. He took a moment to check in with Jon Hatton while he was away from her.

"Everything okay with Caroline?" Jon asked by way of greeting.

"Yes, no problems. It looks like your Freihof guy either doesn't know she's out here or has decided not to make a play. But I'll still be keeping my eyes peeled."

"Last time he used someone else to do a lot of his dirty work, Zane. So just be careful."

He finished his conversation with Jon, then hustled back to Caroline, who was ready to go.

She turned to him, everything already packed up. "What were you doing back there, writing poetry? Let's get a move on, Wales."

Her tone was annoyed, but he saw her smile as she turned away.

"No, I was fixing my hair if you must know. Beauty like this doesn't come without a price." He heard her guffaw as they began their hike. The only trace of the camp was the small ring of ashes from their fire. In wilderness camping you carried all your supplies in and all your trash out.

Big Bend advertised itself as "the other side of nowhere." Over three hundred square miles of all sorts of terrain: rolling hills, cliffs and valleys, desert sections as well as green hills. A hiker's dream if you wanted a variety of terrain and a chance to be alone. Especially now in November. No families camping or large groups led in on horseback.

Caroline had obviously planned out where she would be going. She had a map she glanced at every so often, a compass she brought out more to make sure they were on track. She was prepared, gutsy and strong. Just like she'd always been except...

The image of her rape, of seeing her lying unconscious

on the floor, swamped him. Stole his ability to breathe, to do anything but flounder in remembered panic. In the knowledge of how scared and hurt she had to have been.

She chose that moment to look over at him.

"You okay there, cowboy?"

He tried to shake it off, to make a joke. But he couldn't. He couldn't say anything. He just stopped and stared at her.

Somehow she understood.

"Zane, we're here. We're both here and we're both good."

He just nodded.

"I need you to be in the *now* with me, okay?" she continued. "The *then* costs too much. Takes too much. Be with me—with who I am—*now*."

She reached up and touched his cheek. He stared at her for a long moment before turning his lips to the side and kissing her palm. They both nodded.

She didn't want to stay in the past. He sure as hell couldn't blame her for that. She didn't want him to keep her there, either.

He realized he'd been doing that for a year and a half. Keeping her inside the box of the attack.

She turned and began walking again.

Obviously she refused to stay in the box any longer. He needed to stop trying to fit her there.

They walked the next few hours chatting easily, at least mentally. Physically, the pace they set as they hit higher ground made talking more breathy.

Midafternoon, Caroline stopped abruptly.

"Everything all right?" he asked.

"Yeah." She nodded. "Just get out your water and let's take a drink."

They'd just stopped for water less than twenty minutes ago. Zane didn't mind stopping, but this seemed odd. Caroline took a swig from her canteen, then walked around so she was standing on the opposite side of Zane.

"Caro, what's going on?"

"I think you better tell me why you're really here."

"Why do you ask that?"

"Because for the last hour there's been someone following us. And I just caught the reflection of the sun off a riflescope again. Whoever it is is getting closer."

"Damn it. You're sure it's not just some other hikers also out here?"

She shook her head. "That's what I thought at first. I'm not sure that the person means us any harm, but someone is definitely following us. Hikers aren't out here for company. Plus, we're on a route I created, not one on any of the normal trail maps. The chances of anyone picking the exact same route I did is pretty slim."

Zane grimaced. Caroline was right. This didn't sound good.

"If you weren't here, I'd double back, sneak behind them and see what was going on."

"Do you think it's just someone in trouble?" Even as Zane said the words, he knew it wasn't true.

"If they fired that rifle in the air, I'd be back to them in no time offering assistance. Whoever it is isn't in trouble. They're gaining in speed."

Zane saw a patch of light shine onto Caroline's shoulder before it quickly moved away. She didn't look at it, although she had to have seen it.

"Was that their scope again?"

She took a sip of water again, looking at him casually, not giving any hint as to the seriousness of the conversation. "Yep. Not someone very familiar with it if I had my guess. I would imagine they're looking at my face right now. Trying to figure out why we stopped."

"Are you in range for them to shoot?" Zane casually stepped to the side so the rifle would be trained at his back, not at Caroline.

"No. If they don't even know they're giving off a glare, I don't think they would try a long-range shot. Right now they're just keeping us in their sights for whatever reason."

"Good."

"So you want to tell me why you're really here so we can formulate a plan and figure out what we need to do?"

Zane hadn't wanted to tell her. Hell, twenty-four hours ago he would've worried that maybe she wasn't strong enough to handle it. He'd been damn wrong about that.

"Jon called me yesterday. He was worried about us."

"Us? Why?"

"Looks like some guy pretty high on the public enemy list has decided to make you and me targets."

Chapter Seven

Caroline appreciated the matter-of-fact way Zane gave her the news. Didn't pull any punches, didn't sugarcoat due to any misconceptions of what might be too much for her *delicate* feelings. He treated her the way he did before the attack.

The news was a little scary, she could admit. Some guy who had already killed or injured multiple Omega Sector agents now seemed to be targeting people who had an attachment in some way to Omega.

And she and Zane specifically. Not awesome.

"So does Jon think this Freihof guy is here now at Big Bend? Is that our rifle friend back there?"

"It seems as though Freihof's MO is to get other people to do his dirty work for him. So it may not be Freihof himself."

Not being here himself wouldn't make them any less dead if the rifle guy started shooting at them. "So what's our plan?"

"First we radio in to the park rangers. See if they know anything about anyone else out here. Maybe it's just someone like you who'd planned to be here the whole time."

She shrugged. "Okay. And the truth is, if the person wanted to shoot us outright, he could've done it before now. We weren't moving fast enough to escape someone."

Zane nodded and looked casually over his shoulder in the direction where she'd seen the rifle glint. "Let's try to put a little distance between us and whoever that is, okay?"

As they restarted walking, Caroline set a pace that was fast but not fast enough to look like they were deliberately trying to get away. Zane contacted the park rangers and they found out no one had filed a hiking plan in this direction but Caroline.

It didn't mean definite bad news, but it wasn't good news, either.

"Damn it, I'm going to have to cut my trip short, aren't I?" She'd been looking forward to this for so long.

"How about when we get this Damien Freihof thing settled, you and I will come back out here for a long weekend?"

Caroline almost stopped midstep at his words. Definitely not what she'd been expecting him to say. She still wasn't sure if he was inviting himself along because he wanted to look out for her or because he wanted to be with her.

But at least he was willing to be in her presence and not treat her like she was about to break. That was all she'd ever wanted from Zane.

She glanced over at his six-two frame, dark brown hair and muscular build. Okay, maybe it wasn't *all* she'd ever wanted. But it was a start.

"I don't know, Wales. What about all the hair product you'd need for a whole weekend? Think you have a backpack that sturdy?" She looked over her shoulder at him.

He grinned and winked at her. "Maybe I'll wear my hat."

Caroline's stomach did the craziest little somersault as much from his smile as his words. She would give anything to see that old cream-colored Stetson back on his head. Even if it didn't mean he was going back to work for the police department. It would just mean he hadn't given up on himself. On life. On there being good in the world.

Whatever it had meant when he'd stopped wearing it.

She smiled back. "Then it's a hiking date."

Less than an hour later, both of them knew they were being hunted. "Whoever it is is gaining," Zane said to her.

"Yeah, I noticed. But I've got a plan formulating. How do you feel about rappelling?"

He gave her a sidelong glance. "I've done it a couple of times, why?"

"There's a cliff edge coming up that has some rappelling ropes and gear already in place. I wasn't planning on using it this trip because it's dangerous alone, but it would get us back down to the river, where we can circle back around to your plane."

Zane glanced back over his shoulder again. "You think we should just give up all appearances of not knowing someone's following us and just make a run for it?"

"Yep. It's our best bet against someone who has a rifle compared to our sidearms. No way we're going to get the same range. We don't want to take a chance on getting into a firefight."

"Smart."

She shrugged. "You know we might be making a mountain out of a molehill. The difference between binoculars and a riflescope is impossible to tell from a sun reflection."

Zane glanced over his shoulder. "You could be right. But to be honest, I'm not willing to take that chance. Not when the person has been steadily gaining on us despite this pace."

"Yeah, my gut says we need to bail. Fast. And if there's one thing I've learned, it's to listen to my gut." It had been one of the first things she and Dr. Parker had worked on: learning to trust her instincts again.

"I agree."

"I say we ditch the packs and run. We can ask the park rangers to come out for them later. Given the psychotic killer possibly targeting us and all, they probably won't mind a trip out here to observe."

He was already stealthily unbuckling his backpack. "They'll probably only laugh at us a little bit."

"Let's hope it's nothing and we can all chuckle. The cliff is about a quarter mile from here. Are you ready to go on my signal?"

He nodded. "Yep, call it and we ditch the packs and run."

They were still walking, but now both of them had moved their hands to the buckles of their backpacks, after Zane grabbed a couple things as casually as he could from the outer side pocket of his. Caroline could feel eyes on them. She unhooked the small strap across her shoulder and moved her hands to the larger one at her waist.

"Now!" she said through gritted teeth. She pulled at the latch at her waist and the pack fell heavily to the ground. Zane's did the same. They both sprinted toward the cliff wall.

Not five seconds later a bullet bit into the ground behind them. Not close enough to be life-threatening, but definitely enough to prove the other visitor definitely wasn't just some lost hiker.

Zane cursed as two more shots hit the ground behind them, ricocheting off the ground. Caroline didn't know if the shooter was just a bad shot or what; she was just glad he wasn't cutting off their route to the cliff edge. As a matter of fact, the shooter was almost guiding them that way.

Because the guy hadn't studied Big Bend like Caroline had. Didn't know there was rappelling equipment at this particular cliff. He thought he was trapping them, but he wasn't.

She and Zane dived behind a large boulder at the edge of the ravine, giving them some cover. No more shots rang out.

He tucked his head to the side and grimaced. "Park rangers are definitely not going to laugh at us."

"Let's just hope we make it back to them."

The rappelling harnesses lay inside a box next to the boulder. They didn't waste any time getting them onto their bodies and clipping the carabiners onto the rope. Zane snatched his shirt off and ripped it into four pieces.

"We need gloves, but this will have to do. We'll burn our hands otherwise."

Caroline took the material, grateful he'd thought of it. She wouldn't have until she'd been over the cliff.

"Do you think he's heading toward us?" she asked as she wrapped the material of the shirt around her hands and refused to gape at how ridiculously sexy Zane looked in just his jeans with no shirt on.

"I think he thinks he has us trapped, so he's probably not hurrying. And might even think we'll be laying down some cover fire. But I don't think we should waste any time."

"He probably doesn't know about the rappelling."

"Let's hope not."

They kept as low as possible as they had to leave the cover of the boulder in order to clip into the rappelling rope. Caroline expected a few more shots but heard nothing.

"It's been a while since I've done this," she admitted as she clipped in and looked over the side of the ledge. Forty yards was a long way to fall.

"Yeah, me too. But it's better than being shot at."

As if the shooter could hear their conversation, a shot rang out near the boulder where they'd just been.

"Take it slow and steady," he told her. "Ready?"

They both got to the edge, then pushed backward, leaping straight back from the top, letting rope go slack as they both slid down about eight or nine feet, then stopped themselves with their hands as they caught their weight against the cliff wall with their feet.

"Good," he told her. "First leap is the hardest. Let's keep moving."

He didn't have to tell her twice. Caroline was well aware of how precarious their situation was if the rifle guy figured out they were no longer behind that boulder and were making a getaway. They would be sitting ducks if he came to shoot at them while they were rappelling down the side of the cliff.

They moved as quickly as their lack of real gear would allow. Caroline was thankful again for the pieces of shirt wrapped around her hands.

Halfway down she began to really believe they were going to make it. She wished she could be doing this under different circumstances because it would be a lot of fun.

She looked over to see Zane grinning like an idiot and knew he felt the same way as she did.

He reached over to high-five her.

Which saved her life as her rope came unattached to its place at the top of the cliff. She immediately began to tumble backward, falling with nothing to catch her and yards to go before the bottom of the ravine.

Zane grabbed for her with his free hand, his quick reflexes allowing him to catch her wrist. Caroline immediately wrapped her fingers around his wrist in a vise and swung her other hand up to latch on to him too.

There was no smile on his face now as he used all his strength to hold on to her.

"I'm okay," she said, and he nodded. She could see sweat breaking out all over his forehead at the exertion of holding both of them.

Suddenly Zane's line jerked also.

Zane said nothing, just pulled her up so they were torso to torso and she could wrap her arms around his shoulders and legs around his waist. He began sliding them both rapidly toward the ground. There was no way he could leap out to get slack on the rope without slamming her against the cliff, so he had to use sheer muscle to get them down.

A few seconds later his rope jerked again, dropping them both five feet.

"Your rope can't hold us both."

"It'll hold," he said through gritted teeth, continuing to work them down. Caroline just tried to keep herself still to not make his job any harder.

The rope sustained them until they were less than ten feet off the ground. Then it gave way with a gentle hiss just as hers had. With nothing now to hold them at all, they both fell backward, landing hard on the ground.

Caroline lay for long seconds just trying to get air back into her lungs, unable to move.

Finally, she looked over at Zane. He was alive, conscious.

"Okay?" he wheezed.

She nodded.

He stood and helped her to her feet, both of them still struggling to take in air. As he wrapped his arm around her shoulders, he began moving them to the east.

"We've got to get back to my plane, but we're going to have to circle around backward to do it. The rifle guy has the higher ground. It won't take him long to figure out we're down here, and once he does, he's definitely going to try to pick us off."

They kept as close to the cliff wall as they could, trying not to give the shooter a target. Without the packs they could move much more lightly and quickly. The hike that had taken them four hours took just half that going back with the punishing pace they set for themselves.

They both had their water canteens, and Zane had grabbed a protein bar before ditching his pack, which they shared without stopping. They never let up the pace even when no shots were fired. Caroline still couldn't shake the feeling that they were being watched.

But that didn't make sense. If this Damien Freihof—or whoever he was working with—was still after them, he would've been shooting. Even if he wasn't good enough to kill them at that distance, he could've still kept them pinned down.

But even though Caroline didn't see any more reflections off riflescopes, she couldn't shake the feeling that danger was only a step behind them.

Zane must have felt it too, because he never once suggested they slow down or that they might have shaken the shooter.

The sun was beginning to set as they got to the plane. They approached it together, both of them with their weapons drawn.

No one was there. No evidence the door had been tampered with or of any problems. Zane did a more thorough check, making sure there weren't any leaks or noticeable trouble before jogging back to her.

"Let's get out of here," he said to her, opening the hatch door so she could climb through. He followed immediately behind her, grabbing a shirt from a small backpack he had in the cockpit. "I know it sounds crazy, but I feel like we're about to be ambushed at any moment."

Caroline shook her head, still looking through the window. "No, it's not crazy. Even though no one has been shooting at us, I feel the same way."

They buckled themselves into the harness-type seat belts and slipped on the communication headphones as Zane started the engines. He eased the plane to the farthest end of the open area where he'd landed. Caroline held on to the seat belt straps where they crossed over her chest as he eased the throttle back and sent the plane speeding down the field. Moments later they were airborne.

As they climbed into the air, she relaxed. She had no doubts whatsoever about Zane's ability as a pilot.

"Okay, I have to admit I was expecting bullets to be flying at us or something," Zane said into the headphones.

"Yeah, me too."

"I've got to call in to the nearest air traffic control. Declare an emergency flight plan. There's going to be a crap ton of paperwork to fill out with this, but—"

A deafening roar and loud popping sound came from the engine to their left before it stuttered to silence.

"What just happened?"

"Engine flameout," Zane said, both hands wrapped in a death grip on the steering column, struggling to keep the plane steady. "We can still fly with one engine, but it's not optimal. I'll need to inform ATC so we can declare it and get back on the ground as soon as possib—"

His words were drowned out by another roar, this time from the right engine. Caroline could see the glare of the flames out of the corner of her eye for a minute before it went out.

Now they were flying with no power in either engine, the silence in the cockpit giving new meaning to *deafening*.

Zane struggled to control the Cessna at all now. "Get the radio and call out a Mayday." He nodded toward the GPS unit between them. "Give them our closest coordinates."

Caroline grabbed the radio and turned it to the frequency she'd used for the ranger station. No one was manning it, since it wasn't her check-in time, but she kept repeating the Mayday and coordinates just in case.

She could see Zane looking around for anywhere they could possibly land. Big Bend wasn't set up for planes and most of the ground wasn't flat, especially in the direction they'd been heading before the engines blew.

"What do we do?" Caroline asked. It was much easier to hear her now with no engine noise.

"We need to find a place to put her down. Fast. Any open area. No big rocks or trees."

That wasn't going to be easy.

"I think that dried-up riverbank is our best option. It's probably our only option." Zane motioned to the left with his head and maneuvered the plane, almost by sheer willpower, toward it.

"C'mon, baby," he muttered as the plane shuddered slightly, resisting his ease toward the opening in the earth in front of them.

An eerie shadow joined the already eerie enough quiet as the plane dipped lower and cliff walls surrounded them on either side.

"Caro, we're going to be coming down fast and hard. Make sure your harness is on as tightly as possible." Zane did the same to his own.

Caroline did all she could do, which basically was not scream at the top of her lungs and distract Zane, as the ground kept moving rapidly toward them. He needed every bit of concentration he could get.

"You can do this, Zane."

She didn't know if he heard her as the Cessna hit roughly along a higher section of the creek bed, then bounced hard against the ground. The force flung Caroline back against the seat as the plane flew back up, then came down roughly again. The impact was bone-jarring, but at least they were still alive.

Zane slowed the plane as much as he could and then turned the yoke sharply so they began to slide to the side. Working against their own speed snapped them around hard, collapsing one side of the plane as the landing gear gave out, slowing them down. She didn't know if it would be enough to stop them from slamming into the ravine wall.

Zane took his hands off the yoke; there wasn't anything he could do to steer now. The weight of the plane teetered forward as they continued their rapid approach toward the wall.

He reached out his hand to grab hers. "Hang on, we're going to flip," he said. Caroline grasped his hand, doubtful they'd live through the next thirty seconds.

The plane flipped, ripping their hands apart as they slammed into the ravine wall.

Then there was only blackness.

Chapter Eight

Zane's eyes opened and it took him a minute to get his bearings. He was hanging in the seat sideways, the harness holding him in. The entire cockpit tilted at a precarious angle. But he was alive.

His attention immediately focused on Caroline. Her much smaller body may not have withstood the impact so well. He couldn't see her from where he was trapped against the seat. Now that the plane had flipped, Caroline was above and a little bit behind him. And the plane was rapidly filling with smoke.

"Caro?" Nothing. "Caroline? Talk to me."

He pushed himself up from the seat so he could get a glimpse of her. She hung limp against the harness holding her, her arms and her hair just fell forward, lifeless.

Zane forced panic out of his system as he reached down to unhook his safety harness. After a tug-of-war of brute force, Zane won. He slipped his arms from the belts, ignoring the pain, grateful he could move at all.

"Wake up, Caroline. Can you hear me?" She still hadn't moved or said anything.

He worked his way up to Caroline's seat, where she lay motionless against the belts. He didn't see any blood or any obvious injuries but knew they could be internal.

He was reaching for her pulse when she moaned and

moved slightly. Zane felt relief wash through him. She wasn't dead.

But smoke was definitely filling the cockpit at an alarming rate. He needed to get them out of the plane immediately.

"Caro? Baby, can you hear me? We're alive, but we've got to get out of here."

He tried pulling at the release mechanism of her harness, but it was jammed. Breathing was getting more difficult.

Zane grabbed his army knife from his jeans pocket. Bracing his legs against the small side window, which was now on the ground, he used his strength to lift Caroline's unconscious form, then sawed through the canvas of the harness belts.

It wasn't an easy process. Even as light as she was, holding her dead weight up so he could cut the straps without cutting her took all his strength. The smoke was really becoming an issue. It was coming from the back of the plane, but once it hit the engines, this thing would be a fireball.

He felt one of Caroline's arms brace herself on his shoulder, holding part of her weight. He looked up from where he was cutting the straps to see her green eyes peering down at him.

"Hey."

"We're alive," she whispered.

"Yes. But it's just a matter of time before the fire makes its way to the engines. We've got to get out of here."

"You're bleeding." Her voice was tight.

He looked over at his arm where he'd been cut. "I'll be fine. Push yourself up as far as you can."

"I can only do it with one arm, I'm pretty sure the impact knocked my other shoulder out of joint."

Zane muttered a curse. "Okay, just hang in there."

She grimaced at his poor choice of words.

Cutting the side where she could hoist herself became much easier with her assistance. He had to brace his arm against her chest and push to get the other side. He could tell by her labored breathing that his actions were hurting her. When the last of the belts finally gave way, she fell heavily on him. He caught her as gently as he could.

"You okay?" She nodded and he put her gingerly on her feet and helped her gain her balance as he began to climb over the pilot seats. Both of them were coughing now.

"Let's get out of here," Zane wheezed. He grabbed his small backpack—it didn't have much in it in the way of usefulness, but it was better than nothing.

He pulled himself up and through the flimsy cockpit door that had broken away and into the main cabin, reaching back to help Caroline. They could both see flames now.

"I'm fine," she told him. "You get the outer door open. I'll get myself out of here."

Zane nodded and proceeded to put all his effort into opening the door that would lead them outside. It was caught against the ravine wall and didn't want to budge. When using his back and shoulders didn't do much, Zane leaned his weight against one of the passenger seats and used the muscles in his legs to try to force open the door. Caroline made her way out of the cockpit and added her strength to the effort.

Damn it, they couldn't survive the crash just to die here from smoke inhalation.

Their eyes stung and lungs burned, but finally the crushed door gave way on the hinge side and slid open enough for them to fit through. Zane steadied her as much as he could as they half ran, half stumbled away from the burning plane.

He knew the moment his livelihood blew up. The force

literally swept them off their feet and threw them forward onto the ground. He heard Caroline cry out as her injured shoulder hit the ground hard. Zane wrapped his arm up over her head as pieces of the plane became projectiles all over the ravine.

The quiet after the explosion was unnerving. Both of them lay on the ground trying to catch their breath for a long while. Finally, Zane flipped himself over and sat up, gently helping Caroline to do the same.

She reached over and touched her injured shoulder, wincing. "Definitely out of the socket. It's going to need to be put back in."

That didn't sound good in any way. "Like you running into a wall and knocking it into place?"

She rolled her eyes. "You've seen *Lethal Weapon* too many times. No, the acromioclavicular joint can be eased back into place with much less violence."

He noticed she didn't say with much less pain.

"You're going to have to do it, Zane."

"Hang on a second, I'm not the medical professional. You are." Plus, the thought of hurting her made him almost physically ill.

"I can't do it. It takes two hands to slip the joint back in properly."

She was already looking pale, and he could tell every time she gave a residual cough from the smoke it was causing her more pain.

"I don't want to hurt you."

She took a step toward him. "Once you do it, it will hurt a lot less, believe me. And there's no way I'm going to be able to climb out of here with a dislocated shoulder. Plus, the longer we wait, the more swollen and aggravated it will get. It's an anterior dislocation, so that's good."

He didn't know what that meant, but didn't see anything good about it.

"I'm going to lie on the ground so there's no weight on this shoulder." He helped her get down on the ground as she explained what he needed to do. Which way to pull her arm and which way to twist once he did. He knelt down next to her injured arm.

She reached up with her good arm and pulled his face down so their foreheads were touching. "Thank you," she whispered. "Remember, slow and easy, no quick, jerky movements."

He shifted slightly and kissed her forehead. It was time to get this done so both of them could stop hurting. "Ready? One, two, three."

Zane did exactly as she'd instructed, wishing to God roles were reversed so he could take the pain instead of her. He heard a broken sob come out of her mouth at the very last moment before the joint slipped back into place.

He wiped her hair off her brow as her breath shuddered out. But he could tell immediately by the way all the muscles in her body relaxed that she was in much less pain now.

"Thank goodness," she murmured.

"Does it still hurt?"

"Not nearly as much as it did thirty seconds ago."

They both sat there, just catching their breath.

"How about you? Are you okay? I know you have that cut on your arm."

He looked down at it. "It's already stopped bleeding."

Zane did a physical inventory of the rest of his body. Everything seemed to be moving, even now that adrenaline wasn't fueling all his thoughts and actions. No sharp or overwhelming pains, but a ton of little ones.

"You doing okay?" he asked her.

She grimaced and didn't open her eyes. "My entire

body hurts, but I don't think I have any life-threatening wounds."

"That's basically how I feel."

Now she opened her eyes. "But considering we just crashed into a ravine, I think we're in pretty good shape."

"Damn straight."

They both sat up although neither of them were very interested in doing more. "How exactly did that happen anyway? I'm going to assume that us being shot at and then both engines of your plane blowing out on the same day are not a coincidence."

Zane shook his head. "There's no way in hell it's a coincidence. If one engine had blown, I might have called it suspiciously bad luck. Both engines? That's sabotage."

They both stared off at the wreckage in silence for long minutes. "I know you didn't have time to do a full walkthrough before we took off, but did you see anything suspicious?"

"No." Zane stretched his shoulders, trying to work out some of the stiffness. "I looked for obvious problems—leaking fluid that would signify cut lines—but didn't see anything. But if someone knew about planes, there are easy ways—like putting sugar in the gas tank, which clogs the fuel lines as it dissolves—to bring a plane down."

"Now we know why our shooter didn't take any more shots at us. He wanted us to make it back to the plane."

Zane nodded. "And now we know we're likely dealing with more than one person. Someone with the rifle and someone who sabotaged the plane. And I don't think it was coincidence that our rifle friend decided to wait until we were at the rappelling equipment before taking his first shots."

Caroline grimaced. "He was leading us there."

"Yep. And then that equipment just happened to be

faulty? I don't think so." Zane shrugged and stood. "We've had two attempts on our lives today and neither of them have been by rifle shot. All the shots did was lead us where they wanted us to go. Someone wanted us dead but wanted it to look like an accident."

He reached down a hand to help Caroline up also, careful of the arm that was still sore. "What happens now?" she asked.

"That Mayday you got off to the ranger station will give them a rough idea of where we are."

"Yeah. I've studied the topography maps of Big Bend for weeks, and unfortunately, we are pretty far from any of the ranger stations."

"And none of them have a helicopter or rescue plane just sitting around, I'm sure. Even if they go to the coordinates you gave them in the Mayday, we're still twenty-five miles away from that. It's going to take them a while to find us, even once they have the right equipment to do so."

She tucked a strand of hair behind her ear the way she'd always done when she was thinking. "We don't have any supplies and a storm set is supposed to move in tonight. It's part of the reason I studied the maps so extensively. I wanted to be able to change course as needed based on weather. Where we were before wouldn't have been in the line of the storms, but here…"

"Then let's get out of this ravine in case the storm does come our way. Climbing out of here when it's dry is going to be hard enough." He looked up and around them.

They were in a much more remote and rugged section of the park. No rappelling equipment would be found around here. They would have to take it very slowly and carefully up the steep walls of the ravine. It wouldn't exactly be rock climbing, but it would be close.

Plus, they were overstimulated, hungry and tired. This wasn't going to be fun.

"You ready to do this?" Zane asked as they found the least steep section of the ravine. It was still thirty feet, but at least not at a ninety-degree angle.

Caroline nodded.

"You go up ahead of me." Zane wished he could go first, to help find good footing, but still be under her in case she fell. He couldn't be in two places at once. "Just take it slow. Stop and rest whenever you need to."

He looked up and over at the sky. Zane didn't tell her that time was of the essence—it was getting dark and a storm would be coming in soon. Caroline already knew.

Too slow and they'd be halfway up the ravine and caught in the dark and a dangerous storm. Too fast and one or both of them might fall and seriously injure themselves.

She took her first steps toward the wall, walking at first, then hoisting herself as it became more vertical. They talked through different hand and foot holds, especially as they made it ten, then fifteen feet up the ravine.

A fall now could prove just as deadly as the crash had been. But Caroline never wavered. It was one of the things he'd always admired about her: her ability to focus, set her mind to a task and complete it. It made her one hell of a paramedic.

Not to mention her body had a toned strength to it now that she hadn't had before. She'd always been slender, too skinny in his opinion, but not anymore. A couple of years ago she would've had a difficult time making it up this cliff, even despite her slight size.

But now she had a strength, in both her arms and legs. Even with the injured shoulder, he could tell by the way she was able to stretch, hoist herself up. To use both her arms and legs to lift her body weight. He'd noticed her strength earlier when the repelling gear had given way. Without her grasp on him, keeping herself supported, he wouldn't have been able to get them both down safely.

He could see her lithe muscles moving under her pants and long-sleeve shirt and had to force the thought of what her body would look like now—no clothes at all—out of his head. Now wasn't the time to be doing anything but focusing completely on the task at hand. Not that fantasizing about Caroline was ever appropriate.

About ten feet from the top of the ravine they came to a large crevasse in the rock. An opening big enough for them both. It gave them a chance to rest and sit down.

And realize that the storm was approaching faster than either of them had thought. The temperature had dropped ten degrees since they'd started their climb.

"I think we better stay in here and ride out this storm," Zane said. "Even if we make it up to the top, there's not much shelter up there at all. At least here we'll have a better chance of staying dry."

They needed supplies. Water-resistant material, warmer clothes, sleeping bags. But all those items were still in the packs they'd dropped when they ran. All they had was what Zane had taken out of his hiking pack and left in the small backpack in the plane. In other words, stuff that hadn't been good enough to make first string.

He took the backpack off his shoulders and brought it around to unzip it. He had a second pair of jeans, an extra pair of socks, a sweatshirt and a half-full water bottle. But best of all, a rain poncho.

"Don't guess you have a satellite phone in there?" she asked as he set the items out.

"I wish. Nothing particularly great."

"But added warmth and element protection. So better than nothing."

They decided that Zane would put on the extra pair of jeans under his current hiking pants. It wouldn't be comfortable, but at least it would be an added layer. Caroline slid on his socks which came up to well over her knees and put on the sweatshirt. Her smaller frame would need the warmth more than his would.

She pulled the hood of the sweatshirt up over her head. "At least it's not yellow," she murmured.

Zane had forgotten about that. Caroline's attacker had worn a yellow hoodie. In her pain from the attack, and the way the man had blitzed her, hitting her before she could truly react, she had mistaken a yellow hoodie for blond hair. It had caused the police to arrest the wrong man at first—someone with long, bright blond hair.

Zane wasn't sure exactly what to say. "Are you okay?"

Caroline nodded. "Yeah, believe me, if it will keep me warm, I don't give a damn what color the hoodie is."

"Good. Because that storm is looking uglier every minute." They both looked out at the dark clouds rolling in.

They split the water in the water bottle between the two of them, then Zane set it on the outside of the ledge, where it would catch some rain. He braced it with some of the little rocks around.

Then they slid back as far as they could, about two feet from the outer edge. They lay down nearly on top of one another and cocooned themselves as much as possible in the rain poncho.

And waited for the storm to hit.

Chapter Nine

Hours later, rain pouring all around them in the inky blackness of the night, Caroline lay in Zane's arms.

Somewhere she'd never thought she'd be again.

She wanted to enjoy it, she really did. But huge waves of agony kept pouring over her. Every way she shifted to try to get comfortable on the wet, hard ground of the crevasse just made some other pain worse.

It was everything she could do not to cry. And Caroline was not a crier.

"What if I lie on my back and you ease onto my side. Will that help any?" Zane asked.

"That's just going to cause you to get more wet and cold."

"I'm feeling a little too hot anyway, so why don't we try it?"

She tried to give a small laugh, but it just came out as a puff of air. There was no way Zane was feeling too hot. The weather had dipped another fifteen degrees since nightfall and even in the partial shelter of their overhang they were both still getting wet.

But Zane still moved onto his back, careful to keep the poncho around both their heads and torsos to keep them as dry as possible. Caroline was able to shift some of her weight onto his chest and almost moaned out loud at how good it felt to be more comfortable.

When Zane's arm reached around her and forced her head down on his chest, taking even more of her weight, she couldn't stop the moan.

"That's right. Never let it be said that I don't know how to show the ladies a good time."

Now Caroline did chuckle. He sounded as physically miserable as she felt. "If this is a date, you've definitely got the excitement factor down pat. I'm waiting for a lion to jump up here and attack us, just to finish this day off."

"That's not scheduled for another hour, so you can relax." He shifted a little so more of her weight rested against him. "Are you doing all right? I know your shoulder has to hurt."

"I'd give a lot of money for some ibuprofen right now," she admitted, but didn't want to complain anymore. "How about you?"

"Not comfortable, but considering what we went through? Very grateful we're both alive. I'm sorry your hiking trip was ruined."

"I'm even more sorry that you were right and it ended up being dangerous." She made a sour face.

Zane laughed and pulled her closer. "If it helps, I don't consider myself to be right. I think having one of federal law enforcement's most wanted criminals personally targeting you counts as extenuating circumstances. Otherwise I think your trip would've been perfectly safe."

"Definitely added some factors I didn't plan for. And by the way, thank you. If you hadn't come out here, I would've been dead a couple times over."

"I wouldn't be too sure of that. I think it's possible that Freihof and his partners followed me. Or that I at least tipped them off as to where you were. It's interesting that you didn't have any trouble at all until after I got here."

"Maybe."

"I can promise you that we're going to catch this guy once we make it back to civilization."

Caroline wondered if Zane knew how much like law enforcement he sounded. Not that she doubted him.

"I believe you. Although it sounds like you might have to get Captain Harris to reinstate you, super cop." She snuggled a little closer. "You always make me feel safe, Zane."

She probably shouldn't admit such a thing; it would make him uncomfortable given how he'd kept himself away from her for so long. It must be the exhaustion or pain getting to her. But it was still the truth.

She couldn't see his face but heard the derision in his laugh. "You're kidding, right?"

"About Harris reinstating you? He would be beside himself with ex—"

"No. About feeling safe with me. Don't joke about that, Caroline. It's not funny."

She shifted her head up slightly, wishing she could see him in the darkness. She might as well tell him the truth; it wasn't like he could be around her any less than he'd been the last year and a half.

"I've always felt safest around you."

"Maybe before you were attacked."

She shrugged painfully. "The attack changed how I saw and thought about pretty much everything. Changed my very DNA, I think, sometimes. But around you is where I have always felt safest."

She could feel tension flood his body. "God damn it, Caroline, you were raped and nearly beaten to death because of me."

Tension flooded her. "What are you talking about? I was attacked because Trumpold was a psychopath."

"Trumpold overheard our conversation, Caro. He knew

you had invited me over that night. Knew you would expect *me* to be knocking on your door when I got off my shift. But I decided not to go."

His voice dropped lower.

"We'd been arguing about something that day. For the life of me I can't remember what it was. You were winning, as usual, so I thought I would get the upper hand by not showing up that night."

"Zane, don't—"

His voice rose much louder than needed to be heard over the storm. "You cannot tell me that you didn't open your door to that sicko because you thought it was me knocking."

She heard the agony in his words and would give anything to be able to tell him that. If only to give him the peace of mind he obviously so desperately searched for. But she couldn't. No matter what she and Zane were or weren't to each other, no matter how tumultuous their relationship, they'd always been honest.

"Yes, I opened the door because I thought it was you," she said softly.

She felt his arm drop from her completely. Felt him almost deflate. Wither.

"How can you say that you feel safe around me after that?" he finally asked. "The night you needed me most I was too busy plotting how to get the upper hand in our relationship."

They lay there for long minutes, silence surrounding them as completely as the storm.

Caroline thought Zane had distanced himself after the attack because he couldn't stomach what had happened to her. That he thought she was too delicate to go back to what their relationship had always been: passionate and sometimes almost violent in its intensity. And maybe that was still true. But she realized now that guilt was the bigger part of what had driven him away all these months.

"Zane, it was Dr. Trumpold. He blitzed his way through the door as soon as it was cracked open. He hit me immediately in the face, and I never saw it was actually him."

"I know." The words were ripped out of Zane's chest. "And you cracked the door in the first place because you thought it was me."

"Maybe." She had to make him understand. To help Zane realize why it had never occurred to her to even partially blame him for what had happened. "Zane, I *knew* Dr. Trumpold. Worked with him almost every day. Yes, I opened the door thinking it was you. *But I would've opened the door to him anyway.*" She spaced out each word to make sure he understood.

It hurt to say them, to even think about that man. She hated that a knock on her door still caused her to blanch and that her first instinct everywhere she went now was to look for danger.

Zane didn't say anything and she didn't really expect him to. He had to process this at his own rate. She didn't blame him; she never had. But she couldn't force him to accept that. They lay there in silence, but eventually Zane's arms found their way back around her, moving in gentle circles on her waist.

"We were fighting that day over which was better, A&M or Austin," she finally said. "I'd insulted your precious Longhorns." She knew that because as she'd come out of the coma, before she'd remembered anything about her attack or felt any of the pain, she'd thought of another point in her argument in the superiority of the Aggies over the Longhorns.

They'd never finished that argument.

She heard Zane curse softly. "I should've known it was about a stupid football team."

"If it hadn't been that, it would've been one of the other hundred topics you and I bickered about on a daily basis. We fought, we made up. We were rough. It's just how we always operated, Zane. It's what worked for us."

Right up until it didn't. Until he stopped fighting. She felt him nod from where she still lay against his chest.

"Our relationship was always so volatile," he whispered softly.

Yes, their passion for each other had been almost violent in its intensity sometimes. She'd loved that they hadn't always made it to the bedroom because they couldn't wait to get at each other. "I remember. Believe me. I remember."

"You say that like it's a good thing."

"Who cares if it was good or bad? It was *us*. And whether people understood it or not, we were good together. Even during our loudest screaming matches."

"But then everything changed." The sadness was pronounced in his tone.

"It didn't have to."

"You told me to stay away from you." He shifted slightly under her. "Not that I blamed you for that. Still don't."

She sighed. "I didn't tell you to stay away from me. I told you to stop treating me like I was some sort of delicate doll."

"God, Caro, I watched your broken body lying on the ground. I sat by your hospital bed for two days while you were in a coma. And I was the lead detective on the case, so I've seen all the photos of everything else."

She sat up, wanting to be close to him but needing a little distance. At least the rain was starting to back down some.

He continued as if she hadn't moved. "Nobody would've

blamed you for never wanting to be around another man ever again. Much less be with me. Not only was it partially my fault…"

She wasn't having any of that. "No. It wasn't."

"But our relationship always bordered on rough anyway. How in the world could I think you would ever want that?"

"So you tried to make it into something it wasn't."

"I wanted to be what you needed." He scrubbed a hand across his face.

"What I needed was someone who didn't treat me like I was never going to be anything but a recovering rape victim! I thought that person was you. It was everything I held on to in the hospital and all through my physical therapy."

"Caro—"

All the feelings and frustrations were flooding out of her now, her own violent storm. She couldn't stop it if she wanted to. "I waited and waited, but you never showed up, Zane. Someone who looked like you did. He held my hand and talked to me. But it was just a pale copy of the original. I needed *you*. I needed *us*. So you're right, when you couldn't provide that, I didn't want you around. I wanted you to treat me like I was *me*."

Zane sat up with her, pulled her closer. She didn't resist. "Caroline."

"But when I told you to go, I never meant for you to stay away forever. I just wanted time to heal. For both of us to heal. Because you needed to just as much as I did."

"You're right. I did." He nodded, still holding her against him.

"But you didn't heal, Zane. You quit the job you loved, the one you were so good at, where you made a difference, and you never came back. You just vanished. You left me too."

"I thought being away from you was the best thing I

could do. That you wanted me away. It was the only gift I had left to give."

She wanted to cry. For the past that couldn't be changed. "That was never what I wanted."

He pulled her tighter to his chest, laying them both back down. "I see that now. I didn't handle the situation very well. I know that. My only excuse is that I thought I was doing what you wanted—keeping away from you."

"Maybe we both didn't handle the situation very well." She sighed.

"You had enough to deal with, just getting through every day."

"I would've rather had you there with me."

"I'm here with you now."

She could hear his heartbeat under her cheek. He was with her now. Maybe that was enough.

"You can't treat me like I'm fragile, Zane. Everyone else still does. Like I'm going to crack at any moment. I'm not. I'm strong. That's part of the reason I was hiking out here. To prove I was okay."

"Everyone knows you're strong."

"Do *you*? Do you really, Zane?"

"Yes. I've always known it. But what I saw you do today? Hold it together as the plane was coming down? Direct me with how to get your shoulder back in joint, then climb up a ravine wall? I don't think any sane person could doubt you're strong."

She wanted him to prove it. Prove that he believed it.

Not with words. She knew he could say the words. Knew he even believed the words.

She needed him to show her—to show *both* of them—right now that she wasn't breakable.

The pain in her shoulder didn't matter, the aches and bruises they both had weren't relevant. Caroline wanted to feel alive on the inside. Wanted to feel alive, feel strong and womanly, the way only Zane had ever made her feel.

The storm had slipped by. All they had left was night. Tomorrow the rescue would come.

Tomorrow they'd be going back to real life.

But first she would enjoy Zane the way she had in the past. Before they'd let someone take much more from them than they ever should have given up.

She shrugged the poncho from over her shoulders and threw it to the side. Then she slid up from where she was lying on her side against him so she was straddling his hips. The narrow spacing of the crevasse didn't give her room to sit straight up, so she was forced to hover over him, her breasts pressed against his chest.

"Whatcha doing?" he murmured, his face only inches from hers.

"You've got to prove it."

"Prove that I want you?" His hands gripped her hips and pulled her down harder against him. "I don't think there can be any doubt of that."

"Prove that you really think I'm strong. That you're not afraid I'll break at the least little thing."

"I know you won't."

"Prove it, Zane. Prove that you can still get lost in me. That we can get lost in each other."

His hand reached up and tangled in her hair, bringing her lips down hard against his. His tongue thrust into her mouth and she moaned. Yes. Yes, this was what she wanted.

His teeth nipped at her lips and his arms wrapped more tightly around her.

Their harsh breaths filled the alcove when he broke away after long minutes.

"You want this? Us?" he whispered, pulling her hips more tightly against his.

"Yes. Hard. Now, Zane."

"Fine. But we do it my way."

She cocked an eyebrow. "Your way? Have things changed so much that your way and my way are no longer the same?"

He pulled her down for a punishing kiss. One that bruised her lips.

One that eased something inside her. Revived places in her that had lain dead for too long. She moaned into the kiss and his groan soon joined hers.

"You still have the smartest mouth, that's for sure," he said against her lips. "Here's my deal. I won't hold back. And believe me, Caro, that won't be a problem."

"Good. That's what I want too."

"But…"

She didn't want to hear the but. She covered her lips with his to shut him up. And it worked. For a couple of minutes.

But then his hand wrapped more fully in her hair and pulled her back so he could talk.

"But," he began again as if she hadn't stopped him before. "You're injured from what happened today. So if something starts to hurt too badly, you tell me immediately, okay?"

That she could handle. "Yes."

His fingers eased from where his fist had gripped the roots at her skull. His other hand moved up from her hip and soon both hands were cupping her face, dwarfing her cheeks.

"And if anything else starts to bother you, darkness starts to creep in, anything gets too overwhelming, you have to tell me."

"I thought that you believed I was strong enough to handle it."

"I do. But part of that strength is being willing to speak up if it's too much. You want me to let go? Fine. You're not fragile and I'm not going to treat you like you are. But I have to know, hell, Caro, *you* have to know that at any point a single phrase can stop this."

"Like a safe word?"

"I don't care what you call it, but we've both got to know you've got the means to stop this at any time necessary."

He was right. It was what they should've done years ago. What they should've worked through together from the beginning, but they'd been too stubborn and stupid.

Of course, they'd been that way before the attack too.

"Airplane," she said.

"What?"

"Airplane. That's what I'll say if I'm getting too over-whelmed."

He laughed. "Perfect. At least it's not 'Zane is a jack-ass.'"

She reached down and kissed him again. "I say that too often for it to be a safe phrase."

"You promise you'll use *airplane* if you need it."

"I promise. You promise not to treat me like I'm going to break."

He kissed her again and her breath whooshed out as he wrapped his arms around her tightly and spun them both so that she was pinned underneath him.

"I promise," he said against her lips. "Tonight we both burn."

Chapter Ten

Waking up with Caroline in his arms was something Zane had given up on ever happening again.

Happening in an alcove in the wilderness twenty-five feet off the ground after their plane had crashed and someone had been shooting at them didn't make it more believable.

The sun was coming up, the worst of the storm had passed and at least rain wasn't pelting them any longer, although Zane knew the low clouds would slow the rescue effort.

Caroline's small body rested, sprawled almost completely on top of his. The low temperatures had demanded they get all their clothes back on before sleeping, but having her this close was almost like skin to skin.

Somewhere in the midst of their lovemaking he'd understood what she'd been trying to tell him. What she wanted from him. From them.

She hadn't wanted him to hold back. But she hadn't been talking just about physically.

Lovemaking between them had always been raw and passionate—rarely ever soft and sweet—and last night hadn't been an exception, as visceral as always. But that wasn't necessarily what Caroline had meant when she'd asked him not to hold back.

She'd wanted him not to hold back *mentally*. Not to let the past take any more away from them than it already had. To not look at her and wonder if she was okay, if something was scaring her, was hurting her, was bringing back memories of the attack.

She wanted him—*them*—to be like it was before those were ever questions in his mind.

She wanted him to want her. Zane wanting Caroline.

And he had.

God, how he had.

And he'd trusted her to tell him if things got to be too much. To use her safe word, airplane. It hadn't been easy to trust her. At first he'd been studying her, pausing, moving with deliberate care to make sure everything was okay with her.

But then he realized that was exactly what she'd been talking about. That was exactly what she *didn't* want.

So he'd let go. Trusted her. Trusted her strength.

Trusted that she would tell him if something didn't work for her. But evidently everything worked for both of them, because once he'd let go, he'd *really* let go and Caroline had been right there with him.

He pulled her closer onto his chest, wincing for her when she moaned slightly in pain even in her sleep. Their escapades last night definitely had not helped all their minor injuries. But neither of them had complained at the time.

He would let Caroline sleep as long as she could, then get the bottle that had collected the water from the storm. It wouldn't be much, but it would be enough.

As soon as the rain cleared, they'd need to make it the rest of the way up the ravine and try to light some sort of signal fire. It would be the most assistance they could offer the rescue plane that would come after them. And Zane knew they would as soon as the storm cleared. Which thankfully wouldn't be too much longer. They had limited food, limited water and no shelter besides this crevasse.

Holding his arms steady around Caroline, staring up at the rock just a couple feet over his head, Zane knew he had to accept that his means of livelihood now lay as charred pieces of metal in the bottom of the ravine. Until he worked out the insurance paperwork and issues, he was without a job.

Which was fine, since he planned for his new full-time job to be protecting Caroline until this Damien Freihof guy was caught. It had nothing to do with not trusting her to take care of herself. Zane would be damned if he would leave her to face this alone.

He held her for the next couple of hours, dozing himself. When he woke again, the rain had completely stopped.

As much as he didn't want to, it was time to get moving.

"Hey, sleepyhead." He rubbed a hand gently up and down her back. "It's time to get up."

He could tell the exact moment she woke up. Her entire body tensed. Zane wasn't sure what it meant: if she was scared, hurt, embarrassed. All?

He slid his hands off her so she wouldn't feel like anything was trapping her in any way.

"Zane?" she asked hoarsely as she pushed away from his chest, then gasped, he was sure, at the pain it caused her shoulder.

He kept his tone even. "Just me, sweetheart. Hanging out with you here in our little alcove."

He felt her relax as she remembered, although not nearly as relaxed as when she'd slept. "That's right. I remember."

He chuckled. "I hope so. If not, I wasn't doing my job right."

She snuggled a little closer to him like he'd hoped. "I

think you did it just fine. But man, I need a toothbrush." Her stomach growled. "And something to eat."

"I have a packet of crackers in my backpack and hopefully the water bottle got filled in the rain. But no toothbrush, sorry."

"Then you definitely won't want to kiss me."

He reached down and tilted her head up until they were face-to-face. "Believe me, I want to kiss you. No matter what the circumstances, I always want to kiss you." And he did, not giving her a chance to get embarrassed and pull away.

He wanted it to go further. Could tell they both wanted it to go further. But he eased back after a few minutes. They couldn't take a chance on missing the rescue plane when it came by.

"We need to get up to the top," he said as he helped her sit up. "That last part is the steepest, and with your shoulder, it's going to take longer."

He crawled over and got the water bottle, glad to see it was full. They both drank from it, then Zane got the cracker packet out of the backpack. Sharing three peanut butter crackers apiece wasn't going to satisfy hunger very long.

"Do you think they'll find us today?" she asked between bites of cracker.

"Yes. We need to build a fire if we can. Something really smoky will be easier for a pilot to spot than just two people."

"That's good." She nodded. "Because with as wet as the wood is going to be, a smoky fire is going to be the only thing we can get."

They finished their meager meal and began the slow progress of making it up the last ten feet of the ravine wall.

Caroline's arm had stiffened while she slept and the swelling from joint trauma had left her hardly able to move it.

To get her up, Zane stood right behind her, supporting her body with his as she hoisted herself up with one arm.

He could tell she was worried and uncomfortable as they made their way up. He didn't blame her. She had to lean all her weight back on him as she moved her one workable arm from one holding point to another. If he lost his grip, they would both fall to almost certain death.

"You're doing great, you know that?"

"Whatever." Her tone was short. He had no doubt if he could see her face she'd be rolling her eyes. Caroline didn't like feeling weak.

But he couldn't see her face because he was behind her, with his body pulled flush against hers. He used that as a method of distracting her, nuzzling his face into her neck.

"I'm in no hurry to get up the wall if it means I can be this close to you."

He felt her ease just slightly.

"You're lucky I have to keep my grip on the rocks or you might be in trouble," he continued. "Do you remember that shower in Houston?"

She'd had a weekend class she was taking to further her paramedic training. Zane had surprised her by meeting her at the hotel and upgrading the room to a special suite. The shower had a rock facade for one of the walls. And Zane had wasted no time getting Caroline's body pressed up against it, not unlike how he had her pressed against the cliff now.

"Yeah, but there I wasn't about to cause us both to fall to our death because I couldn't get my stupid arm to work properly."

"Trust me, darlin', I'm not going to let either of us fall."

She relaxed back against him more and then climbed

the last few feet up to the top. He could tell the effort had taken quite a bit out of her. She needed painkillers, something to reduce the swelling, a full meal and a hot shower.

Zane prayed they had a capable pilot in whoever was working the rescue attempt. These low-lying clouds would make everything more complicated. If the pilot wasn't good at his job, finding them would take a lot longer.

Starting a fire took a long time, since all the wood was wet. Once they did get it started—using every skill Zane had learned as an Eagle Scout and had him swearing he would trade his firstborn child for a set of matches—Caroline was right; it smoked like hell.

But it would be a signal. No one could doubt it was a man-made fire.

Which was good because Caroline's pallor concerned him more with each passing hour. He knew she felt bad when she didn't argue with him about resting rather than helping him gather more firewood. She just nodded.

So when they heard a low-flying plane a couple hours later, Zane's relief was profound. He immediately began fanning the fire with his backpack. Caroline jumped up and waved her good arm. As the plane passed over them, its wings tilted back and forth like a drunk stumbling down the sidewalk. It then flew out of sight.

"Oh no," Caroline cried. "Did they miss us?"

"No, the pilot saw us. That's what the tilting of the wings signified. His best way to signal us."

"But he just left."

"As we found out the hard way yesterday, there's no real place to land around here. Too many trees, and the ravine didn't prove very fruitful as a runway. The pilot will radio in our location. Someone will be here as soon as they can."

Zane was right. A few hours later a park ranger vehi-

,cle showed up at their location, complete with food, water and a first aid kit.

After twice the normal dosage of ibuprofen and a relatively full belly, Caroline fell asleep in the back seat of the vehicle as they headed to the ranger station.

"We appreciate the effort you guys put in to finding us," Zane told the park ranger, whose name was Ron Nixon, as they neared the ranger station. They'd kept quiet much of the way to allow Caroline to sleep.

"We're just glad you're both all right. Captain Harris from the Corpus Christi police station had put in a special request to us to keep an eye on Ms. Gill."

"You mean like having her check in with you every few hours?"

Ranger Nixon gave a guilty grimace. "Actually, he asked us to drive out to see her every day. Just make sure she was okay. Told us what had happened to her."

Zane shook his head. Now he understood even more Caroline's insistence on him not holding back, on treating her as if he trusted her to be able to handle the situation put before her.

Because evidently, based on Captain Harris's actions, people were still trying to smother her.

But none of that was Ranger Nixon's fault, so there wasn't any point getting upset with him. He was just doing what had been asked of him. Captain Harris shouldn't have been so quick to share Caroline's personal story. She'd be mortified if she knew.

She just wanted to leave the past behind her. But evidently it was the people she cared about the most who wouldn't let her do that. Zane had been one of those people until last night.

He turned to Nixon. "I think she would've been fine under normal circumstances. No need for anyone to look out for her. This was a case of someone specifically chasing us."

"We're just glad you were able to land the plane. When we got your Mayday, we knew there was trouble based on the location."

"I think *landing* may be too polite of a word for what we did."

Nixon shrugged. "Anything you walk away from is a landing, right?"

Zane smiled. "I'm thankful you could find us this morning. I'm surprised you had a plane out as soon as you did. I thought you might have to bring one in as well as a pilot."

Ranger Nixon pulled the vehicle down the drive to the ranger station. "Normally, we would. But this morning a plane and a couple of pilots showed up on our little landing strip here. Evidently news about your Mayday had gotten around."

"Let me guess. To Captain Harris?" The Corpus Christi PD didn't have an airplane, but Zane wouldn't put it past the man to beg, borrow or steal one to come look for him and Caroline.

"No, not Harris. Much bigger than that."

Nixon didn't need to say any more; the people walking out the door of the ranger station said everything Zane needed to know. Jon Hatton and Lillian Muir from Omega Sector. They'd been the ones who had delivered the plane. One of them had been piloting it, which explained how he and Caroline were found so quickly. There wasn't anyone better in all the country when it came to search and rescue.

As Nixon pulled to a stop, Zane got out of the SUV. He went to shake Jon's hand as the man walked up, but Jon pulled him in for a quick, hard hug instead.

"I'm glad you're okay, brother," Jon murmured. "You and Caroline both."

Hard to believe this was a man Zane had fought with so hard when they'd first met nearly two years ago.

"Me too. She's conked out in the back. Had a dislocated shoulder I had to slip back into joint. That helped, but she was still in a lot of pain."

"Ouch," Lillian murmured.

Zane smiled at the petite woman, a member of the Omega SWAT team. She was damn tough. Zane wouldn't doubt she'd had a dislocated limb at some point in her past. "Thanks for coming, Lil."

"Glad to get away from all the wedding craziness happening at Omega. Steve Drackett got hitched last month. Now this one—" she nudged Jon "—and Sherry. Then Brandon Han and Andrea Gordon are scheduled for February. It's like there's something in the water."

Zane smiled. "By all means, let's get to some more fun stuff, then. Like catching the psychopath who's trying to kill us."

Chapter Eleven

Damien Freihof couldn't have orchestrated this situation any better if he had planned the whole thing himself.

Oh, wait, he *had* planned the whole thing himself, and yep, it had worked exactly how he'd envisioned it.

Damien read again the report given to him from the secretive Mr. Fawkes, a mole inside Omega Sector working with Damien to take the organization down. Damien still didn't know the man's real name, but as long as he kept providing valuable information, he could remain as taciturn as he wanted.

Profiler Jon Hatton and SWAT team member Lillian Muir had rushed down to Texas from Omega Sector headquarters in Colorado to help when they'd heard trouble had found Zane Wales and Caroline Gill. To offer their assistance in any and every way possible, including the use of the search and rescue airplane.

Evidently a Mayday report had come from Zane Wales's plane to the ranger station. The ranger station had notified the Corpus Christi Police Department, who had notified Omega Sector, who in turn, inadvertently of course, had notified Damien.

Damien didn't much care if Zane Wales and Caroline Gill were dead already or not. If they weren't yet, they would be soon. Besides, they were just a means to an end.

Making Omega Sector pay. Making the members of Omega Sector understand the agony of losing people they love. Damien had already taken the life of one Omega agent, but his plan wasn't to kill off agents one by one.

He wanted to kill the people they *cared* about. Snatch them away. Gut Omega from the inside.

Just like they'd done to him when they'd killed his Natalie. Omega thought the battle had started with him when Damien had gone after SWAT member Ashton Fitzgerald and his lover, Summer Worrall. But it had really started seven years ago with Damien's wife's death in an Omega raid on his home.

Natalie had been his most prized possession. She'd made him the envy of all his friends when she'd married him. He could still picture her beautiful face, her long blond hair, her beautiful blue eyes. The classic American beauty. And she'd been *his*. Only his.

Until Omega took her life.

And now they would pay. One loved one at a time. And then when they knew the agony of love lost, Damien and the mole, Mr. Fawkes, would destroy Omega for good. Mr. Fawkes had his own political agenda, but Damien didn't care much about that.

A text came to Damien's burner phone. He knew it had to be one of two parties. Either Mr. Fawkes or the Trumpolds, the people who wanted to kill Zane and Caroline.

Mr. Fawkes.

Wales and Gill are still alive after the plane crash. Jon Hatton and Lillian Muir are going with them from Big Bend to CC.

Of course Jon Hatton would go with his friends to Corpus Christi, even with his own wedding coming up next week. After all, Zane and Caroline meant so much to Jon. They meant a lot to many people at Omega Sector.

That was why this entire plan would work. If Omega didn't care, killing the couple in Texas wouldn't make any difference.

Now he had another call to make. To Nicholas Trumpold. Brother of the late Paul Trumpold, the man who had attacked and raped Caroline Gill.

Damien had spent considerable time over the last few weeks convincing Nicholas and his sister, Lisette, that their beloved brother had been framed. That Caroline Gill had lied about the attack and Zane Wales, as an officer of the Corpus Christi PD at the time, had helped frame Paul.

That the police department had been so desperate to make the public think they had put the serial rapist terrorizing the city behind bars they'd looked the other way at evidence that would've exonerated their brother.

None of that was true, of course. Paul Trumpold had been a psychopath intent on hurting women. The hospital photos of the women he'd attacked told a story of sick violence and desire for their humiliation. Trumpold, about to be caught and arrested, had then attacked Jon Hatton and his fiancée, Sherry Mitchell, and nearly killed them both.

But Paul Trumpold's siblings, who had idolized their big brother, had been easily convinced of their brother's innocence.

They'd just wanted to believe it so badly. That he couldn't possibly be the monster he'd been made out to be. Paul had died early in prison and hadn't been around to tell them anything.

The falsified documents Damien had created, making it look as if Caroline and Zane had both lied about the entire situation, had just sealed the deal. From there it hadn't taken long for Damien to convince the Trumpold siblings to get revenge on their brother's behalf.

Of course, they had no idea that them taking revenge would also suit Damien's purpose—it would tear at a piece of Omega.

Omega knew Damien was behind the attacks on their loved ones. Heaven knew, he'd left them enough clues, a whole wall's worth. They even knew about Damien's ability to change his appearance. To make himself look like someone completely different every time he stepped outside. That was what had kept him ahead of law enforcement, and all their facial recognition software, for the past year, since he'd escaped from prison.

Sometimes he went out with no disguises on whatsoever just to mess with them. It was fun to hear about them scurrying around trying to find him like ants.

But now he had a business call to make. He dialed Nicholas Trumpold's number to give them the news that Zane and Caroline were still alive.

"Hello, Damien."

"Where are you, Nicholas?"

"We're outside of Big Bend, if that's what you're worried about. After we sabotaged Wales's plane and led them back to it, we didn't stick around."

"I'm sorry to inform you that Mr. Wales and Ms. Gill made it out of the crash alive." Damien wondered how the other man would take the news.

Silence for a long moment. "Good."

"Good?" That wasn't what Damien had been expecting to hear.

"Lisette and I discussed it. That we had been rash in our decision to kill Wales and Gill and make it look like an accident."

It sounded like the Trumpolds were having second

thoughts. Damien had very little patience for people who deviated from the plan.

Especially when those people were expendable in the overall strategy like the Trumpolds. But Damien kept his patience. "Nicholas—"

"What I mean by that is that if Zane Wales and Caroline Gill had died in either the rappelling accident or the plane crash we set up for them, then the world wouldn't know the truth about our brother. Wouldn't know they lied."

Damien's eyebrow rose. Interesting. "That's true."

"So it's good that they made it out alive. Lisette and I have a new plan."

"And what is that?"

"We're going to get them to confess. To state publicly what they did and clear Paul's name."

There was no way in hell that was ever going to happen, but Damien kept that knowledge to himself. "They've kept it a secret for over eighteen months now. I don't think they're just going to confess."

"Lisette and I have already talked about that. We'll force them to confess."

"Sounds painful." Damien smiled.

"I'm sure it will be."

Evidently Paul hadn't been the only psychopath in the Trumpold family. Sounded like Nicholas was pretty excited about the thought of torturing Zane and Caroline. To get them to confess to something that was completely untrue.

Damien grinned. It was unfortunate for the Texan couple. But it worked just perfectly for him.

FORTY-EIGHT HOURS after Zane's plane had crashed, they made it back to Corpus Christi. Caroline had barely had time to say hello to Jon and Lillian at the ranger station before she was immediately whisked off to the local hospital just outside of Big Bend. An X-ray and MRI had shown that she had no breaks or fractures and that Zane had done a pretty damn good job getting her joint back into the socket.

The doctor gave her a prescription-level painkiller and sent her on her way, calling her very lucky.

Caroline already knew that. Not just because they'd survived the crash, but because of what had happened afterward between her and Zane.

Their lovemaking had been downright fantastic. Not just the physical aspect of it, although that had been awesome too, but the fact that for the first time since the attack Caroline had just felt *normal*.

Maybe not actually normal, since they'd been in an overhang on the middle of a cliff surrounded by a storm after surviving a plane crash. But normal as in Caroline and Zane.

Not rape survivor Caroline. Just *Caroline.*

And it had felt amazing.

In all possible ways.

She knew it didn't solve all the problems, particularly the fact that they had someone trying to kill them. But damned if Caroline didn't feel better than she had in months.

Zane had made love to her like he used to. Like he wasn't afraid she would break or run screaming. She peeked over at him from where she sat in the passenger's seat now, his strong arms gripping the steering wheel, easing them through Corpus Christi traffic. They'd just come from the police station.

"Captain Harris looked pretty giddy to have you back." She couldn't help but tease him. They'd dropped Jon and Lillian at the department so Jon could brief Harris and the other officers about what was going on. Harris, once

he'd heard about Zane's plane, had told him the only logi-
cal thing—given the circumstances—was for Zane to be
reinstated as law enforcement.

Kill two birds with one stone: Zane needed temporary
employment, and Corpus Christi needed one of their best
detectives back on the job.

Zane grimaced. "I thought he might actually break out
into a jig when I said I would come back temporarily."

"He never filled your detective position, you know.
Hemmed and hawed about budget cuts, but we all knew
he was hoping you would return."

She saw his fingers tighten on the steering wheel. "I
don't think Harris or anybody else should put too much
faith in me. Not only am I rusty, I wasn't at the top of my
game when I left."

Caroline studied him. She'd lost so much in the attack,
but Zane had lost a lot too. The difference had been that
her wounds were visible and she'd therefore gotten all the
help and support she'd needed.

Had Zane gotten any help or support? Would he even
have accepted it if anyone offered? Knowing him, probably not.

"Airplane," she said to him.

"What?" He glanced at her before looking back at the
road. "Wait. Is there a reason why you're using your safe
word? Are you okay?"

"No, I'm fine. But you need a safe word. Have you ever
thought of that?"

"What?"

"Okay, maybe not a safe word. But you know how I had
to almost force you into treating me normally in the ravine?
When we—" She floundered, unable to get the words out,
suddenly feeling a little embarrassed.

He glanced at her again, eyebrow raised. "Had incredibly awesome sex?" He reached out and grabbed her hand, entwining their fingers.

She flushed but grinned. "Yes. That. It wasn't until I demanded you treat me normally that you did it."

"Okay, I still don't understand what this has to do with me needing a safe word."

"You don't need a safe word. But you do need to force yourself to start treating *you* normally."

He glanced at her with one eyebrow raised. "I'm pretty sure I don't know what you're talking about."

But he did. She knew he did. "I'm pretty sure you do. Enough, Zane. Just like you had to stop treating me like I was broken, you have to stop treating yourself that way."

He let go of her hand, making it look like he needed both of his on the wheel, but she knew him well enough to know that he didn't like to think she might be right.

"You have to admit what you lost in the attack, Zane."

"I lost you."

"You lost more than that. You lost your faith in yourself. Your confidence as a law enforcement officer. Things were taken from *you* in my attack too."

Zane scoffed. "Oh, boo-hoo. Compared to what you lost, who gives a rat's ass what I lost."

"It's not a damn competition, Zane. Nobody gets a trophy for losing the most." Her voice was rising. His was too.

But she didn't mind fighting with him. It was just more proof that he wasn't holding back.

"I know that." He slid his fingers through his hair in a frustrated gesture. "But I also know that what I lost was nothing compared to what you did."

"And I had people lining up down the block to help me. To talk to me. Do you know that Grace Parker, the top psychiatrist at Omega Sector, has been counseling me?"

"No." He glanced at her again. "I assumed you had

someone you talked to, but I didn't know it was someone with Omega."

"She's the best there is. I love her."

"I'm glad you have someone. That's important in a situation like this."

"Exactly." She paused for just a minute. "Who do you have, Zane? Who have you talked to?"

He didn't answer, just stared out the windshield.

"This was too big to tackle on our own. For either of us," she said quietly. "Even now."

"Well, I'm fine. People have different ways of coping. You talked to a shrink. I—"

"Ran away from a job you loved and moved to the outskirts of town so you would never have to run into me or any of your colleagues unless you wanted to." Now it was her turn to raise an eyebrow at him.

"Just leave it alone, Caroline. I did what I thought I had to do."

Knowing what he thought, how he blamed himself for her attack, Caroline understood that. But it was time for a change.

"Do you still feel like it's what you have to do? Even after what happened between us at Big Bend?"

"I feel like right now we need to focus on keeping Damien Freihof and whoever he's working with from carrying out their plans to kill us. The rest can wait."

"You're avoiding, Zane."

"I'm working on keeping us safe."

Caroline had meant to tell him where her new town house was, the one she'd moved into just a couple of months ago. But she realized Zane already knew.

"You know where I live." Her tone was accusatory.

"Yes."

"I only moved there six weeks ago."

He shrugged. "I knew when you moved. I've always known. I knew when you moved to the place before that. And the other. I knew when you moved out of your parents' house. Although I wasn't surprised at that."

"I couldn't live there anymore. None of us ever wanted to set foot there again. They sold it."

"I don't blame you. Don't blame them."

"Then the other places... I just had a hard time. Tried living with a roommate, and that didn't work. Moved on my own. Tried a second-floor apartment. Just trying different things to see what worked for me."

"And this new place?"

"I've come to discover it's not really the place that makes that much of a difference. It's my frame of mind. Sometimes I have no problem for days or even weeks. But then sometimes..." Caroline shrugged. "The other night when we saw each other at the Silver Eagle, I was there because I couldn't force myself to go into my town house alone."

"I'm sorry."

"I have good days and I have bad days. That would be true for you too if you came back to law enforcement, you know. You would have some bad days. But some would be good."

"Give it a rest, Caro. I'm already temporarily reinstated."

"Maybe I miss your white hat."

"You hated that hat. Knocked it off my head every chance you got."

Only so she could run her fingers through his hair, but she didn't have to tell him that. "Well, now I miss it."

He pulled up to her town house. "I'm not leaving you here, by the way."

"I can take care of myself."

"That's great. You can take care of yourself with me at your side. Keys."

She rolled her eyes. "Whatever. I just want to get into some different clothes. We can fight about this later."

She tossed him the keys and he opened the truck door before turning back to her. "Wait here. Just in case."

He drew his gun from his belt holster and moved into the town house. Just a couple minutes later he came back out.

"Okay, looks like we're clear."

Entering her town house was quite a bit easier with Zane by her side, she had to admit. But even then she felt compelled to do her normal safety routine as soon as she walked in.

She looked at him. "Um, airplane."

He immediately stepped closer, face concerned. "What's going on? How can I help?"

She wanted to kiss him for knowing the perfect thing to say without even thinking about it. She knew he took her seriously without wanting to fix it himself.

"I have a process. Something I do every time I come home. I need to do that now, if it's okay."

He looked relieved. "Sure."

"It's a little weird."

"Does it involve you getting naked and dancing in the middle of the living room?"

She smiled. "No, sorry."

"Damn it. Whatever, then. Do your boring little weird thing."

Caroline began walking around the living room, running her fingers along the bottom of each of the window-sills where they met the apron—the little ledge sticking out. By the time she got to the third one she knew Zane had to wonder what exactly she was doing, but he waited patiently.

After she'd checked all the windows she walked to the back door and crouched down. She looked toward the bottom of the door and froze at what she saw. "Zane?"

"Yeah?" He was to her in a second. "What's going on?"

"Someone has been in my town house."

Chapter Twelve

Zane immediately had his sidearm out again. He'd already checked her small place pretty thoroughly.

"There's no one in here now, that's for sure. How do you know someone has been in here?"

She showed him a piece of clear tape she'd put at the bottom of her back door. Immediately he realized how it worked. The tape was unnoticeable when the door was closed, covering both the door and frame. But if the door opened, the tape came unstuck from the door frame.

Very simple but very effective. It was what she had been checking for at each of her windows also.

"I always have this on the back door and windows." She grimaced. "It's one of the coping mechanisms Dr. Parker and I came up with."

He put his gun away. "To know if someone has been in the house?"

"About eight months after the attack I started waking up at night terrified someone was in the house with me. That was the second time I moved into a place that had as few windows as possible." She shrugged. "The tape was a simple method that allowed me to know for sure, to convince my terrorized mind at three o'clock in the morning that no one could possibly be inside."

He reached over and yanked her into his arms, thankful when she didn't stiffen or pull away, as emotion nearly overwhelmed him. Her words broke his heart and yet made him so damn proud of her at the same time.

"I think it's brilliant if you ask me."

He felt her good shoulder shrug slightly. "At first I considered myself a coward. I could understand and condone moving out of my parents' beach house, where the attack happened. But moving to the second place, with less windows, just seemed cowardly."

"But it wasn't."

"No. It took me a while to figure that out. Recovery is not a straight line. It's sometimes one step forward and half a mile back. Setbacks are part of the process."

Zane realized *he* should have been part of her process too. Maybe he could've helped her through some of this if he'd chosen to really listen to her needs rather than give her what *he* thought she needed.

Maybe the tape still would've been necessary. But maybe knowing he was there would've been enough.

"Hey, in the now, Wales."

"What?"

"Whatever it is that has you all stiff? Let it go. We can't change the past. We can only change what we choose to do today."

She was right. And today, right now, involved the fact that someone had been inside her town house. He reluctantly let her go.

"I assume you didn't ask anyone to water plants or bring in your mail while you were gone?"

"No. No plants. And I had asked the post office to hold my mail."

"It could be innocent. Smoke detector malfunctioned and the landlord came in. Something like that."

But after someone had tried to kill them multiple times,

neither of them actually believed that was the case. And since he hadn't planned on leaving her alone anyway, he might as well take her with him instead.

"Let's get what you need. Try to touch as little as possible. I'll send the CSI team in here to see if we can get any prints. Since the perp didn't think you'd know he was in here at all, maybe he didn't wear gloves."

"I hadn't thought of that. I have a landline if you want to call it in." They'd both lost their phones at Big Bend.

"Really? Most people don't anymore. Just use their cell phones."

She shrugged. "Another coping mechanism. Knowing I would always have two different ways of calling for help if needed."

"Smart again."

"One of the first things Dr. Parker and I discussed was that I didn't need to apologize for how I chose to survive. I wasn't doing drugs. Wasn't drinking obsessively or breaking any laws. So anything I did to help cope wasn't anything to be ashamed of."

He kissed her forehead. "Damn straight."

He helped her gather a couple of changes of clothes and toiletries.

"Where are we going?"

"We'll go to my place. But first things first, we've got to get both our phones replaced."

They left Caroline's town house and took care of the tedious job of getting new phones. By that time Caroline was looking pretty tired and Zane was feeling it too. They needed a good night's sleep to face what was ahead.

Not to mention he very much looked forward to having Caroline in an actual bed.

But when they arrived at Zane's house, he didn't need

a broken piece of tape on the door to know someone had been in his place.

Someone had completely trashed it.

Once he got the door open and saw the damage, he immediately drew his weapon. "Caro, go wait outside."

"What? What is it?"

"Someone's been in here."

"I'll call Captain Harris."

"Call Jon and Lillian too."

Zane's house on the outskirts of town wasn't much. Two bedrooms, one bath. He'd basically rented it because of its proximity to the airfield he spent so much time at with his business. And because he hadn't been able to force himself to live at the house he'd bought.

Whatever care the intruders had taken at Caroline's house to make sure they would go unnoticed, they'd done the opposite here. Furniture was overturned, dishes broken, contents of drawers strewn everywhere.

Someone had been pissed off when they did this.

"Jon and Lillian are on their way. ETA about ten minutes. Captain Harris said he would have the crime lab techs come over here as soon as they're done with my town house."

"Okay."

"Is it all right for me to come in or should I stay outside?"

In most cases Zane would have people wait outside. Less chance of contaminating possible evidence. But he didn't want Caroline out there exposed in case the person who did this wasn't done with their little temper tantrum.

"Do you mind coming in but just staying by the door?" They'd still be able to see and hear each other.

"Sure."

He heard Caroline's low whistle when she saw the state

of his house. "Unless your housekeeping skills took a sharp turn for the worse after we broke up, someone was really angry in here."

Zane nodded. "Generally speaking, destruction of this magnitude would suggest that the perp knows me personally. Has a personally directed anger toward me."

"You and the contents of your fridge." She pointed toward the kitchen, where everything that had been in his refrigerator now lay all over the floor.

"Sometimes someone can be searching for something and when they can't find it they go into a rage. But this is extreme even for that."

"And what would someone have been looking for in your house?"

"I have no idea. And especially Damien Freihof. I didn't even know who he was until Jon told me about him."

"Me neither. And I can't figure out what he has to do with us."

"Only that we have ties to Omega. That seems to be it." Zane looked through his bedroom and the bathroom—same sort of destruction, no discernible pattern—before coming back out to the kitchen.

"Did the same person who broke into my house do this to yours?" Caroline asked from where she still stood just inside the door.

"Probably."

"Why were they so destructive here but not at my place?"

He stood in the middle of the room, turning so he could see everything, trying to look at it from a detached, professional opinion.

"Either they escalated in anger, maybe starting with something at your place, then ending it here. Or…" He trailed off, not liking where his thoughts were heading.

"What?"

"Or they've been after me from the beginning and I led them straight to you at Big Bend."

"I thought Jon said both our names were found in whatever clues Damien Freihof left for Omega."

"Yes, but you can't deny that there's definitely an anger here that wasn't present at your house."

"But maybe they came here first."

Zane had to admit that could be true. There were too many unknown variables. But one thing would give him some information: the food.

He walked into the kitchen and bent down to where the half gallon of milk had been thrown onto the ground and spilled.

He smelled it.

"I'm SWAT and don't really do much detective work, but I'm going to go with my gut on this one and say that's milk," Lillian said from the door.

Zane got back up from the ground. "Hey, guys."

"Wow, they really did a number on this place," Jon said, pulling on a pair of gloves.

"Yeah. Forensics team is on their way over," Zane told him. Lillian stayed near Caroline at the door. "The milk has no smell."

"None? Not the least bit of souring?"

"No. As a matter of fact, it's still a little cool."

Both men now had their hands near their sidearms. It was warm enough in Zane's house that milk that had been out for a day or two would've at least been room temperature. Not cool.

This had happened recently. Whoever had broken into Zane's house had done it in the last few hours.

Jon crouched down next to Zane to touch the milk himself.

"Whoever it was could've been here waiting to ambush

you or figured you would both be here," Jon said in a volume that wouldn't carry to the door.

Zane glanced over to where Lillian and Caroline were talking to each other. "Yeah, if we hadn't had to replace our phones, we would've been here hours ago. I've got to take Caroline somewhere safe."

"Hotel?"

"No. I have someplace else in mind." A place he'd never planned to tell Caroline about. But it would be much more comfortable than a hotel. "It will be better, since we don't know how long it will take to catch Freihof and his goons."

"About that." Jon grimaced.

"What?"

"We had a confirmed sighting of Freihof in Colorado Springs at the same time your trouble was happening in Big Bend. I mean obvious. Freihof is pretty brilliant when it comes to disguises and he definitely wanted to make sure we knew it was him and we knew he was in Colorado."

"So whoever tried to kill us wasn't him."

Jon shrugged. "He wasn't physically present in Texas is all I'm saying. The last person who came after someone at Omega wasn't actually Freihof—it was someone he had convinced needed to take revenge."

Jon explained about SWAT member Ashton Fitzgerald and how he'd been hunted down by Curtis Harper, the son of a man who'd been killed in an Omega SWAT raid years ago. Freihof had told Harper he would help the man get his revenge.

Harper had nearly died in the process, since Freihof hadn't mentioned that he would blow up Harper along with any nearby Omega agents.

"Lillian is here, if needed, as a sort of protection duty for Caroline. I thought Caroline might be more comfortable with a woman," Jon continued. "If you weren't around."

And there it was again. The good intentions Caroline spoke about. People—even her best friend's fiancé—wanting to protect her, but it made her feel weak, breakable.

But on the other hand, Zane knew what Lillian could do. Could kill a man with her tiny bare hands and not break a sweat. As far as protection detail went, very few could beat Lillian Muir, man or woman. And right now, no matter why Lillian was the one chosen, they needed all the help they could get.

"So if Freihof didn't do it, then he's either hired someone to come after us or has found someone from my past. I've arrested a lot of people. Quite a few who would be pretty pissed off. A couple who it wouldn't take much to talk into coming after me."

Both men stood. "And honestly, brother, it wouldn't take very much observation to realize that the best way to get to you, to cause you pain, is through that lady over there." Jon pointed at Caroline.

"I've got to keep her safe, Jon. I can't stand the thought of anything happening to her. Not again."

"I know. You get her someplace safe, away from her house or here. And until we know more, telling as few people as possible where that place is might be a good idea. Lillian and I will wait for the crime scene team here."

Zane nodded. "Thanks, Jon. I'll be in touch tomorrow."

Jon slapped him gently on the shoulder as Zane turned toward Caroline.

He would keep her safe no matter what. Knew where it was that he would take her. Even if it meant giving up the secret he never meant to share with anyone. Especially her.

Chapter Thirteen

"Zane, where are we going?"

They'd been driving around in his truck for nearly an hour now. Every time she thought she knew where they were headed, Zane would make a sudden turn, leading them to another part of town.

Not that Caroline minded riding around in his truck like old times, but Zane was becoming more tense as they drove.

"I don't think either my house or yours is safe. As a matter of fact, Jon and I both feel whoever broke in did it after the attempt on our lives at Big Bend, not before. Maybe even earlier today."

Suddenly the danger seemed even closer and she understood why Zane was driving them around. He was making sure no one was following them. That would also explain his tension.

"So a hotel? Somewhere to hang out?" They needed rest. She needed rest. She needed to feel Zane's arms around her again.

She realized they were headed toward the beach, maybe a hotel nearby. She hadn't been there in a long time. She sighed. Yet another thing she'd allowed to be taken from her in the attack. But it would be different with Zane with her.

Zane's presence always made everything different.

Zane didn't answer her question, and she didn't push. He obviously had a plan and she trusted him. It wasn't long before they pulled up to a house a couple blocks from the oceanfront, and only a couple of neighborhoods over from where her parents' house used to be.

There weren't any hotels in this area of the beach. Just houses.

"Where are we going? There aren't any hotels here."

"We're not staying at a hotel."

She looked around, unable to decide if this area should make her uncomfortable or not. It wasn't anything at the beach that had hurt her. The man who had caused her such pain was dead.

"A safe house? Something of the department's?"

She didn't think they would have an oceanfront safe house, but crazier things had happened.

"No, it's not the department's. But it is safe."

They pulled into the drive of a small house, about a block and a half from the actual waterfront. Like many of the houses so close to the ocean, there was no full bottom floor. It was built on glorified stilts to keep the water from doing much damage during hurricane season. The entire living area started on the second floor. This allowed Zane to pull his truck all the way under the house to park.

They both got out and Zane grabbed their duffel bags from the cab behind his seat. He led her up the stairs and pulled out a key on his normal key ring and unlocked the door, holding it open for her, and walking in behind her.

She looked around, taking in the open floor plan with the cozy living room—complete with couch and love seat—opening up into the kitchen. From first glance there looked to be three bedrooms, two on one end of the living room, a master bedroom on the other side.

Zane wasn't looking around at all, obviously familiar with the house and its layout.

"What is this, a rental? A friend's place?"

He set the bags down. "No. Actually, I own it."

She spun to stare at him. "You own a house at the beach." She couldn't help but laugh. "You hate the beach. I used to have to drag you here whenever I wanted to go. What, did you buy it as an investment property or something?"

"Something like that."

"I guess it's hard to rent it out during the winter."

Zane just shrugged, walking over to get a bottle of water out of the refrigerator. Except, why would he know there was water in the fridge? He shouldn't be that familiar with what was on the inside of the rental property.

There was something Zane wasn't telling her.

"Does anyone know we're here?"

"I gave Jon and Lillian the address, but not anybody from the department. Why?"

She walked over and opened the refrigerator. It didn't have a lot of stuff in it, but neither was it empty. "I just wondered if you had someone come stock the house for us."

"No, I wanted to keep our whereabouts as tightly guarded as possible."

She turned around to face him, crossing her arms over her chest. "You don't rent this place out, or at least you haven't for a while."

Zane took a chug of his water. "No. You're right. I don't rent it out."

"Do you live here too?" Caroline couldn't figure out what piece of the puzzle she was missing. "Two houses or something?"

"No. I've slept here occasionally when I haven't wanted

to drive all the way back out to my house. But, no, I don't live here."

"So let me see if I understand. You own a pretty nice beach cottage. It would make a great place to live, but you don't live here. It would also make a great rental property, but you don't rent it out."

"Just leave it alone, Caroline."

She shook her head. "Why? What is there to leave alone? It's weird, Zane. And not very financially smart."

"Yeah, I'm well aware of the fact that a mortgage and a separate rent payment every month, even though my place near the airfield is pretty negligible in terms of rent, is not the best plan."

This was ridiculous. "Then why the hell are you doing it? Move here."

"I can't. Like you said, I don't like the beach."

She rolled her eyes. "Then sell or rent this place, for heaven's sake."

"I can't do that, either."

"Why the hell not?" Her volume was going up, but she couldn't help it.

His fist slammed down against the kitchen island. "I bought this place for you, okay? For us."

"What?" She reared back a step.

The anger in his voice had disappeared. "I closed on this house two weeks before you were attacked. I had planned on asking you to move into it with me. But then…"

But then everything changed.

She took a step closer, but it felt like a chasm separated them rather than one small kitchen. "You never told me. Even after."

"There was never a good time. First you were in recovery. Then you wanted nothing to do with the beach. Then…" He trailed off, turning away and walking over to the massive doors that led out to the deck. He opened them and glanced back at her over his shoulder. "Then you wanted nothing to do with me."

Caroline watched as he walked outside, bracing his forearms on the rail of the deck, looking out at the view of the ocean the house afforded.

She looked at the house with new eyes. He'd bought this for *them*.

It was perfect, she realized. Would've been just what she would've wanted to start a life together with Zane.

She wanted to yell, to scream out her pain. To find that she'd lost even more than she'd ever known was almost too much to bear.

She'd already lost so much. They both had.

She looked at Zane standing out on the deck, staring at the sea. Standing on the deck he'd known she would love. Hell, she already did and she hadn't stepped foot out there yet.

Could she walk out there to Zane right now, on the deck that should've been theirs, and try to make everything right? To make their relationship what it was?

No, she couldn't. Too much time had passed. For both of them. Things were too different. Their relationship could never be what it once was.

But that didn't mean it had to be nothing.

She'd spent a lot of time with Dr. Parker in those first few months just trying to get things back to standard, to ordinary. Except Caroline had no idea what ordinary was. She and Dr. Parker had worked long and hard on establishing a new baseline of normal. Of accepting that things would never go back to the way they were, but that didn't mean you were never okay again.

She and Zane had to establish a new baseline of normal. Starting right now.

She began walking toward him just as he turned to look at her. They were in sync, the way they'd always been. She stepped out onto the deck and he reached his hand out toward her. Neither of them said anything, just held on to one another's hand.

Finally, Zane pulled Caroline against his chest as he leaned back on the railing. She wrapped her arms around his trim waist, hooking her thumbs into the back belt loops of his jeans. The beat of his heart under her ear reassured her of her safety much more than the waist holster she'd felt briefly as she'd slipped her arms around him.

She wished she could just stay against him forever.

But her phone chirped obnoxiously from her pocket.

"Text?" he asked.

"Yes," she murmured, her mouth half against his shirt. "Just ignore it."

"It might be Jon or the precinct." He slipped his fingers into her pocket to pull it out. "Or, God forbid, your parents."

Caroline smiled, letting him read the text. Her parents hadn't ever really liked Zane. Or at least hadn't liked how volatile their relationship was. But they would have no idea he was around, so she doubted it would be anything about Zane.

But she felt him stiffen beneath her. "What the hell, Caroline?"

"What?"

He spun the phone around so she could read the message.

You're a liar and you deserve everything you've got coming to you. Don't think you've escaped.

Caroline grabbed the phone. "Oh yeah. I forgot about these stupid texts. I keep meaning to ask someone how to block this number."

"How long have you been getting them?"

"I don't know." She pulled away, the peace she'd known just a few moments before, gone. "A week? Why are you getting all angry? It's just a wrong number."

"A wrong number? Someone is trying to kill you, Caroline. You should've told me about this. They've got to be connected."

"I didn't think about it, okay? And then I didn't have my phone, so I didn't get any messages."

She looked up at him, ready to blast into him again, but realized there was something else. "What? What aren't you telling me?"

He reached into his pocket and held out his phone so she could see the message that had just arrived for him.

What you hid will come to light. Soon the whole world will know.

She grabbed the phone out of his hand. "What? Is this your first message?"

"No. Like you, they've been coming for a week."

"Zane—"

He took her hand and led her inside. "Yeah, I know. This means we're both being targeted. We've got to get these phones to the station, see what info the tech department can get from them."

"Do you think it's someone local?"

"I don't know. But I plan to find out."

Chapter Fourteen

"Okay, I know this is a hard question, but I need honesty from both you guys," Jon said to them as they sat around the table in the Corpus Christi PD conference room.

They'd brought the phones back last night and left them for tech—happy to get the overtime—to sort through. Zane had let Jon and Lillian know about the texts but then had explained they were going back home.

Home. Zane didn't let himself think too much about that. For nearly two years he hadn't let himself think about the beach cottage and what it represented and how he hadn't been able to let it go. A shrink would have a field day with that one. Maybe that was why he'd never gone to talk to anyone about his feelings.

But taking Caroline home with him, despite the danger, had just felt right. And getting her into a bed with him and making love, slowly, softly—such a different pace for them—had definitely felt right.

But now the time for tenderness was over. It was time to do whatever was necessary to find who was targeting them and make sure Caroline was safe again.

"Despite what the texts imply, Jon, I don't think either Caroline or I have anything to hide."

Jon leaned back in his chair. "I don't doubt that. But I thought we should start with the opening. If either of you took up shoplifting or ran over your neighbor's cat and buried it in your yard, now is the time to come clean with that."

It was good to have Jon here with them. It eased some of the pressure. He knew them, they didn't have to go through the awkward stages of building up trust. Jon wanted to protect Caroline and stop whoever was behind this almost as much as Zane did. After all, Caroline was the best friend of Jon's bride-to-be. The wedding was scheduled for this weekend.

"All right," Caroline said. "I'll admit, the first bridesmaid dress your fiancée picked out? I threatened to kill her if she went with that one. Pretty sure I said it publicly."

Jon chuckled. "The powder blue one?"

Caroline rolled her eyes. "For an artist, she had some pretty big missteps there for a while. Fortunately, she finally picked a great one and I didn't have to kill her."

Jon smiled. "But seriously. Zane, any corners you cut as you got your business started? Caroline, any accidents where maybe you covered a bad call by telling a lie?"

Zane could see both he and Caroline becoming defensive. Nobody liked to have their integrity questioned.

Jon held out a hand. "Listen, you guys are like family to me. And I would personally vouch for both of you without question. But if you've got something you need to get off your chest, now is the time."

"I've got nothing, Jon." Caroline sat up taller in her seat as she said it. "There was a drunk who was threatening to get me fired a few days ago at an accident scene, since I wouldn't stay and look at his dislocated pinkie when I had a bunch of other people around me with serious injuries. But that's the only incident I can recall in the recent past. Since the attack, I've basically just spent most of my time surviving and coming to grips with reality."

Jon nodded, then turned to Zane. "You? I remember

you had quite the hot temper when we worked together nearly two years ago."

Zane shrugged. "Still do. But I've kept to myself. Hell, I can't even remember having a real conversation with anyone outside my friends on the force for the past six months."

"Okay." Jon put both hands down on the desk. Obviously, he believed them and wasn't going to belabor the point. "Then let's talk about what the tech folks found out about the texts to your phones."

Jon pulled out papers and handed Zane and Caroline both copies. "Here's a list of all the texts that both of you received and the day and time they were sent."

"They were all sent close to the same time to both of us," Caroline pointed out.

"Yes." Jon nodded. "And they all came from the same phone. Not listed as registered to anyone, unfortunately."

Zane looked at the list of messages. There had been fourteen sent over the last eight days. Each one called Caroline a liar in some way and accused Zane of hiding something.

"So is this a dead end?" he asked Jon.

"We've got Omega looking into it. They've got more sophisticated technology to pull data from the phones. Maybe they can get something Corpus Christi couldn't."

"Okay." Zane sat back in his chair. "Did the CSI crew find anything at my house? Fingerprints?"

He appreciated that Jon had been keeping an eye on this so that Zane and Caroline could get a night of much-needed rest.

"Nothing usable. I stayed with them to see if I could figure out any patterns. See what the perp's overall plan was. But it honestly just looked like a fit of rage to me."

One of the CSI personnel came rushing into the room.

"Detective Wales, Agent Hatton, we have something you need to see in the lab."

Zane grabbed Caroline's hand and they rushed with Jon down the hall to the lab. They were met by Susan McGuinness, head of the CCPD crime lab.

"Zane, good to have you back here. We've missed you."

"Thanks, Susan. What's going on? Did you find something at my house?"

"No, actually, we found something at Caroline's house."

"Mine?" Caroline asked. "There wasn't any damage at my house."

"If it wasn't for Caroline's trick with a piece of tape, we wouldn't have known anyone was in there at all."

Susan nodded. "No doubt that's what the person who broke in wanted."

"Tell me you found a fingerprint, Susan."

"Would that be enough to get you to agree to return to the force full-time?" the older woman asked.

Zane could feel Caroline's smile and her eyes on him. He just shrugged. "Maybe."

"Well, unfortunately, it's not a fingerprint we found. But it is something much more interesting."

"What?" He, Jon and Caroline all asked at the same time.

"Transmitting devices. Hidden in two of Caroline's lamps."

Of all the things Jon was expecting to hear, this didn't even make the list. "Are you serious?"

"It wasn't us who found them, actually. It was that other Omega Sector agent. The lady," Susan said.

Jon looked closer at the bugs. "Lillian Muir. She's actually SWAT, not an investigator."

"Well, she was the one who found the bugs after we'd already left."

Jon nodded. "She and I agreed to split up. This morning we wanted to make sure no one was returning to the scene of the crime looking for either of you. She probably went inside to check."

"When she found something unusual, she went out and called us," Susan continued. "Smart on her part. We were able to figure out they were transmitting devices and that they were still actively transmitting."

Zane turned to Caroline and Jon. "That was probably why they trashed my house. To keep us focused over there instead of at your house, Caro. I never even thought to look for transmitting devices."

She shrugged. "I wouldn't have, either."

Jon turned back to the crime lab director. "Can we get any information from the devices? Anything specific about them?"

Lillian walked through the door. "You guys hear about the bugs at Caroline's house?"

"Susan was just telling us," Zane responded. "We're trying to figure out if there's anything usable in the bugs."

Susan looked over at Lillian. "We don't know."

"When will you know?" Zane asked.

"Well." Lillian smiled. "The lab doesn't know anything about the devices because I talked them into leaving them functional at Caroline's town house."

Caroline's eyes flew to Zane's, distress clear, but Zane already knew what Lillian was thinking. "So we can set a trap," he said.

"Yep." Lilian nodded. "I was very careful not to report finding the bugs while I was inside the house, and I made sure none of the nerds—" she turned to Susan "—no offense, said anything while we were inside."

"None taken," Susan responded. "It's a solid plan."

"So the perp doesn't know we know," Zane said, reaching for Caroline's hand. "This could be the break we need."

Caroline still didn't look convinced. "So we, what, go back to my house and give who is listening false information?"

Zane nodded. "Sort of. We can tell them whatever we want. They've got no reason not to believe it."

"We'll fabricate a situation where you guys are away from the department," Jon said. "Dinner or a walk or something."

"I don't want to take a chance with Caroline."

"Zane—"

He cupped her cheek with his hand. "It has nothing to do with not trusting you or thinking you can't handle yourself. I swear to you I would say this about any civilian. You don't have the training to be used as bait. It's too dangerous."

"Caroline, Zane's right," Lillian said. "It's a much better plan to let me wear a wavy brown wig and pose as you. We're roughly the same build. Until someone got right up on us, they wouldn't know it wasn't you."

Jon smiled kindly. "And once the perp is close enough to know the difference, we'll have officers waiting to arrest him."

"How do we know the guy won't just shoot? He was shooting at us at Big Bend," Caroline pointed out.

Zane could see her point. "He was trying to make our deaths look like an accident. Shooting us won't give him that."

"But he could decide to take his chances," Lillian pointed out. "We'll have to give a situation where you're vulnerable, but long-range shooting isn't an option."

Zane nodded. There were a lot of options. They just needed to figure out the best one. He didn't mind putting himself in danger if it meant catching the person intent on hurting Caroline.

"I don't like you setting yourself up," Caroline looked up at him with her big green eyes. "The same way you don't want me to do it, I don't want you to, either."

He smiled gently. "If I'm law enforcement, it's what I do."

She kissed the palm of his hand cupping her cheek. "Law enforcement or not, you watch your back."

"I won't have to. I've got the best doing that for me."

THEY DIDN'T WASTE any time putting their plan into action, knowing every moment they didn't make a move gave the killer more time to scheme.

So a few hours later Caroline found herself and Zane back at her town house, playing out a script they'd already formulated at the station.

"I just need a break, Zane," Caroline said as they walked in the front door. "This was supposed to be my vacation."

"It's not my fault someone is trying to kill you," Zane said, playing his part. "It's just not safe for you to go anywhere alone right now."

"I spent the entire day at the police station. I don't like the station. You know that. It brings back bad memories." Those words didn't require much acting. She still felt uncomfortable around the police station. "It makes me feel like a victim. Powerless."

Zane's eyes flew to hers. He knew she was speaking the truth now, having gone slightly off script.

"You might always feel that way," he said softly. "It might never be a place you're totally comfortable with."

She shrugged. "I have to admit, it's easier when you're there."

He walked over and wrapped his arms around her. "But I know you can handle it either way."

She needed to get them off her personal feelings and back on script.

"I know what I want to do!" This was it. The part of the plan Zane and Jon thought whoever was after them would go for. All Caroline had to do was sell it to whoever was listening.

Zane chuckled. "Wow, haven't seen you this excited for a while. What do you want to do?"

"There's that new shop, Taste Unlimited, downtown. It sells all sorts of foods made for picnics, but also wines and desserts."

"Sounds great to me."

"Let's go there and I'll pick out the food and you pick out the wine and dessert. It'll be a crazy hodgepodge and perfect for a picnic. We can even have the picnic in the station if you want to, since I'm sure going to the beach or a park is off-limits for a while."

"I just want to keep you safe."

His statement was part of the script, but she also knew it was true.

"But I guess a little shopping before locking us away at the station isn't a problem. And it sounds like we might come up with some crazy combinations."

Caroline reached over and kissed him. "That will make it even better."

Zane looked at his watch as if he was considering the time. "Okay, let's shower and I want you to take a little nap first. We'll leave for your Taste Unlimited place and their vast offerings in, say, three hours? Then we have to go to the station so I can get some work done."

He phrased it as though he wanted to make sure that was okay with her. As though they hadn't carefully discussed how much time to give whoever was listening so he could have a chance to investigate the store, see if it would be a great place to try to grab Caroline or Zane and formulate a plan.

There were already officers at the store waiting. Watching for anyone who might come in looking to scope out the place. Especially aware of what Damien Freihof looked like.

Caroline and Zane had laid the bait. Now it was time to see what they would catch in their trap.

Chapter Fifteen

A little more than three hours later, Zane was pulling into a spot in Taste Unlimited's parking lot. Lillian sat in the passenger seat next to him. Her normal dark hair was covered by a brown wig and she wore a pair of large sunglasses.

Not much could be done about her darker skin—Lillian's heritage was Latina, as opposed to Caroline's light skin and freckles. Lillian wore a long-sleeve shirt and a maxi skirt that covered most of her legs, but that was as much as could be done.

If anybody got a close look at Lillian, they would know she wasn't Caroline. But hopefully it would be enough. And thankfully Caroline currently waited at a safe house a few miles away. A protection detail with her. Knowing she was safe was the only thing that allowed Zane to be able to focus on this mission.

"Ready?" Zane asked Lillian.

"Yep. Let's get this son of a bitch."

Zane smiled. Nobody messed with Lillian who didn't live to regret it.

"So far we haven't seen anything unusual," Jon's voice said inside Zane's ear. He was in a van with a painter's logo, parked just outside the front door of the shop. Inside were detectives Wade Ammons and Raymond Stone, one working the register, the other the sandwich counter. The owners of Taste Unlimited had been fully cooperative, a fact for which Zane was truly grateful.

"Okay, Jon. We're going in."

"Roger that."

Another undercover officer would enter the store after Zane and Lillian and together they'd all be looking for anyone who seemed suspicious or overly interested in either Zane or Lillian's Caroline.

"All right, let's do this," Zane said to Lillian. She also could hear Jon through her earpiece.

Zane jumped out of the truck and hustled around it to open the door in a grand romantic gesture. Knowing the guy might be watching them even right now, Zane immediately tucked Lillian into his shoulder. She did her part, burying her head into his chest, wrapping both her arms around his waist.

To anyone else it would just look like a loving couple on their way to pick up food for a picnic with just a tad too much PDA. He hoped.

Zane glanced around without trying to give the appearance he was doing so. There was only so much he could do without giving himself away. He had to trust the people on the team. They were good at their jobs and had a much more natural vantage point, able to watch without being noticed.

He'd worked with Wade and Raymond for years in the department. Jon was also top at his job. Zane knew he could trust them all.

Once inside the store, he and Lillian split up.

"Pick us out something good," Lillian said to him, playing her part. She was keeping her sunglasses on even though she was inside. It would look unusual, but better than giving someone a clear picture of her face.

They were inside the store for about five minutes when Jon reported.

"Okay, we've got an SUV with tinted windows pulling up on the east side of the parking lot. Near the back exit. Single male, midforties, about to enter through the front door."

"Roger that," Zane murmured as everyone else did the same.

Zane positioned himself in a row where he could see the front entrance while appearing to be studying a label on a bottle of wine. He saw the man enter.

Nothing about the man's actions could be considered casual. He looked down one aisle, then another. He didn't do anything overtly suspicious, but neither did he look like the other customers. If they weren't looking for someone who had nefarious intentions, no one would probably take much notice of the man at all.

But expecting a killer? This man fit the bill.

He glanced over at Zane, then looked away quickly. Zane pretended to study the wine bottle as he watched the man pick up a jar of olives and do the same.

"Lillian, get in position by the back door. Let's see if we can tempt him into making a move." Jon's voice came over everyone's earpiece. "I'm running this guy through facial recognition, but unless we get super lucky, we're not going to get a response in time for it to be helpful."

The man set the olives on the shelf and began walking.

"He's coming your way, Lil," Zane whispered.

"Roger."

Zane moved through the aisle, wanting to be near in case something went down.

"You've got another couple coming in through the front," Jon said seconds before the door opened and the electronic chime gave its short whistle.

Counting the one pair who had already been inside the store, the man and the new couple, they had a total of five potential suspects.

Jon said what Zane was thinking. "Remember, we might not be dealing with a lone suspect. So don't discount these couples."

Zane heard Wade talk to one duo as they selected products. Lillian still had her back to the man to keep her face hidden. The man was slowly working his way up toward her.

"Lil, he's about seven feet behind you," Zane said, wanting to give her as much of an advantage as possible. From where he stood, he could see her nod her head just the slightest bit.

The new couple who came in knew exactly what they wanted. Grabbed a meat and cheese platter and a bottle of wine and were soon paying Wade at the register.

The suspicious man still hadn't made any moves, but neither were his actions normal. He was staring at different items up and down the aisles, as if he had no idea what he wanted.

Or he wasn't in here to buy anything at all. Maybe just like the team, he was scoping things out, checking to see if anything was fishy before he made his move.

Zane eased himself back just as Jon made the same call. "Everybody, the main suspect might be scoping, so don't do anything suspicious or draw attention to yourself. We've got a group of three women coming in the door, early twenties. And another single man, African American, midthirties."

Having more people in the store both helped and hurt. It made Zane and the crew less conspicuous, but it also gave them more people to have to watch. Even the group of women couldn't be ruled out.

"Roger," Raymond whispered into the comm unit before turning to the new customers and offering his assistance. Zane looked at the man he still found most suspicious. He seemed to be easing his way toward Lillian.

"He's about five feet from you now, Lil," he said softly. "Why don't you go check out that counter near the back door? I'm going to hang out near the front door in case he decides he wants to take me instead."

They were counting on the fact that the man would probably use a concealed sidearm to try to get either Zane or Lillian, or both, to leave with him. But in case he had other plans and decided shooting within the store was acceptable, the team all had their own weapons ready. Not to mention SWAT outside, who could be called in on a moment's notice.

Lillian moved toward the back door and Zane followed, still holding the bottle of wine he'd been studying but with his left hand so he'd be easily able to draw his gun from the holster with his right.

When the guy shifted his weight back and forth on his feet—deciding if this was worth it?—then moved toward Lillian, Zane was sure they had their guy.

"I think he's about to make a move," Zane said into his comm device. "Get ready to lock it down, Jon."

"Roger."

Zane could see Lillian, looking so much like Caroline with the brown wig, tense just slightly, not enough to be noticeable to a bystander but enough for Zane to be sure she was ready.

"Zane," Jon said. "We've got another single male entering the store. Parked where I would if I was the perp. Backed his car in for an easier getaway."

Damn it, Zane didn't want to split his focus between the guy almost on Lillian and the new one. He couldn't talk easily into his comm unit without the first guy hearing him.

"Zane," Wade said when he got a visual on the man entering the store, "This guy was at the store earlier. Came in, bought a sandwich and left. Big guy. Caucasian. Midtwenties."

That changed things. Someone who had scoped out the store earlier and then parked in a way that made an escape easier?

Suddenly they had two equally potential perps.

"I'm sending in another undercover officer, Joanna Cordell," Jon said. "Zane, you stay with Lillian and the first guy, and Joanna will be on the second."

Joanna had been on the force for a long time. She was in her fifties but was a good officer. Not to mention no one would pay much attention to her. She just looked like a friendly motherly type.

Zane turned and took a couple steps back so he couldn't be heard. "Remember, we need them to make a move before we take them down. We can't arrest anyone for being creepy."

"Roger that," Jon said. "She'll be coming through the door in fifteen seconds. Raymond, you work with her on the new guy. Wade, you get ready to go whichever way is needed."

"Roger." Both men's muffled responses came through.

Zane turned his attention back to Lillian and the agitated guy. He was still moving closer to her and seemed to be more nervous. He picked up one more bottle, then put it down, before walking right over to Lillian.

"Excuse me, miss?" Zane's hand was at his weapon before the guy even tapped her on the shoulder. But Zane kept his cool. Asking someone a question wasn't a crime.

"Contact," he murmured into his mic for the team to hear.

"Yes?" Lillian responded, keeping her face slightly averted from the guy. Depending on how familiar he was with how Caroline looked, this would play out for only a minute at best before he realized it wasn't really her.

"Do you know anything about capers?"

Capers?

To Lillian's credit, she kept her wits about her. "You mean, like the stuff that goes in Greek salads?"

The guy looked visibly relieved. "Yes. Exactly. My wife is seven months pregnant and she sent me out demanding capers. And hell if I know what capers are. I thought they might be olives."

This could still be a ploy, but if so, it wasn't a very strategic one. The guy was leading Lillian away from the back entrance, where it would've been so easy to just grab her arm and pull her out, and back toward the middle of the store. Where the damn olives were.

"I'm pretty sure this first guy isn't our perp," Zane said into his comm unit. "I think he's just freaking out because his wife is pregnant and is craving specialty food. But I'll keep watching."

"Joanna is moving in toward guy number two," Wade murmured. "We probably need to get Lillian close to the back entrance again if we're eliminating guy number one as a suspect."

"Let's have someone tail guy one when he leaves, just in case he got spooked." Seeing if the guy really did have a pregnant wife and asking him some general questions about Taste Unlimited wouldn't be hard.

"Roger that," Jon said from out in the van.

Zane turned to the side so no one could tell he was speaking. "Wade, can you move over to help the pregnancy guy out? That will free Lillian to move back toward the exit to see if we get a rise out of suspect two."

Over the comm unit Zane could hear Wade ask Lillian and the pregnancy guy if they needed any help. The guy told Wade about the capers and Lillian eased away, wishing him luck. Wade did his best to figure out what the hell capers were and where they were located.

"The second guy is staring at Lillian," Jon said. Zane couldn't see them from the aisle he was located in. "Be sure to keep your face averted toward the east wall, Lil. He's studying you pretty hard."

"Roger," Lillian said. She moved from the olive section, away from Wade and the pregnancy guy, back to where she'd been perched before, right by the exit. She studied the trail mix and different bags of nuts and seeds there. Carefully picking up one container after another and reading the back.

Zane worked himself closer so he could have visual contact with Lillian and the guy.

He was definitely studying her.

He took a few steps down the aisle toward her, but then the three twentysomething gals came around the corner. They were laughing and joking and asked his opinion about something.

As soon as he had the attention of three attractive women, the man obviously forgot about Lillian altogether. Zane watched discreetly for a few more minutes to make sure this wasn't part of a ploy.

It wasn't. The guy was here because either he liked the sandwich he'd gotten earlier or he figured out a lot of attractive women hung out at Taste Unlimited. Or both.

"You see this, Jon?" Zane asked.

"Yeah. Doesn't look like he's our perp, either. Just out trolling for women. I'll still have someone follow him, just in case."

They stayed at the shop another thirty minutes, watching as a number of people came in and out, but none of them approached either Lillian or Zane. When they'd been there over an hour total, Zane finally decided to call it.

"This is a bust, you guys. Whoever was listening isn't coming. Perp either decided it wasn't worth the risk or somehow spotted us and left."

"I agree," Jon said. "But in case you're still being watched, you and Lillian buy some stuff and head back out to your vehicle. The bugs might still be useful. We'll try again soon."

It just meant another night where Caroline wasn't safe. Another day where they couldn't get on with their lives. Couldn't be together just as a normal couple.

He wanted to give her that—give them *both* that—so badly he could taste it.

They got a bottle of wine and threw in a few food items, paid Wade at the register and walked out the front door.

"Sorry, Zane," Lillian murmured. "Maybe I didn't look enough like Caroline to draw the perp in."

Zane shrugged. That might be true, but there wasn't anything they could do about that. "Maybe. But if so, it wasn't due to lack of effort on your part."

"Like Jon said, we'll try again. Just because it didn't work this time, doesn't mean it won't work at all."

"Yeah. We've just got to come up with another location that is secure but also—"

Jon's voice interrupted their conversation. "Zane, we've got a problem."

"What?"

"I just received an SOS from the safe house. Caroline's in trouble."

Zane and Lillian both dropped their groceries and sprinted for the truck.

Chapter Sixteen

Caroline didn't like being out of the action, but she understood the need for it. She wasn't a trained law enforcement officer. Yes, she'd done some significant self-defense training since the attack, but that didn't mean she knew enough for undercover work. She was nowhere as good as Zane and Lillian and Jon.

They were capable. More than capable. Skillful. But still it was hard being protected here inside the safe house knowing they were out there facing possible danger.

It had all been very cloak-and-dagger. She and Zane had napped at Caroline's town house—although neither of them had really slept—then gotten up and ready for their date, talking about normal stuff.

Zane had been crisp and collected, helping lead Caroline into conversations that seemed mundane, normal. Helping her forget there was someone trying to kill them listening on the other end of those transmitting devices.

He rescued her every time she started to flounder, panicked that she might say something wrong. Once when she'd been getting too flustered, he'd backed her up against the refrigerator and kissed her senseless.

That had made her forget her own name, much less that they were on some supersecret mission.

When it was time to leave, having given the bad guys

plenty of time to scope out Taste Unlimited and figure out how to make their move, Zane mentioned he needed to go to the bank before their date. He and Caroline had walked into the bank together.

A few minutes later, Zane and Lillian, wearing the same outfit as Caroline, had walked out and gotten into Zane's truck.

Caroline had been escorted out of the bank by a plain-clothes officer named Gareth Quinn about fifteen minutes later and taken to a safe house, which was actually just a couple miles from the Taste Unlimited store. He'd explained how he understood why she wouldn't want him staying in the house with her and would stay out in the car.

Captain Harris's—her adoptive uncle Tim's—doing, no doubt. She loved the man and had known him since birth, but he couldn't seem to let her attack go. Did he really think that Caroline was so fragile that she wouldn't even want to be around a male police officer for a couple hours? So the captain had ordered Quinn to wait outside.

That was the problem with family, wasn't it? Even adopted family, like Tim. They loved you, but they never allowed you to change. Caroline was always going to be the victim to them. To her uncle especially, since he worked in law enforcement and saw the worst of humanity. Which sucked, since he was also the captain of police and worked very closely with her bosses.

Zane and Lillian would've been at the shop for almost an hour now. She hoped no news was good news. That not hearing from them meant they had caught whoever was behind all this and were in the process of throwing the book at him. Or them. Whatever.

She knew Zane would call as soon as he had something concrete to tell her. This safe house wouldn't be her home for more than a few hours. She and Zane had considered taking her to his place at the beach but decided the fewer people who knew about that, the better. But she would've rather been there.

A knock on the door froze Caroline's blood. Damn it, would that happen for the rest of her life? Would her mind always automatically go back to the day of the attack whenever she heard a knock? It was one of the things she hadn't been able to get any control over. No matter what, when she heard a knock on the door, her entire body clenched in panic.

She walked to the door, trying to get her fear under control. She was in a safe house with an officer outside. Nobody but law enforcement knew where she was.

But when she opened the door just the slightest bit, a man came crashing through.

Just like what had happened the day she was attacked.

If she thought panic assailed her just at the knock, it was nothing compared to the sheer terror that sucked her under now. Every self-defense move she'd learned, every means of protecting herself, vanished from her mind.

The man pushed her to the ground and Caroline cried out. Scurrying back, getting away from him, was all she could think to do.

She couldn't scurry away fast enough. The man walked over to her and gripped her by her hair. Caroline cried out.

"It's time for you to come with me."

He began pulling and she began to struggle, kicking out toward him, which he just easily sidestepped.

Her terrified mind waited for the blows to come. The blows that would break her bones, deliver pain she hadn't thought was possible, like it had before. Somewhere in the back of her mind she knew this wasn't Paul Trumpold. He'd been younger, stronger. Had delighted in her pain.

This man was not as fit, was older. Didn't seem intent on delivering physical blows.

But when she looked up into the doorway, she swore she saw Trumpold. His dark hair and good looks that had fooled everyone, hiding a monster. Caroline wretched, vomiting up the entire contents of her stomach.

She struggled to remember a self-defense move, to force herself to do more than just squirm and kick at the man. She sobbed in frustration as he pulled her toward the door, grabbing at his hand to relieve the pressure in her scalp.

"If you don't come with me, I'll be forced to kill you here."

The man sounded like he almost regretted that fact, but Caroline knew she couldn't let him take her from the safe house. She knew firsthand the sort of pain the human body could endure before death. She didn't want to die here, but she couldn't let him take her from this house.

But then he was gone, his hold of her scalp ripped free as he went flying past her deeper into the room.

It took her a moment to realize there was a tangle of two bodies. And the other one was Zane.

Lillian stood in the doorway, gun raised. "Are you okay, Caroline?" she asked, her eyes surveying the room rather than looking at her.

"Y-yes. I'm okay."

Zane was fighting with the other man, if you could call it much of a fight. Zane was younger, stronger and obviously enraged.

Lillian stepped in, gun still raised to chest level. She scoped out the rest of the room.

"Did the guy come in alone?" she asked, ignoring the punches being thrown by Zane and the intruder.

"I... I don't know." Caroline barely got the words out. "I thought I saw a second man standing at the door, but I'm not sure." She also thought the man was Paul Trumpold, but he was dead. Caroline knew she couldn't trust her own mind.

Lillian quickly made her way into the one bedroom of the safe house, the bathroom and the kitchen.

"We're clear here," she said into some sort of communication unit.

Jon came running through the door, looked at Caroline huddled up against the wall and Zane and the other man still rolling on the ground throwing punches at each other.

"Zane, enough," Jon said. "We need to question him, not put him in the hospital."

Caroline watched Zane pull himself together and get off the man, who lay moaning on the floor. Both Lillian and Jon had their weapons trained on him. He wasn't going anywhere.

"Cuff him," Zane told Jon, then walked over to Caroline.

She wanted to go to him, to meet him halfway, but couldn't seem to get herself off the wall.

He held his arms out in front of him, the way someone would do if they were proving they meant no harm or sudden movement. She knew then that she must look as frightened and horrified as she felt.

"Zane," she whispered his name and fell into him. He caught her and lowered them both to the ground, his arms wrapped securely around her.

"Are you hurt?" he asked. "Do we need to get you medical attention?"

"No," she whispered. "He didn't hurt me."

For the longest time they said nothing else, just held each other. She could hear Jon read the guy his rights before they cuffed him. Multiple officers came in and out of the safe house, including Gareth Quinn, who evidently had been knocked unconscious in the car on the street but then came to and called in reinforcements.

Zane just sat against the wall holding Caroline the whole time.

"Let's get you home," Zane finally said.

"Don't you need to go question that guy or something?"

"It will wait. They'll get all his info, but they won't start questioning him without me."

Caroline just tucked herself into his arm. She didn't want to look around. Didn't want everyone to know that they'd been right to be so protective of her. That when literal push came to shove, Caroline had frozen.

That she was as weak as everyone thought.

She'd sworn she'd never be a victim again. Had gone through hundreds of hours of therapy and physical training to keep from being a victim again, but when the crisis moment had come, she'd just folded and begun to cry.

Caroline wanted to cry now. Huddled against the door of Zane's truck, staring blankly out the window, she wanted to bawl her eyes out. She'd been fighting so hard for her independence, swearing she could handle herself, that she was so strong.

One knock on a door and two minutes of a man pushing through had shown her otherwise. She was never going to be okay again.

"Caro," Zane whispered, not trying to touch her. "Are you sure you're not hurt? Don't hide it if you are. Tell me."

"No, he didn't hurt me. Didn't hit me at all. Was just pulling me out the door by my hair. You're more hurt than I am." She didn't look away from the window as she said it.

They rode in silence until Zane eventually pulled up to his beach house. They went up the stairs, Zane unlocking the door, then checking to make sure the house was secure. Caroline didn't wait outside for him to finish this time. She entered, then crossed all the way to the living room to the outside deck. She crossed to the railing, staring out at her beloved ocean. From this direction she couldn't see the sun that was beginning to set but knew it was by the purple hues being cast over everything.

"Caro." She heard Zane from the doorway. "Tell me what's wrong. It's more than just the guy breaking in, isn't it?"

She could hear him come a little closer.

"Although, that's upsetting enough for anyone. To think you're safe, that the danger is elsewhere, but it's not. That's scary. And not just to you, to anyone."

He fell into silence when she didn't say anything. How could she make Zane understand? He'd always been so strong, so capable. Never plagued by doubt or frozen into inaction.

Not like her.

It was a crippling thing to realize all the progress you thought you'd made—you'd worked and scraped and clawed for—was just a figment of your imagination.

"He knocked on the door." The words were out of her mouth before she could stop them.

Zane didn't push, just came and stood by her at the railing.

"Trumpold knocked. The day he attacked me, he knocked on my door." Caroline knew this was a sore spot for Zane. That he blamed himself for not being the one who had knocked on her door that day. But he didn't draw the conversation to him or his guilt. She appreciated it. Appreciated the strength in his silence.

"So when this guy knocked, I panicked. I should mention that I always panic when someone knocks on my door. God forbid you be the poor package delivery guy in my neighborhood. He must think I live on the verge of a nervous breakdown." She tried to laugh, but it didn't sound the least bit amused even to her own ears.

"It's an understandable trigger, Caro. You know that, right?" he said softly.

"Oh, God, yes, I understand that. I have spent more time in therapy talking about knocks on doors than anything else. It's ridiculous." She tapped her knuckles against the railing. "Even knowing it's me, watching my own knuckles hit the wood, I still get slightly nauseous at the sound."

Zane nodded, not saying anything. She couldn't blame him. What could you say to that?

"But I thought it was probably that officer, Gareth Quinn. And I knew I was being a complete coward. So I opened the door."

She took a deep breath.

"It was only opened a crack when he pushed his way through, slamming the door open."

"Just like Trumpold," Zane finished for her.

"Yes." Caroline could barely get the syllable out.

Zane put his hand over hers on the railing. "I'm so sorry."

She pulled her hand out from under his. "But that's not it, not really. If that is what had happened and the dude had scared the life out of me and you'd gotten there just in time to save the day, I'd be fine with that."

"I don't understand. I thought he didn't hurt you."

"He didn't, Zane. He was planning on dragging me out of the safe house, told me he was going to kill me, but you got there in time."

"That's good, right?" He obviously couldn't understand the distress tainting her tone.

"I froze."

He didn't ask what she meant. He'd been in law enforcement too long not to understand.

"I've spent so much time studying self-defense since the attack. Months of classes. Hundreds of hours. But when he forced his way in, it was like I forgot it all."

"Caro—"

She shook her head. "I can see it all playing in my head like it's a movie. And I want to scream at that girl on the ground, 'What's the matter with you? You know how to break his hold. Hell, you know how to break both his arms. Do it!'"

Her hands clenched into fists. "I just laid there on the ground, crying, Zane. I even vomited. That guy wasn't as fit as Trumpold, wasn't as strong, hadn't stunned me the way Trumpold had with his first two punches. But I just laid there, blubbering. I don't know what would've happened if you hadn't gotten there when you did."

"Caroline, it happens. People freeze up. Even in law enforcement it happens."

His matter-of-fact tone, devoid of anything that could be considered condescending or pitying, helped her in ways he couldn't possibly know.

"I hate myself. I hate myself for being so weak. A victim." She turned away from the view of the ocean and leaned her back against the railing. "Again."

Zane came to stand right in front of her, his hands on her shoulders. "There's nothing about you that's weak, Caro. And you're no victim. You were stunned. A situation you couldn't possibly have expected caught you off guard. It happens."

She didn't want to look at him, but he caught her chin with his thumb and finger and forced her to look up. Forced her to look into those rich brown eyes, where she didn't see anything close to pity or concern. Didn't even see love.

She saw respect, and it meant more to her than all the other emotions could've meant combined.

"We got there when we did, and thank goodness," Zane continued. "Because those punches I got in on that guy, I needed them, and they're probably the only ones I'll legally get."

She couldn't help but smile a little at that.

"But I have no doubt you would've bounced back, Caro. That training you've done, it would've filtered its way back into your mind, into your muscles. You wouldn't have let yourself be taken by that guy. I would bet every cent I have in this life and the next one that you would've taken him down in the next few minutes."

Caroline leaned into his chest. "I just wish I had a replay button. That I could go back and do it again. Make it different."

He wrapped his arms around her like he planned to never let her go. "Believe me, I've wished for one of those too. But we can only move forward. All I know is that you have the inner strength to withstand damn near anything."

Chapter Seventeen

Zane didn't go back into the station that night. Caroline and her needs were more important to him than questioning the perp they'd caught right away. Plus, Zane probably needed a little more cooling-down time anyway.

He'd probably lose his newly reinstated status pretty quickly if he started punching on a suspect in custody.

He had let Jon and Captain Harris know he wasn't coming in until this morning and both had agreed it was the best thing to do. The suspect—Jon informed Zane that the guy's name was Donald Brodey, a name that sounded vaguely familiar to him—would wait.

But now Zane was ready. Wanted some answers. Lillian was hanging out with Caroline so Zane could be at the station getting them. He didn't want to take any chances until they knew exactly what was going on. After what happened yesterday, Caroline wasn't as resistant to having Lillian around, which broke his heart.

Caroline's reaction to the break-in at the safe house wasn't unheard of and certainly wasn't anything that should cause her shame. He'd gotten through to her the best he could about that, but he knew she regretted how she'd reacted. But any law enforcement officer knew full well that practicing, drills, sparring were all well and good, but that in the heat of the moment, training didn't always translate to perfect real-world responses.

He wished Caroline could have another chance to fight down the guy breaking through the door, but he damn well hoped it would never happen again. Zane would help her find other ways of making sure she didn't freeze up again that didn't involve her being in actual danger.

Zane found Jon back at the little corner desk beside the copying machine, where the department had so rudely put him when he'd come here initially working the serial rapist case. Nobody in the Corpus Christi PD had wanted an outsider coming in to help with the case. They'd thought Jon would be a hotshot know-it-all.

He'd been neither.

"You know we'll get you a regular desk, Jon. You don't have to be all Harry-Potter-living-under-the-stairs anymore."

Jon smiled. "This desk holds some pretty fond memories for me. Led me to my soon-to-be wife, you know."

Zane smiled too. Couldn't argue with that. Sometimes bad circumstances were what ended up pointing you in the right direction.

"So does the name Donald Brodey seem familiar to you?" Jon got up and handed a file to Zane.

"Vaguely."

"That's because you arrested him eight years ago. Felony breaking and entering coupled with burglary."

Zane opened the file. "Yes. Now I remember. It was one of my first cases as a detective." He studied the mug shot of Brodey from nearly eight years ago. He'd been in his late thirties then, which put him in his midforties now.

"Looks like a pretty cut-and-dried case. His prints were at the scene. He'd already done a couple of years for misdemeanor B and E charges."

Zane's eyes narrowed. "But he always said he didn't commit this particular crime. I remember that."

"Did you believe him?" Jon asked.

Zane shrugged. "Not really. But I have to admit, I might have been more interested in proving my worth to the department than I was interested in listening to some repeat offender argue about his innocence."

"Looks like he served six years. He's been out for about a year and a half."

"Honestly, I haven't thought about Brodey since he went to prison. I definitely wouldn't have pegged him for trying to kill me. For a damned B and E conviction." Zane closed the file.

"Well, he wanted to talk to you."

"Then let's give the man what he wants."

They cleared it with the captain and had Brodey brought to an interview room from holding. The man was definitely bruised from their tussle yesterday, but then again, so was Zane.

"Detective Wales." Brodey smirked as Zane and Jon entered.

"Brodey." Zane took the seat directly across from him. Jon took the one at the corner of the metal table. Jon read the man his rights.

"Not going to call for your lawyer, Brodey?"

The older man sat back in his chair. "Nope. Ain't got nothing to say that a lawyer will change."

"I suppose you're innocent of this just like you were innocent all those years ago?"

Brodey's eyes narrowed. "I was innocent of that B and E and you know it."

Zane shook his head. "Is that why you've been sending me all those texts? My 'secret' that would come to light."

"Yeah. You can't hide your secrets forever, Wales." He crossed his arms over his chest.

"And Caroline Gill? What does she have to do with my secrets?"

"Everybody knows the best way to get to you is through Caroline Gill. That's why I was trying to take her yesterday. I knew if I could get her, it wouldn't be any problem to get you to surrender."

"And what were you going to do once I surrendered?"

"You were going to pay for them permanently, Wales. For the lies you told. For the years I lost."

Zane glanced over at Jon, who looked as surprised as he did. For someone who'd always claimed his innocence about a crime eight years ago, Brodey had just confessed to a much bigger one.

"What are you doing, Brodey? Why are you telling me this? You know it's just going to get you sent back to prison."

"Maybe it's worth it. Maybe seeing you pay for your sins is worth the risk of going back to prison."

"You've been out of jail for eighteen months. Why did you decide to just come after me now?"

"Somebody made me see the light. A fellow I think you guys know. Name is Freihof. Damien Freihof."

Brodey had their attention now.

"Freihof put you up to this? To trying to kill both me and Caroline?"

Brodey smiled. "Yep. Helped me to understand that you needed to pay for what you'd done. That I lost years of my life thanks to you."

"But what about Caroline? She never did anything to you, Donald. Why take out some sort of misguided revenge on her?"

Brodey looked down for just a minute and shifted in

his chair. Then he looked back up at Zane. "Did you know I had three kids when you put me in jail, Wales? They needed their daddy and they lost him. Because of you. Sometimes innocent people get hurt. Your girlfriend was like my children."

"How did you know where Caroline would be yesterday?"

"I planted bugs in her house so I could listen to what you said."

"We found those. But we never said anything about where Caroline would be staying." Zane knew full well they wouldn't have given that information away in their conversation, knowing someone was listening.

"Yeah, but you didn't find the device I put in your truck. I could hear all your conversations there too. I knew you were using that other lady as bait to try to draw me out."

Zane grimaced. They hadn't even thought about a transmitting device in their vehicles. But they should have.

"So I followed you to the bank yesterday," Brodey continued. "Then followed her from there instead of you."

It was a smart plan and had almost worked. If Brodey had moved a little quicker. If he'd knocked Gareth Quinn a little harder on the head so the other man didn't wake up so quickly and report the problem, Brodey would've gotten away with it.

Zane and Jon spent the next few hours questioning Brodey, trying to get as much information as they could about Damien Freihof. Brodey wouldn't admit to anything that happened in Big Bend but gave fairly consistent answers to questions about yesterday's attack.

Two days ago he'd broken into Caroline's town house and planted the transmitting devices. He'd then immediately gone over to Zane's house and trashed it. They'd missed catching him by only thirty minutes.

Brodey knew his best bet was to get Caroline alone. To kidnap her and draw Zane out. Realizing the info Zane and Caroline were providing in her town house was a trap, Brodey decided to use their own plan against them.

And Damien Freihof was at the heart of it all. Encouraging Brodey. They'd never met, but Freihof had spent the last two weeks by phone and video messaging convincing Brodey of the justice of taking Zane down. Brodey had agreed.

By midafternoon, Zane had done all the questioning he could. Brodey had written down his confession. His intent. Brodey would be going back to jail, probably for the rest of his life.

Zane and Jon filed the paperwork they needed, then went to Zane's house to break the good news to Caroline and Lillian.

It wasn't often in a law enforcement officer's career where the bad just up and admitted to a crime, even signing a confession. Sure as hell made the case easier.

They explained everything while Caroline cooked a simple spaghetti dinner with salad.

"So it looks like Brodey will be going away for a long time," Zane finished.

"Omega Sector still has to catch Freihof, but Brodey's failure to kill you at least slows his plans considerably. It will take a lot of time and effort to convince someone else to take on the job of trying to kill you," Jon said.

"Is that what you think this Freihof guy will do? Just keep trying to find people to convince to hurt us?" Caroline asked.

Jon shook his head. "Honestly, no. I think this is a game for Freihof, with rules. Rules that he establishes, but rules nonetheless. I think for each target he has one puppet—for lack of a better word—that he's created and molded."

"With Fitzy, that was Curtis Harper," Lillian said.

Jon nodded. "Exactly. Freihof convinced Harper to kill SWAT member Ashton Fitzgerald. When that didn't work, I think that part of the game was over. Freihof doesn't seem to be going after the same people more than once."

Zane looked over at Caroline, loving the relief that was evident on her face. He reached over and grabbed her hand.

"Until we arrest Freihof, none of us are completely safe, but probably the part of the game involving the two of you is over for him."

"Thank goodness," Caroline murmured under her breath. "I mean, I know that's probably wrong of me to say, since if he's finished with us, it means he's just moving on to someone else."

"Nothing wrong with being thankful that you're out of a madman's scope," Lillian said around a bite of pasta. "And we're going to do our damnedest to make sure Freihof doesn't have the time or means to target someone else."

Caroline smiled. The first real smile he'd seen from her since they were hiking in Big Bend, before all of this started. Zane squeezed her hand. "I'm going to have to take you out so you can finish your Big Bend hike."

"Maybe in a few months. I'm itching to get back to work right now. Back to some sort of normal."

Zane didn't blame her. Caroline needed the parts of her life she had control over. Her job as a paramedic was a big aspect of that. "I'm sure the hospital won't mind having you back a couple days early from vacation."

"Speaking of, I've got to go back to all that wedding nonsense at Omega. It's out of control." Lillian sighed dramatically.

Jon smiled. "Excuse you, I happen to be a big part of that 'wedding nonsense.'"

"I know. You're almost as bad as Sherry."

"Be sure to tell Sherry I can't wait to see her," Caroline said. "Just a few more days."

"I will. It will be nice to have a drama-free weekend for a change."

Chapter Eighteen

The first sight of a broken ankle at a bike accident the next day had Caroline feeling great. That probably made her a little weird, but she didn't care. She was back at work, at a job she knew she was good at. She hated that the cyclist was in so much pain but loved having something to physically do with her hands. With her brain.

How she'd reacted when Donald Brodey broke into the safe house two days ago still stung. But Zane was right: she couldn't let that paralyze her. Couldn't let that stop her forward progress or growth. He'd talked about helping her with some situational awareness exercises and training where she could be caught off guard.

She smiled as she helped brace the young man's foot in preparation to move him into the ambulance. Zane helping her improve these skills would make her more ready for anything that came her way. Any training that made her less of a victim, she was up for.

But more important, it meant that Zane wasn't planning on running back to his little pocket of Corpus Christi after this was all over, never to be seen again. She didn't know if he was going to continue to work for the police department—although everyone had to admit, he'd flowed right back in as if he'd never left—but he wasn't going to disappear again.

She wasn't exactly sure where that left them personally. Eventually they'd need to broach the subject. But right now, sleeping in his arms every night in the house he'd bought for them, the house he hadn't been able to force himself to sell or even rent to someone else? It was enough for her.

They drove the cyclist back to the hospital and Caroline and Kimmie made a beeline for the coffee shop. They'd already been going for four hours in a twelve-hour shift, and you never knew when an emergency call would come in. So you took advantage of coffee breaks while you could.

"I don't think you've stopped smiling all day," Kimmie said as they paid for their brew, preferring the specialized coffee at the shop over the muck that often waited in the free areas of the hospital.

"I'm sorry. I'll start frowning immediately."

Kimmie smacked her lightly on the arm. "You know I think it's great. Although I'm sure that guy with the broken ankle thought you were some sort of sadist—so happy about his pain."

Caroline chuckled. "Yeah, that probably wasn't sensitive."

"I'm assuming your happiness has to do with the arrest of the guy who was trying to kill you."

Caroline added sugar to her coffee. "It's definitely a relief."

Kimmie nudged her. "And don't think it escaped my notice that Zane Wales dropped you off at work this morning."

Caroline tried not to blush. "It was on his way, since he's working at the police station."

"And because you guys were making wild, passionate monkey love all last night, weren't you? Gosh, he is so gorgeous, Caroline. Sigh. I want a super hunk like that."

Out of the blue, Caroline pulled Kimmie in for a hug.

Kimmie hugged her back—as Caroline had no doubt she would—and laughed as they broke apart. "What was that for? We've been partners for nearly eighteen months and I don't think we've ever hugged."

Caroline had resented being partnered with Kimmie. She'd known Uncle Tim had done it because he'd deemed that, after the attack, Caroline needed to work with a woman. Someone nonthreatening and lighthearted. Caroline had tried to never let her resentment show to Kimmie; after all, it wasn't Kimmie's fault she was the most perky, sweet partner they could find. Tim had done what he'd thought was best for Caroline.

Ended up he'd been right. Kimmie was probably the best partner Caroline could've had for the past year and a half. Not because she wasn't a man, but because she was hardworking, enthusiastic, and wanted to learn what Caroline had been ready to teach.

Caroline smiled. And Kimmie was always perky.

"You're a great partner, Kimmie. And a good friend. I just wanted to hug you."

Kimmie hugged her again quickly. "I just wanted to get another one in before you go back to non-hugging mode." She pulled away and they walked down the hallway with their coffee.

They'd barely finished half their cups before they got the call. A warehouse fire down near the oil district. Multiple injuries, utter chaos. An all-hands call.

Caroline and Kimmie dumped their coffee and ran for the ambulance, pulling out of the hospital parking lot rapidly along with other ambulances. Fire and rescue vehicles would be joining them on-site.

As they pulled up to the location, Caroline could see it was worse than she'd thought.

She turned to Kimmie. "The fire chief will be calling

out orders. It will be pretty chaotic, so just take it one patient at a time. Don't get overwhelmed."

Caroline had worked only one other fire like this, about five years ago. She'd gotten a little panicked and didn't want the same thing to happen to Kimmie.

They jumped out of the ambulance and reported over to the fire chief, who was barking out orders. He pointed at Caroline and Kimmie.

"Office workers. Southeast corner." He pointed in the general direction. "Smoke inhalation mostly. Evaluate, get the most severely injured to the main hospital. Gill, coordinate and see who needs to go to the local medical center if the main hospital ER can't take them."

It was a big job, to coordinate what patients would go where, but Caroline appreciated the trust the fire chief was putting in her. She was one of the most seasoned paramedics out here. She wouldn't let him down.

"Let's go, people." The EMTs and paramedics—EMTs with more schooling—all followed after Caroline. She split them up into groups and soon everyone had a job to do caring for the injured.

Caroline spent the next six hours coordinating between hospitals and the EMTs, evaluating burn and smoke inhalation victims and getting them where they needed to be. This fire couldn't have happened at a worse spot for casualties. A factory with hundreds of people inside had been affected.

Things were just starting to slow down enough for Caroline to eat a protein bar, something every paramedic kept stashed for situations just like this where a meal wasn't possible. She washed it down with another bottle of water, although she'd been careful to keep herself hydrated throughout the day. She didn't want to end up as someone needing medical attention rather than giving it.

When she had a short break, she grabbed her phone to text Zane.

Massive fire in oil section. Won't be done for a while.

His response was almost immediate.

Be safe. Text me when you're done.

She looked over at the firefighters. They seemed to be getting it under control. Most of the critical victims had been seen and escorted to hospitals and medical centers in the greater Corpus Christi area.

Caroline scoped out the scene. They'd done a good job here today. Loss of life had been minimal thanks to the work of the firefighters and EMTs.

"Hey, Caroline, somebody was looking for you. An EMT," Kimmie said. Caroline had been split up from her partner for most of the day. She pointed to the far side of the building. "Around the corner there. Someone else told me, so I don't know what it's about. Sorry. Want me to go ask?"

Caroline grabbed a protein bar. "No, you stay here and eat this. Take five minutes. You've been working hard today. We all have. I'll go see what's needed."

Kimmie smiled. "Thanks. Wanna hug?"

Caroline rolled her eyes, knowing the woman was kidding. "Yeah. It can be our new thing."

She jogged over to the far side of the building. It was much quieter over there, away from the action. An EMT was crouched down near the back corner.

"Hey, is everything okay?" Caroline asked. "I heard you needed me."

The woman glanced over her shoulder at Caroline.

"Yeah, do you mind coming over here? I think you should see this."

Caroline prayed it wasn't a body, although she didn't see how it could be in such a small space.

She squatted next to the woman and looked into the hole where she stared. Caroline didn't see anything but dirt.

"What are we looking at?" she asked.

Caroline felt a prick at the back of her neck and swatted at whatever bug had bitten her. A few seconds later the woman stood. Caroline tried to stand too, but found herself dizzy.

"Whoa. I think I need to eat something besides a protein bar." She looked back at the hole again. "I'm sorry. What did you want me to see here?"

The woman didn't answer and Caroline turned to look at her again.

She was spinning.

The entire world was spinning.

This wasn't low blood sugar from not eating enough. She'd been drugged.

Caroline looked at the woman again and realized she wasn't really wearing an EMT uniform, just similar colors.

"Who are you?" Getting the words out were more difficult than they should be.

"I'm the person who's going to show the world what a liar you are, Caroline Gill. Finally show everyone what you've done and how my brother's death was your fault."

Caroline tried to stand again but couldn't. She began to crawl away, but much more slowly than she wanted. Her muscles refused to work. She held on to consciousness for as long as she could, even knowing she was fighting a losing battle against whatever drug the woman had given her.

"My brother was a doctor, so I know a little about temporary paralytic drugs," the woman said, inching her face closer to Caroline. "You should never have lied about him, Ms. Gill."

Through the fuzziness in her mind Caroline realized who the woman was. She was the sister of Paul Trumpold, the man who viciously attacked and raped Caroline.

And she thought Caroline had made up the whole story.

She clawed through the dark to try to keep hold of consciousness, knowing this woman intended to harm her, but couldn't do it. Her panic got even worse as she saw someone who looked just like Paul Trumpold standing behind her. As Caroline laid her face on the ground, the woman did the same, facing her.

"Don't worry. We'll talk soon."

The vicious hatred in the woman's eyes was the last thing Caroline saw before the darkness overtook her.

Chapter Nineteen

Zane sat back in the chair at his desk in the Corpus Christi Police Department. When he'd come back in this morning, instead of having to work in the conference room, since he had no desk assigned to him, he'd found his old desk back in place. His old chair at it and nameplate on the front.

Almost like he'd never left.

He would've thought there would've been some hard feelings, either about him returning or about him leaving in the first place. And maybe there was. But as a whole the department had banded together and welcomed him back into their midst.

Zane had to admit leaving again would be difficult. He missed detective work. Even now that they had found the person trying to hurt him and Caroline, he didn't know if he could walk away. The people he worked with here were family. They understood what the attack on Caroline had cost him and supported him—then and now—the best way they could.

Today that had been dragging his desk and chair back to where they'd once been.

But the part of him that enjoyed sitting in this chair, the part of him that had missed law enforcement work every day for the past eighteen months since he'd quit, knew that something wasn't right.

Donald Brodey's arrest. His confession. All of it. As much as Zane wanted it to be perfect and tidy, it wasn't. It just didn't sit well with him.

Something wasn't right.

Jon walked over and leaned on the corner of the desk. "Looks like they're carving out a permanent place for you here."

Zane leaned back, stretching his legs out in front of him. "Nice of them, I have to admit."

"You going to stay?"

"I think so. It's not like I have any other job around right now. They're still picking up pieces of my Cessna in Big Bend."

"Not to mention you miss police work." Jon's eyebrow rose, daring him to deny it.

Zane shrugged. "It's true. I do."

"You're good at it, Zane. Got a natural talent and a good temperament for it."

"I know."

"Plus, that incredible humbleness."

Zane chuckled, but then it faded out. "The only problem is, right now my detective spider senses are telling me there's something wrong with Donald Brodey."

Jon sat at the chair by Zane's desk. "What about him?"

Zane shrugged. He wasn't exactly sure what he meant and didn't want to bog Jon down if his fears amounted to nothing. "I know you need to go. I don't want Sherry getting mad at me because I kept the groom away for too long."

"I've got an hour before I need to leave for my plane. Plus, Sherry is capable of handling anything thrown her way. One of the things I love most about her."

Jon and Sherry were a good fit. Partners in every sense of the word.

"Do you have any wild parties coming up? In your last few days of singlehood?"

Jon shook his head. "Nah. The guys and I will probably go out for a few beers, but I'm not interested in a strip club or the 'normal' bachelor stuff."

Zane wasn't actually surprised. "Oh yeah?"

"Once you have the one you really want, all of that seems ridiculous, you know? I have no interest in seeing any other naked or partially naked woman besides Sherry."

Zane knew what he meant. He wouldn't go to a strip club now if someone dragged him. It wasn't what he wanted.

Caroline was what he wanted. Today. Tomorrow. The rest of their lives.

Jon leaned back in his chair. "So tell me what you think is going on with Brodey."

"I reviewed his case again this morning. From the original B and E."

"And?"

Zane shifted slightly. "Now, with nearly a decade more experience, I'm looking at the arrest in a different light. Brodey claimed his innocence the whole time. Said someone planted his fingerprints at the scene."

"Do you believe him?"

"I believe we caught another burglar six months later and the evidence suggested he'd been placing fingerprints that weren't his around crime scenes to make himself less of a suspect. I think it's possible that Brodey was telling the truth. That someone did put his prints on the scene."

"Brodey had already been convicted two other times, you know. So it's not like this was some innocent guy off the street who got thrown in jail."

"Actually, that's what convinced me. I went back through his other case files, cases I wasn't part of at all, to see if he claimed his innocence then. To see if that was just his MO."

"And?"

"Nope. Served his time, never claimed innocence once."

Jon shifted in his chair. "Okay. Then, that just supports his claim that he was out for revenge. That's why he came after Caroline—to get back at you."

Zane picked up a pencil on his desk and began twirling it between his fingers. "That's what I thought too. That this Damien Freihof guy had just gotten his claws into Brodey and twisted his thinking. And I have to admit, that's possible."

"But something has you questioning it."

"Brodey wasn't ever violent, Jon. All of his crimes involved breaking into houses where no one was home. The man has a family. Kids."

"You're thinking that it's a pretty big jump to go from a family man with no history of violent crime to kidnapping and attempted murder."

"Yes. Exactly. And moreover, I can see why he would still be mad at me. But Caroline? It would take a pretty hardened criminal to kill her for something I did."

"People change. Jail hardens them. Then someone like Freihof comes along and pushes them in a certain direction, even one they wouldn't normally take on their own."

"Yeah, I guess you're right."

Wade Ammons walked through the door of the detective section.

"Hey, Wales, you look pretty good sitting in your old spot. Does that mean you're going to be staying?"

"I'm thinking about it. If you guys and the captain really want me back around."

The younger man smiled. "We do, believe me. It's been hard trying to make this place look good all by myself."

Jon stood. "I've got to move if I'm going to catch my plane. Call me if you need to talk some things through. I'll also keep searching with Omega resources. Make sure we're not missing something."

Zane shook Jon's hand. "Thank you, for everything. I guess Caroline and I will be up this weekend to see you get hitched."

"See you then."

Jon headed out and Zane sat back down at his desk. "Where is everybody, Wade?"

The detectives' desks were on the second floor of the building that housed the police department. It was generally more quiet here than all the uniformed officers' desks and general processing. But it was never this quiet.

"Huge fire down in the oil district started an hour ago. Most of the station is down helping."

"Casualties?"

"Yeah, a lot. A bunch of office workers got trapped. Caroline's down there. Last report was that she was directing ambulance traffic to different hospitals."

It was a crazier day than she'd expected to go back to, but Zane knew she could handle it. She was probably glad to have such a busy day. Caroline liked to keep focused. She excelled at it.

"Let me know if you need any help with anything or if I'm needed at the oil district."

"Will do. Sounds like the worst of it has passed, though."

"I'm going to get Brodey out of holding and talk to him one more time. I feel like we're missing something."

Wade nodded. "We're gathering everything we know about the last eighteen months of Brodey's life since he made parole. As soon as the file is ready, I'll get it to you."

Interviewing Brodey again wasn't hard, since he was

still being housed in the temporary cells inside the department until his bail hearing date. But the man was much less cooperative this time. Sullen almost.

"You still have a right to an attorney, Brodey. You know that," Zane finally said when Brodey hadn't given him nearly as open answers as yesterday. "Do you want a lawyer?"

The man had already signed a confession, so it wouldn't help much. But it was still his right.

"Naw. I don't want no lawyer."

"Tell me more about Damien Freihof. How did he contact you?"

Brodey looked down at his hands. "Freihof called me on the phone. Said he'd been over my case. That he thought you were a crooked cop and that I should take my revenge on you."

"I see."

"I lost a lot of years of my life because of you."

"You already had two strikes before you even came across my radar. So it's difficult to believe that you think I'm responsible for all your woes."

Brodey just crossed his arms and leaned back in his chair, staring at the table.

Zane decided he needed to take another tack. "But okay. What if I said, looking back at the case now, I can see why you said you were innocent. That I agree with you that someone should've looked more closely into your case when we discovered someone was, in fact, planting prints of other criminals."

Brodey straightened for just a moment, looking Zane in the eye. "That's what I told you from the beginning."

"And I was wrong, Brodey, I should've listened. But I was young. Yours was one of my first solo detective cases. I wanted to make a splashy arrest maybe more than I wanted to make sure justice was served."

"You tell my wife that, okay, Wales?" It was the first time Brodey hadn't seemed dour. Seemed legitimately invested in what he was saying. "You tell her that I wasn't lying about not being the one who broke into that house."

"You're going away for attempted murder, Brodey. Why the hell will your wife care about a B and E from eight years ago?"

Brodey seemed to wilt right in front of him. "You're right, I guess. But if it ever comes up, you tell her that, okay?"

Zane tried to get more details from Brodey after that. About Freihof, about Big Bend. But the man wasn't talking.

"I signed a confession. I don't have anything more to say." And that was it. The longer Zane talked, the more silent the older man became.

Zane got a text from Caroline telling him she would be running late and texted her back. He spent some more time with Brodey trying to get him to spill any more details, but the man obviously was done talking.

Finally, Zane had him sent back to his cell. He left the interview room with no more information than when he'd started, besides an odd statement about letting Brodey's wife know he was innocent of a crime that in the greater scheme of things didn't really matter.

As promised, Wade had left a file on Zane's desk about Brodey's whereabouts and activities since he'd been released from prison. He'd been out for eighteen months, unemployed. He and his wife were separated, but not divorced. She'd stayed with him even when he'd been incarcerated. They had three teenage children.

Their financial situation was pretty grim, Zane had to admit. The wife and kids were living in a two-bedroom apartment, and they had missed multiple rent payments. Zane didn't doubt they'd be evicted soon.

There was only one picture of the family. The youngest, Brodey's son, seemed to be using some sort of braces in order to walk. Zane grimaced. Medical bills for an illness or disability could cause even further financial hardship.

He turned the page and everything made more sense for him.

Two months ago, Donald Brodey had been diagnosed with cancer and had less than six months left to live.

No wonder Brodey had wanted him to pass along the message to his wife. The way things were going, with his confession, he would probably never see her again. At least would never see her as a free man.

Maybe Jon was right; maybe finding out he was dying had changed Brodey. Instead of wanting to right any wrongs before he died, he wanted to exact his revenge on Zane. Freihof just happened to contact him at the right time.

Zane leaned back in his chair, the one in which he'd done his best detective work over the years. There was a big piece of the puzzle he still wasn't seeing. He knew that with every fiber of his being.

He just hoped he'd figure it out before disaster struck.

Chapter Twenty

Caroline woke up slowly, feeling like she'd had way too much to drink the night before. But she couldn't remember any drinking.

And why was she sitting if she was waking up the morning after with a huge hangover? Shouldn't she be lying in bed?

She finally pried her eyes open, then immediately closed them again when dizziness and nausea assailed her. She couldn't help the groan that fell from her lips. She tried to raise her hand to her head to help relieve some of the pressure but found she couldn't move her arms.

Then it all came back to her. Not drinking. Drugged. By the sister of the man who had tried to destroy her life.

"Yeah, that chloral hydrate is a bitch, isn't it?" Caroline couldn't tell exactly where the woman's voice was coming from. She was evidently walking around the chair Caroline was bound to. Not helping the dizziness. "Quick to knock someone out, but a little more difficult to recover from."

Caroline felt a sting in her scalp as the woman grabbed her hair and yanked her head back. "But that queasiness? Trust me, that's the best you're going to feel all day. It's just going to get worse from here."

"Who are you?" Caroline pushed the words past the

dryness of her throat, her voice sounding strange even to her own ears.

"That's right, we haven't formally met, have we? I'm Lisette Trumpold."

"Paul Trumpold's sister."

The woman snatched Caroline's head back by the hair again. "Don't even say his name." The woman's voice was rising in both pitch and volume. She slung Caroline's head forward. "You ruined his life with your lies. You don't deserve to say his name."

Now it was more than just the drugs that made Caroline want to vomit. After living through the vicious attack by Paul Trumpold, to hear someone defend him—even a family member—made her want to hurl her guts out.

"I never lied about your brother and what that sick bastard did."

The world spun wildly out of control as the back of Lisette's hand connected with her cheek. If she hadn't been tied to the chair, she would've flown out of it.

"Liar!" Lisette screamed right in Caroline's face, spittle flying everywhere. "I've seen the truth, the real medical reports, not the ones you and your boyfriend fabricated and gave to the police."

Caroline tasted blood in her mouth from where her teeth had scraped the inside of her cheek. She tried to gather her thoughts, figure out exactly what this crazy woman was talking about.

Caroline breathed deeply, trying to take in as many details as possible. Lisette hadn't killed her outright at the fire scene, so evidently she wanted Caroline alive for some reason. That was good. Gave her time to figure out some way of escape.

And she was talking about different medical reports? Caroline had no idea what the hell that meant. Her medical records had definitely been a part of the case against Paul Trumpold, but there had been only one set.

She needed to figure out exactly what Lisette wanted. Then she could better formulate a plan.

"Recognize where we are yet?" Lisette asked.

Caroline forced herself to open her eyes despite the dizziness and nausea it caused. She breathed in and out through her nose, lifting her head and looking around. She knew immediately where she was.

She was in the house where she'd lived when Trumpold attacked her. On the floor right under the chair that she was tied to right now, he had beaten her into a coma and raped her.

Caroline could feel the onslaught of panic. Looking at the door just a few feet in front of her, she could easily envision the day she'd opened it just a crack and he'd forced his way through. Could feel the pain—a thousand times worse than the slap Lisette had just given her—as his fist connected with her jaw, shattering her cheekbone.

She heard herself whimper, struggling through the effects of the drug to know what was now and what was then. She closed her eyes again, trying to hold on to her sanity.

It was Zane's face in her mind, his voice in her subconscious, that got her through.

All I know is that you have the inner strength to withstand damn near anything.

The words he had said to her after Donald Brodey attacked her at the safe house. She held on to them like a lifeline.

Inner strength. Inner strength. Withstand damn near anything.

Caroline opened her eyes, no longer picturing Trumpold pushing his way through the door.

Paul Trumpold was dead. He could never hurt her again.

His psycho sister, on the other hand, was alive and circling Caroline like some sort of predator. Caroline fought hysteria, knowing she had to work the problem in front of her, just like she did every day as a paramedic.

"You brought me to the house where I used to live," Caroline said as evenly as she could, studying Lisette.

"Yes." Lisette actually looked pretty excited that Caroline recognized it. "I rented it from the new owners."

Caroline resisted the urge to point out how sick that was. "Are you working with Donald Brodey?"

Lisette began pacing back and forth. "To a degree. He had his usefulness."

That didn't make any sense to Caroline, and it ultimately didn't matter, since he wasn't here to help Lisette, so Caroline decided to try a different tack. The most direct one. "What do you want, Lisette?"

"I want you to pay for what you've done. I want you to tell the truth."

That sounded like what Zane had told her Donald Brodey had said. But Brodey wasn't connected to the Trumpolds in any way that they knew of.

"And what truth is that exactly?"

"I want you to admit to the world that you lied about my brother. About what you said he did to you. I know you lied."

She could see the other woman getting worked up just thinking about it. "Lisette, why do you think I lied? What reason would I have to lie about something like that?"

Lisette stopped her pacing and stared at Caroline. "He said you would say that. That you would say you had no reason to lie."

"Who said that? Brodey?"

Lisette didn't even listen to Caroline, just kept on talking. "But he showed me the reports. He showed me how you and Zane Wales got together and faked the whole thing."

Caroline shook her head. She didn't want to make Lisette angry, because God knew the woman was already unstable enough, but she honestly had no idea what she was talking about.

"Lisette, I think there was some mistake. Maybe you got the wrong medical reports by accident or something. Mine were very clear about what happened to me."

Lisette stormed over to a nearby table and brought a file back, opening it and holding it in front of Caroline's face.

"This is the medical report that went to the police department."

Caroline didn't need to look at it for long to recognize it. That was very definitely her battered face in the picture. Very definitely pictures of bruises and welts covering half her body. She didn't even try to read the trauma that had been done by the rape itself.

"Yes, that's my medical report." Caroline kept her voice as even as she could, swallowing the tremors.

Lisette flew back to the table and picked up another medical report, holding it in front of her again. "But this is the actual medical report after your so-called attack, isn't it?"

Caroline studied the file, unsure at first of what she was looking at. It was definitely her, but with much less trauma.

Then she remembered.

"Lisette, this is also a medical report for me. But it wasn't after my rape. This was from two months before. I was accosted by a man during one of my calls as a paramedic. He was robbing a convenience store and pushed me over trying to flee from police. My medical report was going to be used as part of his prosecution."

Lisette just stood there, smiling.

"What?" Caroline finally asked.

"That's exactly what he said you'd say. He was right about everything. You don't have any remorse at all, do you?"

"Look, those medical reports are two separate incidents."

"Not according to the dates," Lisette spat.

"What?"

"The dates are the same."

"Then it was a mistake. A typo. Or someone deliberately changed them to try to trick you."

"Or you and Zane Wales turned in a completely false medical report in order to get my brother arrested. You weren't nearly as hurt as you pretended to be."

Caroline tried to reason with her. "Lisette, I know you don't want to hear this about your brother. I'm sure you loved him."

Caroline had a brother and loved him. Of course, he would never attack a woman and beat her until she went into a coma. But she had to stay focused on reaching Lisette and making her understand.

"Brodey or someone else is feeding you lies, Lisette. Someone is trying to trick you into believing that Zane and I did something we didn't do. We had no reason to frame your brother."

"Donald Brodey has nothing to do with this!" Lisette screamed.

And suddenly it all became so clear to Caroline. No, not Brodey.

Damien Freihof.

He was the one who had manipulated Lisette like this. Or had taken what the woman so desperately wanted to hear and given her reason to believe it.

"Damien Freihof has been lying to you." Lisette's eyes

flew to Caroline's at the mention of his name, confirming Caroline's suspicions. "He's using you."

"Freihof has done nothing but show me the truth. You are the one who has been telling lies. But I'm going to make sure the world knows the truth."

"And how are you going to do that?"

"You're going to admit what really happened while I record it."

Caroline wanted to point out that even if she retracted her entire account of what Paul Trumpold did to her, it wouldn't change anything. Trumpold had attacked Jon Hatton and Sherry Mitchell. Had admitted to raping Caroline and six other women. He had stabbed Jon and Sherry both and been about to kill them when Zane arrived and shot him.

In the overall process, Caroline's version of the story didn't even matter. Paul Trumpold would've gone to jail with or without her medical record or testimony.

Although she'd been glad to give both to help make sure Trumpold went to prison for as long as possible.

But bringing this to Lisette's attention would probably just cause her to kill Caroline.

"I don't think changing my statement alone would do anything to clear your brother's name." Not that Caroline would do it anyway. There was no way in hell she would amend, modify or otherwise revise even one single line of the truth about what happened to her.

She looked Lisette straight in the eye. "And I won't change it anyway. If you hurt me, people will be able to tell I was only doing it under duress."

"We'll see about whether you won't change your lies when I start cutting off Zane Wales's fingers." Lisette laughed as Caroline blanched. Caroline had no doubt she meant it. "That's why I want you to call him and tell him to meet you here."

Caroline shook her head. "You might have wanted to ask me to do that before you told me you were going to cut off his fingers."

Lisette reached into the pocket of Caroline's paramedic jacket. "I sort of thought you might say that. So I guess I'll just text him with your phone."

She spoke as she typed. "I need you to come to my old house ASAP. Something important to show you. Can't talk now."

Caroline watched as Lisette sent the text, then cringed when the phone buzzed in response a few seconds later.

"What is it?" Caroline asked. Lisette read the text from Zane out loud.

"We won't answer him." Lisette smiled at Caroline. "How about that? It'll make it seem all so intriguing."

A few minutes later Caroline's phone rang. No doubt Zane calling when she didn't respond to his text. Lisette just held it until it went to voice mail. It rang again a few seconds later, and Lisette just threw it on the table.

"A missed text and two calls?" Lisette smiled. "A mysterious request to meet him at the scene of the crime? I think it's fair to say our white-hatted hero is on the way."

Lisette walked over to the table and began taking out an assortment of knives and guns. "I'll just get everything ready for when he arrives. I bet he'll knock on the door just like you said my brother did. But this time he'll get the surprise of his life."

Chapter Twenty-One

When Zane got another text from Caroline a few hours after the first telling him about the fire, it was because he figured she'd finally finished her shift, a twelve-hour one that had turned into closer to fourteen hours. He hadn't minded staying to do some more work. Trying to figure out what was missing with Brodey and glancing at some other cases. Detectives rarely got to work one case at a time.

But when he looked down at his buzzing phone for the text he thought would be a request to come get her, he did a double take.

I need you to come to my old house ASAP. Something important to show you. Can't talk now.

Zane couldn't think of any reason Caroline would set foot into that house again. Especially without at least talking to him about it first. He texted back.

What is it?

No response. He waited a few minutes in case she was busy with something, but when she didn't answer at all, he called.

Straight to voice mail.

Called again. Same thing.

Zane didn't panic. It had been a long day for both of them. The fire in the oil district wasn't terribly far from the beach section. Maybe she hadn't wanted to come all the way out here to the station just to drive all the way back to the house for whatever she wanted him to see. He began walking to his truck.

Caroline didn't have her truck, so she couldn't have driven herself over there. Someone had to have taken her, so that might explain why she wasn't answering her phone—she was talking to someone else.

But his gut told him that Caroline wouldn't enter that house again casually. Wouldn't just drive by and go inside for no reason. She was strong enough to handle a visit there, but she wouldn't go without planning.

Zane picked up his pace. Something wasn't right here.

"Wade," he called to the other man as he passed him. He gave him Caroline's previous address. "I need you to look up that address and see who owns it now. Any info. It's where Caroline lived when she was attacked."

"Got it."

"I need it fast, Wade. She just texted me from there."

"She in trouble?"

"Nothing to indicate it. But she wouldn't just go back there without a reason."

"I'll call you with the info."

Zane ran out of the station and to his car. The more time that passed without hearing from Caroline, the more worried he became. She should've at least seen he'd called or texted and responded by now. Given all that was going on, the danger they'd faced, she wouldn't just leave him without any communication.

He was just pulling out of the parking garage when his phone rang. He switched his phone to the hands-free speaker so he could continue to drive without looking at the number.

"Caroline?"

"No, man, it's Jon. Were you expecting a call from her?"

Zane explained what was going on and where he was headed.

Jon cursed under his breath. "I put in a request for Donald Brodey's financial records before I got on the plane. I just got to the Omega office and the report was ready."

This couldn't be good, not if Jon was calling so fast. "What?"

"Last week Brodey had a sizable deposit put into his bank account."

"How sizable?"

"Half a million dollars."

Zane whistled through his teeth. For a man who was about to go back to prison, that would help his family out quite a bit.

"Well, I discovered Brodey is terminally ill. Only a couple months left to live. So Freihof must have paid him to come after Caroline and me. Which makes more sense to me than him wanting revenge enough to want to kill us."

"That's just it, Zane. I tracked down the money. It didn't come from Freihof."

"Are you sure? I can't imagine he'd just use his real name on an account."

"Someone did use their real name, but it wasn't Freihof who paid Brodey."

"Who was it?"

"A Lisette Trumpold. Younger sister to Paul Trumpold."

Zane stomped on the gas, no longer caring about breaking any speed limits. "Damn it, Jon. Caroline texted me from the house where Trumpold attacked her."

"I think Lisette paid Brodey to take the fall for her

handiwork in Big Bend. She knew once we had someone in custody—someone who admitted to the crimes—your guard would be down."

"That's why Brodey didn't really have a lot of details today when I went to talk to him. I thought he was just regretting signing the confession. But really it was because he didn't have details to tell."

"And because he didn't want to lose his payoff," Jon finished for him. "I'll call Captain Harris and have him send uniforms to the address."

"Tell him to keep them quiet. If this is a hostage situation, I don't want Lisette to panic. I'm only five minutes out."

Another call beeped in. "I've got to go, Jon."

"Be safe, brother."

The call disconnected and Zane connected to the other one, praying it would be her. "Caroline?"

"No, sorry, man, it's Wade."

"Did you find out anything?"

"The house is owned by a Jack and Marty Smith. They rent it out. Current rental for the month of November is…"

"Lisette Trumpold."

"Yeah, do you know her?"

Zane gritted his teeth, wishing he could make the miles fly by faster. "She's the sister of Paul Trumpold, the man who attacked Caroline."

Wade let out a string of obscenities. Zane couldn't agree more.

"Jon Hatton is calling the captain even as we speak to get squad cars out here. They can't come in blazing, Wade."

"I'll make sure they don't."

"I'm not waiting for backup. I'm going in."

"Be careful."

Zane parked his car two houses down from where he needed to be. If Lisette had Caroline, which at this point he couldn't doubt was the case, he sure as hell wasn't going to just go knocking on the front door. Then Lisette could just kill them both.

Not to mention a knock on that door would scare Caroline. He never planned to knock on any door around her for the rest of their lives.

If Lisette had been sending those texts about Caroline being a liar and Zane keeping secrets, then Freihof had obviously gotten his hooks into her. Convinced her somehow that her brother was innocent and he and Caroline were at fault.

As utterly untrue as that was, it at least made sense.

But Lisette had made a tactical error in bringing Caroline here to this house. Caroline had lived here for years before the attack, and Zane had spent so much time here that it was like he had lived here too. He knew which windows creaked and which deck beams would hold his weight as he climbed up.

Weapon drawn, Zane made his way to the bathroom window on the side of the house. He and Caroline had joked and called that window a pervert's delight. If a Peeping Tom got lucky, he could catch someone in the bathroom, if not, he'd still have a view of almost the entire bottom floor.

He saw Caroline tied to a wooden chair in the middle of the hallway. The pressure in his chest eased. She was alive. That was the most important thing.

And he was damn well going to make sure she stayed that way.

He wasn't sure if Lisette was working alone or not, and he could bet she was armed to the teeth, so he couldn't just barge in. He prayed the squad cars would follow instructions and not come in lights and sirens blazing.

He slipped up the back outer stairs to the far bedroom. It had a door that led out to the deck and was his best chance of getting into the house unnoticed.

It still wasn't going to be easy.

He put his gun back in its holster as he arrived at the door. He let out a sigh of relief when he realized the new owners hadn't been willing to spring for a new, more fortified one. Applying the right pressure at an angle, he was able to slip his credit card in between the handle and the frame and popped open the door.

Caroline had once locked herself out and had shown him the trick. He'd told her how ridiculous she was not to get that door fixed. If she could get in the door like that, then a burglar could too. She'd laughed, saying it was so much more likely that she would forget her keys than it was for someone to break into her house.

He'd always meant to get that door fixed, even if just to piss her off. Thank God he hadn't had the chance and the new owners hadn't, either.

The door creaked slightly as he opened it and he immediately paused, wincing. But he could hear Caroline downstairs, talking to Lisette pretty loudly. He didn't know if she was doing it to help him, but either way it would cover the noise he was making trying to get to her.

He eased the door closed behind him, not wanting to take a chance on the wind blowing something over if he left it open.

"If your boyfriend doesn't get here soon, maybe I'll just start with your fingers."

"Maybe he's not coming. Maybe he has other things to do with his time besides run over here just because he got a cryptic text from me."

"He'll be here. I have no doubt about it. I've seen the way he looks at you. I saw you kissing in the parking lot of the Silver Eagle last week. That's when I realized what Damien told me had to be the truth."

"Just because Zane and I have a physical relationship?"

"Damien told me that you guys had kept apart for all these months to throw off suspicion about your lies. He told me that once you thought it was safe, you'd get back together. He was so right. Damien was right about everything."

"Damien Freihof is a pathological liar and genius using you to get back at a law enforcement group called Omega Sector. You're his pawn, Lisette. You don't have to be."

Zane grimaced as he heard Lisette strike Caroline. "Don't try to talk to me like you know me. You cost my brother his life. I loved him and you cost him everything."

Zane eased down the hall while Lisette paced back and forth in a frenzy. Then she went over to a table and pulled out a gun and pointed it right at Caroline's head.

Ice flowed through Zane's veins. He could jump from where he stood at the banister, but Lisette would definitely have time to shoot Caroline before he landed.

Caroline cleared her throat. "All right, Lisette, you want your confession from me? I'll give it to you. Set up the camera."

Zane could finally breathe again when Lisette removed the gun and walked over to set up her camera. Caroline was keeping her head, biding more time. Zane eased down a couple of stairs, staying in the shadows. The next time Lisette came close to Caroline, he would be able to pounce and catch her.

"Start from the beginning," the other woman said. "And if you tell the truth, maybe I'll kill your boyfriend quickly and you won't have to watch him suffer."

Caroline looked into the video camera Lisette had set up on a tripod a few feet in front of her. "My name is Caroline Gill. I am here to set the record straight about Dr. Paul Trumpold and my claim that he attacked me."

Zane could tell getting the words out were difficult for Caroline. She was doing her best just to keep it together.

"I need some water, Lisette. I can't get through this whole thing with my throat this dry. I was working at a fire all day today."

"Fine." Lisette did something to the camera, then stormed into the kitchen. When Zane heard the sink faucet come on, he stuck his hand over the banister.

"Caro," he whispered.

She looked up, eyes wide. He put his finger over his lips. "Anybody else here?" he asked as quietly as he could.

"No, just her." He could tell she wanted to say more, but there wasn't time.

"I'll jump her when she gives you the water."

He'd barely moved back into the shadows before Lisette came out of the kitchen. "You know, it's good that we stopped. It reminded me you can't be tied up when you give your confession. Then everyone is just going to think you were coerced."

Zane cursed under his breath as she picked up a knife and the gun again. She held the gun to Caroline's head once more as she cut the binds on her wrist. Zane couldn't risk the jump. She cut the rope on the other wrist before handing Caroline the water.

"Now, let's try this again. Take two." Lisette laughed wildly, like some demented film director.

They needed to get Lisette to come back over to the stairs but without the gun. Zane didn't know how to get her to do that without risking Caroline's life.

Caroline started talking again.

"My name is Caroline Gill. I'm here to set the record straight about my claim that Dr. Paul Trumpold attacked me."

Lisette's eyes narrowed as she paused the camera again. "I will come over there and cut you if you don't give me the truth."

"Okay, Lisette, the truth. You deserve that."

"Damn straight I do."

"Here's the truth." Caroline paused and took a deep breath. "I was standing right about here when someone knocked on my door. Do you know that hearing someone knock on a door still has the power to make me cower on the inside? Because right after I opened the door, your brother burst in, his fist striking my face before I could even react."

"Tell the truth, you bitch!" Lisette screeched.

"I am telling the truth. He hit me so hard that the bones in my cheek shattered. I fell to the floor, ironically, right here. Right here under my feet was where your brother attacked and raped me, Lisette."

Lisette stormed at Caroline, knife in hand. But a knife wasn't a gun and Zane was faster. He leaped over the banister, placing himself between Caroline and the madwoman rushing toward her. Lisette obviously wasn't expecting that. She brought the gun in her other hand up, but it was too late. With one quick uppercut Zane had the woman laid out on the floor.

He quickly took both weapons from her. She was already regaining consciousness and moaning as Zane handcuffed her hands behind her back.

"He hit me just like that, Lisette, but your brother didn't stop with just one punch," Caroline said hoarsely.

Then she sat down on the ground, on the floor where so much pain and humiliation had happened to her, and cried.

Chapter Twenty-Two

It was a beautiful day for a wedding.

Caroline had known Sherry Mitchell since they were both in college. They'd remained close through the years. Standing up here as part of the bridal party was an honor. She was delighted to be a part of her friend's special day.

A couple of weeks ago Caroline might have been nervous about standing in front of a hundred people. In a dress. In heels. None of those were things she was comfortable with. But given everything that had happened over the last two weeks, standing here didn't seem like such a terrorizing event after all.

Besides, she knew she looked good in the dress, especially if the way Zane couldn't take his eyes off her was anything to go by.

Maybe she'd have to start wearing dresses more often. Her paramedic uniform involved blue cargo pants and a blue button-down shirt. When she wasn't in that, she tended to be in jeans and a T-shirt.

No one would ever accuse Caroline of being too girlie.

But Zane hadn't taken his eyes off her from where he sat in the second row since the moment she'd walked down the aisle in front of Sherry a few minutes ago. He was still staring. And damn if she didn't like that hungry look in his eyes.

It was definitely enough to make a girl wear a dress more often.

Jon and Sherry had decided on a small wedding in a simple church just outside of Colorado Springs. Even being small there were nearly a hundred people here, many of them Omega Sector agents who worked with Jon and Sherry. They were more than just colleagues; it was easy to tell. They were family.

The wedding official was starting the charge to the bride and groom when Caroline caught sight of the videographer making his way straight up the middle aisle. The photographer had taken a much more conservative post in the back of the church.

Caroline tried to ignore the videographer, with the camera stuck to his face, but the guy seemed to be coming straight toward her, not caring at all about the service.

When she got married, she didn't want any disruptions like this guy. She would make sure that the videographer and photographer both knew she and Zane wouldn't tolerate a disruption like this.

Caroline's eyes flew to Zane's. Had she just made wedding plans with him in her mind? She ought to wait until he actually asked her.

The videographer looked like he was going to come all the way up onto the platform with the minister. Caroline just rolled her eyes as he did exactly that. But instead of having his camera pointed at the bride and groom, it was pointed at her. And then he dropped it from the front of his face.

Caroline felt terror shoot through her.

It was Paul Trumpold. And he was coming toward her, gun now in hand.

She forced herself not to let the panic take her under.

She needed her wits about her. No, this wasn't Paul Trumpold. He was dead.

But it was the man who had been in the doorway at the safe house and who she saw before the drugs had knocked her unconscious at the oil fire.

"That's right," he said. "I'm Nicholas. Paul and Lisette's brother."

How many violently crazy people could one family have?

She heard gasps and movements as Nicholas pulled her down in front of him, using her as a shield as he pointed his gun toward her head.

"You lied about my sister and my brother. He's dead and she's in jail because of you."

His voice, so similar to the one she heard in her nightmares, brought waves of terror. But this time she refused to give in.

She'd frozen the last time a man had grabbed her. Forgotten all her training and panicked. She wouldn't let that happen again.

Nicholas obviously wasn't expecting any fight out of Caroline. She certainly hadn't given one as he'd watched Brodey try to take her from the safe house.

This idiot probably didn't know that he'd walked into a church full of highly trained special agents. Caroline didn't know if any of them were carrying weapons, but she knew Zane was. He'd balked about having to get a special permit for his ankle holster for the plane ride here yesterday. But he wasn't planning on going anywhere without a weapon after what had happened recently.

All she had to do was give Zane a chance and not let this guy drag her out of the building.

Caroline met eyes with Zane, who gave her the slightest nod. He knew what she was planning, in sync with her the way they always had been. He trusted her to be able to do it.

Without warning she let all her weight go limp in Trumpold's grasp around her throat. When he shifted his stance to get a better hold on her, she made her move. She threw her heeled shoe back as hard as she could, gouging him in the shin, causing him to loosen his hold. She spun in his loosened grip, bringing her elbow around to clock him in the jaw.

When his head snapped around at her strike, she continued her momentum, swinging her arms around in a double fist, knocking the gun out of his hand and straight toward Zane. Then Caroline dropped to the ground, out of the way.

She hadn't been there the day Zane shot Paul Trumpold, saving Jon's and Sherry's lives and ending Trumpold's reign of terror over so many women.

But she was here this time when he put a bullet in Trumpold's chest before he could get his gun up and pointed at her. She was sure it was just as impressive.

That was *her* man. And she loved him.

In the aftermath of the situation, it was easy to tell who was an Omega Sector agent and who wasn't.

Everybody from Omega came forward to make sure Nicholas Trumpold was secure. Everybody who wasn't an agent made a mad rush to an exit to get away from a possibly dangerous situation.

Knowing Trumpold was taken care of, Zane moved quickly to Caroline, his face worried. His hands were gentle, ready to pull away if she seemed overwhelmed by what had happened.

"Caro, are you okay?"

Was she okay? Was he kidding? She knew she was grinning like an idiot but couldn't find it in her to care.

She had not been another damn victim.

"Did you see that move? Would've been a hell of a lot easier if I hadn't been in this dress."

The worry slid out of his eyes and he pulled Caroline against his chest. "It was pretty impressive. Trumpold definitely didn't expect it."

"But you did. You knew I could do it."

He kissed her forehead. "Of course you could do it. You just had to believe in yourself."

He wrapped his arms tighter around her as a couple of agents handcuffed Trumpold.

"I guess he's not dead."

Steve Drackett, head of the Critical Response Division of Omega, shook his head. "No. He'll soon be joining his sister in prison. Charged with attempted murder and ruining a perfectly good wedding day."

They all looked up at the bride and groom. Sherry looked white as a ghost and Jon was holding her tightly.

"I'm so sorry, Sherry." Caroline left Zane's arms and walked toward her friend. "He ruined your wedding."

"No, that's not it," Sherry said, looking at Caroline, then over at Steve and the other Omega agents. "I saw Damien Freihof. He was in the back corner of the church." She pointed in the direction. "He gave me a wave, then left in the middle of the panic."

Zane could hear the muttered curses of the agents around him, toned down because they were in a church.

"How did he know about this wedding?" Steve asked. "How did either of them know about this?"

The wedding hadn't been a secret, but it hadn't been made public in any way, either. Omega had too many enemies for that, Freihof being number one of them.

"We've got a mole, Steve," Jon said. "We can't deny that anymore. Damien is working with someone inside Omega Sector."

THE WEDDING WAS moved to the Omega Sector chow hall. It was the only place big enough to hold all one hundred guests.

And after what had happened, nobody minded having to go through a metal detector to get to the ceremony.

Jon and Sherry were determined that their wedding would go on. Today. Exactly one year to the day from when Jon had proposed. Damien Freihof would not stop them from getting married on the day they had planned.

Zane had to admit it was the most unique wedding he'd seen, but that didn't make it any less beautiful. Maybe it was because the bride and groom were so obviously in love with each other.

The caterers had transported the food over from the original reception site, and the musicians had just packed up their instruments and brought them over. The cafeteria opened into a small terrace, so people flowed both inside and out.

After the ceremony Zane planted an arm around Caroline and didn't plan to let her go from his side for the rest of the night.

Hell, he didn't know if he was going to let her go from his side for the rest of forever.

"That was some pretty impressive teamwork you two showed at the church today," Steve Drackett said as they mulled around talking to people and eating the finger food.

"Thank you," Caroline said. "Although, we didn't plan it, believe me. I'm just glad I didn't freeze up."

"Well, if you two decide you're ready to get out of Corpus Christi, be sure to come see me about openings here at Omega. We could always use people who stay cool under pressure." Steve turned to Caroline. "And we could use a good medic for our SWAT team."

Zane loved Caroline's smile, and if she had expressed an interest in Steve's offer, Zane would've followed her lead.

"Sorry, afraid we're Texas folk, through and through. I don't think we could ever truly leave," Caroline said.

"I certainly respect that. But let me know if you change your mind."

A beautiful lady with a dark-haired baby in her arms came up to Steve. "No shoptalk at the wedding. I could tell from across the room you were talking business."

Steve reached down and kissed her and took the baby from her arms. "Busted." He smiled at Caroline and Zane as he led his wife back to the action.

Caroline turned to him, worry in her eyes. "I shouldn't have spoken for you, Zane. I'm sorry. Omega Sector might be a dream come true for you."

He wrapped his arms around her and pulled her closer. "No, I don't want to leave Texas. Especially not now just as I'm getting re-situated in the police department. Tim Harris would have my ass if I quit now, even for Omega Sector."

"You're really going to go back to the department full-time?"

"Yeah. It's where I belong. We both know that."

Her smile beamed. "Stay right here. I brought something with me and I think it's just about time."

"What is it?"

"I'll get it and show you."

"Maybe I don't want to let you go."

"I'm just going across the room." She rolled her eyes.

He pulled her up tight against him. "Maybe I'm not just talking about here. Maybe I'm talking about forever."

She reached up and put both her hands on his cheeks. "I can't promise you forever, Zane. Not yet. There's something missing."

He fought to tamp down the disappointment that swamped

him at her words. She needed more time, he had to understand that. After what she'd been through, who could blame her for needing more time?

It was hard, but he let her go. He watched as she scurried across the room to a gift bag she'd brought and left by one of the doors. She'd had it on the plane and even had it at the church earlier. He'd assumed it was a gift for Jon and Sherry, but now she was bringing it back to him.

She held the string of the bag with one hand as she stopped directly in front of him. She reached into it and pulled out his white cowboy hat.

Zane didn't know what to say. She must have grabbed it from his house, although he hadn't seen her do it. Before he could think of anything, she slipped it onto his head.

"Now," she whispered, dropping the bag and smiling up at him.

"Now what?" he said, unable to stop the smile spreading all over his face. He pulled her to him, knowing he would never be able to let her go again.

"Now you're ready to rejoin the force, and you and I are ready for our forever."

* * * * *

CARDWELL CHRISTMAS CRIME SCENE

B.J. DANIELS

With utmost appreciation I dedicate this Cardwell book to Kimberly Rocha, the craziest, most loving, generous, truly beautiful fan I've yet to meet.

Chapter One

DJ Justice opened the door to her apartment and froze. Nothing looked out of place and yet she took a step back. Her gaze went to the lock. There were scratches around the keyhole. The lock set was one of the first things she'd replaced when she'd rented the apartment.

She eased her hand into the large leather hobo bag that she always carried. Her palm fit smoothly around the grip of the weapon, loaded and ready to fire, as she slowly pushed open the door.

The apartment was small and sparsely furnished. She never stayed anywhere long, so she collected nothing of value that couldn't fit into one suitcase. Spending years on the run as a child, she'd had to leave places in the middle of the night with only minutes to pack.

But that had changed over the past few years. She'd just begun to feel...safe. She liked her job, felt content here. She should have known it couldn't last.

The door creaked open wider at the touch of her finger, and she quickly scanned the living area. Moving deeper into the apartment, she stepped to the open bathroom door and glanced in. Nothing amiss. At a glance she could see the bathtub, sink and toilet as well as the mirror on the medicine cabinet. The shower door was clear glass. Nothing behind it.

That left just the bedroom. As she stepped soundlessly toward it, she wanted to be wrong. And yet she knew someone had been here. But why break in unless he or she planned to take something?

Or leave something?

Like the time she'd found the bloody hatchet on the fire escape right outside her window when she was eleven. That message had been for her father, the blood from a chicken, he'd told her. Or maybe it hadn't even been blood, he'd said. As if she hadn't seen his fear. As if they hadn't thrown everything they owned into suitcases and escaped in the middle of the night.

She moved to the open bedroom door. The room was small enough that there was sufficient room only for a bed and a simple nightstand with one shelf. The book she'd been reading the night before was on the nightstand, nothing else.

The double bed was made—just as she'd left it.

She started to turn away when she caught a glimmer of something out of the corner of her eye. Ice ran down her spine as she dropped the gun back into her shoulder bag and stepped closer. Something had been tucked between the pillows and duvet. Gingerly picking up the edge of the duvet, she peeled it back an inch at a time. DJ braced herself for something bloody and dismembered, her mind a hamster on a wheel, spinning wildly.

But what she found was more disturbing than blood and guts. As she uncovered part of it, she saw familiar blank eyes staring up at her. Her breath caught in her throat as tears stung her eyes.

"Trixie?" she whispered, voice breaking, as she stared at the small rag doll's familiar face.

On the run with her father, she'd had little more than the clothes on her back except for the rag doll that had been her only companion since early childhood.

"We should throw this old thing away," her father had said after a dog tore the doll from her hands once and he'd had to chase it down to retrieve what was left because she'd been so hysterical. "I'll buy you another doll. A pretty one, not some stuffed fabric one," he'd pleaded.

She'd been so upset that he'd relented and let her keep the doll she'd always known as Trixie. But she could tell that he would have been happier to get rid of the thing. She wondered if it brought him bad memories, since it was clear that the doll was handmade. Even the clothing. She liked to pretend that her mother had made it for her. If her mother hadn't died in childbirth.

Was that why her father wished she didn't care so much for the doll? Because it brought back the grief, the loss? That might explain why he had seemed to want nothing to do with anything from the past, including her doll. Not that she'd ever understood her father.

Life with him had been sparse and sporadic. He had somehow kept her fed and clothed and managed to get her into school—at least for a while until they were uprooted again. But the incident with the doll now made her wonder.

From as far back as she could remember, she'd believed that the doll with the sewn face and the dull, dark stitched eyes needed her as much as she needed it.

Now she half feared all she would find was Trixie's dismembered head. But as she drew back the covers, she saw that the body was still intact. Someone had left it for her tucked under the covers almost...tenderly. With trembling fingers, she picked up the treasured rag doll, afraid something awful had been done to her that would spoil one of the few good memories she had of her childhood.

Cupping the precious doll in her hands, DJ began to cry—for herself and for Trixie. The doll was in incredible shape for how old she was, not to mention what she must have been through over the years. DJ thought of her being lost, someone discarding her in a trash can as nothing more than junk and that awful feeling she'd had that she would never see her again.

So how had Trixie miraculously turned up again?

Heart in her throat, she looked closer at the doll.

Something was wrong.

The doll looked exactly like Trixie, but... She studied the handmade clothing. It looked as pristine as the doll. Maybe whoever had found it had washed it, taken care of it all these years...

For what possible purpose?

As happy as she'd been to see the doll again, now she realized how unlikely that was. Why would anyone care about some silly rag doll? And how could someone possibly know she was the one who'd lost it all those years ago?

After being her constant companion from as far back as she could remember, Trixie had been the worse for wear before DJ had misplaced her. The doll had spent too many years tucked under one of DJ's chubby arms. So how—

With a jolt, she recalled the accident she'd had with the doll and the dog that had taken off with it all those years ago. The dog had ripped off one of Trixie's legs. With DJ screaming for help, her father had chased down the dog, retrieved the leg and later, at her pleading, painstakingly sewn it back on with the only thread he could find, black.

Her fingers trembling, she lifted the dress hem and peered under the only slightly faded red pantaloons. With both shock and regret, she saw that there was no black thread. No seam where the leg had been re-attached.

This wasn't her doll.

It surprised her that at thirty-five, she could feel such loss for something she'd been missing for so many years.

She stared at the rag doll, now more confused than ever. Why would people break into her apartment to leave it for her? They had to have known that she'd owned one exactly like it. Wouldn't they realize that she'd know the difference between hers and this one? Or was that the point?

DJ studied the doll more closely. She was right. This one and Trixie were almost *identical*, which meant that whoever had made them had made *two*. Why?

She'd never questioned before where her doll had come from. Trixie was in what few photographs she'd seen of her childhood, her doll locked under her arm almost like an extension of herself.

Like hers, this one looked more than thirty years old. The clothing was a little faded, the face even blanker than it had been all those years ago, but not worn and faded like Trixie had been when DJ had lost her.

DJ felt a chill. So who had left this for her?

Someone who'd had this doll—a doll that was identical to hers before Trixie's accident. Someone who'd known there had been two identical dolls. Someone who knew this doll would be meaningful to her.

But why break in to leave it for her tucked under the covers? And why give it to her now? A life on the run had taught her one thing. The people who had left this wanted something from her. They could have mailed it with a note. Unless they had some reason to fear it could be traced back to them?

Regrettably, there was only one person she could ask, someone she hadn't spoken to in seven years. Her father.

She took a couple of deep breaths as she walked back into the living room. She'd left the door open in case she had needed to get out fast, but now she moved to close and lock it.

With her back against the door, she stared at the apartment she'd come to love. She'd made a life for herself here, and just the thought of being forced to give it up—

She was considering what her intruder might want from her when she felt a prick and dropped the doll. Sucking on her bleeding finger, she stared down at the rag doll. The dress had gaped open in the back to expose a straight pin—and what looked like the corner of a photograph.

Carefully picking up the doll so it didn't stick her again, she unpinned the photo and pulled it out. There were three people in the snapshot. A man and two women, one young, one older, all dark-haired. The young woman, the only one smiling, was holding a baby.

She flipped the photo over. Written in a hurried hand were the words: *Your family.*

What? She quickly turned the photograph back over and stared at the people pictured there.

She'd never seen any of them before, but there was something familiar about the smiling woman holding the baby. DJ realized with a start that the woman looked like her. But how was this possible if her mother had died in childbirth?

If it was true and these people were family…was it possible she was the baby in the photo? Why would her father have lied if that were the case? He knew how much she would have loved having family. He'd always said it was just the two of them. But what if that wasn't true?

Still, she thought as she studied the photo, if it was true, wouldn't they have contacted her? Then she realized they *were* contacting her now. But why wait all these years, and why do it like this?

The reason hit her hard. No one had wanted her to know the truth.

But someone had decided to tell her.

Or *warn* her, she thought with a shiver.

Chapter Two

"Are you sure it's the same doll? I thought you lost it years ago."

DJ gripped the utilitarian standard black phone tighter as she looked through the thick Plexiglas in the prison visiting room at her father.

Walter Justice had been a big, handsome man who'd charmed his way out of trouble all his life—until it caught up with him one night when he'd gotten involved in a robbery that went badly and he ended up doing time for second-degree murder. He had aged well even in prison, and that charm was still there in the twinkle of his blue eyes, in his crooked-toothed smile, in the soft reassuring sound of his voice.

She hadn't been able to wait until visiting day, so this was the best that could be done on short notice with the prison warden. But as surprised and pleased as her father had been to see her, he'd given the doll only a cursory look.

"It's the same doll," she said impatiently into the phone. "It's just not *mine*. Apparently someone made two of these dolls. The clothes are handmade—just like my doll. Everything is identical except the doll isn't mine," she explained impatiently. "So whose is it?"

"How should *I* know?"

"You have to know where *my* doll came from," she argued.

"DJ, you don't really expect me to remember where we picked up a rag doll all those years ago, do you?"

"Yes, I do." She frowned, remembering a photo she'd seen of when she was a baby. Trixie had been lying next to her. "I had it from as far back as I can remember. You should remember if someone gave it to me when I was a baby."

He glanced away for a moment. "Look, if you think it is some kind of threat, then maybe you should disappear for a while."

She hadn't said she thought it was a threat. Her eyes widened in both alarm and anger. What wasn't he telling her?

"That is all you have to say? *Run?* Your answer to everything." She thought of the cheap motels, the carryout food, the constantly looking over her shoulder, afraid someone would either kill her father or take him from her. First sign of trouble—and there was always trouble when your father is a con man—and off they would go, usually in the middle of the night. She'd spent too many years on the run with him as a child. This time she wasn't running.

"No," she said, gripping the phone until her fingers ached. "This time I want answers. If you don't tell me, I'll get them on my own."

"I only want you to be…safe."

"*Safe?* So this doll *is* a threat." She cursed under her breath. For years she'd had to deal with people her father had swindled or old partners he'd shortchanged or screwed over. Half the time she didn't know who was after them or why they had to keep moving, always on the run from something. She'd felt as if she'd had a target on her back all her life because of this man. "What have you gotten me into now?"

"You can't believe this doll is my doing."

Why had she thought that her father, a man who lied for living, would be honest with her? Coming here had been a mistake, but then again, she'd had no one else to ask about the doll—or the photo.

She reached into her pocket. She'd come too far to turn around and leave without at least trying to get the truth out of him. "Who are these people in this photograph, and why would someone want me to have it?" she demanded as she pressed the crinkled photo against the Plexiglas between them.

DJ watched all the color drain from his face. Growing up, she'd learned to tell when he was lying. But what she saw now on his face was pain and fear.

His gaze darting away from the photo as he lowered his voice. "I don't know what this is about, but what would it hurt if you just got out of town for a while?"

She shook her head. "Stop lying to me. You recognize these people. Tell me the truth. Is this my mother? Don't you think I noticed that she looks like me? Am I that baby?"

"DJ, how is that possible? I told you, your mother died in childbirth."

"Then this woman isn't my mother?"

"On my life, you aren't the baby in that photo." He crisscrossed his heart. "And those people are not your family."

She'd been so hopeful. She felt like crying as she peeled the photo off the grimy glass and dropped it back into her bag along with the doll. She'd had to leave her gun in her car and felt naked without it. "But you did recognize the people in the photo."

He said nothing, which came as little surprise.

"I have no idea why I came here." She met his gaze. "I knew you'd lie."

"DJ, whatever you think of me, listen to me now," he pleaded.

DJ. That had been his nickname for her, and it had stuck. But hearing him say it had her fighting tears. She'd once thought her father was the most amazing man in the world. That had been a very long time ago.

She got to her feet, shaking her head at her own naïveté as she started to put the phone back. She'd fallen for his promises too many times in her life. She'd made a clean break when he'd gone to prison, telling him she never wanted to see him again.

Drawing the phone to her ear, she said, "It is clear to me that you've lied to me my whole life. What I don't know is why. But I'm going to find out."

"I did the best I could, just the two of us," her father said, his voice breaking. "I know I could have done better, but, DJ—"

She'd heard this before and couldn't bear to hear it again. "If I have family—" Growing up, she'd often dreamed of a big, boisterous family. Now, with Christmas coming, she felt nostalgic. If she had family, if that's why they'd left this for her now...

She'd seen an ad in a magazine of a family around a beautifully decorated tree on Christmas morning. That night she'd prayed to the starlit night that she could be that little girl in the ad.

But her prayer hadn't been answered, and now she

no longer believed in fairy tales. If anything, life had taught her that there were no happy endings.

"DJ, you have to listen to me." He'd raised his voice. The guard was making his way down the line of booths toward him. "You don't know how dangerous—"

"Dangerous?" she echoed.

The guard tapped him on the shoulder. "Time to go."

"DJ—"

"Just tell me the truth." She hated how vulnerable she sounded. She'd seen his face when he'd looked at the people in the photograph. He *had* recognized them. But if they were her family, then why had he looked so...hurt, and yet so frightened? Because he'd been caught in a lie? Or because she had something to fear from them?

She'd had to become strong and trust her own instincts for so long... Growing up on the run with her father had taught her how to survive.

That was, until she'd found the doll and the photo of three people she didn't know, one of them holding a baby who, no matter what he said, was probably her. But what about that would put her in danger?

"Last chance," she said into the phone.

The guard barked another *"Time to go."*

Her father's gaze locked with hers. She saw pleading in his eyes as he quickly said into the phone, "There's a reason I lied all these years, but the truth is...you will be hearing from my family in Montana soon. Go to them until you hear from me." The guard grabbed the phone from her father's hand and slammed it down.

DJ stood staring at him, his words rooting her to the floor. Her father had family in Montana? *She* had family? A family that would be contacting her? If this was another lie…

Slowly she hung up her phone as she watched Walter Justice being led away. Frowning, she pulled out the photo. He's sworn these people weren't her family. Then who were they? Her mother's family? A cold dread filled her at the memory of her father's reaction to the photo.

The doll and the photo proved that they knew about her. That at least someone in that family wanted her to know about them. And now she was going to find them. That she was on her own was nothing new.

And yet the fear she'd seen in her father's eyes almost burned through her resolve.

IN BIG SKY, MONTANA, Dana Cardwell Savage braced herself as she pushed open the door to her best friend Hilde's sewing shop. Christmas music played softly among the rows and rows of rich bolts of fabric. For a moment she slowed to admire the Christmas decorations that Hilde had sewn for the occasion, wishing she had time to sew. She missed quilting and the time she used to spend with Hilde back when they were partners in Needles and Pins.

Seeing her friend at the back, she moved on reluctantly. She needed to tell Hilde the news in person. Her only fear was how her friend was going to respond. Their relationship had taken a beating three years ago. Hilde had only begun to trust her again. And now this.

"Dana!" Hilde saw her and smiled, clearly pleased to see her. Raising four children, Dana rarely got down to the shop that she and Hilde had started together. Hilde had bought her out long since then, but Dana still loved coming down here, where it was so peaceful and quiet.

She moved to the stools by the cash register and pulled one up to sit down. There were several people in the shop, but fortunately, Hilde's assistant, Veronica "Ronnie" Tate, was helping them.

"Where are the kids?" Hilde asked.

"With Stacy." She loved that her older sister was so good about taking all of the children to give Dana a break. Stacy's daughter, Ella, was almost five now. Dana's twins were four, Mary was eight and her oldest, Hank, was nine. Where had those years gone?

"So, you're out on the town?" Hilde asked and then seemed to notice how nervous Dana was. "What is it? What's happened?"

"My cousin Dee Anna Justice, the *real* one. Except apparently she goes by DJ. I talked to my uncle, Walter, whom I was led to believe was dead." She didn't want to bias Hilde against the real Dee Anna Justice any more than she might already be, given the past. But she also couldn't keep anything from her. "Walter called from prison."

"Prison?"

Dana nodded. "He assured me that his daughter is nothing like him. In fact, she hadn't talked to him in years until recently. She doesn't know she has family, he said. She was never told about us. My uncle was hoping that I would contact her and invite her to come to Montana for the holidays so she can get to know her family."

Paling, Hilde's hand went to her protruding stomach and the baby inside her. Three years ago, a young woman claiming to be Dee Anna had come to the ranch. Dana, who had so desperately wanted to connect with a part of her family she hadn't known even existed, had fallen for the psychopathic, manipulative woman's lies, and they had all almost paid with their lives.

But Hilde had suffered the most. Dana still couldn't believe that she'd trusted the woman she thought was her cousin over her best friend. She would never forgive herself. The fake Dee Anna, it turned out, had been the roommate of the real Dee Anna Justice for a short period of time. The roommate had opened a piece of her mail and, since they resembled each other, had pretended to be Dee Anna. Dana had believed that the woman was the real Dee Anna Justice and almost lost everything because of it.

"Why would he keep something like that from her?" Hilde finally asked.

"Because his family had disowned him when he married a woman they didn't approve of. He thought his family would turn both him and his daughter away, apparently."

"But now?"

"Now, he said with Christmas coming, he hoped I would reach out to her and not turn her away as his family had done. She doesn't have any other family, he said." She saw Hilde weaken.

"I told my uncle about the woman who pretended to be Dee Anna. He was so sorry about what happened," Dana said quickly. "He said he'd never met DJ's former roommate, but that he was shocked, and his daughter would be, too, to learn that the woman was capable of the horrible things she did."

Hilde nodded. "So, you've contacted her?"

"No, I wouldn't do that without talking to you first."

Her friend took a breath and let it out. "It's all right."

"I won't if it upsets you too much," Dana said, reaching for Hilde's hand.

"You're sure this time she's the real Dee Anna Justice?"

"Hud ran both her and her father through the system. She has been working as a travel writer, going all over the world to exotic places and writing about them under the pen name DJ Price." One of the perks of being married to the local marshal was that he wouldn't let anyone else come to visit without first finding out his or her true identity.

"So Colt knows that the real Dee Anna has turned up?"

The only good thing that had come out of that horrible time three years ago was Deputy Marshal Colt Lawson. He had believed what Hilde was saying about the fake Dee and had ended up saving her life as well as Dana's and the kids'. Now the two were married, and Dana had never seen Hilde looking happier, especially since she was pregnant with their first child.

"I talked to Colt *first*. He said it was up to you, but none of us wants to take any chances with this baby or your health."

Hilde smiled. "I'm as healthy as a horse and the baby is fine. As long as we're sure this woman is the real Dee Anna and not a murdering psychopath."

The other Dee, the fake Dee Anna Justice, had set her sights on Dana's husband, Marshal Hud Savage, planning to replace Dana. So Dana and her children had to go, and Hilde, the interfering friend in the woman's mentally disturbed mind, along with them. Dana shivered at the memory.

She had nightmares sometimes, thinking they were all still locked in that burning barn. "*That* Dee Anna is dead and gone."

Hilde nodded. "But not forgotten."

"No, not forgotten. It was a lesson I will never forget, and neither will Hud." She smiled and squeezed her friend's hand. "I'm just glad you and I are okay."

"We're more than okay. I know how much family means to you. Contact your cousin and tell her she's welcome. I would never stand in the way of you finding more of your relatives on your mother's side."

"I want you to meet her. If for any reason you suspect anything strange about her—"

Hilde laughed. "I'll let you know if she tries to kill me."

Chapter Three

Beau Tanner had always known the debt would come due, and probably at the worst possible time. He'd dreaded this day since he was ten. Over the years he'd waited, knowing there was no way he could deny whatever request was put to him.

The sins of the father, he thought as he stared at the envelope he'd found in his mailbox this morning. The return address was for an attorney in San Diego, California. But the letter inside was from a California state correction facility prisoner by the name of Walter Justice.

He wondered only idly how the man had found him after all these years, forgetting for a moment the kind of people he was dealing with. Beau could have ended up anywhere in the world. Instead, he'd settled in the Gallatin Canyon, where they'd first met. He suspected Walter had kept track of him, knowing that one day he would demand payment for the debt.

The letter had been sent to his home address here on the ranch—instead of his office. So he knew before he opened it that it would be personal.

Telling himself just to get it over with, Beau studied the contents of the envelope. There were two sheets of paper inside. One appeared to be a travel article about Eleuthera, an island in the Bahamas. The other was a plain sheet of paper with a printed note:

Take care of my daughter, DJ. Flight 1129 from LA arriving in Bozeman, Montana, Thursday at 2:45 p.m. Dana Cardwell Savage will be picking her up and taking her to Cardwell Ranch. I highly advise you not to let her know that you're watching out for her—and most especially that it was at my request.

It was signed W. Justice.

Under that he'd written, "Cell phone number for emergencies only."

Today was Thursday. DJ's flight would be coming in *this* afternoon. Walter had called it awfully close. What if Beau had been out of town? If he'd questioned whether Walter had kept track of him, he didn't anymore.

He read the letter again and swore. He had no idea what this was about. Apparently Walter's daughter needed protection? A small clue would have been helpful. And protection from what? Or was it from whom?

Also, he was surprised Walt's daughter would be coming to Montana. That was where their paths had crossed all those years ago. He thought of the dark-haired five-year-old girl with the huge brown expressive eyes and the skinny ten-year-old kid he'd been.

He remembered the way she'd looked up at him, how he'd melted into those eyes, how he'd foolishly wanted to rescue her. What a joke. He hadn't even been able to rescue himself. Like him, she'd been trapped in a life that wasn't her doing.

"Any mail for me?" asked a sleepy-sounding female voice from behind him.

He folded the letter and article and shoved them into his jean jacket pocket before turning to look at the slim, beautiful blonde leaning against his kitchen counter. "Nope. Look, Leah—"

"I really appreciate you letting me stay here, Beau," she said, cutting him off. "If this package I have coming wasn't so important and I wasn't between places right now…"

Beau nodded, mentally kicking himself for getting involved when she'd shown up on his doorstep. "Leah, I wish you hadn't put me in the middle of whatever this is."

"Please, no lectures," she said, raising a hand. "Especially before I've had my coffee. You did make coffee, didn't you? I remember that you always made better coffee than Charlie." Her voice broke at Charlie's name. She turned away from him, but not before he'd seen the tears.

She pulled down a clean cup and poured herself a cup of coffee before turning to him again. He studied her in the steam that rose from the dark liquid. He'd met Leah Barnhart at college when his best friend and roommate, Charlie Mack, had been dating her. The three of them had become good friends. Leah and Charlie had later married and both taken jobs abroad. Over the years, they'd kept in touch for a while, then just an occasional Christmas card. The past few years there hadn't even been a Christmas card.

No wonder he'd been so surprised and caught off guard to find her standing on his doorstep last night.

"And you're not in the middle of anything," she said after taking a long drink of her coffee.

"Why *are* you here?"

"I told you. I'm expecting an important package. I happened to be in Montana and thought about our college days…" She met his gaze and shrugged.

He didn't believe any of it. "Where's Charlie? You said he's still in Europe. I need his number."

She looked away with a sigh. "I don't have it."

He glanced at her bare left-hand ring finger. "Are you *divorced*?"

"No, of course not." She let out a nervous laugh. "We're just— It's a long story, and really not one I'm ready to get into this early in the morning. Can we talk about this later?"

He agreed, since he needed to get to work. DJ Justice would be flying into Montana in a few hours. He had to be ready. He had no idea what was required to keep her safe. It might come down to some extreme measures. Since he didn't know why she even needed protection—or from whom—now was definitely not the time to have a houseguest, especially one who knew nothing about his life before college. He wanted to keep it that way.

"You don't decorate for Christmas?" Leah asked as she looked around the large log home he'd built back in a small valley in the mountains not far from Big Sky. He'd bought enough land that he could have horses—and privacy. That was another reason he'd been surprised to find her on his doorstep. His place wasn't that easy to find.

He raked a hand through his thick, unruly mop of blond hair. "I've never been one for holidays."

She nodded. "I thought you'd at least have had a tree and some lights."

He glanced at his watch. "If you need anything, call my office and talk to Marge."

Leah made a face. "I called your office on my way here. Marge scares me."

He doubted that. He'd known Leah a lifetime ago. Was this woman standing in his kitchen the same Leah he'd toasted when she and Charlie had married? "Marge is a little protective."

"I should say. So you really are a private investigator?"

"That's what my license says."

She studied him with narrowed eyes. "Why do I get the feeling there is more to it?"

"I have no idea," he said. "Are you sure you'll be all right here by yourself?"

"I'll be fine." She smiled. "I won't steal your silverware, if that's what you're worried about."

"I wasn't. Anyway, it's cheap flatware."

She sobered. "I've missed you, Beau. Charlie and I both have. But I honestly do have a package coming here, and it's important or I wouldn't have done it without checking with you first."

"Then we'll talk later," he said and left. It made him nervous, not knowing what was going to be required of him over the next few days or possibly longer—and having Leah here was a complication.

Turning his thoughts again to DJ Justice, he realized he was excited to see the grown-up DJ. He'd thought about her over the years and had hoped her life had turned out all right. But if she was in trouble and needed his help, then there was no way of knowing what her life had been like the past thirty years. He hated to think what kind of trouble she had gotten into that required his help.

Since her father was calling in a promise... Beau was betting it was the dangerous kind.

ANDREI LOOKED AT the coin in his hand for a long moment. His hand shook a little as he tossed the coin and watched it spin before he snatched it from the air and slapped it down on his thick wrist.

He hesitated, mentally arguing with himself. He had a bad feeling this time. But the money was good, and he'd always gone by the flip of a coin.

Superstition dictated that he went through the same steps each time. Otherwise...

He knew too well the *otherwise* as he slowly lifted his palm to expose the coin. Heads, he went ahead with this hit. Tails...

Heads. A strange sense of both worry and disappointment filled him. But the coin toss was sacred to him, so he assured himself he should proceed as he pocketed the coin.

Stepping to the table, he picked up the information he'd been given on the woman he was to kill.

He noticed that a prison snitch had provided her whereabouts. He snorted, shaking his head and trying to ignore that little voice in his head that was telling him this one was a mistake. But he'd worked with the man who'd hired him before, so he pushed aside his doubts and picked up the photo of Dee Anna Justice, or DJ as she was apparently called.

Pretty. He wondered idly what she had done to warrant her death—but didn't let himself stay on that thought long. It had never mattered. It especially couldn't matter this time—his last time.

Maybe that was what had him on edge. He'd decided that this one would be it. With the money added to what he'd saved from the other hits, he could retire at forty-five. That had always been his goal. Another reason he'd taken this job. It would be over quickly. By his birthday he would be home free. He saw that as a sign, since this would be his last job.

Encouraged, he took the data over to the fireplace and lit it with a match. He would already be in Montana, waiting for a sign, by the time Dee Anna Justice arrived.

DJ LEANED BACK into the first-class seat, wishing she could sleep on the airplane. Her mind had been reeling since finding the doll and the photograph. But now, to discover after all these years that she had family, a cousin…

She'd been shocked and wary when she'd gotten the message on her voice mail. *"Hi, my name's Dana Cardwell Savage. I'm your cousin. I live in Montana, where your father was born. I'd really love to talk to you. In fact, I want to invite you to the Cardwell Ranch here at Big Sky for the holidays."*

Instantly she'd known this call had been her father's doing. But how had he gotten her cell phone number? She mentally smacked herself on the forehead as she recalled the guard at the prison searching her purse. The only thing he'd taken was her cell phone, saying she could pick it up on the way out. She should have known her father had friends in prison.

She'd thought about ignoring the message. What if this was just some made-up relative? She wouldn't have put it past her father.

But the voice had sounded…sincere. If this Dana Cardwell Savage really was her cousin…would she be able to fill in the gaps about her father's family? What about her mother's family? Wasn't there a chance she might know something about the doll and photograph?

She'd always had the feeling there was some secret her father had been keeping from her. If Dana Savage had the answer…

After doing some checking, first to verify that Walter William Justice had been born in Montana near Big Sky and then to see if there really was a Cardwell Ranch and a Dana Cardwell Savage, DJ had finally called her back.

A few minutes on the phone and she'd agreed to fly out. "I can't stay for the holidays, but thank you for asking. I would like to meet you, though. I have to ask. What makes you so sure we're cousins?"

Dana explained about discovering an uncle she hadn't known existed until she'd found some old letters from him to her grandparents on her mother's side. "There'd been a falling-out. I hate to say this, but they'd disowned him. That's why I'd never heard of your father until a few years ago, when I found the letters."

His family had disowned him? Was it that simple, why she'd never known about them? "Do you still have those letters?"

"I do."

She had felt her heart soar. Something of substance she could use to find out the truth. She wanted answers so badly. "I've never known anything about my father's family—or my mother's, for that matter, so I'd love to learn more."

"Family is so important. I'm delighted that your father called. I'd heard he had died. I'm so glad that wasn't true."

Little involving her father was the truth, DJ thought. But if his family had disowned him, then maybe that explained why he'd kept them from her. She had a cousin. How many more relatives did she have that he hadn't told her about?

She tried to relax. Her cousin was picking her up at the airport and taking her to the family ranch where her father had been born. These people were his family, *her family*, people she'd never known had existed until recently. She wanted to pinch herself.

Pulling her purse from under the seat in front of her, she peered in at the rag doll. If only it could talk. Still, looking into its sweet face made her smile in spite of herself. It wasn't hers, but it was so much like hers...

She thought of Trixie and remembered leaving a motel room in the middle of the night and not realizing until later that the doll wasn't with her.

"You must have dropped her," her father had said as they sped out of town.

"We have to go back," she'd cried. "We can't leave her."

He'd looked over at her. "We can't, sweetie. If I go back there... We can't. I'll get you another doll."

She hadn't wanted another doll and had cried herself to sleep night after night until she had no more tears.

"It was just a stupid doll," her father had finally snapped.

"It was all I ever had that was mine."

Now, as she looked at the doll resting in her shoulder bag, she wondered where it had been. Had another girl had this doll as she suspected? But how would that girl know about DJ and Trixie? Trixie was lost, while this doll had been well cared for all these years. Why part with it now?

Her head ached with all the questions and a nagging sense of dread that she wasn't going to like what she found out.

It made no sense that people had given her this doll and the photograph unless they wanted her to find out the truth. But the way they'd left it, breaking into her apartment...

She had tucked the photo into a side pocket of her purse and now withdrew it to study the two women, the one man and the baby in the shot. The man and women were looking at the camera, standing next to a stroller. There was nothing in the background other than an unfamiliar stone wall to give her any idea of where it had been shot—or when.

With a start, she saw something in the photo that she hadn't noticed before. She'd always looked at the people in the photo, especially the woman holding the baby.

But now she saw something in the stroller that made her heart pound. A doll. The doll she now had tucked in her purse. Her father hadn't lied. She *wasn't* this baby, because it wasn't her doll in the stroller. But who was the baby, if not her?

Chapter Four

It had snowed last night, dumping another six inches. Fortunately Highway 191 through the Gallatin Canyon had already been plowed by the time Beau dug himself out and drove to his office on the second floor of an old brick building in downtown Bozeman.

"Good morning, boss," Marge said from behind her desk as he came in. Pushing sixty, solid as a brick wall and just as stout, Marge Cooke was as much a part of Tanner Investigations as the furniture.

"I'm on my way to the airport soon," he said, taking the mail and messages she handed him. "I'll probably be out of contact for a few days," he said over his shoulder as he headed for his office. He heard her get up and follow him.

As he sat down behind his desk, he looked up to find her framed in the doorway. She lifted one dark penciled-in eyebrow and asked, "Since you never take any time off and I know you aren't busy decorating for Christmas, I'll assume you're working. You want me to start a client file?"

"No, this is…personal."

Just when he thought her eyebrow couldn't shoot any higher, it arched toward the ceiling.

"It's not personal like *that*," he said, giving her a shake of his head.

"I have no idea what you're talking about."

He laughed. "I'll be checking in, but I know you can handle things until I get back."

"Whatever you say, boss. Far be it from me to suggest that you haven't been on a date since a Bush was in office."

"Clearly you forgot about that brunette a few months ago."

"That wasn't a date," she said as she turned to leave. "And she made such an impression that you don't even remember her name."

He sat for a moment, trying to remember the brunette's name. Sandy? Susie? Sherry? Not that it mattered, he told himself as he sorted through his mail and messages. He wouldn't be seeing her again.

There wasn't anything in the mail or messages that couldn't keep.

Taking out the letter and the article Walter Justice had sent him, he read them again, then flattened out the article, wondering why it had been included until he saw the travel writer's byline: DJ Price.

So was he to assume that DJ Justice's pseudonym was Price? He typed DJ Price into his computer's search engine. More articles came up, but no photo of the author. From the dates on the articles it would appear she was still employed as a freelance writer for a variety of publications. If DJ Price was DJ Justice.

He returned the article and letter to the envelope, folded them into his pocket and shut off his computer. As he walked out of his office past Marge's desk, she said, "Shelly," without looking up as he passed.

"Wouldn't want you straining your brain trying to remember the woman's name all the way to the airport."

Beau chuckled to himself as he made the drive out into the valley. He couldn't help feeling anxious, since he had no idea what he was getting himself into. Nor did he know what to expect when it came to DJ Justice.

At the airport, he waited on the ground floor by the baggage claim area. There were a half-dozen people standing around holding signs. Dana Savage was one of them. The sign she held up read, CARDWELL RANCH. DJ.

He hung back as the arrivals began coming down from upstairs. On the drive here, he'd told himself there was no way he would be able to recognize DJ. She'd just been a kid of five all those years ago. He'd been a skinny but worn ten.

But the moment he laid eyes on the dark-haired woman at the top of the escalator, he recognized her. Dee Anna Justice. That brown-eyed girl had grown into a striking woman. Her hair was long, pulled back in a loose bun at the nape of her neck. Burnished strands had come loose and hung around her temples.

Silver flashed at her ears and her wrists and throat. She was wearing jeans, winter leather boots that came up to her knees and a teal blue sweater. She had a leather coat draped over one arm, and there was a carry-on in her hand.

She looked up in his direction as if sensing him staring at her. He quickly looked away. This was not what he expected. DJ didn't look like a woman on the run. She looked like a woman completely in control of the world around her.

So what was he doing here?

DJ HAD STILL been upset as the flight attendant announced they would be landing soon. She'd stuffed her purse back under the seat. Out the window, she'd seen nothing but white. Snow blanketed everything. She'd realized with a start that she'd never felt snow. Or had she?

Now she surveyed the small crowd of people waiting on the level below as she rode the escalator down. She knew she was being watched, could feel an intense stare. But when she looked in the direction it came from, she was surprised to see a cowboy.

He stood leaning against the stone wall next to the baggage claim area. He was dressed in jeans, boots and a red-and-black-plaid wool jacket. His dark Stetson was pulled low, his blond hair curling at the neck of his jacket.

As he tilted his head back, she saw the pale blue familiar eyes and felt a shock before he quickly looked away. There had been a moment of...*recognition*. Or had she just imagined that she knew him? She tried to get a better look at him. Why had she thought she recognized him?

She had no idea.

He was no longer paying any attention to her. She studied his profile. It was strong, very masculine. He held himself in a way that told her he was his own man. He was no urban cowboy. He was the real thing.

She scoffed at the idea that she knew him. She would have remembered a man like that. Still, she couldn't take her eyes off him and was startled when she reached the end of the escalator.

Turning toward the exit, she spotted a woman about

her own age holding a sign that said CARDWELL RANCH on it, and in smaller letters, DJ.

The moment her cousin saw her, she beamed with a huge smile. DJ was surprised how that smile affected her. Tears burned her eyes as she was suddenly filled with emotion. She had the crazy feeling that she'd finally come home. Which was ridiculous, since she'd never had a real home life and, as far as she knew, had never been to Montana.

She swallowed the sudden lump in her throat as she wound her way through the small crowd to the young woman. "Dana?"

"DJ?"

At her nod, Dana gave her a quick hug. "Welcome to Montana." She stepped back to stare at DJ. "You don't look anything like the last Dee Anna Justice."

DJ heard relief in her cousin's voice.

"I'm sorry. I shouldn't have said that," Dana said, then must have noticed that DJ didn't know what she was talking about. "Your father did tell you about your former roommate pretending to be you."

"No, I guess he failed to mention that."

"Well, it's water under the bridge… I'm just glad you're here and I finally get to meet you."

"Me, too," DJ said, feeling that well of emotion again.

"We'll get your luggage—"

"This is all I have." Traveling light wasn't the only habit she'd picked up from her father. She had stopped by the bank before she'd left San Diego. She took cash from her safe-deposit box, just in case she might have reason not to use her credit card. But that would mean that she was on the run and needed to hide.

Dana glanced at the overnight bag. "That's it? Not to worry. We have anything you might need. Ready to see the ranch?"

She was. "I'm looking forward to it." Again she felt someone watching her and quickly scanned the area. It was an old habit from the years when her father used her as a decoy or a lookout.

"Always watch for anyone who seems a little too interested in you—or the ones who are trying hard not to pay you any mind," he used to say.

She spotted the cowboy. He had moved from his spot against the wall and now stood as if waiting for his baggage to arrive. Except he hadn't been on the flight.

"Do you need anything else before we head out?" Dana asked, drawing her attention again.

"No, I'm good," DJ said and followed Dana toward the exit. She didn't have to look back to know that the cowboy was watching her. But he wasn't the only one.

BEAU WATCHED DJ LEAVE, curious if anyone else was watching her. Through the large window, he could see Dana's SUV parked outside. DJ was standing next to it, the two seeming to hit it off.

No one seemed to pay her any attention that he could tell. A few people were by the window, several taking photographs. In the distance, the mountains that surrounded the valley were snowcapped against a robin's-egg-blue sky.

He watched DJ climb into the SUV. As it pulled away, there was the clank of the baggage carousel. The people who'd been standing at the window all turned, pocketing their phones. One man took a moment to send a text before moving to the baggage claim area. Everyone looked suspicious, and no one did.

Beau realized he was flying blind. He had to know why Walter Justice had hired him. He had to know what kind of trouble DJ was in.

Pulling out his phone, he stepped outside into the cold December afternoon. The air smelled of snow. Even with the winter sun shining against the stone wall of the airport, it was still chilly outside.

Beau was glad when the emergency number he'd called was answered. It took a few minutes for Walter to come on the line. He wondered what kind of deal the inmate had made that allowed him such service. Con men always found a way, he thought, remembering his own father.

"Have you seen her?" Walter asked at once.

"I have. But you might recall, I've seen her before."

"She was just a child then."

"She's not now," he said, thinking of the striking woman who'd come down those stairs. "That's just one reason I need to tell her the truth."

"No. That would be a mistake. You don't know her—she doesn't trust anyone."

"Whose fault is that?" Beau asked. "If you want me to get close to her, you have to let me do it my way. Tell me what kind of danger she's in."

"That's just it. I don't know."

Beau swore under his breath. "You expect me to believe that? I have to know what I'm up against." Walter knew enough that he'd "hired" Beau.

Silence filled the line for so long, he feared the inmate had hung up. "It could have something to do with her mother."

"DJ's *mother*?"

"Sorry, not DJ's mother. Carlotta is dead. Her grandmother Marietta is still alive. Marietta might have found DJ."

"Found her?"

"It's complicated."

"I'm sure it is. But if you expect me to keep your daughter safe, you'd better tell me."

There was a sound of clanging doors. Then Walter said, "I have to go. Call me tomorrow." And the man was gone.

Pocketing his phone with a curse, Beau headed for his pickup. He couldn't wait until tomorrow. He would have to do this his way—no matter what Walter Justice had said. He thought of the woman he'd seen. Years ago he'd yearned to save that brown-eyed girl. He was getting a second chance, but he feared he wasn't going to have any more luck than he'd had at ten.

What the hell had he gotten involved in?

DANA CARDWELL SAVAGE was a pleasant surprise. DJ saw at once the family resemblance in this cheerful young woman with the dark hair and eyes. She was so sweet that DJ felt herself relax a little.

"We are so happy to have you here," her cousin was saying. "Your father said that he's been wanting to get us together for years, but with your busy schedule…" Dana glanced over at her and smiled. "I'm glad you finally got the chance. This is the perfect time of year to visit Cardwell Ranch. We had a snow last night. Everything is pretty right now. Do you ski?"

DJ shook her head.

"That's all right. If you want to take a lesson, we

can certainly make that happen. But you ride, your father said."

"Ride?"

"Horses. It might be too cold for you, but it's always an option."

The SUV slipped through an opening between the mountains, and DJ was suddenly in a wonderland of white. Massive pine branches bowed under the weight of the fresh white snow. Next to the highway, the river was a ribbon of frozen green.

DJ had never seen anything like it. Or had she? At the back of her mind, she thought she remembered snow. The cold, soft flakes melting in her child-sized hand. That sense of wonder.

Dana was telling her about the Gallatin Canyon and some of its history. "I'm sorry," she said after a few minutes. "I talk too much when I'm excited."

"No," DJ said quickly. "I'm interested."

Dana smiled at her. "You are so different from the last Dee Anna Justice who visited us. Sorry. You said you hadn't heard about it."

"What happened?"

DJ listened and shuddered to think that she'd lived in the same apartment with someone like that. "I'm so sorry. I didn't really know her. We shared an apartment, but since my job is traveling, I was hardly there."

Her cousin waved that off. "Not your fault. That's why we're excited finally to meet the real you."

The real you? DJ almost laughed. She hadn't gone by her real name in years. She wasn't sure she even knew the real her.

Chapter Five

Jimmy Ryan could hardly hold still, he was so excited. He couldn't believe his luck as he saw the man come into the bar.

"You bring the up-front money?" he asked the moment the man took the stool next to him at the bar. The dive was almost completely empty this time of day. Still, he kept his voice down. This was serious business.

When the man had told him he was looking for someone with Jimmy's...talents, he'd never dreamed how perfect he was for the job.

"Montana? Hell, I used to live up there, you know, near Big Sky," Jimmy had bragged. He hadn't been there since he'd flunked out of high school after knocking up his girlfriend and being forced into a shotgun marriage, but that was beside the point.

"I remember you mentioning that. That's why I thought of you. So maybe you know the area?" the man had said.

"Like the back of my hand. I might even know the target."

"Ever heard of the Cardwell Ranch?"

Jimmy had felt a chill as if someone had walked

over his grave. This *was* too good to be true. "Are you kidding? I used to...date Stacy Cardwell."

"Well, maybe you won't want this one."

As desperate as he was for money, he would have killed anyone they asked, even Stacy herself, though not before he'd spent some quality time with her for old times' sake.

He'd thought it was fate when the man told him the hit was on a woman named DJ Justice, a cousin of the Cardwells. "Don't know her. Don't care even if I did. Just get me some...traveling money and then let me know how you want it handled."

The man had said he'd get back to him, but it had to be done soon. Jimmy had started making plans with what he would do with all that money.

Now, though, he felt his heart drop as he saw the man's expression. "I'm sorry. The client has decided to go with someone else."

"Someone else?" Jimmy cried loud enough that the bartender sent him a look. "Come on," he said, dropping his voice. "I thought I had it? I'm perfect for the job. Shouldn't it be a case of who gets her first? If it's the money—"

"They went with a pro, all right?"

"Excuse me?" Jimmy demanded, mad at the thought of losing the money and taking it as an insult. "I grew up in Montana. Do you have any idea how many deer I killed? You ever kill a deer?"

"A deer is a lot different than killing a woman." The man threw down some bills on the bar. "For your time." He slid off his stool and started to step away.

"You think that bothers me?" Jimmy had known

some women he would have loved to have put a bullet in. He wouldn't even have flinched.

As the man started through the empty bar toward the back door, Jimmy went after him, trotting along beside him, determined not to let him leave without getting the job.

"I'll do it for less than your…pro."

"I don't think money is the issue," the man said without looking at him. "She just wants it done fast."

She? He was thinking jealousy, revenge, a catfight over some man. "So what did this DJ Justice do? Steal some broad's old man?"

The man stopped at the door. Jimmy could tell that he was regretting giving him the details. "Look, forget this one, and maybe the next time I have something…" The man pushed open the door.

"You want to see a pro? I'll show you a pro. I got this one," he called after him. "I'll find her first and I'll be back for the rest of the money."

STACY CARDWELL WIPED her eyes as the movie ended. She couldn't help blubbering, not at the end of a touching love story. Maybe she was a sucker for a happy ending. Not that she expected one for herself. She'd picked the wrong man too many times.

But she was just happy to have her daughter, Ella, who was almost five years old. Ella had the biggest green eyes she'd ever seen and had stolen her heart even before she was born. Sure, Stacy got lonely sometimes, but she had her sister, Dana, and brothers, Jordan and Clay. Jordan just lived up the road. Clay was still in California but visited a couple times a year.

Years ago they'd had a falling-out over the ranch.

Stacy still regretted it. But Dana had forgiven her, and now they were closer than ever.

"Hello?"

She quickly turned off the television as Burt Olsen, the local mailman, stuck his head in the front door of the main ranch house, where Stacy was curled up watching movies.

"Got a package for Dana," he said. "Need a signature."

Stacy waved him on into the house, smiling as he stomped snow off his boots on the porch before entering. Burt was always so polite. Dana was convinced that Burt had a crush on Stacy, but he was just too shy to ask her out. She was glad Dana wasn't here to tease her about him.

"How's your day going?" Burt asked, then quickly lowered his voice. "The kids asleep?"

She laughed and shook her head. "That would be some trick, to get them all to take naps at their ages. No, their grandpa took them sledding. I'm just holding down the fort until my sister gets back."

"Saw your car out front," Burt said. "Figured you might be sitting the kids. What'd ya think of that snow last night? Really came down. I've already been stuck a couple of times today. Glad I have chains on my rig."

She nodded as she signed for the package. "Can I fill up your thermos with coffee? I have a pot going."

"That would be right nice of you," Burt said, blushing a little. He was a big man with a round red face and brown eyes that disappeared in his face when he laughed. He wasn't handsome by anyone's standards, but there was a warmth and a sincerity about him.

"He will make some woman a fine husband," Dana

had said more than once. "A smart woman would snatch him up."

Stacy had never been smart when it came to men, and her sister knew it. But she liked Burt. If she had been looking for a husband... But she wasn't.

When he returned from his truck with the thermos, she took it into the big farmhouse kitchen and proceeded to fill it with hot strong coffee. Burt had followed her only as far as the kitchen doorway.

"Having electrical problems?" Burt asked.

She turned to frown. "No, why?"

"I saw some feller up a pole not far from the house."

Stacy shrugged. "Here, I made sugar cookies. I'll put a couple of them in a bag for you."

"Oh, you don't have to..."

"Dana would insist if she was here," Stacy said.

"Well, thank you." He took the thermos and the plastic bag. "Shaped like Christmas trees," he said, holding up the bag to see the cookies. "You did a real nice job on them."

She felt her cheeks heat. Burt was so appreciative of even the smallest kind gesture a person did for him. "Thank you."

"Well, I'll be getting along, then." He nodded, not quite looking at her. "Might want to dig out some candles in case that lineman turns off your power. You have a nice day now."

"I'm going to try." She watched him drive away, wondering when Burt was going to get around to asking her out and how she was going to let him down easy.

In the kitchen, she got herself some cookies and milk. Going back to the television, she found another

Christmas love story and hoped Burt was wrong about the power man cutting off her television. She didn't get that much time alone to watch.

But this show didn't hold her attention. She wondered when Dana would be back with their cousin Dee Anna Justice and what surprises this cousin might bring to the ranch.

As Beau climbed into his SUV and began the drive out of the airport on the newly constructed roads, his cell phone rang. The roads were new because Gallatin Field was now the busiest airport in the state. "Beau Tanner."

"What is your hourly rate?"

He recognized Leah's voice and imagined her standing in his living room. "You can't afford me. Seriously, what is this about?"

"I lied to you. Charlie and I...we're in trouble."

Beau wasn't surprised. "So, there isn't an important package?"

"There is, kind of. I hate involving you in this."

"I can't wait to hear what this is exactly, but can we talk about it when I get home?"

"Yes. But I insist on hiring you. I have money, if that's what you're worried about."

"That isn't it. I have something right now that is going to take all of my attention."

He got off the call, cursing under his breath. If this was about marital problems between her and Charlie...

He really couldn't deal with this right now. Ahead he could see Dana Cardwell's black Suburban heading toward Big Sky. Beau followed, worried about Leah and Charlie, even more worried about DJ Justice.

What kind of trouble was DJ in? Her father thought it might have something to do with her grandmother? That her grandmother had *found* her? He cursed Walter. Who knew how many skeletons the man had in his closet?

But what did that have to do with his daughter?

If Beau had to lay money down on it, he would have bet there was a man in DJ Justice's story. A man with a jealous wife or girlfriend? Or had DJ chosen a life of crime like her father? At least Beau's father had reformed somewhat after that night here in the canyon when Beau had made the deal with Walter Justice.

Since becoming a private investigator, he'd thought he'd heard every story there was. Where it got dangerous was when the spouse or lover would do anything to cover up an affair—or even a score. Usually money was involved. And passion.

So what was DJ's story?

MARIETTA PISANI STOOD at her mirror, considering the almost eighty-year-old woman she saw reflected there. *Merda!* She looked as cranky as she felt, which almost made her smile. When had she gotten so old? She didn't feel all that different than she had in her twenties, except now her long, beautiful, raven-black hair was gray. Her once-smooth porcelain skin was wrinkled.

She knew what had aged her more than the years— her only child, Carlotta. That girl had seemed determined to drive her crazy. It had been one thing after another from an early age. She shook her head, remembering the hell Carlotta had put her through, and then softened her thoughts as she was reminded that her beautiful, foolish daughter was in her grave.

Not that she hadn't left a storm in her wake. And now Marietta had to clean it up.

"Can I get you anything else, Mrs. Pisani?" asked a deep, elderly voice behind her.

She glanced past her reflection in the mirror to Ester, who'd been with her for almost fifty years. Ester had grayed since she'd begun working here as a teen. Sometimes Marietta mixed her up with her mother, Inez, who'd been her first housekeeper right after her marriage.

"No, Ester, I don't need anything."

"What about you, Mr. Douglas?" Ester asked Marietta's solicitor.

Roger shook his head. "I'll be leaving shortly."

"You can turn in," Marietta told the housekeeper.

"Just ring." The sixty-seven-year-old woman turned to leave. "Sleep well." She'd said the same thing every night for the past fifty years.

As Ester closed the door behind her, Marietta focused again on her own reflection. Nothing had changed except now her brows were knit into a deep frown. Ester hadn't been herself lately.

The thought caused Marietta a moment of alarm. Was the woman sick? Marietta was too old to train another housekeeper. Not that Ester kept house anymore. A housecleaning crew came in once a week, and she employed a full-time cook, as well. Ester's only job now was to see to her mistress.

Of course, Ester didn't see it that way. She resented the housekeeping crew and the cook and often sent the cook home early so she could take over the kitchen. She would then make Marietta's favorite meals, just as her mother had done.

The thought that Ester might leave her for any reason was more than she could stand. Ester was the only person in the world Marietta trusted—other than her granddaughter Bianca. She tried to put her worries aside, assuring herself that she'd be dead before Ester went anywhere.

Still, it nagged at her. Not that Ester had said anything. It was more of a…feeling that something was wrong. Unfortunately she knew nothing about the woman's personal life—or if she even had one. Ester had married some worthless man years ago, but she'd had the good sense to get rid of him early on. Since then, as far as Marietta knew, there was no one else in her life. Ester had doted on her and Carlotta and thought that the sun rose and set with Bianca.

When Carlotta had died a few months ago, Ester had taken it harder than Marietta. The housekeeper had loved that child as if she were her own. She'd helped raise her and was the first to make excuses when Carlotta got into trouble, which was often.

But the one Ester loved even more than life itself was Bianca.

It was her thirty-four-year-old granddaughter Marietta worried about now because of Carlotta's death-bed confession.

She clenched her gnarled hands into fists at the memory. The stupid, stupid girl. The secret she'd kept from them all could destroy the legacy Marietta had preserved for so many years—not to mention what it could do to the family fortune.

That was why the mess her daughter had left behind had to be cleaned up. For the family's sake. For Bianca's sake and the generations to come.

"I should go," Roger said.

She'd forgotten he was even still in the room. A slight man with an unmemorable face, he practically disappeared into the wallpaper. "You're sure you can handle this properly?" she asked as she looked past her own image to his.

He sighed. "Yes."

"I don't want Bianca ever to know. If that means paying this woman to keep quiet—"

"I told you I would take care of it. But it is going to cost you. Your daughter left us little choice unless you want to see your family's reputation destroyed by a complete stranger."

A complete stranger. That was what Dee Anna Justice was to her. Marietta had never laid eyes on this… granddaughter, hadn't even known she existed until her daughter's deathbed confession. "Just see that it's done and spare me the sordid details."

"Don't I always?" As he started to leave, she heard a rustling sound and looked up in time to see Ester skittering away.

DANA WAS TELLING her about the "canyon," as the locals called the Gallatin Canyon. It ran from just south of Gallatin Gateway almost to West Yellowstone, some fifty miles of twisting road that cut through the mountains. Sheer rock cliffs overlooked the highway and the Gallatin River.

The drive was breathtaking, especially for DJ, who'd never been in the mountains before—let alone in winter. The winding highway followed the river, a blue-ribbon trout stream, up over the Continental Divide.

"There used to be just a few places in the canyon, mostly ranches or dude ranches, a few summer cabins, but that was before Big Sky," Dana was saying.

DJ could see that luxury houses had sprouted up along the highway as they got closer to the ski resort and community that had grown around it.

"Our ranch was one of the first," her cousin said with obvious pride. "It is home. The only one I've known. And I have no intention of ever leaving it."

DJ couldn't imagine what it must have been like living her whole life in one place.

Dana slowed and turned not far past the sign for Big Sky Resort. Across the river and a half mile back up a wide valley, the Cardwell Ranch house sat against a backdrop of granite cliffs, towering snow-filled pines and bare-limbed aspens. The house was a big, two-story rambling affair with a wide front porch and a brick red metal roof. Behind it stood a huge new barn and some older outbuildings and corrals.

"Hud, my husband, keeps saying we need to build a bigger house, since we have four children now. But… well…"

"It's wonderful," DJ said and tried to imagine herself growing up here.

"You'll be staying in one of our guest cabins," her cousin said and pointed to some log buildings up on the side of the mountain. "I think you'll be comfortable there, and you'll have your privacy."

DJ was overwhelmed by all of it, so much so that she couldn't speak. As Dana parked, a dark-haired woman came out on the porch to greet them.

"Stacy," Dana called. "Come meet our cousin."

Chapter Six

DJ thought Stacy looked like an older version of her sister. She'd been prettier at one time, but her face told of a harder life than Dana had lived. Seeing how much she resembled both of her cousins gave DJ a strange feeling. For once, her father had told the truth. These people were her *family*.

Dana introduced them and then asked her sister, "How were the kids?"

"Dad came by and took them sledding," Stacy said. "He called just before you drove up to say he's decided to take them to Texas Boys Barbecue, since they say they're too starved to wait for supper. The café is owned by our cousins from Texas," she said to DJ. Turning back to her sister, she said, "I'm working this afternoon at the sewing shop, so I'd better get going, since I need to pick up a few things before then."

"Go, and thanks."

Stacy looked to DJ, who'd been taking in the ranch in a kind of awe. "It was great to meet you. I'll see you later?"

"You'll see her. DJ's staying for a while," Dana declared and climbed the porch steps to open the door and usher DJ in.

She stepped into the house and stopped. The decor was very Western, from the huge rock fireplace to the antler lamps and the Native American rugs on the hardwood floors. Even the Christmas decorations looked as if they'd been in the family for years.

There was also a feeling of déjà vu as if she'd been here before. Crazy, she thought, hurriedly wiping at her eyes.

"It's so…beautiful," DJ said, her voice breaking.

Dana laughed. "*My Christmas tree? I* know it's hard to put into words," she said, considering the misshaped evergreen in the corner, decorated with ornaments obviously made by children. "But I've always been a sucker for trees that would never have gotten to be Christmas trees if it wasn't for me."

DJ managed to laugh around the lump in her throat. "I meant your house," she said, smiling at the sight of the ungainly tree, "but your Christmas tree is…lovely. An orphan tree that you brought home. It's charming."

Her cousin smiled at her. "Let's have a late lunch, since I know you couldn't have gotten much on the plane, and we can visit."

She followed Dana into the large, cheery kitchen, wondering if she hadn't been here before. It felt strangely…familiar. Had her father brought her here at some point? Why else was she feeling so emotional about this large, rambling old house?

"I can't tell you how surprised I was when I found some letters from your father and realized that my mother had a brother I'd never known existed," Dana said as she opened the refrigerator and pulled out a large bowl. "I hope you like shrimp macaroni salad." DJ nodded and Dana continued. "It wasn't like my mother, Mary Justice, to keep a secret like that. Then to find out that he hadn't actually died…" Her cousin put the bowl on the table and got out plates, forks and what looked like homemade rolls. "Coffee, tea, milk?"

"Milk." She couldn't remember the last time she'd had milk, but it sounded so good, and it felt right in this kitchen. Everywhere she looked she saw family history in this house. One wall was covered with photos of the children, most atop horses.

"Sit, please." Dana waved her into one of the mismatched multicolored wooden chairs in front of the long, scarred table.

"I didn't know about you, either," DJ said as she pulled out the chair and sat. Dana joined her after filling two plates with pasta salad. DJ took a bite. "This is delicious."

They ate in a companionable silence for a while. The house was warm and comfortable. From the window over the sink, DJ could see snow-laden pines and granite cliffs. It was all so beautiful, exactly how she had pictured Montana in December. She hadn't thought she was hungry, but the salad and the warm homemade roll dripping with butter quickly disappeared. This felt so right, being here, that she'd forgotten for a while why she'd accepted the invitation.

DJ was running her finger along one of the scars on the table when Dana said, "I can't understand why my grandparents would disown their son the way they did. They were a lot older when they had your father. Maybe it was that generation…but not to tell us…"

DJ took a sip of cold milk before she asked, "Who told you he was dead?"

"I didn't speak to your mother personally, but her assistant—"

"My *mother's assistant*?" DJ asked, abruptly putting down her milk glass. "When was this?"

Her cousin thought for a moment. "That would have been in the spring three years ago. Her assistant, at least, that's who she said she was, told me that your mother couldn't come to the phone."

"I was always told that my mother's been dead since I was born," DJ said. "It's what I've believed all my life, so I don't understand this."

"I don't understand it, either. Then whose assistant did I speak with, if not Marietta Pisani's?"

"She told you my mother's name was Marietta?" She shook her head. "Where did you get the number to call her?"

"From…from the woman who'd pretended to be you, Camilla Northland. After she was caught, I asked her where the real Dee Anna Justice was. I thought she was telling me the truth." Dana put a hand over her mouth. "Why did I believe anything that woman told me? I feel like such a fool."

"No, please don't. So my roommate gave you the number?"

Dana nodded. "She said a woman had called the apartment asking for you before she left to come out here to Montana to pretend to be you. When your roommate asked who was calling, she said her name was Marietta."

"That's my grandmother's name, but she is also deceased. At least, that's what my father told me. But since he kept all of you from me…" Her life felt like one big, long lie. "My father told me that my mother's name was Carlotta."

Her cousin looked flummoxed. "Camilla seemed to think Marietta was your mother. Either she lied, or—"

"Or the person who called lied."

Dana nodded thoughtfully. "I believed Camilla, since she also told me that the reason my uncle had been disinherited was that he'd married a foreigner. The woman who said she was Marietta's assistant had an Italian accent. I asked about her daughter. I'm not even sure I called you by name. She said you were in Italy—or was it Spain?—visiting friends. Is any of this true?"

DJ shook her head. "I've been in San Diego all this time except when I was traveling for work. I have no idea where my former roommate could have gotten her information, but that she knew my grandmother's name… I don't think she was lying about the phone call. Do you still have that number?"

Dana shook her head. "I'm sorry."

"I was hoping you could help me piece together more of my family history. My father told me that he and I were the only two left. Until he told me that you might be calling, I had no idea that wasn't true."

"Well, you have me and Stacy, plus my brothers, Jordan and Clay, as cousins, plus our cousins from Texas. You'll meet Jordan tonight. Clay lives in California, not that far from where you live now. So, you never met anyone on your mother's side of the family?"

"No. All I knew was that my mother's name was Carlotta and my grandmother's was Marietta. My father's never been very…forthcoming with information. He let me believe I didn't have *any* family."

"Oh, DJ, I'm so sorry," Dana said, reaching across the table to take her hand. "Family is…my heart. My father and uncle, my father-in-law, are often…trying," she said and smiled. "I've fought tooth and nail with my siblings, lost them for a few years, but finally have them back. I can't imagine not having any of them in my life. I'm so glad that now you have all of us."

DJ's eyes burned as she squeezed her cousin's hand.

"All of us *and* Cardwell Ranch," Dana added and let go of her hand.

DJ picked at her lunch for a moment. Was it possible that her grandmother Marietta was still alive? Then wasn't it also possible that her mother, Carlotta, was alive, as well? She could see why her father might have kept her from his family, since they had disinherited him, but why had he kept her from her mother's family?

DJ remembered the night she'd finally badgered her father into telling her about her mother. He'd had too much to drink. Otherwise all he'd ever said was that her mother had died and it was too painful to talk about. That night, though, he told her that Carlotta had been a beautiful princess and the love of his life.

"She was too beautiful," he'd said. "Too spoiled, too rich, too much of everything. Her family didn't think I was good enough for her. They were right, of course." He'd let out a bitter laugh. "It cost me my family as well, but I will never regret loving her." He'd blinked back tears as he looked at DJ. "And I got you. I'm a lucky man."

She'd been full of questions. How could he have lost Carlotta and his family, too?

"Do you understand now why I don't want to talk

about your mother? So, no more," he'd said with a wave of his hand. "I can't bear it." His gaze softened as it fell on her. "Let's just be grateful that we have each other, because it's just you and me, kid."

Even now, she couldn't be sure any of his story was true. Her heritage was a puzzle with most of the pieces missing. "I'm surprised that you'd never heard of my father before you found the letters," she said.

"I was shocked. Like I said, I still can't believe my mother would have kept something like that a secret."

"You said you still have those letters?"

"I can dig them out, along with that number—" At the sound of a vehicle, followed by the eruption of children's voices, Dana added, "After I corral the kids."

DJ cleaned up the dishes while Dana went to greet the children. She could hear laughter and shrieks of playfulness outside. She couldn't help but smile to herself.

Drying her hands, she pulled out the photo and studied it in the light from the kitchen window. With her cousin's help, she was going to find the family she'd been denied.

She gazed at the photo of the baby—and the doll in the stroller. If she wasn't the baby the smiling woman was holding, then who was, and why had someone wanted her to believe they were family?

Whoever had left her the doll and the photo knew the truth—and wanted her to know it. But what was the truth? And what was the motive? To help her? Or to warn her?

She felt a sudden chill. She would find out, but at what cost?

ON THE WAY to the small resort town of Big Sky, Stacy couldn't get DJ off her mind. There was a distinct family resemblance because of the dark hair and eyes, but still…she had the feeling that she'd met her when they were kids.

At the drugstore, she got out and was about to lock her car when she heard the sound of footfalls in the new snow behind her.

"Stacy?"

She started at the familiar male voice directly behind her. Turning, she came face-to-face with her old boyfriend from high school. *"Jimmy?"*

He grinned. "I go by James now. I'm surprised you remember me."

How could she not remember Jimmy Ryan? He'd dumped her right before her junior prom to go back to his old girlfriend, Melody Harper. He'd been the first in a long line to break her heart.

"Are you here for the holidays?" He and Melody had gotten married right after high school. Melody, it turned out, had been pregnant. He'd taken a job with Melody's uncle in California, and that was the last Stacy had heard or seen of him.

He was looking at her the way he used to, unnerving her. "I wondered if you were still around."

"I left for a while. How is Melody?"

"Wouldn't know. We're divorced. How about you?"

For a moment she couldn't find her voice. "Divorced." More times than she wanted to admit. "I have a daughter, Ella."

"Lucky you. It turned out that I couldn't have children."

She blurted out in surprise, "But I thought Melody was pregnant."

"Turns out she wasn't," he said bitterly. "She told me that she'd miscarried, so we spent a lot of years trying before the truth came out."

"I'm sorry."

His gaze met and held hers. He was still the most handsome man she'd ever known. His dark hair was salted with gray at the temples, which only seemed to make his gray eyes more intense. "Could I buy you a cup of coffee?"

Stacy felt that old ache. Had she ever gotten over Jimmy? Wasn't he why she'd jumped into one relationship, one marriage after another? "I have to get back to the ranch soon."

"Just a quick cup of coffee. I've thought about you so often over the years and regretted letting you down the way I did."

How many times had she dreamed that he would say those words—or at least words much like them?

She glanced at her watch. "I suppose a cup of coffee wouldn't hurt."

"YOU'RE TIRED FROM your long trip," Dana said after introducing DJ to all the children and her father, Angus Cardwell. "Dad, if you don't mind staying around for a few minutes, I'm going to take DJ to her cabin so she can get some rest."

"You're in good hands," Angus said. "Trust me."

DJ couldn't help but smile. Trust wasn't something that came easy for her. But Dana and this family inspired trust.

"The kids want to go see a movie in Bozeman,"

Angus said. "Maybe we'll do that and really make a day of it."

There were cheers from the five children. Dana laughed. "You haven't had enough of them? Fine. But we're all going to The Corral tonight. Stacy has agreed to babysit."

As they stepped outside, DJ on impulse turned to her cousin and hugged her. "Thank you for everything."

"I haven't done anything yet," Dana said. "But I am so glad you're here. Families need to stick together."

With that, her cousin walked her up to her cabin on the mountainside.

DJ couldn't believe the cabin as her cousin opened the door and ushered her in. Someone had started a fire for her. It blazed bright in a fireplace on the other side of a seating area. There was a small kitchen that she knew would be stocked with anything she might need even before Dana opened the refrigerator door to show her.

But it was the bedroom that stole her heart. "Oh, that bed." It was huge, the frame made of logs, the mattress deep in pillows and quilts. "I won't want to get out of it."

Her cousin smiled and pulled out a step. "This is how you get on the bed. I told them it was too high, but my brother Jordan made the beds, and so far everyone loves them."

"I can see why," DJ said, laughing. "This is amazing. Really, thank you so much."

"It's my pleasure. You'll get to meet Jordan and his wife, Liza. Clay, your other cousin, as I told you, lives in California. He'll be flying up for Christmas. But we'll get to all of that." She smiled. "I'm just happy you're here now. We can talk about Christmas later."

"I can only stay for a few days. With the holidays coming, I don't want to be in the way."

"In the way?" Dana exclaimed. "You're family. You'll make this Christmas even more special."

DJ couldn't help being touched.

"Get settled in and rest. We have something special planned for tonight. The Corral has the best burgers you've ever tasted, and the band playing tonight? It's my uncle and father's band—more relatives of yours I thought you'd enjoy meeting in a more casual atmosphere."

Dana was so thoughtful that DJ couldn't say no.

"I'll drop by some clothing and Western boots that should fit you before we go."

DJ started to tell her that this was all too much, but Dana cut her off. "You have to experience Montana and canyon life. I promise that you'll have a good time."

There was nothing more DJ could say, since she didn't want to disappoint her cousin. Dana had been so welcoming, much more than she should have been for a relative she'd never met before.

She watched Dana walk back down to the main house. Something in the distance flashed, the winter sun glinting off metal. She could see a repairman hanging from a power pole in the distance.

Emotional exhaustion pulled at her. The past few days had been such a roller-coaster ride. She closed the door and locked it. For the first time, she felt...safe.

The cabin was so warm and welcoming, she thought as she walked into the bedroom. The bed beckoned to her. Smiling, DJ pulled back the homemade quilt, kicked off her shoes and crawled up under the covers. She was asleep almost at once.

MARIETTA KNEW SHE wouldn't be able to sleep. She kept thinking about this granddaughter. She realized she knew nothing about her other than what Roger had told her. A father in prison. The young woman writing stories for travel magazines.

"Not married?" she'd asked.

"No. Lives alone. Stays to herself."

She tried to imagine the girl. Did she look like Carlotta or that horrible father of hers? What if she looked like Bianca?

Reaching over, she rang the bell for Ester. It was late, but she knew she'd never get to sleep without some warm milk.

"Is something wrong?" Ester asked moments later from her doorway.

"I can't sleep."

"I'm not surprised."

She stared at her housekeeper. "I beg your pardon?"

Ester shook her head. "I'll heat some milk. Would you like anything else?"

Marietta gritted her teeth as she shook her head. It wasn't her imagination. Ester was acting oddly.

When she returned with a glass of warm milk and a biscuit with butter and honey, Marietta asked, "Roger hasn't called, has he?"

"I'm sure you would have heard the phone if he had, but no."

"You don't like him." She realized she'd given voice to something she'd known for a long time. Not that she normally cared if her housekeeper liked her attorney or not. But tonight, it struck her as odd. Almost as odd as the way Ester was behaving.

"No, I don't like him. Nor do I trust him. You shouldn't, either." Ester started to leave.

"Why would you say that?" she demanded of the housekeeper's retreating back.

Ester stopped and turned slowly. "Because he's been stealing from you for years." With that, she left the room.

Marietta stared after her, dumbstruck. Was Ester losing her mind? It was the only thing that made sense. The woman had never talked to her like this. She would never have dared. And to say something so...outrageous.

She took a sip of the milk, followed by a bite of the biscuit, until both were gone. Neither was going to help her sleep tonight.

Chapter Seven

The Corral turned out to be an old-fashioned bar and restaurant that looked as if it had been there for years. DJ liked the idea of a place having a rich history—just like the ranch Dana had grown up on. She couldn't imagine having that kind of roots. Nor could she imagine knowing the same people for years like Dana did—which quickly became obvious as they climbed out of the large SUV.

The parking lot was full of pickups and a few SUVs. Several trucks drove up at the same time they did. The occupants called to Dana and were so friendly that DJ felt a stab of envy.

"Do you know everyone in the canyon?" she asked.

Her cousin laughed. "Hardly. I did once upon a time. But that was before Big Sky Resort."

The moment they walked through The Corral door, the bartender said hello to Dana, who quickly set them both up with light beers. "You're in Montana now," she said, clinking her beer bottle against DJ's. The band broke into an old country song, the lead guitarist nodding to them as he began to sing.

"You already met my father, Angus Cardwell, on lead guitar," Dana said as she led her to the only empty table, one with a reserved sign on it that read Cardwell Ranch. "And my uncle Harlan is on bass tonight. They switch off. They've been playing music together for years. They've had other names, but they call themselves the Canyon Cowboys now, I think." She laughed. "They're hard to keep track of."

They'd barely sat down and had a drink of their beers when Dana's brother Jordan came in with his wife, Liza, a local deputy still in her uniform. Jordan was dark and good-looking and clearly in love with his wife, who was pregnant.

"We came by to say hello, but can't stay long," Jordan said. "I'm sure we'll get to see you again while you're here, though."

"Is your husband coming?" DJ asked after Jordan and Liza had left.

"Hud's working tonight. But you'll get to meet him." Dana ordered loaded burgers as the band kicked into another song. "Oh, there's Hilde." Her cousin rose to greet her very pregnant friend. They spoke for a moment before Dana drew her over to the table.

Hilde looked reluctant to meet her. But DJ couldn't blame her after everything she'd heard about the pretend Dee Anna Justice.

"I'm so sorry about my former roommate," DJ said. "I had no idea until Dana told me."

Hilde shook her head. "It's just nice that we finally get to meet you. How do you like the ranch?"

"I love it, especially that four-poster log bed I took a nap in earlier."

Hilde laughed as she sat. Her husband came in then, still wearing his marshal's office uniform, and went to the bar to get them drinks.

A shadow fell across the table. When DJ looked up, she was surprised to see the cowboy from the airport standing over her.

"Care to dance?" he asked over the music.

DJ was so startled to see him here that for a moment she couldn't speak.

"Go ahead," Dana said, giving her a friendly push. "Beau Tanner is a great dancer."

Beau Tanner. DJ didn't believe this was a coincidence. "Did you have something to do with this?" she whispered to her cousin.

"Me?" Dana tried to look shocked before she whispered, "Apparently he saw you at the airport and wanted to meet you."

So that was it. DJ pushed back her chair and stood. Maybe his interest in her was innocent. Or not. She was about to find out either way.

He took her hand and pulled her out onto the dance floor and into his arms for a slow dance. He was strong and sure, moving with ease, and definitely in control.

"Dana told me you would be here tonight," he said. "I was hoping you would dance with me."

"Why is that?" she asked, locking her gaze on his.

His pale blue eyes were the color of worn denim, his lashes dark. Looking into those eyes, she felt a small jolt. Why did she get the feeling that she'd looked into those eyes before?

"I saw you at the airport. When I heard that you were Dana's cousin, I was curious." He shrugged.

"Really? You just happened to hear that."

"News travels fast in the canyon."

"What were you doing at the airport? I know you

weren't on my flight. I also know you weren't picking anyone up."

He laughed. "Are you always this suspicious?"

"Always."

She lost herself in those eyes.

"You want to know why I was at the airport? Okay." He looked away for a moment before his gaze locked with hers. "Because of you."

"So much for your story that you just happened to see me at the airport and were curious."

"I don't like lying. That's just one reason we need to talk," he said as he pulled her close and whispered into her ear. "Today at the airport wasn't the first time I'd seen you. We've met before."

She drew back to look into his face. "If this is some kind of pickup line…" Even as she said it, she remembered thinking at the airport that he looked familiar. But she was always thinking people looked like someone from her past. That was normal when you had a past like hers.

"It was years ago, so I'm not surprised that you don't remember," he said as the song ended. He clasped her hand, not letting her get away as another song began.

"Years ago?" she asked as he pulled her close.

"You were five," he said next to her ear. "I was ten. It was only a few miles from here in this canyon."

She drew back to look at him. "That isn't possible. I've never been here before." But hadn't she felt as if she had? "Why would I believe you?"

He looked her in the eye. "Because a part of you knows I'm telling the truth. It's the reason you and I need to talk." Without warning, he drew her off the dance floor, toward the front door.

She could have dug her heels in, pulled away, stopped this, but something in his tone made her follow him out the door and into the winter night. He directed her over to the side of the building where snow had been plowed up into a small mountain. "Okay, what is this about?" she demanded, breaking loose from his hold to cross her arms over her chest. "It's freezing out here, so make it fast."

He seemed to be deciding what to tell her. She noticed that he was watching the darkness as if he expected something out there to concern him. "All those years ago, your father did me a favor," he said.

She laughed, chilled by the night and this man and what he was saying. "Now I know you're lying. My father didn't do favors for anyone, especially for ten-year-olds."

"Not without a cost," he agreed.

She felt her heart bump in her chest and hugged herself tighter to ward off the cold—and what else this man might tell her.

"Your father and mine were…business partners."

"So this is about my father." She started to turn away.

"No, it's about you, DJ, and what your father has asked me to do."

She stared at him. She'd come here wanting answers. Did this man have them? If he was telling the truth, she'd been to Montana with her father years ago. It would explain why some things and some people seemed familiar—including him.

She could see the pale green frozen river across the

highway, the mountains a deep purple backdrop behind it. Everything was covered with snow and ice, including the highway in front of the bar.

"If our fathers were business partners, then I don't want anything to do with you."

"I wouldn't blame you, but my father got out of the…business after the night we met. I'm assuming yours didn't, given that he is now in prison."

She flinched. "How do you know that?"

"I told you. He did me a favor—for a price. He contacted me. It's a long story, but the night we met, your father and I made a deal of sorts. He helped me with the understanding that if he ever needed my help…"

"You said he did a favor for you? My father made a deal with a ten-year-old?"

"I promised to do whatever he wanted if he let my father go."

DJ felt a hard knot form in her chest. "I don't understand." But she feared she did.

"My father had double-crossed yours. Your father was holding a gun to his head."

"And you threw yourself on the sword, so to speak, by promising my father what, exactly?" What could her father have extracted from a boy of ten?

"He asked me to make sure that nothing happens to you."

She laughed, but it fell short. "That's ridiculous. Why would he think *you* could keep me safe?"

"I'm a private investigator. I have an office forty miles away in Bozeman. I'm good at what I do."

"And humble." She rubbed her arms through the flannel shirt her cousin had given her to wear. But it wasn't her body that was chilled as much as her soul.

Her father, the manipulator. He'd gotten her here. Now he was forcing this cowboy to protect her? She shook her head and started to step away again. "I can take care of my—"

A vehicle came roaring into the parking lot. As the headlights swept over them, Beau grabbed her and took her down in the snowbank next to them, landing squarely on top of her.

JIMMY RYAN RUBBED his cold hands together. He'd already spent several hours of his life sitting outside a bar, hoping to get a shot at DJ Justice. Finding out where DJ would be tonight had been child's play. Over coffee with Stacy he'd listened distractedly as she'd told him what she'd been up to since high school.

"So you're living at the ranch?" he'd asked. "How's that working out with family?"

"Fine. Another cousin has turned up. They seem to be coming out of the woodwork," she'd said with a laugh. "First my five male cousins from Texas. They opened Texas Boys Barbecue here in Big Sky. Have you been there yet?"

"Not yet. But you said another cousin has turned up?"

"Dee Anna Justice. DJ. I haven't gotten to spend much time around her and won't tonight. I'm babysitting the kids so Dana can take her out."

"Oh, yeah? Your sister taking her to someplace fancy?"

"The Corral. My father and uncle are playing there. You remember that they have a band, right?"

The Corral. "Sure, I remember. So what does this cousin look like?"

She'd described DJ. Sounded like he couldn't miss her, so to speak.

He'd glanced at his watch. "I'm going to have to cut this short. Maybe we can see each other again." If things went right tonight, that wouldn't be happening. But he hadn't minded giving Stacy false hope. And who knew, he'd thought, maybe they could hook up before he left. She was still pretty foxy, and he could tell she still wanted him.

Now, sitting across the highway in his rented SUV, his rifle lying across his lap, he just hoped he got another chance at DJ. Earlier she'd come out of the bar. But she'd been with some man.

He'd still been tempted to take the shot, but the man had stayed in front of her. When a car had come racing into the parking lot, the cowboy had thrown them both in a snowbank. What was that about?

"WHAT IN THE—" DJ's words were cut off by the sound of laughter as several people tumbled from the vehicle.

"Shh," Beau said, pulling back to look at her. She saw a change in his expression. Still, the kiss took her by more than surprise. She pushed against his hard chest, but his arms were like steel bands around her.

Worse, she felt herself melting into him, into the kiss, into the warmth of his mouth and the taste of beer on his lips. She was vaguely aware of music and laughter and the sound of people as they entered the establishment before he let her go.

She was shaken by the kiss and everything he'd told her as he rose and pulled her to her feet. "What was that?" she demanded as she began to brush cold snow off her backside.

"A kiss. Apparently it's been a while for you, as well," he said with a cockiness that was downright aggravating. He began to help her with the snow, his big hand brushing over the Western shirt, vest and jeans she wore.

"I can do it myself," she snapped and took a step away from him. She wanted to tell him that she'd only kissed him back because he'd taken her by surprise. But he didn't give her a chance to lie.

"Don't look so shocked. It was just a kiss, right?" His blue eyes gleamed in the light from the neon sign over their heads. "It wasn't like you felt anything. Like either of us felt anything."

The man was exasperating. She hadn't come looking for any of this. "I was asking why you thought you could get away with kissing me like that. Or was that part of the bargain you made with my father?" she asked, hoping he caught the sarcasm.

"I wasn't sure who was driving up just then. I was merely doing my job. Protecting you, since the one thing your father didn't make clear is whom I'm protecting you from. As for the kiss, it just seemed like a good idea. It won't happen again."

"You're right about that, because I don't need your so-called protection." With that, she pushed past him and started for the bar as Dana opened the door and called, "DJ, your burger's ready."

JIMMY RYAN WASN'T the only one watching some distance from The Corral. Andrei had learned to be patient, studying his mark, waiting for a sign that the situation was perfect.

He would get only one chance to pull the trigger.

Rushing it would put the mark on alert and make his job next to impossible. That's if he didn't get caught trying to get away after blowing it.

He'd seen Dee Anna Justice, or DJ, as she was called, go into the bar with her cousin. He wasn't even tempted to take the shot. Later everyone would have been drinking and that would add to the confusion about where the shot had come from.

He'd been surprised when DJ had come back out so soon—and with a man. They seemed to be in an intense conversation.

Who was this cowboy?

What happened next turned Andrei's blood to ice. A vehicle came roaring into the bar's parking area. The cowboy with Dee Anna threw her into the snowbank next to where they had been talking.

Andrei sat up straighter, tightening his grip on the binoculars. Why was the cowboy so jumpy? It made no sense.

He swore. Had there been another contract out on her—one that had failed? How else could he explain why the man with her had reacted like that?

What had he gotten himself into?

BEAU STOOD NEXT to the snowbank, cussing under his breath. Walter had warned him not to tell her. Now he understood why. The woman was stubborn as a danged mule.

He touched his tongue to his lower lip and tasted her, smiling as he thought of the kiss. No matter what she'd said, he'd felt her kissing him back.

Another vehicle pulled into the parking lot, dragging him back to the problem at hand. DJ Justice. How was he going to keep her safe? And safe from what? Or whom? He cursed Walter Justice. Tomorrow he would call him back, but in the meantime, all he could do was keep an eye on the man's daughter.

Good luck with that, he told himself as he went back into the bar. She was sitting again with her cousin. He went to the bar, taking a stool where he could watch her in the mirror behind the counter. She looked up and their gazes met for a moment.

She touched her tongue to the corner of her mouth and licked away a dollop of ketchup. Then she smiled as if she knew exactly what that had done to him. It was clear that she understood how their kiss had affected him. Because it had affected her, as well? Not likely.

He pulled his gaze away to nurse his beer. This woman was going to be the death of him.

Chapter Eight

Jimmy cursed and told himself to stay calm. He was going to get his shot. He'd been ready, but the damned man kept blocking his shot. He'd decided to try to take them both out when he got his chance.

He put the crosshairs on her head. His finger teased the trigger. He took a breath. He couldn't blow this.

A semi roared past between him and the bar, kicking up a cloud of snow. When he looked through the scope again, the woman had pulled away from the man and gone back into the bar, the man right behind her. Who was this guy, anyway?

Jimmy swore, hauled his rifle back in and closed his window. He tried not to be discouraged. He had Stacy, which meant he had a standing invitation to Cardwell Ranch. Why rush it? What was another day?

He was getting cold and tired by the time the door of the bar opened again. He put his window down, lifted the rifle and looked through the scope. Two women. He recognized Stacy's sister, Dana, leading the way. Right behind her was…DJ Justice.

His heart began to pound. His finger on the trigger began to shake. Before he could get the crosshairs on her, the door of the Suburban opened and she was gone.

He beat the steering wheel with his fist, then whirred up the window. He'd get his chance. He had to. A thought struck him. He'd find out where DJ was staying on the ranch and take her out quietly, he thought as he tested the blade with his thumb. A bead of blood appeared on his skin at the mere touch.

The idea of cutting her throat appealed to him. He was good with a knife. It would be better this way. Better chance of killing her and then making a clean getaway before anyone was the wiser.

He just had to make sure that the pro didn't get to her first. Maybe their paths would cross. He sheathed the knife, smiling at the prospect of surprising the pro.

DJ WATCHED THE winter landscape sweep past under a full moon. "I really like your friend Hilde."

Dana smiled as she drove them toward the ranch. "I'm so glad. Hilde liked you, too. So, what did you think of Beau Tanner?"

She shot a look at her cousin. "How long have you known him?" she asked, avoiding the question.

"Not all that long. His family is from the canyon, but he returned only about five years ago. You two seemed pretty close when you were dancing."

DJ smiled. "You aren't playing matchmaker, are you? You know I'm going to be in town only a few days."

"You'll be here a lot longer than that if I have my way," Dana said and laughed.

When they reached the house, the porch light was on, but everyone appeared to have gone to bed hours ago.

"I should probably go on up to my cabin," DJ said, getting out of the Suburban.

"I saw that my sister made sugar cookies. I'm thinking cookies and hot cocoa. Interested? It's not that late."

DJ couldn't resist. "If you're sure we won't wake everyone up."

"The kitchen is a long way from the upstairs bedrooms. Come on," she said, leading DJ inside.

A few minutes later, nibbling a sugar cookie, DJ watched her cousin make hot cocoa. Her mind kept returning to Beau Tanner and what he'd told her earlier, not to mention the kiss. That she'd felt something—not just something, but *something*—made her angry with herself. Worse, he'd known she felt it.

But she suspected he had, too. She smiled to herself as she recalled his expression as he'd watched her lick the dab of ketchup from the corner of her mouth.

"DJ?"

She realized she hadn't been listening. "I'm sorry?"

"Do you want me to get out the letters or is it too late?" Dana asked.

"No, I would love it, if you can find them."

"I found them earlier and put them in the desk down here," she said. "I know you're anxious to learn everything you can about your family. Me, too. Pour us each a cup and I'll get them."

DJ filled two mugs with hot cocoa and, with a plate of cookies, sat down at the table. Dana returned, sat down next to her and pushed a bundle of letters toward her.

The envelopes were yellowed with age and tied together with a thin red ribbon. DJ looked at her cousin as she picked them up with trembling fingers. "They must have meant something to your grandmother for her to keep them like this."

Dana nodded. "I thought the same thing. I can't imagine turning my back on my children, no matter what they did."

"You haven't met my father," she said with a sad smile. "I'm sure he sounded charming on the phone. But he was a born con man. He never did an honest day's work in his life. That's how he ended up in prison."

"My grandparents were hardworking ranchers, up before dawn, so they must have been horribly disappointed that their only son wasn't interested in staying on the ranch," Dana said with such diplomacy that DJ loved her all the more for it.

"You don't mind if I open these and read them?" she asked.

"Of course not. They're from your father. If they can help, please. I just don't want them to upset you."

DJ laughed, thinking of all the things she'd been through tonight, Beau being one of them. "I was raised by my father. Nothing about him would surprise me." She knew that wasn't quite true. When he'd mentioned Montana, what she'd heard in his voice—longing, regret, love—*that* had surprised her.

She opened the first letter. Something about her father's precise handwriting made her ache inside. It was clear even before she read the first few words that he was trying hard to make amends. He wanted his parents to get to know his wife.

DJ put that letter away and picked up another. This one was along the same lines as the first. He talked about wanting to return to the ranch, to raise a family there.

The next letter was even more heartbreaking. He was pleading with his parents to forgive him. She saw that the letters had been written only weeks apart.

DJ wasn't sure she could read the last letter. The writing was so neat, so purposeful, so pleading. In this letter, he said that he desperately wanted his family to meet his baby girl, DJ.

Don't punish her for my mistakes. Please don't deny your grandchild because of mistakes I've made. I will do anything you ask of me. I'll do it for my child… I'd do anything for DJ. All she has is me.

As she read the last lines, her eyes burned with tears, the words blurring before her. She quickly closed the letter and put it back into the envelope. He had pleaded for their forgiveness and asked if he and his baby could come home. Clearly they hadn't forgiven him, since her cousin had never met him.

But she and her father must have come to Montana later, when she was five. How else could she have met ten-year-old Beau Tanner? How else could her father have forced such a promise out of him?

He'd tried to give her family. She didn't think his words could break her heart any further and yet they had. He'd poured his heart out to his parents and yet they hadn't budged. No wonder he'd never told her about his family. But what had he done to make them so cold to him?

"He must have done something they felt was unforgivable. I can't believe it was simply for marrying a woman of Italian descent," she said and looked at her cousin.

"I don't know. I never really knew my grandparents. I was young when they died, but they were very strict, from what my mother told me. However, I'm with you. I don't think it was the marriage. I think something else happened. Maybe if you asked your father—"

"He isn't apt to tell me, unfortunately, since I knew nothing about any of this," she said quickly and got to her feet. "There is something I'd like to show you." She picked up her bag from the chair where she'd dropped it. "Do you recognize this?" she asked as she held out the doll to her cousin.

Dana took the rag doll so carefully, holding it gingerly as she looked into its innocent face. "It's old, isn't it? Was it yours when you were a child?" she asked as she studied the construction and clothing.

"You've never seen it before?"

"No, I'm sorry. I can tell that it is handmade." She pointed to the small embroidered red heart, almost like a birthmark, on the doll's chest, under the collar of her dress. "Did someone make the doll for you?"

"That's what's so...frustrating. I had an identical doll, but I lost it years ago. When I first saw this one, I thought it was mine. It's not, though. Mine had an accident with a dog."

"How odd. So, how did you come to have this one?" Dana asked.

"I recently found it in my bed in my apartment."

Her cousin quickly rubbed her arms as if chilled. "That is spooky. And you have no idea who could have left it for you?"

She shook her head. "None. But this was pinned to the rag doll's body, under her dress." She took out the photo and handed it to her cousin. "What about the people in this photograph? Do you recognize them?" DJ asked hopefully.

Dana studied the old photograph for a long moment before shaking her head. "I'm sorry, but I've never seen them before."

Taking the photo back, she felt a deep sense of disappointment. She'd hoped that her cousin would have the answers she desperately needed.

On the table was one of the first letters she'd opened. "Did you see this part?" she asked her cousin. "There was another woman my father had been in love with that summer. Apparently it was someone his parents adored. If he broke that woman's heart..." She looked back through the letter. "He mentions a Zinnie." Glancing up at Dana, she asked, "Do you know anyone by that name?"

Her cousin thought for a moment. "Could be Zinnia Jameson. Well, at least, that's her name now. She married a local rancher. She would be about the right age. They live about ten miles up the canyon. It's too late to ask her tonight."

"But we could go tomorrow?"

Dana smiled and rose. "Tomorrow, though if your father broke her heart, she might not want to talk about it."

"It was more than thirty-five years ago."

"As if that makes a difference when it comes to a broken heart," her cousin said. "Maybe Zinnia is why Walter's parents couldn't forgive him."

ROGER DOUGLAS HAD just poured himself a drink when his phone rang. He couldn't help being nervous. If he didn't get rid of Dee Anna Justice... Paying her off wasn't an option. That would mean opening up the financials. He couldn't let that happen. All he needed was a little more time to win the money back. There was a poker game tomorrow night. High stakes. With a little luck...

The phone rang again. He pulled it out of his pocket, expecting it would be Marietta. He really wasn't in the mood to talk to her tonight.

With surprise, he saw that it was the man he'd hired to find him a killer. Was he calling to say the deed was done? His heart soared. With Dee Anna Justice dead, he would have the time he desperately needed to cover his tracks.

"Tell me you have good news," he said into the phone without preamble.

"We have a problem."

"I don't want to hear—"

"He thinks you put an earlier hit out on her."

"What? That's ridiculous."

"Well, something's wrong. He says there's this cowboy dogging her like he thinks someone is going to try to kill her."

"I have no idea what that's about, let alone who this cowboy might be. You said that other man you talked to about this...contract could be a problem."

"It's not him."

"You sure about that?"

"Look, I'll talk Andrei down. He's a pro. He'll complete the contract."

"What about the other guy?"

"Jimmy? Who knows? He might get lucky and take her out. He's cheaper, and with the pro getting cold feet, this could work out better for both of us."

"It had better."

"Easy, Roger. The only reason you and I are pals is that you owe my boss a potful of money. So remember who you're talking to." He hung up.

Roger downed his drink and poured himself another. If this blew up in his face…

BEAU WOULDN'T HAVE been surprised to find his house empty when he finally got home. Leah had shown up like a ghost out of the past. He half expected her to vanish the same way.

The house was dark as he entered. As he turned on the light, he was startled for a moment to see a shadowy figure sitting by the window.

"You could have turned on a light," he said, annoyed with her for showing up, for only hinting at whatever was wrong and now for startling him.

"I like the dark," she said, turning to look at him. "Also, you can't see the northern lights with a lamp on. Didn't you notice them?"

He hadn't. He'd had too much on his mind.

"Rough night?" she asked as he hung up his Stetson and coat.

"You could say that. Look, I'm not staying, so now probably isn't the best time for you to tell me what's going on with you and Charlie."

She nodded, making him wonder if she was ever going to tell him. "Is everything all right?"

"Just work."

Leah nodded as if to say she knew he was putting

her off and it was okay. She got up and followed him into the kitchen. In the overhead light, he could see that she'd been crying.

"Once I finish this job—"

"It's all right. But I do appreciate you letting me stay here."

He nodded as he made himself two sandwiches and bagged them with a couple of colas. "I'm going to grab a quick shower."

"I was just headed for bed. I didn't realize how late it was. Beau, if there is anything I can do—"

"No. Thanks for cleaning up after yourself."

She laughed. "I didn't mean in the house. I have some experience with undercover operations."

He stared at her. "As what?"

"An operative. But we can talk about that when this job of yours is over."

An operative? He realized how little he knew about her and Charlie as he watched her head for the guest bedroom. He'd thought that she and his former best friend were having marital problems. Now he didn't know what to think.

He didn't have time to speculate. Right now, his number one problem was DJ Justice.

Chapter Nine

It was after midnight. The snow-covered mountainside shone like day in the light of the huge white moon hanging overhead.

"Let me walk you to your cabin," Dana said as DJ started to leave.

"No, it's late and I can get there just fine on my own." She smiled at her cousin and gave her a hug. "But thank you. For everything."

"I'm sorry I wasn't more help with the doll and photo. Tomorrow, though, we'll pay Zinnia a visit."

"We'll get it figured out," DJ said, hoping it was true. At least she knew more now than she had before coming here. Her father's letters still broke her heart. What had he done?

"So you liked Beau?" Dana asked almost shyly.

DJ chuckled and shook her head. "The truth is, my father asked him to look after me while I'm out here."

"Really? What did he think might happen to you? Or," she said, smiling, "was he trying to throw the two of you together?" From the glint in her cousin's eyes, it was clear that she thought Walter was also playing matchmaker.

DJ shrugged. She really had no idea. If she hadn't

seen her father's fear… "Again, thank you for everything. See you in the morning." As DJ stepped out on the porch, closing the door behind her, she caught movement out of the corner of her eye. For a startled moment, her hand went to her bag. Unfortunately she'd had to leave her gun behind in California.

Beau Tanner rose from the chair he'd been sprawled in, his boots scraping the wood porch as he tipped his Stetson. "Didn't mean to scare you."

"What are you doing here?" He *had* scared her, but she was trying hard not to show it.

"My job. I told you. Your father—"

"And I told you. I can take care of myself. I release you from any promise you made when you were ten." She started off the porch but heard his boots right behind her. She spun on him. "What are you planning to do? Follow me everywhere?"

"If that's what it takes to make sure you're safe."

She thrust her hands on her hips. "This is crazy. Look, I'm fine. There is nothing to protect me from."

"You sure about that? Well, I'm not. And until I am…"

"Fine. Follow me if it makes you happy." She started up the mountainside, breathing hard from her anger and just seeing him again. The last thing she needed right now was some man who…who irritated her. Her heart was beating faster at just the sound of his long strides as he easily caught up to her.

"Let's just keep to the shadows of the pines," he said, pulling her out of the moonlight.

She indulged him and his paranoia, filling her lungs with the cold night air as she tried to ignore him. The cowboy wasn't the kind who was easily ignored. She caught a whiff of his scent, a mixture of the great out-doors, fragrant soap and a powerful maleness.

DJ hated the effect it had on her as her body be-trayed her. She felt an ache inside her like something she'd never felt before. Maybe it was from years of not feeling safe, but she wanted to be in his arms again. She wanted to feel again like she had that moment in the snowbank when his mouth was on hers. She wanted to feel…protected, and she had in his arms.

Which was why she couldn't let herself give in. She would be here only a few days, and then she would be returning to California and her life there.

"This is where we part company," she said as she climbed the steps to her cabin and started to open the door.

He'd taken the steps in long strides, and now his large hand closed over hers. "Not until I make sure the cabin is secure."

She opened the door, turning on the light as she stepped inside, Beau right behind her. She couldn't be-lieve how far he was taking this. "It's late and I need to get some rest."

He didn't seem to be paying any attention to what she was saying. She hadn't wanted him in her cabin. Earlier the place had felt spacious, but it didn't now. "This is silly. You can see that there is no one in here."

He turned to look at her. "I think you have some idea who might want to harm you. That's information I need. Tonight. Before this goes any further."

She heard the determination in his voice and sighed inwardly. *Let him have his say and then send him on his way*, she thought. "Fine."

It had been a long day, but after the nap earlier and

everything that had happened, she felt more wired than tired, in truth. She moved to the small kitchen and opened the refrigerator, remembering the variety of beverages and snacks her cousin had shown her.

"Wine or beer?" she asked, knowing the only reason she was asking was that she needed the distraction.

"Beer." He had moved to the small breakfast bar and taken a seat on one of the stools. She handed him a bottle of beer and took one for herself. Twisting off the top, she took a drink. It was icy cold and tasted good.

Leaning against the kitchen counter, she studied the handsome cowboy. It was his eyes, she thought. She had remembered them because they were so unusual. Worn denim. Maybe also because there was kindness in those eyes that she would have recognized even as a child of five.

"I'm sorry you got involved in this," she said as she picked at the label on her bottle for a moment. When she looked up, she realized he'd been studying *her*.

"Why does your father think you need protecting?" Beau asked and watched her take another drink of her beer as if stalling. He understood she was holding out on him. He'd been in this business long enough to know the signs. DJ was running scared, but she was trying damned hard not to show it.

"You say you met me years ago?" she finally asked. "Did you know anything about my family before that? Or after that?"

He had removed his Stetson and tossed it on one of the other stools. Now he shrugged out of his coat, the same one he'd worn to the airport. He could see that this was going to take a while.

"Are you going somewhere with these questions? Or just avoiding mine?" he asked after draping his coat over a stool. He locked gazes with her. "I have to wonder why you aren't being straight with me. I hate getting myself killed without knowing why."

She looked chagrined as she put down her beer and turned to him. "I'm not sure what this has to do with anything, but before I left California, my apartment was broken into. The intruder left something for me."

He held his breath as he waited, imagining all kinds of nasty things.

"It was a doll with a photo pinned to it." She nodded as if she could tell that wasn't what he'd expected. "I used to have a rag doll identical to it. It wasn't a commercial doll. Someone had made it. Made two, apparently. Because as it turns out, this one wasn't mine. But it is so much like mine..."

"...that you wondered whose it had been."

She smiled. "Glad you're following along."

"And the photo?"

She reached into her shoulder bag and took out the doll and photo. She handed him the photo. "I don't recognize any of them or have any idea who they might be. I asked my father, but..."

"He said he didn't know them."

"But from his expression when he saw the photo, he knows who they are. He suggested I get out of town."

Beau studied the photo. "You think you might be this baby?"

"My father swore I wasn't."

"But you don't believe him."

She sighed. "I don't know what to believe. For years he told me I had no family. A couple of days ago I find out about the Cardwells—and the Justices. My father was born here, apparently. His family disowned him after he married my mother. He wrote a few letters trying to get back into their good graces. He must even have come here if you and I met all those years ago."

"You think he was here trying to make amends?"

"It doesn't sound like making amends was the only reason my father came here. Otherwise I doubt we would have met."

Beau nodded as he picked up the doll she'd set on the breakfast bar. "I called your father after I saw you at the airport today."

That surprised her. She took a drink of her beer and seemed to be waiting for what was coming.

"I told him that in order to protect you, I needed to know what I was protecting you from," he said. "Your father swore that he didn't know, but when I pressed him, he said it might have something to do with your mother's family. He said they might have…found you."

She shuddered. *"Found me?"*

"That's what *I* said. Unfortunately he had to go before he could tell me anything further. I thought you might know why he would say that."

DJ stepped past him to move to the window that looked out over the ranch. As she drew back the curtain, he said, "I wish you wouldn't do that."

She let the curtain fall into place and turned to look at him. "You think this has something to do with my *mother's* family? Why would they leave me the doll and the photo if they didn't want me to know about them?"

"Maybe they didn't leave them. Maybe some well-meaning person did." He shrugged. "I got the impression that your father thought you had something to fear from them."

She took another sip of her beer. "Well, that's interesting, given that all my life he's told me I didn't have any family. Not just that," she said as she walked back to the counter where she'd been leaning earlier. "I always felt growing up that we were running from something, someone. A few times it was one of my father's...associates. But other times..."

"You think it might have been your mother's family?"

She shrugged and toyed with the label on her beer again. He saw her eyes fill with tears. "That would be something, if the people I have to fear are...family."

"We don't know that." He got up, moved to her and took the nearly full bottle of beer from her. He set it aside. "You should get some rest."

He expected her to put up a fight, but instead she merely nodded. "It has been a long day." Her gaze met his. He did his best not to look at her full mouth.

Stepping away from her, he reached for his coat and hat.

"As it turns out, my father had a girlfriend before he married my mother," she said behind him. "Dana and I are going to visit a woman named Zinnia in the morning. I have a bad feeling he broke her heart. Still, I'm hoping she might be able to help me put another piece into the puzzle that is my father."

"I'm going, too, then."

"I told you. I release you from any promise you made my father years ago."

He nodded as he shrugged into his coat. "Just the same, I can go with you or follow you. Your choice."

Beau snugged his Stetson down over his blond hair. His boots echoed on the hardwood floor as he walked to the door, opened it and turned. "I'll be right outside if you need me." He tipped his hat to her.

She opened her mouth, no doubt to argue the point, but he was out the door before she could speak. As he settled into the swing on the porch, he listened to her moving around inside the cabin and tried not to think of her in that big log bed he'd seen through the open bedroom doorway.

"STACY? DID I wake you?" Jimmy knocked over the bottle of whiskey, swore and grabbed it before most of it ended up in the motel carpet. "You still there?"

"Jimmy?" she said sleepily.

"James. I told you, I go by James now." He took a drink and pushed aside his irritation at her. Tonight hadn't gone as he'd planned, and he felt the clock ticking. Who knew what the pro was doing tonight, but getting into the ranch wouldn't be easy for him—especially at night. There were hired hands, ranch dogs, lots of people living there. Unless they knew you... He told himself he still had the upper hand.

"What do you want?" Stacy asked, sounding irritated with him now.

He quieted his voice. "I was thinking about you. Thinking about old times. You and me." He could almost feel her soften at his words. Whatever he had back then, he still had it—at least where Stacy was concerned.

"So you decided to call me in the middle of the night?" She didn't sound irritated anymore. Maybe she was a little touched by the gesture.

"Yeah, sorry about that. I just couldn't get you off my mind. I wanted to hear your voice."

"You didn't say what you were doing in town. Are you living here now?"

He'd been vague, letting her think he was looking for a job, a place to live, letting her think he might be staying. "We can talk about that sometime, but right now I want to talk about you."

"What about me?"

"I still remember the way you felt in my arms."

"You do?"

"Uh-huh. Do you remember...me?"

She made an affirming sound.

He could imagine her lying in bed. He wondered what she had on. Probably a flannel nightgown, but he could get that off her quick enough.

"You are the sexiest woman I've ever known," he said and took another sip of the whiskey. "You said you live on the ranch now. In one of those cabins on the mountainside that I can see from the road?"

"Jim—James."

"I was thinking maybe—"

"My daughter. Ella, I told you about her. She's here in the cabin with me."

"I would be quiet as a mouse." There was just enough hesitation that it gave him hope, but she quickly drowned that idea.

"No. If that's all you wanted, I really need to get some sleep."

He realized that he'd come on too strong. He cursed under his breath. "No, that's not all I want. I shouldn't have called tonight. But after seeing you... I want to take you out to a nice dinner. That is, if you're free."

Silence, then, "When?"

"Tomorrow night. I figure you'll know a good place to go. Nothing cheap. I want to make up for this call."

"Okay."

He shot a fist into the air. "Great. I'll pick you up. What time? And hey, I want to meet your daughter." He'd almost forgotten about the kid again.

"Sure," she said, sounding pleased. "Tomorrow, say, six? My sister will babysit Ella."

"See if she'll take her for the night, because I want to get you on a dance floor after dinner. I can't wait to get you in my arms again."

Stacy laughed. "I've missed you."

He smiled to himself as he hung up and picked up the hunting knife from the bed. "Tomorrow night." He would mix a little pleasure with business.

Chapter Ten

The next morning, just after sunrise, Dana found Beau on DJ's porch. She handed him a mug of coffee and a key. "Go over to the cabin next door. I can stand guard if you think it's necessary."

He smiled at her, glad to have Dana for a friend. "I don't think you need to stand guard." He figured DJ should be safe in broad daylight with so many people on the ranch. And he didn't plan on being gone long.

"Thanks for the coffee—and the key. But I think I'll run home and get a shower and a change of clothing. DJ said the two of you are going to visit Zinnia Jameson. I'd like to come along."

"Fine with me. I'm glad you're looking after her." Her smile seemed to hold a tiny surprise. "She's special, don't you think?"

He laughed. "You're barking up the wrong tree. It isn't like that." He thought about the kiss and quickly shoved the memory away.

"That's what they all say—until love hits them like a ton of bricks."

Beau left, chuckling to himself. He'd heard that Dana Savage was one great matchmaker. She'd helped all five of her cousins find the loves of their lives. But she'd apparently failed with her older sister, Stacy, he thought.

And she would fail with him.

On the way home, Beau put in another call to the number Walter Justice had given him. A male voice answered just as before. He asked for Walter Justice.

A moment later another male voice came on the line. The gravelly voice informed him that Walter couldn't come to the phone.

"I need to talk to him."

"Not sure if that is ever going to happen. He got shanked last night. They've taken him to the hospital."

"Is he going to be all right?"

"Don't know." The line went dead.

Beau held his phone for a few moments, listening to the silence on the other end. DJ's father was in the hospital, possibly dying? There might never be any answers coming from that end.

He pocketed his phone, telling himself that he needed to let DJ know. She said she didn't care about her father, but having been through this with his own, he knew it wasn't true. When the man was your father, no matter how much he screwed up, his loss…well, it hurt. He remembered feeling racked with guilt because he hadn't kept in touch with his father. For years he'd wanted nothing to do with him.

Ultimately it all came down to blood and a built-in love that came with it.

Reaching his house, he climbed out of his pickup, thinking about the Walter Justice he'd known years ago. He wondered how he'd aged since he'd been in prison. He doubted he'd changed, which could explain why he was in the hospital now.

Beau swore under his breath. He didn't know what to do. He had to keep DJ safe. It was a debt that he wouldn't renege on—even if Walter didn't survive. He wasn't the kind of man who went back on his word. But he also knew there was more to it. He kept thinking about that brown-eyed little girl and the woman she'd become.

He would tell her about her father. But not until after their visit to Zinnia Jameson's house. He wasn't sure how she would take the news. Maybe there was no connection between what had happened to her father and whatever Walter feared might happen to his daughter.

Either way, Beau was even more concerned for her safety.

ANDREI SNIFFED THE WIND, waiting for a sign. He clung to the utility pole, careful not to attract any undue attention.

This job had turned out to be harder than he'd thought. For some reason Dee Anna had picked up an overprotective cowboy. Because of that, he was having trouble getting the right shot.

That alone should have made him quit the job.

But his birthday was coming, and he'd planned this for too long. His last hit. He would feel incomplete if he didn't finish. Also, he never quit a job once he'd flipped the coin and it had come up heads. It felt like a bad idea to do it now. He never liked to test luck.

So he would finish it and celebrate his birthday as he hung up his gun.

All he had to do was kill Dee Anna Justice. But not today, he thought as he sniffed the wind again.

She and the cowboy had to feel safe. Then they would make the mistake of letting him get a clean shot. He would bide his time.

"This couldn't wait until a decent time of the day?" attorney Roger Douglas demanded as he joined Marietta in the library. He stepped to the table where Ester had put out coffee and mini citrus muffins. He poured himself a cup and took two muffins on a small plate before sitting down.

"I wanted an update on the…situation," Marietta said. She felt calm and in control, more than she had in the few months since Carlotta had confessed.

"It's a little early to—"

"I assumed you would be handling this yourself and yet here you sit."

He picked up one of the muffins. She noticed that his hand shook as he popped it into his mouth. Clearly he was stalling for time.

"Have you even found her?" she demanded.

"Yes, of course. She's at a place called the Cardwell Ranch near Big Sky, Montana. She's staying with a cousin on her father's side of the family. I've had her apartment bugged for several months—ever since you asked me to find her."

"But you haven't gotten around to offering her money?"

"What is this really about?" Roger asked patiently, as if she was a child he had to humor.

"Have you offered Dee Anna Justice the money or not?"

He studied her for a moment before dragging his

gaze away. "Maybe we should discuss this when you are more yourself."

"Actually, I am, and for the first time in a long time. I am going to want to see all the financials on the trust funds." He paled, confirming what she'd feared. Her nosy housekeeper knew more than she did about what was right in front of her eyes. "But on this other matter…"

Roger rose. "I don't know what's gotten into you, but I told you I would handle it."

"How much are you planning to offer her?" She saw something in his eyes that made her heart drop. How much money had he stolen from her? Was this why he was dragging his feet? Because there wasn't enough money left to bribe Dee Anna Justice?

"What did you do?" she demanded.

He began to pace the room. "You're not thinking clearly, so I had to take things into my own hands. Trying to buy off this woman is the wrong approach. She would eventually bleed you dry. You know what kind of woman she is given that her father is Walter Justice. I told you I'm taking care of it and I have. I've hired someone to make sure she is no longer a problem."

For a moment Marietta couldn't catch her breath. "You did what?"

He dropped down into a chair next to her and took one of her hands. "It is the only way. I've kept you out of it. I—"

She jerked her hand free. "You stupid fool." Her mind raced. "Is it done already?"

"No, but I should be hearing from him—"

"Stop him!" She shoved to her feet. She was breathing hard, her heart thumping crazily in her chest. She tried to calm down. If she had a heart attack now...

"You stop him or I will call the police."

Roger looked too shocked to speak. "You wouldn't do that."

"Try me. Call him now!"

"My job is to protect you."

She shook her head. "Protect me? Give me your phone. I will stop the man myself." She held out her hand.

"You can't do that, Marietta." He sounded scared. "You don't know what this man is capable of doing if he feels you're jerking him around."

"You think he is more dangerous than me?" She let out a chuckle, feeling stronger than she had in years. "Roger, get your affairs in order. You're done, and if I find out what I suspect, that you've been stealing from me, prepare for spending the rest of your life in prison. You're fired, and if you try to run, I'll send this man after you."

All the color had drained from his face. "You don't know what you're saying."

"I do, for the first time in a long time. I've depended on you to make decisions for me because you made me question myself. But I'm clearheaded now, Roger." He started to argue, but she cut him off. "Make the call."

She watched, shaking inside. But whoever he was phoning didn't answer. She listened to him leave a message calling off the hit.

"This is a mistake," Roger said as he pocketed his phone. "I've been with you for years. I've—"

"Get out." She pointed toward the door. "Don't make me call the police to have you thrown out. And you'd better pray that the man you hired gets the message."

As he left, Marietta heard a floorboard creak. Ester. The nosy damned woman. She thought about firing her as well, but she was too upset to deal with another traitor in her midst right now.

THE WOMAN WHO answered the door later that morning at the Jameson house was tiny, with a halo of white-blond hair that framed a gentle face. Bright blue eyes peered out at them from behind wire-rimmed glasses. "Yes?" she asked, looking from DJ to Beau and finally to Dana. She brightened when she recognized her.

"Sorry to drop by without calling," Dana said.

"No, I'm delighted." She stepped back to let them enter.

"This is my cousin DJ."

"Dee Anna Justice," DJ added, watching the woman for a reaction to the last name. She didn't have to wait long.

Zinnia froze for a moment before her gaze shot to DJ, her blue eyes widening. "Wally's daughter?"

DJ nodded. She'd never heard anyone call her father Wally.

"And you know Beau Tanner," Dana said.

"Yes," Zinnia said. An awkward silence fell between them, but she quickly filled it. "I was just going to put on a pot of coffee. Come into the kitchen, where we can visit while I make it." Her eyes hadn't left DJ's face.

They followed her into the kitchen. DJ had been so nervous all morning, afraid that this might be another dead end. But now, from Zinnia's reaction to her, she had little doubt this woman had been the one her father's parents had hoped he would marry.

"Dana is helping me piece together my past—and my father's," DJ said, unable to wait a moment longer. "You were a part of the past, if I'm not wrong."

Zinnia had her back to them. She stopped pouring coffee grounds into a white paper filter for a moment. "Yes." She finished putting the coffee on and turned. "Please sit."

DJ pulled out a chair at the table. Her cousin did the same across from her. Beau stood by the window.

Zinnia came around the kitchen island to pull up a chair at the head of the table. When she looked at DJ, her expression softened. "I loved your father. Is that what you wanted to hear?"

"And he loved you."

The woman nodded, a faraway look in those blue eyes. "We'd been in love since grade school." She chuckled. "I know that sounds silly, but it's true. We were inseparable. We even attended Montana State University in Bozeman together. Everyone just assumed we would get married after college."

"Especially my father's parents," DJ said.

"Yes. I had a very good relationship with them. I was like another daughter to them, they said." She smiled in memory.

"What happened?" DJ asked, even though she suspected she already knew.

Zinnia straightened in her chair as if bracing herself. "Wally got a job as a wrangler taking people into Yellowstone Park. His parents were upset with him because they needed him on the ranch, but Wally was restless. He'd already confessed to me that he didn't want to take over the ranch when his parents retired. He wanted to travel. He wanted..." She hesitated. "That's just it. He didn't know what he wanted. He just...*wanted*." Her gaze locked on DJ's. "Then he met your mother. She and some friends were touring the park." Zinnia shrugged, but her voice cracked when she added, "Apparently it was love at first sight."

The coffeemaker let out a sigh, and the woman got up.

DJ rose, too. "May I help?"

Zinnia seemed surprised. "Why, thank you. There are cups in that cabinet."

She took out four cups and watched as Zinnia filled each. DJ carried two over, giving one to Dana and the other to Beau as he finally took a seat at the table. She'd expected to see him on her front porch when she got up this morning, but to her surprise, he'd come driving up, all showered and shaved and ready to go wherever she was going.

He'd been so somber, she wondered if he wasn't having second thoughts about getting involved with her father—and her. She couldn't blame him. It seemed ridiculous for him to tag along, since she seemed to be in no danger. Maybe her father had overreacted.

She'd said as much to Beau, but he'd insisted that he had nothing else planned that day except spend it with her.

Because of some promise he'd made a con man when he was ten? What kind of man would honor that?

Beau Tanner, she thought, turning her attention back to Zinnia.

"My grandparents must have been horribly disappointed," DJ said after taking the cup of coffee the woman handed her and sitting back down.

Zinnia sat, cradling her cup in her two small hands. "They were as brokenhearted as I was," she said with a nod and then took a sip of her coffee, her eyes misty.

DJ wanted to tell her that she'd dodged a bullet by not ending up with her father. But even as she thought it, she wondered what kind of man her father might have been if he'd married Zinnia and gotten over his wanderlust.

"I had no idea that my mother had a brother," Dana said into the awkward silence. "Then I found some old letters. That's how we found you."

Zinnia nodded. "Wally's parents did everything they could to get him not to marry that girl, to come back to the ranch, to help them, since they were getting up in age. Mostly they wanted him to marry me." She smiled sadly. "But in the end…" Her voice broke. "Sadly, I heard the marriage didn't last long." Her gaze was on DJ again.

"My mother died in childbirth."

The older woman seemed startled to hear that.

DJ stared at her. "That is what happened, right?"

"I only know what Wally's parents told me."

"It would help if you could tell us what you do know," Dana said.

Zinnia hesitated for a moment and then spoke quietly. "As you might have guessed, I stayed friends with Wally's parents. They were such sweet people. They were devastated when Wally didn't come back." She took a sip of her coffee as if gathering her thoughts. "Wally called at one point, asking for money. I guess he thought they would give him what he felt was his share of the ranch." She scoffed at that. "He always made things worse."

Seeming to realize that she was talking about DJ's father, Zinnia quickly added, "Forgive me for talking about him like that."

"There isn't anything you can say that I haven't said myself. I know my father. He didn't get better after he left Montana."

"Well," the older woman continued. "When he called for money, he told them that Carlotta—" the name seemed to cause her pain even after all these years "—had left him to go spend time with an aunt in Italy."

DJ reached into her shoulder bag and took out the photo. As she passed it over to Zinnia, she asked, "Do you recognize any of these people?"

Zinnia studied the photo for only a moment before she put it down. "The young woman holding the baby is Carlotta Pisani Justice. Or at least, that had been her name. I saw her only once, but that's definitely her. You can see why Wally fell for her."

Picking up the photograph, DJ stared at the young woman holding the baby. This was her *mother*. "My father swears that the baby she's holding isn't me."

Zinnia looked at her with sympathy. "We heard that her wealthy family had gotten the marriage annulled somehow and threatened that if she didn't go to Italy, they would cut off her money. It seems she met someone her family liked better in Italy, quickly remarried and had a child with him."

"So this child would be my half brother or sister," DJ said more to herself. When she looked up, she saw Zinnia's expression.

The older woman was frowning. "But if her family had the marriage annulled… Why would they have done that after your mother and father had a child together?"

DJ felt an odd buzzing in her ears. She thought about what Beau had told her. Her father feared that her mother's family had "found" her.

"Is it possible they didn't know about me?" DJ asked, finding herself close to tears. Her gaze went to Beau's. She saw sympathy in his gaze but not surprise. All those years on the run. Had they been running to keep the truth from her mother's family?

The doll and the photo meant *someone* knew about her. Not only that, they also wanted her to know about them.

BEAU DROVE DJ and Dana back to the ranch after their visit with Zinnia. Both were quiet on the short drive. The sun had come out, making the snowy landscape sparkle like diamonds. As he drove, he chewed on what they'd learned from Zinnia. He felt for DJ. Apparently her mother had walked away not only from her father but also from her.

But what part had her father played? He could only guess.

He hated that the news he had to give her would only make her feel worse. But he had no choice. He couldn't keep something like this from her. She had to know.

As he pulled into the Cardwell Ranch and parked, Dana's children all came running out. They were begging to go see Santa at the mall in Bozeman.

Stacy was with them. "I didn't put it in their heads," she said quickly.

Dana laughed. "Looks like I'm going to the mall," she said as she started toward the kids. "DJ, you're welcome to come along. You, too, Beau."

Beau shook his head. "Thanks, but DJ and I have some things we need to iron out."

Dana shot her cousin a mischievous look.

"Tell Santa hello for me," DJ said.

Beau said to Dana, "Mind if we take a couple of horses for a ride?"

Dana grinned. "Please. I'll call down to the stables. DJ, you can wear what you wore last night. You'll find a warmer coat just inside the door of the house."

"You do ride, don't you?" he asked her.

"I've been on a horse, if that's what you mean. But whatever you have to tell me, you don't have to take me for a ride to do it."

A man came out of the house just then, wearing a marshal's uniform. Dana introduced them. DJ could tell that something was worrying him and feared it might have to do with her.

"Have you had any trouble with the electricity?" he asked Dana.

"No, why?"

"Burt came by with the mail and told me he'd seen a lineman on one of our poles. By the time I got here, he was gone. Just thought I'd ask. Burt's pretty protective, but still, it did seem odd. Maybe I'll give the power company a call."

As Hud drove away, followed by Stacy and Dana and the kids, DJ turned to Beau. "Seriously, we can't talk here?"

He smiled and shook his head. "Let's get saddled up. We can talk about who's taking whom for a ride once we're on horseback and high in the mountains."

"I'm not going to like whatever it is you need to tell me, am I?"

He shook his head. "No, you're not, but you need to hear it."

WHEN HE'D SEEN Dee Anna and her cowboy saddling up horses, Andrei had known this was the day. Several things had happened that he'd taken as signs. He would have good luck today.

He'd made arrangements the night before to procure a snowmobile. He'd been stealing since he was a boy and still got a thrill out of it. He'd always liked the danger—and the reward. His father had taught him how to get away with it. He smiled to himself at the memory. He missed his father and hoped that he would make him proud today.

Andrei felt good. He was going to get his chance to finish this. He didn't plan to kill the cowboy, too, but he would if he had to. He could tell that the two felt safe here on the ranch. As they rode toward the mountains behind the ranch house, he smiled to himself.

Today would definitely be the day. Last night after stealing the snowmobile, he'd traversed the logging roads behind the ranch. He would be waiting for them on the mountain. He had an idea where they would be riding to. He'd seen horse tracks at a spot where there was a view of the tiny resort town of Big Sky.

He would be waiting for them. One shot. That's all he needed. He would be ahead of schedule. Still, he wanted to get this over with. He knew that feeling wasn't conducive to the type of work that he did. But he couldn't help the way he felt. He was anxious. Once he finished this, he couldn't wait for the future he'd planned since his first job when he was fourteen.

His cell phone rang. He ignored it. He could almost taste success on the wind as he climbed on the snowmobile and headed up one of the logging roads toward the top of the mountain behind Cardwell Ranch.

FROM THE WINDOW Marietta watched her granddaughter come up the circular drive and park the little red sports car that had been her present for her thirtieth birthday.

"She can buy her own car," Ester had said with disapproval. "She has a job. It would be good for her and mean more to her."

Marietta had scoffed at that. "I have no one else to spoil." Which was true—at least, she'd believed that Bianca was her only granddaughter at the time. "She is my blood." Blood meant everything in her family. It was where lines were drawn. It was what made Bianca so precious. She was her daughter's child with a nice Italian man whose life, like her daughter's, had been cut short.

At least, that's what she'd told herself, the thing about blood being thicker than water and all that. But that was before she'd found out her daughter had conceived a child with…with that man.

Bianca got out of her car and glanced up as if she knew her grandmother would be watching. Her raven hair glistened in the sunlight as her gaze found Marietta at her window. Usually this was where her granddaughter smiled and waved and then hurried inside.

Today she stood there staring up, her face expressionless, her manner reserved. After a few moments, she looked toward the front door, brightened, then rushed in that direction.

Marietta knew then that Ester must have opened the door. Bianca loved the housekeeper. Maybe even more than she loved her grandmother.

That thought left a bitter taste in her mouth. She turned away from the window. Out of stubbornness, she thought about staying where she was and letting Bianca come to her.

But after a few minutes had passed, she couldn't stand it any longer and headed downstairs.

She found Ester and Bianca with their heads together, as she often did. The sight instantly annoyed her. But also worried her.

"I thought you would come upstairs," she said, unable to hide her displeasure.

Both women turned toward her but said nothing. Marietta looked from Ester to Bianca and felt her heart drop.

"What's wrong?" she demanded. "Has something happened?"

"I know, Grandmother. *How could you?*"

Chapter Eleven

DJ rode alongside Beau through the snow-covered pines until behind them the house could no longer be seen. The world became a wonderland of snow and evergreen below a sky so blue it hurt to look at it.

She didn't think she'd ever breathed such cold air. It felt good. It helped clear her head.

The cowboy riding beside her seemed to be lost in the beauty of the country around them, as well. What was it about him? She felt drawn to him and his cowboy code of honor. Yet all her instincts told her to be careful. He was the kind of man a woman could fall for, and she would never be the same after.

She'd spent her life never getting attached to anything. This man, this place, this Cardwell family all made her want to plant roots, and that terrified her. For so long she'd believed that was a life she could never have. But maybe, if the doll and photo were her mother's family reaching out to her and not a threat…wasn't it possible that she could finally live a normal life?

They rode up a trail until the trees parted and they got their first good view of Lone Peak across the valley and river. This late morning it was breathtaking.

The stark peak gleamed against the deep blue of the big sky. No wonder this area had been named Big Sky.

"It's incredible, isn't it?" Beau said as he stopped to look.

DJ reined in beside him to stare out at the view. The vastness of it made her feel inconsequential. It wasn't a bad feeling. It certainly made her problems seem small.

"Beautiful," she said on a frosty breath.

"Yes, beautiful."

She felt his gaze on her. Turning in the saddle, she looked into his handsome face. He looked so earnest… "Okay, you got me out here. Why?"

"I thought you'd like the view."

She shook her head. "If you're trying to find a way to tell me that you're stepping away from this—"

"I don't break my promises." He pushed back his Stetson and settled those wonderful blue eyes on her. His look was so intense, she felt a shudder in her chest. "We need to talk about what Zinnia told you. But first I've got some bad news. I called your father this morning." She braced herself. "He was attacked at the prison. He's in the hospital."

DJ wasn't sure what she'd been expecting. Not this.

The news was a blow. For years she'd told herself that she hated him, that she never wanted to see him. She blamed him for her childhood. She blamed him for keeping her family from her. She bit her lip to keep from crying. "Is he—"

"It sounds serious."

DJ nodded, surprised how much her chest ached with unshed tears. "You think his attack…" She didn't need to finish her sentence. She saw that he thought whatever she had to fear, he suspected it was connected to her father's attack. "Why?"

"I don't know yet. But I will find out."

He sounded so sure of himself that she wanted to believe him capable of anything. Wasn't that why her father had cashed in on the promise? He must have believed that if anyone could keep her safe, it would be Beau Tanner.

"You think I'm in danger?"

"I do. We need to find out what is going on. We need to find your mother's family."

"But nothing's happened. Yes, I was left a doll and photo of people I didn't know at the time…"

"They broke into your house to leave it."

"But what if it's my mother's family trying to let me know about them?"

He shook his head. "DJ, if that was the case, then why wouldn't they have simply picked up the phone or mailed the doll and the photo with a letter?"

"You see the doll and photo as a threat?" Hadn't she at first, too?

"I agree, someone wants you to know. The question is, why? Given what we learned from Zinnia Jameson…"

She saw where he was going with this. "It could explain a lot about my childhood. I always felt as if we were running from something. What if my father was trying to keep my mother's family from finding us? You don't think he might have…kidnapped me, do you?"

STACY WASN'T SURPRISED when Jimmy showed up at her part-time job at Needles and Pins, the shop that her sister's best friend, Hilde, owned. He pushed open the door, stepped in and stopped dead.

He was taking in all the bolts of fabric as if realizing he was completely out of his element. Stacy watched him, amused. James Ryan afraid of coming into a quilt shop. It endeared him to her more than she would have liked.

"Jimmy?" she said as if surprised to see him. Actually she wasn't. After she'd run into him yesterday, it had been clear he was hoping to see her again. That he had tracked her down… Well, it did make her heart beat a little faster. She'd always thought of him as the love of her life.

He came in, moving to the counter where Stacy was cutting fabric for a kit she was putting together. "James."

"Right. Sorry. Old habits… Do you like the colors?" she asked as she finished cutting and folded the half yard neatly. "Tangerine, turquoise, yellow and brown."

"Beautiful," James said without looking at the fabric. "So, this is where you work?"

"Part-time. I help Dana with the kids and work some on the ranch."

"Busy lady," James said. "I just wanted to make sure we were on for tonight."

She felt her heart do that little hop she'd missed for a long time. "Tonight. Right." She hesitated, torn. Then heard herself say, "Sure, why not?" even though a few not so good memories had surfaced since his call last night.

"Good. I can't wait." He sounded hopeful, and the look in his eyes transported her straight back to high school, when he used to look at her like that.

Stacy felt a lump in her throat. Was it possible they were being given a second chance at love? It seemed too good to be true. "I never thought I'd see you again."

He grinned, that way too familiar grin that had made her lose her virginity to him all those years ago. "Neither did I. Life is just full of surprises. Great surprises. So, I'll pick you up on the ranch. Which cabin did you say was yours?"

"The one farthest to the right on the side of the mountain. You remember how to get to the ranch?"

He laughed. "Like it was yesterday."

MARIETTA HAD TO sit down. She moved to a chair and dropped into it. Her heart pounded in her ears and she feared it would give out on her. She'd feared something like this might happen and had told Roger as much.

"Maybe the best thing would be to tell Bianca," she'd said.

"Have you lost your mind? Once you do that, you're basically admitting that this…woman has a right to part of your estate," Roger had said. "No, there is a better way to handle this, and Bianca never has to know."

Why had she listened to that man?

Bianca brushed back her long, dark hair and glared at her grandmother. "What have you done?"

Marietta's gaze shifted to Ester. She'd never seen such determination in the woman's expression before. Her lips were clamped tightly together and her eyes were just as dark and angry as Bianca's.

"What have you *done?"* she wanted to demand of her housekeeper. Yes, Ester was nosy. And yes, she'd been acting odd lately. But Marietta had never

dreamed that she would go to Bianca. She'd trusted the woman. A mistake, she saw now.

Bianca crossed her arms over her chest. "Isn't there something you want to tell me, Grandmama?"

Use of that pet name was almost Marietta's undoing. She lived only for Bianca. Everything she'd done was for this precious granddaughter.

"Tell you?" she echoed, stalling for time.

"Tell me the truth," Bianca demanded, raising her voice. "Do I have a sister?"

Marietta had known when her dying daughter had confessed she'd conceived a child with Walter that this day might come.

Now she realized how foolish she'd been to think she could keep something like this a secret. Although her daughter and Walter had certainly managed. It was clear that Ester had known about the other child, probably from the beginning. That realization hurt more than she wanted to admit.

It would be just like Carlotta to have shared this information all those years ago with the woman who'd practically raised her. Suddenly she recalled Ester at the sewing machine in her tiny room. She'd been startled and tried to hide what she was doing. Marietta had thought she was trying to disguise the fact that she wasn't working like she was supposed to be.

But now she remembered what the housekeeper had been working on. Dolls. There'd been two identical dolls! Two rag dolls, and yet Bianca had always had only the one.

Betrayal left a nasty taste in her mouth. Her gaze darted to Ester. "I want you out of my house!"

"No!" her granddaughter cried, stepping in front of

the housekeeper as if to shield her. "Do not blame Ester for this. If you fire her, you'll never see me again." The ultimatum only made the betrayal more bitter. "If it wasn't for Ester, I might never have known that I have a sister you've kept from me all these years."

"I wasn't the one who kept it from you all these years. That was your mother—and Ester." She could see now that Ester had been collaborating with Carlotta for years. Had she been stronger, she would have strangled the woman with her bare hands. "It's Ester who has known for so long, not me. Your mother didn't bother to tell me until she was near death. If you want to blame someone—"

"I'm not here to place blame. My mother had her reasons for keeping it from me. I suspect those reasons had something to do with you. But I won't blame you, either." Bianca stepped toward her. "I just want to know about my sister."

"She isn't your *sister*. She's only half—"

Her granddaughter waved a hand through the air. "She's my *blood*."

That it could hurt even worse came as a surprise. "Your *blood*?" she demanded. "Watered down with the likes of a man..." She sputtered. Her contempt for Walter Justice knew no words.

Bianca dropped to her knees before her grandmother and took both of Marietta's hands in hers. "I want to know about her. I want to know all of it. No more secrets. Grandmama, if you have done something to hurt my sister..." She let go of Marietta's hands. The gesture alone was like a stab in her old heart.

"Get me the phone!" she ordered Ester. She called

Roger's number. It went directly to voice mail. She left a message. "Fix this or else."

BEAU COULDN'T HELP but laugh. "Kidnapped you?" He shook his head as he and DJ dismounted and walked their horses to the edge of the mountainside to look out at the view. "I think anything's possible. But I got the impression from your father that somehow your mother's family didn't know about you. And now they do."

"And that puts me in danger?"

He turned to gaze into her big, beautiful brown eyes, wanting to take away the pain he saw there. He'd been trying to save this woman in his dreams for years. Now here she was, all grown up, and he still felt helpless.

"DJ." His hand cupped the back of her neck. He drew her closer, not sure what he planned to do. Hold her? Kiss her? Whatever it was, he didn't get the chance.

The sound of the bullet whizzing past just inches from her head made him freeze for an instant, and then he grabbed and threw her to the snowy ground as he tried to tell from which direction the shot had come.

"Stay down! Don't give the shooter a target," he ordered as he drew his weapon from beneath his coat. Nothing moved in the dark woods behind them. Only silence filled the cold winter air for long moments.

"The shooter?" she repeated, sounding breathless.

In an explosion of wings, a hawk came flying out of the pines, startling him an instant before he heard the roar of a snowmobile.

"Stay here!" he ordered DJ as he swung up into the saddle.

"Wait. Don't…"

But he was already riding after the snowmobiler. He crested a ridge and drew up short. The smell of fuel permeated the air. Below him on the mountain, the snowmobile zoomed through the pines and disappeared over a rise. There was no way he could catch the man. Nor had he gotten a good look at him.

He swore under his breath as he quickly reined his horse around and headed back to where he'd left DJ.

She'd gotten to her feet but was smart enough to keep the horse between her and the mountainside.

"Are you all right?" he asked. He'd been sure the bullet had missed her. But he'd thrown her down to the ground hard enough to knock the air out of her.

Clearly she was shaken. She hadn't wanted to believe she was in any kind of danger. Until now. "Did you see who it was?" she asked.

"No, he got away. But I'll find him or die trying."

Andrei couldn't believe he'd missed. It was the cowboy's fault. If he hadn't reached for her right at that moment… But he knew he had only himself to blame. He'd been watching the two through his rifle scope, mesmerized by what he saw. They were in love.

He'd found something touching about that. He'd been in love once, so long ago now that he hardly remembered. But as he watched these two through the scope, he'd recognized it and felt an old pang he'd thought long forgotten.

Fool! Andrei was shaking so hard he had trouble starting the snowmobile. He'd never really considered that he might get caught. As long as the coin toss came up heads, he'd known his luck would hold.

Now, though, he feared his luck had run out. He ripped off his glove and tried the key again. The snowmobile engine sputtered. He should have stolen a new one instead of one that had some miles on it.

He tried the key again. The engine turned over. He let out the breath he hadn't even realized he'd been holding and hit the throttle. He could outrun a horse.

As he raced through the trees, he felt as if his whole life was passing before his eyes. All his instincts told him to run, put this one behind him, forget about Dee Anna Justice.

But even as he thought it, he knew it couldn't end this way. It would ruin his luck, ruin everything. He would make this right because his entire future depended on it.

He was almost back where he'd started a few miles from the main house on Cardwell Ranch when he lost control of the snowmobile and crashed into a tree.

Chapter Twelve

DJ couldn't quit trembling. It had happened so fast that at first she'd been calm. She'd gotten up from the ground, staying behind her horse as she watched the woods for Beau. Had someone really taken a shot at them? Not them. *Her.*

She'd never been so relieved to see anyone as Beau came riding out of the pines toward her and dismounted. He'd given chase but must have realized there was no way he could catch the man. She'd heard the snowmobile engine start up, the sound fading off into the mountains.

Still, she didn't feel safe. "You're sure he's gone?" she asked now as she looked toward those dark woods.

"He's gone. We need to get back to the ranch and call the marshal. I can't get any cell phone coverage up here."

Her legs felt like water. "If you hadn't tried to kiss me again…"

He grinned. "Maybe next time… That's right. I told you there wouldn't be a next time. I'm usually a man of my word."

She could tell he was trying to take her mind off

what had just happened. "I guess you have a kiss coming."

"Glad you see it that way." He looked worried, as if what had almost happened hadn't really hit her yet. Did he expect her to fall apart? She was determined not to—especially in front of him.

She could tell he was shaken, as well—and worried. His gaze was on the trees—just as it had been earlier.

"Why would someone try to kill me?" she demanded. This made no sense. Nor could the same person who'd sent her the doll and the photograph be behind it. That had to be from someone in her family who'd wanted her to know about them.

But she remembered her father's fear when he'd seen the photo. Who was he so afraid of?

"All this can't be about something my father did over thirty years ago," she said, and yet it always had something to do with him. She thought about what Zinnia had told them. "Apparently this person really carries a grudge." She could see that Beau wasn't amused.

"We're going to have to find your grandmother."

"Marietta Pisani. You think she's hired someone to shoot me? Why now?"

"I wish I knew. But maybe it's what your father said. They didn't know about you and now they do."

She shook her head. "They don't even know me. Why would they want to kill me?"

He shook his head. "From what Zinnia said, it could involve money."

"If that's true, no wonder my father told me my mother died in childbirth. He was actually trying to spare me. How do you like that?" She let out another bitter laugh as she turned to look at the cowboy. "So now they want me dead."

"If your mother died a few months ago, maybe that was when the rest of the family found out about you. It must have come as a shock."

"My mother chose her family and their money over me."

"I'm sure it wasn't an easy choice."

She hated the tears that burned her eyes. "I am their flesh and blood. Wouldn't they want to meet me before they had me killed?"

He reached for her, drawing her into his strong chest. She buried her face in his winter coat. "Let's not jump to conclusions until we know what's going on, okay?"

She nodded against his chest. "Why didn't my father tell me the truth when I showed him the photo?" she asked, drawing back.

"I'm sure he regrets it. He swears that when you came to him, he didn't know what was going on."

She pulled away. "My father lies."

Beau stared at her slim back as she swung up onto her horse. She was reasonably hurt by what she'd learned from Zinnia, but she was trying so hard not to show it. "I don't think he's lying about this."

"Someone else knew about me." She turned to look at him. "That person sent me the doll and the photo."

He hated to tell her that maybe the doll and the photo might merely have been a way of verifying that she was indeed Walter Justice's daughter. When she'd received the items, she headed straight for the prison—and her father, whom she hadn't acknowledged in years.

"But now they're afraid I'll go after the money." She shook her head. "After years of believing I had no family other than my father, now I have so much that some of them have put a price on my head. I don't know what to say."

Beau didn't, either. "You could contact them, possibly make a deal—"

"I don't want their money!" She spurred her horse.

He had to swing up into the saddle and go after her. The woman could handle a horse. He rode after her, sensing that she needed this release. Her horse kicked up a cloud of snow that hung in the air as he caught up and raced like the wind alongside her.

Her cheeks were flushed and there was a steely glint in her eyes that told him of a new determination.

"You'll help me find out who is behind this?" she asked as they reined in at the barn.

"You know I will. But first we have to report this." Swinging down from the saddle, he called the marshal's office. Hud told them to stay there. Good to his word, he was there before the horses were unsaddled and put away in the pasture.

Hud sent several deputies up into the woods to the spot Beau told him about. They'd be able to find it easily enough by following the tracks.

Once inside, he steered them both into the kitchen. "Here," Hud said, shoving a glass of water into DJ's trembling hands. "I have something stronger if that would help."

She shook her head and raised the glass to her lips, surprised she was still trembling. She'd believed she could take care of herself. Now she was just thankful that Beau had been there. What if it had been she and Dana who'd ridden up into the mountains?

"I'll take that something stronger," Beau said to Hud, and he poured him a little whiskey in a glass. Beau downed it in one gulp but declined more.

"This doesn't make any sense," DJ heard herself saying. "It had to have been an accident." She wanted the men to agree with her. But neither did. She could tell that Beau was convinced this was what her father had feared.

She listened while Beau told Hud in detail what he knew. Then she said, "If I brought whatever this is—"

"We'll get to the bottom of this," Hud said. "I'll tell you what Dana would. You're with family. We aren't going to let anything happen to you."

But even as he said it, DJ could see that he was worried. The last Dee Anna Justice had come here and brought trouble. The real Dee Anna promised herself that wouldn't be the case this time. She had hoped she'd find the answers she needed in Montana. Now she worried that she was endangering the family she'd just found.

She would leave as soon as she could get a flight out.

But even as she thought it, she had a feeling she wouldn't be leaving alone—if Beau had anything to do with it.

ANDREI GRIMACED IN pain as he finished bandaging his leg in his motel room. The snowmobile accident was just another bad sign, he told himself. And yet he had survived it with minimal damage.

He'd managed to push the wrecked snowmobile off into a gully where it wouldn't be found—along with some of the debris that had been knocked off it when he'd hit the tree. He'd gotten away. That alone should have been cause for celebration, since it was the closest he'd come to being caught.

Had he not missed, the cowboy would have been trying to save his beloved instead of racing on horseback in an attempt to catch her would-be killer.

He stood now to test his leg and, groaning in pain, sat back down. He wouldn't be climbing any more power poles, that was for sure. But he wasn't going to let this mishap change anything. He'd be fine by tomorrow, he assured himself.

The problem was that now DJ and her protective cowboy would know he was out here. They would be even more careful than they had been at first. He would have to wait—and watch. In good time, he told himself. And he still had time. He could complete this before his birthday, and he would.

He checked his phone. There were two messages from the man who'd hired him. Andrei didn't bother to listen to them. Whatever the man wanted, it didn't matter. This had become personal. Nothing could stop him now.

MARSHAL HUD SAVAGE leaned back in his chair in his den on the ranch to look at Beau. Dana, Stacy and the kids had returned. Not wanting to upset them, he'd suggested the two of them talk in his den. They'd known each other for years—just not well. Their cases had never overlapped until now.

"So, Dee Anna's father hired you?" Hud asked.

Beau liked to keep things simple. He'd learned that years ago when dealing with his father—and the law. He nodded. "He asked me to watch over his daughter."

"He wasn't more specific than that?"

"No."

"And how exactly did he know about you?"

"I guess he could have looked in the phone book under private investigators," he said, dodging the truth.

Hud nodded. "Seems odd, though, asking you to keep an eye on her while she's here where her cousin's husband is the marshal."

"Not really." He softened his words with a wry smile. "Walter Justice is in prison. It could be he doesn't trust law enforcement."

The marshal chuckled at that. "Point well-taken, given what we know about Walter." He studied Beau openly for a moment. "You had taken DJ for a horseback ride."

"To talk. DJ's trying to find out more about her family."

"Dana said the three of you went to visit Walter's high school girlfriend, Zinnia Jameson?"

Beau nodded. "DJ knows nothing about her father's past. We were hoping Zinnia could provide some answers."

"That's what you had to talk to DJ about?"

He could tell that Hud was suspicious, since it had been Beau who'd taken her to a spot where a shooter had almost killed her.

"We needed to talk about what we'd learned, but also, I had to give her some bad news. Her father was shanked in prison."

"I'm sorry to hear that. I get the impression from Dana that DJ and her father aren't close."

"No, but he's still her father."

Hud sighed. "There's something about your story... Tell me again what the two of you were doing right before you heard the shot and felt the bullet whiz past."

Beau laughed. He had great respect for the marshal. The man had sensed he hadn't told him everything. "I was about to kiss her. I'd pulled her closer..."

The marshal nodded smiling. "You were trying to kiss her?"

He grinned. "Unfortunately the shooter took a potshot at us before that could happen."

"So, this is more than a job for you?"

Beau didn't want to get into the whole story of the first time he saw DJ and how he'd never forgotten her. "There's been some attraction from the start."

"I can understand that. It's those Justice women." He turned serious again. "You didn't get a good look at him?"

"No. Nor the snowmobile. Earlier I thought I heard one in the distance, but I didn't think anything about it. It's December. Everybody and his brother have one of the damned things, and the mountains around here are riddled with old logging roads."

"But you're convinced the bullet was for DJ?"

"Depends on how well the man shoots. If he was aiming for me, he can't hit the side of a barn. But if he was aiming for DJ, he's good. Really good. If I hadn't drawn her toward me when I did..."

"You're thinking a professional?"

"I am."

"You have any idea why someone would want Dee Anna Justice dead?"

Beau hesitated. He understood why Hud had wanted to talk to him alone. DJ was Dana's family. Hud would have done anything for his wife.

"It might have something to do with her mother's family," Beau said after a moment. "I'm going to shadow her until we find out what's going on. I don't have much to go on." He told the marshal the names of both mother and grandmother.

Hud wrote them down. Marietta and Carlotta Pisani. "Why would her own flesh and blood want to harm her?"

Beau shook his head, thinking of Cain and Abel. He couldn't help but wonder about DJ's half sister. "There might be money involved."

"GRANDMAMA, YOU'RE SCARING ME. Tell me what you've done," Bianca demanded as her grandmother hung up the phone. "I'm assuming that was Roger you called. He hired someone to find my sister and then what?" She shook her head as if too disappointed in her grandmother to talk for a moment.

Ester had dropped into a chair across from them.

Marietta looked at her precious granddaughter. Her heart was in her throat. What if the man Roger had hired had already accomplished what he'd paid him to do? Now she realized that she could lose the one person who mattered to her.

"Do you have any idea how much I love you, how much I have tried to protect you—"

Bianca's look stopped her cold. "What have you done?"

"It might not be too late."

"Too late for what?"

Marietta waved that off and tried to rope in her thoughts. Roger would already have called if it was done. Of course he'd stopped it. Roger was too smart to go against her wishes on this. She reminded herself he was so smart that apparently he'd been stealing from her for years. She was the matriarch of this family, but Roger was a man she'd leaned on since her husband had died all those years ago.

"Listen to me. I'm trying to make this right." Her fear of losing Bianca's love, though, was a knife lodged in her chest.

"Tell me everything you know about her," Bianca said, sitting down next to her.

There was no keeping it from her now. "I don't know very much, just what your mother told me. Her name is Dee Anna Justice."

"So after Mother told you, did you try to reach her? You just said it might be too late."

So Ester *hadn't* told her everything. Marietta thought she still might stand a chance of regaining Bianca's love, her trust. "You have to understand. Your mother was very young. She fell in love with this man from Montana who was all wrong for her. Fortunately she realized her mistake…" She almost said, *"before it was too late,"* but that had been what she'd thought at the time.

Now she knew that it *had* been too late. Carlotta had given birth to Walter Justice's child—and kept the truth from nearly everyone.

ON HER DEATHBED, Carlotta had cried, saying it was Marietta's fault that she'd had to keep Dee Anna a secret all these years.

"I wanted my child with me. I needed my child with me. But you had made it clear that if I didn't come home, forget about Walter and go to Italy to stay with my aunt…"

"You are going to blame me for this?" she'd demanded.

"I had to give up my child because of you."

No, Marietta had argued. "You gave up your child for *money*. You knew I would cut off your allowance if you stayed with that man. It was your choice."

Had her daughter thought that one day she could just come home with the child and all would be forgiven? Or had she given up on that foolish idea when she'd met the nice Italian man she'd married and become pregnant with *his* child?

"Surely Walter Justice would have gladly given up the child had you demanded it," she had pointed out to her daughter.

"You're wrong. He loved me. He loved Dee Anna. He would never have let you get near her, knowing how you felt about him. But, Mother, now you can make up for the past. Now you have a chance to know your *first* granddaughter."

Carlotta must have seen her expression, because her own hardened. "Or not. Whatever happens, it's on your head now, Mother."

MARIETTA REALIZED BIANCA had asked her a question.

"Why did you hate my sister's father so much?" Bianca asked again, accusation in her tone.

"He was a crook. All he was interested in was our money."

"*Money.* Why does it always come back to that with you?"

"He's serving time in prison. I think that tells you what kind of man he is." She hated that her voice rose, that she sounded like a woman who'd lost control of her life. A woman who was no longer sure of the stand she'd taken. A woman who would die drowning in regret.

Bianca rose. "I want to meet my sister."

"Stop calling her that!" Marietta snapped irritably. "She is merely your mother's mistake."

Her granddaughter looked horrified at her words.

She regretted them instantly. "You don't understand," she pleaded. "This woman isn't one of us. If she is anything like her father, she'll demand part of your inheritance. I know you think you don't care about the money, about the family legacy—"

"It is the family *curse*," Bianca said. "That's what mother called it. She used to wish her family was dirt-poor."

Marietta wanted to laugh. Her extravagant daughter would not have liked being poor, let alone dirt-poor.

Bianca's eyes narrowed. "So this is about money. You're afraid she will want money."

"No, I was willing to give her money. It's about you, Bianca. I don't want you to be hurt. Contacting this woman can only—"

"Tell me how I can find her," Bianca said, cutting her off.

She swallowed and looked to Ester. "Why don't you ask *her*?" she said, pointing to her housekeeper. "She seems to be well-informed."

Ester's gaze met hers, unspoken secrets between them. The housekeeper hadn't told Bianca about the hit man. But she'd hinted at it. Did Marietta really want her to tell everything she knew?

"I'm asking *you*," her granddaughter said.

Marietta sighed. She knew when she'd lost. Wasn't it possible that Dee Anna Justice could already be dead? If so, Bianca would never forgive her. And the family legacy could already be gone, thanks to Roger. She had only herself to blame for all of this. But to lose both Bianca and her fortune would be unendurable.

"She's at the Cardwell Ranch near Big Sky, Montana, but—"

"I'm going to find her," Bianca said with more determination than Marietta had ever seen in her.

As she started to leave, Ester said, "I'd like to go with you."

Bianca shot a look at her grandmother and seemed to hesitate. "Can you manage alone with your bad heart?"

"I've been on my own before," Marietta snapped, wondering how she *would* manage. "Don't worry about me."

"I'll call when I find her," Bianca said.

Everything she cared about was walking out that door. She didn't think her heart could break further. She was wrong, she realized as she saw Ester's suitcase by the door and knew that she might not see either of them again.

"WE HAVE TO find out who's behind this," Beau told DJ before they left Cardwell Ranch. "I thought we'd go by my office in Bozeman. I should warn you about my assistant. She's... Well, you'll see soon enough."

He wasn't surprised when Marge did one of her eyebrow lifts as they walked in. What did surprise him was how quickly she took to DJ.

Like a mother hen, she scurried around, getting coffee, offering to run down to the cupcake shop for treats.

"We're fine. We won't be here long," he told her with an amused and slightly irritated shake of his head. He ushered DJ into the office, saying, "I'll be right back," and closed the door behind her.

Turning to Marge, he said, "What is going on with you?"

"Me?" She gave him her innocent look.

"This isn't a *date*. DJ is a *client*, of sorts. This one is...off the record, but it is still work. Nothing more."

"DJ, huh?"

He shook his head. "Why do you take so much interest in my love life?"

"*What* love life?" she said, fiddling with some papers on her desk.

Beau ignored that jab. "Are you hoping to get me married off?"

"I never said a word."

"You don't have to." He started for his office, but something was bothering him. Turning back to her, he said, "I have to know. DJ walks in and you instantly like her. You've never liked any of the women I've dated, and you've never done more than share a few words with them on the phone. What is different about this one?" he demanded, trying to keep his voice down.

Marge smiled. "You'll remember this one's name."

Chapter Thirteen

DJ pulled up a chair next to Beau as he turned on the computer and began his search. She felt surprisingly nervous sitting this close to him. It brought back the memory of being in his arms, of his mouth on hers. There was something so masculine about him.

"You all right?" he asked as she moved her chair back a little. "Can you see okay?"

She nodded and tried to breathe. "How long has Marge been with you?"

"Since I started. She's like a mother hen." He shook his head. "But I couldn't run this office without her." She heard true admiration and caring in his voice. She also sensed a strong loyalty in him. Look how he'd agreed to protect her based on a promise he'd made so many years ago.

"I like her."

He glanced over at her. "And she likes you. Believe me, it's a first." Their gazes locked for a moment. She could feel the heat of his look and remembered how he'd almost kissed her up on the mountain.

At the sound of his assistant on the other side of the door, he turned quickly back to the computer. "Okay, let's see what we can find out about your grandmother. Marietta Pisani. There can't be that many, right?"

DJ thought about how this had started with the doll and the photo. Her father's letters had led them to Zinnia, who'd told her more about her father—and mother—than she'd ever known. Leave it to her father to tell Beau that the doll and photo might have something to do with her mother's family. Why couldn't he have told her that?

Because he'd been lying to her since birth, she reminded herself. She felt a stab of guilt. He was in the hospital, badly injured. She'd called but hadn't been able to learn much—just that he was in stable but serious condition. She told herself he was tough. He'd pull through. She hoped it was true.

"Your father told you that your mother was dead, but that your grandmother Marietta is still alive, right?" Beau was saying. "Marietta Pisani. Is there any chance she's related to the noble Pisani family of Malta? Descendants of Giovanni Pisani, the patrician of Venice?"

"I have no idea," DJ said.

"Maybe you'll get a chance to ask her," he said and motioned to the screen. "I found only one in the right age group. A Marietta Pisani of Palm Desert, California."

DJ swallowed the lump in her throat. This was the woman who'd had her daughter's marriage to Walter Justice annulled. "What do we do now? You can't think that my grandmother…" Her words faltered. She could see from his expression that he could think exactly that.

Her father had also thought it. Why else would he

have asked Beau to protect her? But surely she didn't need protecting from her own grandmother?

"We call her," Beau said and reached for the phone.

It took Marietta a while to calm down after Bianca and Ester left. At first she was just scared. Scared that she'd lost everything. Then she was furious with Ester for butting into her family business. She'd tried to reach Roger but suspected he was not picking up. The coward.

At some point, she'd have to find out if there was any money left. But right now, it was her least concern. Her daughter would have thought that funny, she realized. The joke was on her, she realized. Roger had stolen her money. All that worry about the family legacy and now she realized that if she lost Bianca, nothing mattered.

When a middle-aged woman arrived with a suitcase in hand claiming to be Ester's younger sister, May, she almost turned her away.

"I'm not like Ester. I'll see to you, but don't think you can browbeat me the way you do her."

Marietta was offended. "I don't browbeat anyone."

May huffed and slipped past her. "Just tell me where my room is. Then I'll see about getting you fed. I cook whatever I can find to cook and you eat it. That's the deal."

With that, the woman had sashayed off in the direction Marietta had pointed.

This was what her life had come to? She almost wished that she'd died this morning before she'd seen that little red sports car drive up.

But then she wouldn't have seen her precious grand-daughter. Not that their visit had gone well.

She tried Roger's number again. Again it went to voice mail. It was in God's hands, she told herself. God's and Bianca's and Ester's and whomever Roger had hired.

She prayed that Dee Anna Justice was still alive. She just didn't want Bianca hurt. But who knew what this Dee Anna Justice was like? She couldn't bear the thought of Dee Anna rejecting Bianca. If there was any money left, she knew her granddaughter would gladly share it with her...sister.

Marietta made the call. She had to take control of her life again, one step at a time, until her old heart gave out.

As STACY DRESSED for her date, she felt torn between excitement and worry. Did she really believe that she and James could start over again after all these years? Maybe she was hanging on to a first-love fantasy James, one who had never existed.

"What has he done for a living since high school?" Dana had asked. She didn't know. "What does he do now?"

"I think he said real estate."

Her sister got that look Stacy knew only too well.

"You remember him," Stacy said. "You liked him in high school, didn't you?"

"I didn't know him," Dana said. "But I do remember that he broke your heart."

"It wasn't his fault. He thought his ex-girlfriend was pregnant..." She stopped when she saw Dana's expression. "He did the right thing by her. He married her."

"I suppose so," her sister said. "Just…be careful. It's not only you now. You have to think of Ella."

She'd thought only of Ella since her daughter's birth. There hadn't been any men, not even one date. But now she could admit that she felt ready. She wanted a husband and a father for Ella and said as much to Dana.

"There is nothing wrong with that," her sister said, giving her a hug. "Maybe James is that man. Maybe he's not. Give it time. Don't let him rush you into anything."

She knew what Dana was getting at. James had rushed her into sex in high school. She hadn't been ready, but she'd feared that she would lose him if she didn't give in to him.

As she finished dressing, Stacy told herself she wasn't that young, naive girl anymore. If James thought she was, then he was in for a surprise.

ROGER SWORE WHEN he saw how many times Marietta had called. He didn't even bother to check the voice mails. He knew she'd be demanding to know what was going on. He'd called the man who'd hired the hit man and had finally heard back.

"He rushed the job and missed," the man told him. "Now he has to fix it. So back off. These things take time. Worse, now she knows someone is trying to kill her. Also, the marshal is involved."

Roger felt sick to his stomach. "You told me that he would make it look like a shooting accident. This isn't what my boss wanted at all. Call him off."

"I'll do what I can. He isn't answering his phone."

Could this get any worse?

"He's going to want the rest of the money. You'd best have it ready for him," the man warned.

"Of course." Roger hung up, sweating. His phone rang again. He saw that this time it was the accountant he'd been working with. Marietta. She was checking the trust funds. He was dead meat, he thought as he let her call go to voice mail.

He decided he'd better listen to Marietta's message. What he heard turned his blood to ice.

"Bianca knows! She and Ester are headed for Cardwell Ranch in Montana. If anything happens to them, I'll have you killed in prison, and you know I can do it. I might not have as much money as I once did, but I still have power."

He disconnected, not doubting it for a moment. He looked around the room. He couldn't wait any longer. She knew that he'd been embezzling money for years from the family trust funds. He'd hoped that he could win it back, but his gambling debts were eating him alive. If the thugs he owed didn't kill him, then Marietta would.

His cell phone rang again almost instantly. He put it on mute, telling himself he would throw it in the ocean the first chance he got and buy a new one. Then he stepped to the suitcase. His passport and the plane tickets were on the table by the door. He picked them up, took one last look at the house he had mortgaged to the hilt and, suitcase in hand, walked out.

MARIETTA LET OUT a scream of pain when she heard an estimate of how much money was missing from the trust funds.

May rushed into the room. "If you're not bleeding, this had better be a heart attack or a killer snake in the room."

"I want to die."

May shook her head. "Let me get a knife."

"I've made a horrible mess of things."

"Haven't we all? If you don't want your supper burned, die quietly while I get back to the kitchen."

Marietta could hear her heart pounding and welcomed death. What had she done? Her mind wouldn't stop racing. All she could think about were the mistakes she'd made. She had another granddaughter. Bianca would have loved having a sister. She used to ask for one all the time. It broke Marietta's heart.

The irony was that Carlotta's second husband hadn't been much of a step up from Walter. Gianni had some shady dealings before his death. But at least he'd come from a good Italian family with money.

She had wanted so much for her daughter.

And yet Carlotta still hadn't married well.

"Playing God wearing you out?" May asked as she brought in her dinner tray.

"Do you always say whatever you think without regard to whether or not it is proper?" Marietta demanded.

May smiled. "Not much different from you, huh?"

"I'm not hungry," she said, trying to push the tray away.

"Too bad. I'm going to sit right here until you eat. Ester said all I had to do was keep you alive. I figure you're too mean to die, but just in case..." May pushed the tray back at her and sat down, crossing her arms.

Marietta glared at her for a moment before picking

up her fork. If she had to eat to get the woman out of her room, she would.

"You know nothing about any of this," she said.

May chuckled.

"If I thought Ester was talking behind my back—"

"What would you have done? Fired her?" May shook her head. "Ester didn't have to tell me anything about you. I saw it in the sadness in her eyes. She's been loyal to you, just as our mother was. You don't realize how lucky you are that she put up with you all these years. Anyone else would have put a pillow over your face years ago."

"I feel so much better knowing you'll be staying with me until Ester comes back," she said sarcastically.

"You think Ester is coming back?"

Marietta stopped, the fork halfway to her mouth. She didn't want to acknowledge her fear that Ester was gone for good. "She won't leave me alone. Not after all these years."

"Because of your sweet disposition? Or because you pay her so much?"

She felt her face heat but said nothing as she concentrated on her food again. This was what her life had come to, she told herself. She was an old woman alone with an ingrate who had nothing but contempt for her. She half hoped the woman had poisoned her food.

Chapter Fourteen

The phone rang. Marietta snatched it up, hoping it was Bianca calling. Maybe she'd changed her mind about going to Montana, about meeting her half sister, about…everything.

"Hello?"

"Is this Marietta Pisani?"

"Yes." Her heart pounded.

"My name is Beau Tanner. I'm a private investigator in Montana. I'm calling about your granddaughter."

"Bianca?" Montana? Was it possible Bianca and Ester had gotten a flight out so soon and were now in Montana?

"No, Dee Anna Justice."

She gripped the phone so hard that it made her hand ache. She held her breath. Hadn't he said he was a private investigator? Shouldn't it be the police calling if Dee Anna Justice was dead?

"What about her?" she asked, her voice breaking.

"You recognize the name?"

"Yes. She's my granddaughter. What is this about?"

"I was hoping you would tell her," the private eye said. "I'm putting her on the phone."

"Hello?"

Marietta heard the voice of her first granddaughter and felt the rest of her world drop away.

"Hello?" the voice said again.

Marietta began to cry uncontrollably.

May came in, saw what was happening and took the phone. "I'm sorry. She can't talk right now." She hung up the phone. Turning, she demanded, "Where do you think you're going?"

Marietta had shoved away the food tray, gotten to her feet and gone to her closet. Pulling out her empty suitcase, she laid it on the bed and began to throw random clothing into it. "I'm flying to Montana."

May took in the suitcase the older woman had tossed on the bed. "Do you really think that's a good idea given your...condition? Let alone the fact that you might be arrested when you land."

So Ester had shared information with her sister. Marietta knew she shouldn't have been surprised. "You've been in on all this?"

May smiled. "It was my son who left the doll and a photo of her mother, grandmother and Carlotta's second husband for DJ." She sounded proud of what she'd done. "Ester was afraid of how far you would go. She said DJ couldn't be brought off. She wouldn't have wanted a cent of your money. So all of this was a huge waste on your part."

Marietta finished throwing a few items in, slammed her suitcase and zipped it closed. She'd been surrounded by traitors. "You couldn't possibly understand why I've done what I have."

"Why you used money to keep your daughter away

from a child that she loved?" May demanded. "Did Carlotta tell you how she cried herself to sleep over that baby you forced her to give up?"

"Forced her? It was her choice. Just like it was her choice to marry the man. So easy to blame me, isn't it?"

May put one hand on her bony hip. "What would your daughter think now if she knew that you were trying to kill that child?"

Marietta swallowed. She wanted to argue that it was all Roger's doing. But she'd trusted him to handle it. Her mistake. All she'd thought about was erasing the existence of Dee Anna Justice to save the family.

"Help me with my suitcase."

May didn't move.

"I'm going to save the woman. Does that make you happy?" she barked.

"*The woman?* She's your grandchild. She's your blood. She's Bianca's sister."

"I don't have time to argue with you." She shook her head. "None of you know this Dee Anna Justice. What if she wants nothing to do with our family? What if she rejects Bianca? What then?"

"Bianca is a strong woman. She will survive. I think you might underestimate the connection they have," May said. "Ester kept in touch over the years with Dee Anna's father. She saw the girl grow up."

"My suitcase."

May stepped forward, slid the suitcase from the bed and began to wheel it toward the front door. "You best hope that you're not too late."

It was already too late in so many ways.

"SOME WOMAN TOOK the phone and said she couldn't talk. Before that it sounded like she was...crying," DJ said as she saw Beau's anxious expression.

He took the office phone and replaced it in its cradle. "At least now we know that she's the right one."

"I guess. She was definitely upset. But upset to hear from me or to hear that I'm still alive?" She could see he was even more convinced that her grandmother was behind what had happened earlier today on the mountain.

"What now?" As if she had to ask. "The would-be assassin will try again, won't he?" She didn't give him time to answer. "I can't stay at Cardwell Ranch," she said as she pushed to her feet. "I can't endanger my cousin and her family—"

"That's why I want you to move in with me."

She blinked. "No, I couldn't."

"If it makes you feel any better, I have a...friend staying with me. Leah."

"I see." A friend, huh? Was that what he called it? She realized how little she knew about this man.

"I can protect you better on my home ground."

"I think everyone would be better off if I just left Montana."

"You're wrong. But if you leave, I'm going with you. Sorry, but you're stuck with me until this is over."

She stared at him even though she'd expected this. "You can't be serious, and for how long?"

"As long as it takes. But if you could just give me a few days and not leave, it would be better. If whoever shot at you is still here, it will give me the chance to catch him."

She didn't like the sound of this. She'd come to care

about this man. She didn't want to see him get killed protecting her and said as much.

"Have more faith in me," he said with a grin. "Let's go get your things." They drove in silence to the Cardwell Ranch.

Dana put up a fight when Beau told her his plan.

"Christmas is only a few days away," she argued. "DJ is family. She should be here with us."

"With luck, this will be over by Christmas," he told her. "Hud thinks it is best, too."

"Hud." With that one word, Dana looked resigned.

DJ hugged her. "I'm so sorry. I would never have come here if I thought it might be dangerous for your family."

"You have nothing to be sorry for," Dana said. "You take care of her," she said to Beau. "I'm depending on you."

"I hate this," DJ said as he drove them off the ranch. "I hate that I involved them and, worse, you. You're only doing this because of some stupid promise you made when you were a boy to a man who had no right to ask anything of you."

Beau was quiet for a long moment as he drove. It almost surprised her when he finally spoke. "The first time we met, I wished that I could help you," he said without looking at her. "I've regretted it ever since."

She spoke around the lump that had formed in her throat. "I don't want you to get killed because of me."

"I don't want that, either," he said with a chuckle. "But I'm not that ten-year-old anymore." He finally glanced over at her. "I can help you. I know what I'm doing."

She looked away, fighting back tears. All this was

because of her father falling in love with the wrong woman? Now he was in the hospital possibly dying and she was... She was in Montana with a cowboy who was determined to save her.

They hadn't gone far when Beau turned off the highway and crossed a narrow bridge that spanned the Gallatin River before driving back into the canyon. At the heart of the valley was a large log house. Behind it was a red barn and some outbuildings. A half-dozen paint horses raced around in a large pasture nearby.

"This is where you live?" she asked, a little awed by the beauty of the scene.

"Do you like?" he asked and glanced over at her.

"I love it." She felt a lump form in her throat. She could see Beau here. "You're a real cowboy."

He laughed. "You're just now realizing that?"

She turned to look at him. She was just now realizing a lot of things, she thought as she stared at his handsome profile in the last light of the day.

JIMMY WAS LATE picking her up, making Stacy have even more second thoughts. But he seemed so glad to see her that she pushed them aside and tried to have a nice time.

He took her to one of the local restaurants, ordered them both a cocktail and drained half his glass before letting out a sigh. He actually looked nervous, which made her laugh and forget her own nervousness.

"So tell me about this cousin staying on the ranch," he said.

"Dee Anna Justice. She's the daughter of my mother's brother, whom we didn't know anything about." She really didn't want to talk about DJ, though. "So, what did you say you're doing in Big Sky again?"

"Working. A brother no one had ever heard of?"

"Working at what?" she asked, wondering why he was so interested in the Justice side of the family.

"This and that." He drained his glass. The waiter came over and before Stacy could look at her menu, James ordered for both of them, including more drinks. "You don't mind, do you?" he asked after the waiter had already left.

She shook her head, although she did mind. "How long did you say you've been back?"

"Did I say? A few weeks. Actually, I'm looking for a job. Anything opening up on Cardwell Ranch?"

She couldn't help but laugh. "What do you know about working on a ranch? As I recall, you hated helping on your uncle's."

"I forgot what a good memory you have." That didn't sound like a compliment. The waiter came with their drinks and he downed his quickly.

"Jimmy—"

"But you can't seem to remember that I go by James now." He was clearly irritated and not trying to hide it.

"Sorry. Why did you ask me to dinner tonight?"

He leaned back, giving her a what-do-you-think look. "I thought for old times' sake..." He shrugged. "You dating someone?"

Fortunately their meals came. They talked little. Jimmy ate as if he hadn't had a meal in days. He devoured his steak and then asked her if she was going to finish hers. She'd lost her appetite early on in the date, so she gladly slid her plate over and let him clean it.

What had she been thinking? Her sister was right.

The Jimmy Ryan she'd been in love with all those years ago wasn't the man sitting across from her.

"Ready?" he asked as he signaled the waiter for his bill.

Turning, she spotted Burt Olsen, their mailman. He nodded and smiled at her. He appeared to be picking up something to go.

Stacy just wanted this date to be over. When Jimmy saw her looking at Burt, he threw an arm around her waist and propelled her toward the door.

"Maybe I should drive," she said as they started toward his truck.

"I don't think you should think." He still had hold of her as they neared the pickup. He opened the driver's-side door and practically shoved her in, pushing her over to get behind the wheel.

"Jimmy—James."

"I remember you being a lot more fun," he said, gritting his teeth.

And vice versa, but she said nothing as she saw Burt getting into his vehicle. He'd been watching the two of them. And she knew that if she said anything to Jimmy, it would turn into a fight. Burt was the last person she wanted seeing her and Jimmy fighting. She told herself that Jimmy hadn't had that much to drink—and it was only a short drive to the ranch.

Neither of them spoke during the drive. As they crossed the bridge, he glanced over at her. "You hear me?"

She hadn't realized he'd said anything. "I'm sorry?"

"I'm sure you are." He drove on into the ranch and pulled up in front of her cabin. "So which one is this cousin of yours staying in?"

She pointed to the last one at the other end of the row. She knew what was coming, but Jimmy was out of luck if he thought she was going to invite him in.

"Thanks for dinner," she said as he shut off the engine. She reached for her door handle. But before she could get it open, he leaned over and grabbed her hand to stop her.

"I'm sorry about tonight. It wasn't you. I got some bad news right before I picked you up. I should have canceled." He drew back his hand.

"What kind of bad news?" she asked out of politeness.

"An investment. It fell through. I was counting on it."

She hoped he didn't ask her for money. "I'm sure you'll be able to get a job."

"A *job*." He said the last word like it tasted nasty in his mouth. "Just not on your ranch, huh? You don't even know what I do for a living."

"A little of this and that is all you told me." She reached for the door handle again.

This time his hand came around the back of her neck. He clamped down hard enough to take her breath away. "You're kind of a smart mouth. I do remember that about you."

Stacy tried to wriggle out of his grasp. "Stop!" she said as he pulled her toward him as if to kiss her. "I said *stop*!" That feeling of déjà vu hit her hard. This was what had happened in high school, only then she'd thought that he was so crazy about her he just couldn't help himself. She knew better now.

Chapter Fifteen

Leah looked up expectantly as Beau entered the kitchen. She smiled quickly as if covering her disappointment. Who had she expected? Her husband? Or someone else?

Her gaze went to DJ, her expression one of surprise and something else. Jealousy?

"This is DJ. She's going to be staying with us. DJ, Leah."

"No last names?" Leah asked, pretending to be amused.

He walked to the stove. "You cooked?"

"Don't sound so surprised. I'm a woman of many talents."

Beau could believe that somehow, even though he hadn't been around Leah in years. She'd always seemed…capable.

"Looks like you made enough for three," he said, lifting the lid on one of the pots and glancing into the oven, where what looked like a Mexican casserole bubbled. Looking up, he said, "You must have been expecting company."

She shook her head, but not before he'd seen that

moment of hesitation. Her laugh wasn't quite authentic, either. But he wasn't about to get into it with her now.

He turned to DJ. "Let me show you to a room."

"It was nice meeting you," Leah called after them.

"You, too," DJ said over her shoulder, and then added only for his ears as they climbed the stairs and rounded a corner, "She doesn't want me here. Wouldn't it be better if I—"

"She isn't my *girlfriend*. She's the wife of my former best friend. I have no idea what she's doing here, so what she wants is really of no interest to me."

DJ WAS SURPRISED at his words. He'd been so protective of her, and yet he seemed angry at the woman they'd left downstairs.

He saw her surprise as they reached the end of the hall, and he started to open a door but stopped. "I don't mean to seem cold, but it's what she's not telling me about her and her husband that has me worried."

"It's none of my business."

He studied her openly. "Come on, let's hear it. I can tell there is something on your mind."

"Did the two of you ever—"

"No. She was always Charlie's girl, and before you ask, no, I was never interested in her."

"It's odd, then, because she seems very possessive of you."

He shrugged and pushed open the door to a beautiful room done in pastels.

"What a pretty room."

He didn't seem to hear her. "I'm right next door if you need me. Leah is downstairs in the guest room."

"Who's room is this?" She realized her mistake at once. "I shouldn't have asked."

"I was engaged to a woman with a young daughter. This was going to be her room, but it didn't work out."

"I'm sorry."

He shook his head. "Looking back, I loved the thought of having a child more than I loved having her mother as my wife." He took a step toward the door. "Get unpacked if you like, then come downstairs. Let's find out if Leah really can cook or not."

After he left, DJ looked around the beautiful room. He'd made it so pretty for the little girl. There was such love in the room. She felt sad for him. How lucky that child would have been in so many ways.

She took her time unpacking what little she'd brought, giving Beau time with Leah. Whatever was going on between them, she didn't want to be in the middle of it. She had enough troubles of her own.

Taking out her phone, she put in a call to the prison. Her father was still in serious condition at the hospital.

She withdrew the photo of her mother from her purse and sat down in the white wooden rocker to study it. This woman had been her mother. She hadn't died in childbirth. No, instead, she'd apparently given up her first child to make her family happy, then married another man and had another child.

But what, if anything, did this have to do with the man who'd shot at her? According to what Beau had been able to find out, her mother really had died recently. So who wanted her dead? The grandmother who'd refused to talk to her? Zinnia had said that her mother's family had money. Surely it couldn't be that simple.

But her father had known the moment he looked at the photo. Her mother's family had found her, and that had terrified him enough that he'd pressured Beau Tanner to protect her.

But what about the other daughter? The one who'd had the doll? What about her half sister?

As JIMMY GRABBED at her, Stacy swung her fist and caught him under the left eye. He let out a curse. His grip loosened and she shoved open the door, only to have him drag her back. He thrust his hand down the front of the dress she'd bought for the date. She heard the fabric tear as he groped for her breasts.

With his free hand, he grabbed her flailing wrists and dragged her hard against him. "You like it rough? You'll get it rough," he said, squeezing her right breast until she cried out.

Stacy hardly heard the driver's-side door open. Jimmy had been leaning against it and almost fell out as the door was jerked open.

"She said stop," a familiar male voice said.

Jimmy let go of her, pulling his hand from inside her dress to turn angrily toward the open door—and the intruder. All he got out was "What the he—" when a fist hit him between the eyes.

Stacy saw it only out of the corner of her eye. The moment Jimmy let go of her, she slid across the seat and climbed out of the pickup. That was when she saw who her savior was. Mailman Burt Olsen's face was set, his voice dangerously calm. "You go on inside now, Ms. Cardwell. I'll take care of this."

She hesitated only a moment before scurrying up the steps. Once on the porch, she turned back. Just as she'd feared, Jimmy was out of the truck and looking for a fight. He took a swing, but Burt easily ducked it and caught Jimmy in the jaw with a left hook. He toppled back toward the open truck door. Burt doubled him over as he fell, shoved him back into the truck and closed the door.

"He won't be bothering you anymore tonight," the mailman called over to her. "But if you need me to stay…"

She almost couldn't find the words, she was so surprised. "No, I'm fine now. But thank you, Burt."

He tipped his baseball cap. Past him, she could see where he'd parked his car and walked up the mountainside. He'd come to her rescue after seeing what had been going on at the restaurant, and all she could think was that he'd let his supper get cold to do it.

Inside the cabin, she locked her door just in case Jimmy—*excuse me*—James, didn't get the hint. The man was a fool, but he wasn't stupid, she told herself. Glancing out the window, she saw that Burt was waiting for Jimmy to leave. She was relieved when a few minutes later she heard his truck start up and drive away.

In the bedroom, she saw that her dress was ruined. She tossed it into the trash. Thinking about Burt Olsen, she had to smile. She'd never seen this side of him before.

JIMMY HAD NEVER been so furious. Who the devil had that man been? Stacy's sweetheart? Nice of her to mention, if that was the case. But he'd called her Ms. Cardwell. Must have been a hired man.

Not that it mattered. He'd sat for a moment, stunned

and bleeding and planning his revenge. The lights went out in Stacy's cabin. He considered breaking down the door but realized he wasn't up to it. There was always another day. The woman would pay.

As he started the truck's engine to drive out of the ranch, he thought about the dude who'd hit him. If he ever saw him again...

He hadn't gone far when his headlights flashed over someone in the shadows of one of the outbuildings. For a moment he thought it was the man who'd attacked him. He slowed and saw his mistake. This man, who ducked behind the barn, was much larger, dressed in all black. He was carrying something. The moonlight had caught on the barrel of a rifle.

Jimmy sped on by, pretending not to have noticed. As he drove down the road to where it dropped over a rise, he realized he'd seen the man before. It was the lineman he'd seen on one of the power poles when he'd driven in earlier.

"Lineman, my ass," he said to himself as he quickly pulled over and cut the engine. He pulled his hunting knife from under the seat.

It was time to take care of the competition. He quietly opened his door and stepped out into the winter night. He could see his breath as he started back toward the barn. The pro must be waiting for DJ Justice to return. Stacy had said earlier that she thought DJ had left with some neighboring cowboy.

Well, Jimmy had a surprise for the man, he thought with a grin. He'd take care of the pro, and then maybe he'd double back for Stacy. He was feeling much better suddenly. And if the bitch thought she would get rid of him that easily, she was sadly mistaken.

BEAU FOUND LEAH setting the table for three. "So, what's going on?"

She looked up as if she'd been lost in thought and he'd startled her. "Supper is almost ready. I made a casserole. I'm not much of a cook, but—"

"I'm not talking about food. What are you really cooking up?"

Leah gave him a blank look. "I told you—"

"You were expecting a package, but…" She started to interrupt. He stopped her with an angry slash of his hand through the air. "What are you really doing here? Earlier you told me that you and Charlie were in trouble and you needed my help."

"I was wrong. This is something that will have to work itself out on its own. I can't involve you."

"You've already involved me. I'm tired of whatever game this is that you're playing. Tell me what the hell is going on."

She slowly put down the plate she'd been holding, straightened the napkin and silverware and then finally looked up at him. "There is a lot I can't tell you. Charlie and I…we've become involved in some…covert work. Our latest…assignment didn't go so well. I got out. Charlie…" Her voice broke. "We made a pact years ago that if we ever got separated, we would meet here." Her eyes glistened. "Because you were always our one harbor even in college."

"Why didn't you tell me that right away?" he asked quietly as he considered what she'd told him.

"Because I didn't come here to involve you in anything. You and your friend aren't in any danger. Charlie's and my work is done far from here. No one knows

I'm here except Charlie. I made sure that I wasn't followed."

He had a million questions, which he suspected she wasn't going to answer anyway, but the creak of the stairs told him that their conversation was over. At least for now.

He'd never been a trusting man—thanks to his father. He hated the way his mind worked. He questioned what most people told him. Leah was at the top of the list right now.

The knock at the door made them both jump. Beau had taken off his shoulder holster and hung it by the door. He stepped to it now and motioned for Leah to go into the den. DJ had stopped on the stairs. One look at him and she'd frozen in midstep.

Another knock, this one harder. Beau strode to the door and pulled his weapon. Stepping to the side, he opened the door, the weapon ready.

He felt a moment of shock when he looked at the rugged, clearly exhausted man standing there. *"Charlie?"*

Chapter Sixteen

Andrei heard the car engine as someone left the ranch. He frowned as he waited for the sound of the vehicle crossing the bridge and didn't hear it. He listened. A chill moved up his spine. He had been watching the house from his hiding spot. But now he stopped at the edge of the barn and sniffed the air.

The vehicle had definitely not crossed the bridge. Nor had it turned back. He would have heard it. That meant that it had stopped. The winter night was so quiet he could hear the ice crack on the edge of the river. He heard the soft click of a car door being closed and readied himself.

The driver had seen him. That rattled him enough. But the driver was also trying to sneak up on him. That meant the person would be armed with some kind of weapon.

All Andrei had was a rifle. But he didn't want to shoot and call attention to himself. So he would wait until the man reached the corner of the barn and then he would jump him. He was ready.

He pressed his back against the side of the barn at the corner and waited. This would complicate things, he thought, on a job that was already complicated as it was. But since his accident, he'd been frustrated. Maybe this was exactly what he needed to let out some of that anxiety.

It had always been more satisfying to kill someone with his bare hands than shoot them from a distance. Given that his leg still hurt like hell, he probably should have walked away. But it was too late now. A twig under the snow snapped close by. No time to make a run for it even if he could have run. This could end only one way. One of them was about to die.

The man came around the corner of the barn. The large knife blade in his hand caught the winter light.

"I'M AFRAID WE won't be joining you for dinner," Charlie said after he and Beau had hugged like the old friends they were. His gaze met his wife's. She stood a few feet away, tears in her eyes and relief etched on her face. She hadn't moved since Beau had opened the door, as if to give the two men some time.

"We need to get going, but it is great seeing you," Charlie said.

"That's it?" Beau demanded as Leah scurried down the hall to the guest room, returning moments later with her overnight bag. She stepped to her husband's side and pressed her face into his neck for a moment, his arm coming around her. The hug was hard and filled with emotion. Clearly this was the package she'd been waiting for.

Charlie had always been good-looking. Now, even though he appeared a little haggard, his smile was infectious. "It is so good to see you. One of these days, we'll be back permanently. I hope we can get together then, have a couple of beers and talk. But right now…"

Beau shook his head. He'd been angry at Leah for not telling him what was really going on. But he couldn't be angry with Charlie, his old friend. "Just be careful." He shook Charlie's hand and watched as the two disappeared down the road. Beau saw car lights flash on and heard the sound of an engine, and then they were gone as if they'd never been there.

He turned to look at DJ.

"Are you all right?" she asked.

He gave her a quick nod. "I hope you're hungry. We have a lot of casserole to eat."

She moved toward the kitchen. "I'd better take the casserole out of the oven, then."

"Maybe we could just sit in front of the fire and have a drink while it cools down a little. I could use one." He moved into the living room and stepped to the bar.

"Wine for me," she said when he offered her a bourbon like the one he'd poured for himself. "You don't have to say anything."

He ran a hand over his face and let out a bitter laugh as they sat in front of the fire. "I didn't trust her. Leah was one of my best friends years ago, and when she showed up..." He met DJ's gaze. "I hate how suspicious I am of people. I question everything."

DJ WAS SILENT for a moment before she said, "Your father was a con man, right?" He nodded, making her smile. "And you expect us to be trusting?" She laughed at that. "We grew up with no stability, no security, no feeling that everything was going to be all right. How did you expect us to turn out?"

"You might be the only person who understands. But you seem to have it all together."

"I *do*?" She laughed again. "It's just an act." The wood popped and sparked in the fireplace. Golden warm light flickered over them. She took a drink of her wine and felt heat rush through her.

"You think we will ever be like other people?" he asked.

"Probably not. But maybe at some point we won't have so much to fear."

"I remember the first time I saw you. Those big brown eyes of yours really got to me. I wanted to save you. I told myself that if I ever got the chance, I would do anything to help you."

She met his gaze and felt a start at what she saw in those blue eyes. Thinking of how it had felt to be in his arms, she yearned for him to hold her. It wouldn't change anything. There was still someone out there who wanted to kill her, but for a while...

Except she knew that just being held wasn't enough. He made her feel things she'd never felt with another man. She would want his mouth on hers, his body—

"We should probably eat some of that casserole," she said, getting to her feet. She no longer wanted temporary relief from her life. Could no longer afford it. Tomorrow morning would be too hard on her. Too hard to let go of this cowboy and the connection between them that had started so many years ago.

Beau seemed to stir himself as if his thoughts had taken the same path as her own. "Yes."

They ate in a tense silence, the fire crackling in the living room, the kitchen warm.

"This is good," she said, even though she hardly

tasted the casserole. She was glad when the meal was over and wished that Beau hadn't insisted on helping her with the dishes.

"I think I'll turn in," she said as soon as they'd finished cleaning up the kitchen.

He looked almost disappointed. "See you in the morning."

She watched him go to the bar and pour himself another bourbon. When she headed up the stairs, he was standing in front of the fireplace, looking into the flames.

Her steps halted, but only for a moment. She *did* understand him. They had a bond that went back all those years. She felt as if she'd always known him. Always...felt something for him.

That thought sent her on up the stairs to her room. But she knew she wouldn't be able to sleep. She felt lost, and she knew that Beau did, too.

She lay in bed, remembering the older woman's voice on the phone. Her grandmother. And hearing the woman crying so hard that she couldn't talk. Was this really a woman who wanted her dead?

BEAU HAD JUST put the coffee on the next morning when he heard DJ coming down the stairs. The phone rang. He'd had a hell of a time getting to sleep knowing that DJ was only yards down the hall. He couldn't help worrying about what the day would bring. A phone call this early in the morning couldn't bode well.

"Beau Tanner," he said.

"It's Marshal Savage, Beau. I've got some news. A man by the name of Jimmy Ryan, a suspected small-time hit man, was found dead on the ranch this morning. Based on the evidence we found in his vehicle, we believe he was the shooter yesterday. He had a high-powered rifle and a photo of DJ with a target drawn on her face."

"You said he's dead?"

"His throat was cut. Earlier last evening, he'd gotten into an altercation with a local man here on the ranch. We suspect the disagreement ended on the road on the way out of the ranch. Jimmy Ryan was found some yards off the road by one of our barns."

He couldn't believe what he was hearing. "So, it's over?" he said and glanced at DJ.

"It certainly appears that way."

"Do we know who hired him?"

"Not yet. We'll continue investigating. I'll let you know if anything new turns up. Dana wanted to make sure that DJ knew. She has her heart set on her cousin staying until after Christmas, and since it is so close…"

"I'll tell DJ and do everything I can to keep her in Montana until after Christmas." He ended the call and found himself grinning in relief. It seemed impossible. The hit man had gotten into an argument with someone and it ended in his death? He wouldn't have believed it if it wasn't for what the marshal had found in the man's vehicle.

"That was the marshal," he said. "They think they have your hit man."

"They caught him?"

Beau didn't want to get into the details this early in the morning, so he merely nodded. "He's dead, but they found evidence in his vehicle that makes it pretty apparent that he was the shooter. I don't know any more than that."

"I heard you ask if they knew who'd hired him."

He shook his head. "I'm sure they'll check his cell phone and bank account. But all that takes time. Hud did say that Dana would be heartbroken if you didn't stay for Christmas. He begged me to get you to stay." He held up his hand as he saw that she was about to argue. "Whatever you decide, I'm sure you don't want to leave until we know more. So…while we're waiting, I have an idea. Have you ever cut your own Christmas tree?"

She looked surprised before she laughed. "I've never even had a real tree."

He waved his arms toward his undecorated living room with Christmas so close. "Never bothered with it myself. But this year, I feel like getting a tree. You up for it?"

DJ HAD A dozen questions, but she could see that they would have to wait. To her surprise, she was more than up for getting a Christmas tree. "After that amazing news, I'd love to go cut a tree."

"Great. Let's get you some warm clothes, and then we are heading into the woods."

She loved his excitement and her own. Clearly they were both relieved. The man who'd shot at her was dead. It was over. She had planned on being gone by Christmas. She still thought that was best. But what would it hurt to help Beau get a Christmas tree?

Dressed as if she was headed for the North Pole, DJ followed Beau through the snow and up into the pine trees thick behind his house. They stopped at one point to look back. She was surprised again at how quaint his place looked in its small valley surrounded by mountains.

"You live in paradise," she said, captured by the moment.

"It is, isn't it?" He seemed to be studying his house as if he hadn't thought of it that way before. "Sometimes I forget how far I've come." He glanced over at her. "How about you?"

She nodded. "We aren't our parents."

He laughed. "Thank goodness." His gaze lit on her.

DJ saw the change in his expression the moment before he dropped the ax, reached out with his gloved hand and, cupping her neck, drew her to him. "I believe you owe me a kiss."

His lips were cold at first and so were hers. The kiss was short and sweet. Their breaths came out in puffs as he drew back.

"You call that a kiss?" she taunted.

His gaze locked with hers. His grin was slow, heat in his look. And then his arms were around her. This kiss was heat and light. It crackled like the fire had last night. She felt a warmth rush through her as he deepened the kiss. She melted against him, wrapped in his arms, the cold day sparkling around them.

When he pulled back this time, his blue eyes shone in the snowy light in the pines. Desire burned like a blowtorch in those eyes. He sounded as breathless as she felt. "If we're going to get a tree..." His voice broke with emotion.

"Yes," she agreed. "A tree." She spotted one. It was hidden behind a much larger tree, its limbs misshapen in its attempt to fight for even a little sunlight in the shadow.

"Dana has this tradition of giving a sad-looking tree the honor of being a Christmas tree." She walked over to the small, nearly hidden tree. "I like this one. It's…"

He laughed. "Ugly?"

"No, it's beautiful because it's had a hard life. It's struggled to survive against all odds and would keep doing that without much hope. But it has a chance to be something special." There were tears in her eyes. "It's like us."

He shook his head as if in wonder as he looked at her, then at the tree.

"Okay, you want this one? We'll give the tree its moment to shine."

"Thank you." She hugged herself as she watched him cut the misshapen pine tree out of the shadow it had been living under.

He studied the tree for a moment before he sheathed his ax. "Come on, tree. Let's take you home."

BIANCA DIDN'T ASK until they were both on the plane and headed for Montana. "You knew about her? My sister? Since the beginning?"

Ester nodded. "Your mother couldn't keep anything from me."

"But you didn't tell Grandmama?"

The housekeeper sighed. "Your mother made me promise, and what good would it have done? I'd hoped that in time… Marietta sent your mother to Italy to stay with an aunt there while she quietly had the marriage annulled. The next time I saw your mother, she was married and pregnant with you."

Bianca shook her head. "How could she have just forgotten about the baby she left behind?"

"She never forgot. When I made that rag doll for you, your mother insisted I make one for your...sister."

"That's why you left my doll and a photograph in her apartment."

"I had a nephew of mine do it. I wanted to tell her everything, but I was afraid."

She turned to look at the older woman. "Afraid my grandmother would find out."

"Afraid it would hurt you. I'd done it on impulse when I realized your grandmother was trying to find DJ."

"DJ? Is that what she calls herself?"

"It was a nickname her father gave her."

"So you saw her occasionally?"

Ester sighed. "Only from afar. Her father insisted. I would tell your mother how she looked, what she was wearing..." Tears filled her eyes. "It was heart-breaking."

"She was well cared for?"

"Well enough, I guess. Her father wouldn't take the money offered him by your grandmother's lawyer at the time the marriage was annulled."

Bianca scoffed. "So maybe he isn't as bad a man as Grandmama makes him out to be."

"Your grandmother had good reason given that he never amounted to anything and is now in prison. But he raised your sister alone and without any help from the family. I admire him for that, even though it was not an...ordinary childhood for DJ. I know he feared that the family would try to take her. I was the only one he let see her—even from a distance."

"I always wanted a sister," Bianca said more to herself than to Ester.

"I know. And I always felt sad when you said that growing up, knowing you *had* a sister. But it wasn't my place to tell you."

"Until now. Why *did* you tell me now?" Bianca asked, turning in her seat to face Ester.

Ester hesitated. Bianca could tell that the housekeeper didn't want to say anything negative about her grandmother.

"Because you were afraid of what my grandmother might do," Bianca said, reading the answer on the woman's face.

"No, I was afraid of what Roger Douglas would do. I knew I couldn't stop him, but you could."

"But did I stop him in time?" Bianca looked out the plane window. *She had a sister.* Her heart beat faster at the thought. How could her grandmother have kept something like this from her? Worse, her own mother?

She'd seen how her grandmother had used money to control Carlotta. She had always told herself that she wouldn't let Marietta do the same thing to her and yet she had taken all the gifts, the Ivy League education, the trips, all of it knowing that she'd better bring the right man home when the time came.

"Do you think she'll be all right by herself?" she asked Ester.

The housekeeper smiled. "Your grandmother is much stronger than any of us give her credit for. But I called my sister while you were getting our tickets. She can handle Marietta."

"Thank you. No matter what she's done, she's my grandmama."

"She is that."

Bianca closed her eyes. She'd lost her father at an

early age, so all she'd had was her mother, grandmother and, of course, Ester. It was Ester who had
kissed her forehead each night, who got her off to
school, who doctored the scrapes and lovingly applied
the medicine. Her mother had always seemed lost in
thought. She assumed that no one noticed how much
wine she had at night before she stumbled to her room
in the huge house overlooking the ocean.

Now Bianca wondered if giving up her first child
had haunted her. When she'd often had that faraway,
sad look in her eyes, was it Dee Anna Justice she was
thinking about?

If so, she knew she should have been jealous of the
hours her mother had been off—if even in her mind—
with her other daughter. Had she loved her more? It
didn't matter. She felt no jealousy.

Opening her eyes, she looked out the plane window again. They were almost there. She wasn't going
to let anything—or anyone—keep her from her sister.

Bianca had always felt as if there was something
missing from a life in which she seemed to get anything she wanted.

What she'd really wanted, though, was a sibling.
She remembered asking her mother once if she could
have more children. She'd wanted a brother or sister
so badly.

"Don't be ridiculous," her mother had snapped.

"I know Daddy's dead, but can't you find another
man—"

"Stop it, Bianca. Just stop it." She'd sent her to ask
Ester about dinner. As Bianca had left the room, she'd
looked back to see her mother go to the bar to pour herself a large glass of wine. Her mother had been crying.

She'd never seen her mother cry before, so she'd made a point of keeping her desire for a sibling to herself after that.

Now she understood those tears. Had her mother ached for that other daughter just as Bianca had ached for her?

The captain announced that they would be landing in the Gallatin Valley soon.

"Maybe we should call this ranch," Ester said, but Bianca shook her head.

"I don't want them to know we're coming." When Ester seemed surprised by that, she added, "If you were my sister, would you want to meet us? I can't take the chance she might leave to avoid us, especially if Grandmama has...done something."

Ester nodded.

Bianca reached over and took the housekeeper's hands. "I hope she likes me."

Ester's eyes filled with tears. "She will love you."

STACY WAS IN SHOCK. When she'd told her sister what had happened last night, she hadn't heard yet about Jimmy. "Burt wouldn't kill Jimmy. He wouldn't kill *anyone*."

"You said yourself that you'd never seen him so angry and that he hit Jimmy twice," Dana argued after she had told Stacy about Jimmy's body being found out by the barn, his throat slit. "Anyway, Hud has only taken Burt in for questioning based on what you told me."

Stacy got up from the kitchen table to pace. She'd lived around her brother-in-law long enough to know how these things worked. Hud would have to go by the evidence. "Burt hit him. Jimmy fought back. Of course there will be some of Burt's DNA on him, but that doesn't mean Burt killed him."

She couldn't believe this was happening. Jimmy was dead. But that wasn't as upsetting as Burt being blamed for it.

"Hud will sort it all out." Her sister eyed her with a mixture of pity and concern. "I thought you weren't interested in Burt."

Stacy hated to admit that she'd felt that way until last night. But she'd seen a different side to him. "He rescued me from Jimmy. He followed us from the restaurant because he was worried about me. And with good reason. I don't know why I agreed to go out with Jimmy. I made excuses for him back in high school when he forcibly took my virginity. He said he was so turned on by me that he couldn't stop himself and it was my fault."

Dana shook her head in obvious disgust. "All while you were saying no?"

She nodded. "I tried to push him off…but I didn't try hard enough back in high school. Last night I would have fought him to my dying breath."

Her sister didn't look pleased to hear that. "I told Hud what you told me, but he will want your side of the story," Dana said, picking up the phone.

Stacy shook her head as her sister started to hand her the phone. She realized that Hud would have questioned her earlier, but she had taken the kids to school. "I'm going down to his office. He's questioning the wrong person."

"I should warn you, he'll want to know where you were last night," her sister said behind her.

She turned slowly. "You can't think *I* killed Jimmy."

"Of course not."

"If I was going to kill him, I would have done it years ago after he raped me. I think until last night, I was still blaming myself for what happened—just as he let me do all these years. Now that I think about it, if Burt hadn't shown up when he did…" She looked up at her sister. "I would have killed him before I let him rape me again."

She went out the door, knowing that she'd made herself look guilty. Better her than Burt.

Chapter Seventeen

Andrei heard the news at breakfast in a small café at Meadow Village. He had tried to go about his day as usual, pretending to be one of the many tourists at the resort for the holidays. No one paid him any mind, since he wasn't limping as badly as he had been.

It wasn't like he could go to Cardwell Ranch. The law was crawling all over the place. Dee Anna Justice wasn't there, anyway. He hadn't seen her or the cowboy since the two had driven away together. But he was convinced she would be back, and the ranch was much easier for his purposes than driving back into the narrow canyon to get to the private investigator/cowboy's house. He assumed the cowboy would take her to his place.

As he ate, he knew that after last night this would be the perfect time for him to just leave, put all of this behind him.

But his pride wasn't going to let that happen.

"The man's throat was cut," a woman whispered to another at the next table. She shuddered and then leaned closer to the other woman. "I heard from my friend at the marshal's office that the dead man was a professional killer."

That caught his interest. His heart began to pound, making it hard to hear what else the woman was saying. So, there had been another contract. He swore under his breath. Things were getting so damned complicated.

"Do they know who did it?" the other woman whispered back.

"Well...you know Burt Olsen?"

"The *mailman*?"

Out of the corner of his eye, he saw her nod. "I heard he's been taken in for questioning. He had gotten into a fight with the man earlier that night."

"Burt Olsen? I just find that hard to believe. That he would...cut a man's throat." She shivered. "Burt always seems so nice."

"You know what they say about deep water."

Poor Burt, he thought. Common sense told him that he'd been given the perfect way out. The cops would think they had their man. Dee Anna Justice would let her guard down. So would her cowboy. He could still finish this job, collect his money and leave the country before his birthday. That's how he had to play this while his luck held.

BEAU STOOD UP the Christmas tree in the living room and stepped back to consider it. "Wow, it looks better than I thought it would. Pushed against the wall like that, it really isn't bad." He turned to see DJ smiling at the tree.

"It's beautiful. It doesn't even need ornaments."

He laughed. "That's good, because I don't own any. I thought we could string some popcorn. I'll pick up some lights when I go to town."

His gaze met hers. That kiss earlier had almost had him making love to her in the snow up on the mountain. He stepped to her now. She moved into his arms as naturally as a sunrise. He held her close, breathing in the fresh-air scent of her.

"DJ," he breathed against her hair.

She pulled back to look up at him. What he saw in her eyes sent a trail of heat racing through his veins. She stood on tiptoes to kiss him. Her lips brushed against his. Her gaze held his as the tip of her tongue touched his lower lip.

He felt a shudder of desire. Taking her hand, he led her over to the fireplace. "Are you sure about this?"

"I've never been more sure of anything in my life."

Golden light flickered over them as they began to undress each other. He could feel her trembling as he brushed his lips across hers.

He trailed kisses from the corner of her mouth down to her round breasts. He found her nipple and teased the hard tip with his tongue, then his teeth. She arched against him as they slowly slid down to the rug in front of the fire. The flames rose. The fire crackled and sighed.

On the rug, the two made love as if neither of them ever had before.

BIANCA AND ESTER landed at Gallatin Field outside Bozeman and rode the shuttle to the car rental agency. While they waited, Bianca looked out at the snow-covered mountains. She'd never driven on snow and ice before. For a moment she questioned her impulsiveness at jumping on a plane and coming here.

Wasn't her grandmother always telling her to slow

down, to think things out before she acted? Just the thought of her grandmother made her more determined to get to Cardwell Ranch—and her sister.

"Here's your key," said the man behind the desk. "Your car is right out there. Do you know where you're going?" he asked, holding up a map.

"Big Sky," she said and watched as he drew arrows on the map and handed it to her.

"Maybe we should call," Ester said as they left. "Just showing up at their door... Maybe we should warn them not only that we're coming but that maybe your grandmother did something she regrets."

Bianca shook her head. "I'd rather take my chances. Anyway, call and say what? We have no idea what is going on. For all we know..." Her voice broke. "I know she did wrong, but I still can't get her into trouble. I keep telling myself that Grandmama wouldn't...hurt her own grandchild."

"In Marietta's eyes, *you* are her only grandchild."

"I'm furious with her, but I can't throw her under the bus," Bianca said, making Ester smile.

"I've wanted to do just that for years, but I understand what you're saying. You don't want her going to prison. I don't, either. It's why I called you and told you what was going on."

"We are only about forty miles away." Bianca shot her a look as she drove, following the man's directions from the rental agency. "Roger was the one who hired someone. Maybe she didn't stop him, but it wasn't her idea, right?"

Ester looked away. "I doubt the law would see it that way. She saw Walter Justice as a problem." She shrugged. "Now she sees his daughter as one."

"But Walter is still alive."

"Last I heard, but he's also in prison."

Bianca shot her a look. "You can't think she had anything to do with that!"

Ester shrugged. "I wouldn't put anything past your grandmother. Let's just hope that phone call she made was…real and that she has stopped all this foolishness."

Bianca stared at the highway into the canyon and the steep mountains on each side. "Look what she did to my mother. Forcing her to keep Dee Anna a secret from me. I'm not sure if I can forgive her if something has happened to my sister."

DJ FELT AS if her life couldn't get any better. It was a strange feeling. After years of holding back, of being afraid really to live, she'd given herself to Beau Tanner completely. Her heart felt so full she thought it might burst.

"It is really over?" she asked him the next morning on the way to Cardwell Ranch. Dana had called and invited them over for brunch, saying the crime scene tape was gone and the ranch was back to normal.

Beau squeezed her hand. "You're safe."

Safe. She realized she'd never felt it before. It was a wonderful feeling, she thought as she looked out on the winter landscape. It had snowed again last night, huge flakes that drifted down in the ranch light outside Beau's home. She'd felt as if she was in a snow globe, one with a cozy little house inside. Wrapped in Beau's arms under the down comforter, she'd found paradise.

Last night she hadn't thought about the future, only the present. But this morning as they neared the turn-off to Cardwell Ranch, she couldn't help but think about her mother's family. What now? If it was true that they'd tried to kill her, fearing she wanted their money… The thought made her heart ache.

Beau reached over and took her hand. "It's going to be all right."

She couldn't help but smile at him. Nor could she help but believe him. With Beau in her corner, she felt she could take on the world.

BIANCA TURNED OFF the highway at Big Sky and stopped a few yards from the Cardwell Ranch sign that hung over the entrance. She glanced at Ester, who quickly took her hand and squeezed it.

"You can do this," Ester said. "She's your sister."

She nodded, smiling in spite of her fear, and drove under the sign and across the bridge spanning the river. She felt as if she'd been waiting for this her whole life. Even with all the lost years, she and DJ still had time to get to know each other. If her sister wanted to.

Bianca felt a stab of fear. What if her grandmother was right and this young woman wanted nothing to do with her family? With her?

A large new barn appeared ahead along with a half-dozen cabins set back in the woods. But it was the rambling old farmhouse that she drove to, with the black Suburban parked in front. She saw a curtain move.

"Tell me I'm not making a mistake," she said to Ester.

"Letting your sister know she's not alone in this can't be a mistake," the older woman said.

Bianca smiled over at her. "I don't know what I

would have done without you all these years." She opened her door, Ester following suit.

The steps seemed to go on forever, and then they were on the porch. Bianca was about to knock when the door opened, startling her.

A dark-haired woman in her thirties looked surprised. Was this DJ? Was this her sister?

"I'm Bianca," she said at the same time the woman said, "I'm sorry, I thought you were…someone else."

The woman looked from Bianca to Ester and back. "Did you say Bianca?"

She nodded. "I'm looking for Dee Anna Justice," Bianca said.

"She's not here right now," the woman said excitedly. "But I'm her cousin Dana."

Feeling a surge of relief at the woman's apparent welcome, she said, "I'm her…sister, Bianca."

Dana smiled. "Yes, her sister. What a surprise."

"I hope not too much of a surprise," she said. "This is Ester, a…a friend of mine. Is my sister here?"

"Please, come in," Dana said and ushered them into the warm living room. "I'll call DJ…Dee Anna, and let her know you're here. Please, have a seat. I was expecting her when you drove up."

Bianca sat in a chair by the fire, glancing around at the Western decor. Until this moment, she hadn't felt like she was in Montana. As Ester took a place on the couch next to her, she spotted the Christmas tree.

Dana turned her back, her cell phone at her ear, and said, "You should come home now," before disconnecting and dialing another number.

When she turned back to them, she saw what they were looking at—and no doubt the expressions on their surprised faces. "That's my orphan Christmas tree," Dana said with a laugh. "It's a long story." She seemed to be waiting for the call to go through, then said, "You aren't going to believe who is sitting in my living room. Your sister! Oh, it's her all right. She looks enough like you that there is no mistake. Okay, I'll tell her." Dana disconnected, smiling. "She's on her way and should be here any minute."

Bianca had never felt so nervous. Ester reached over and patted her hand. "It's going to be fine," the housekeeper whispered.

She nodded, smiling and fighting tears as she heard a vehicle pull up out front. Dana said, "In fact, she's here now."

"ARE YOU SURE you heard right?" Beau asked as he pulled up in front of the house.

Earlier DJ had been sitting cross-legged on the floor in front of the fire, stringing popcorn for their Christmas tree. She had been wearing one of his shirts over a pair of jeans. Her face had been flushed, either from the fire or their lovemaking earlier. She'd looked relaxed, content, maybe even happy. He'd lost another piece of his heart at the sight of her.

Now she looked as if she might jump out of her skin. "My sister. That must be her rental car. Why would she be at the ranch?" she asked, turning to meet his gaze.

"Apparently she wants to see you."

She shook her head, relieved after her call earlier to the hospital that her father was going to make it. "This is crazy. One minute all I have is my father, and now I have cousins and a *sister*?"

"Who might have hired a hit man to take you out." He pulled out his cell phone. "I'm calling Hud."

"No," she said, reaching for her door. "I want to meet her. I don't need the law there. She isn't going to try to kill me."

He hesitated and finally pocketed the phone. "She'll have to go through me first."

"Seriously, I don't think she'd be here now if she was behind this."

"Apparently you haven't dealt with as many criminals as I have."

DJ laughed and leaned over to give him a kiss. "I have a good feeling about this."

He wished he did.

Chapter Eighteen

DJ couldn't believe that she was going to meet her half sister after only recently finding out that she even existed. "How long do you think she's known about me?" she asked Beau as they walked to the porch steps.

He glanced over at her. "I have no idea."

"Sorry, I just have so many questions."

"Ideally she will be able to answer them all for you. Including who hired someone to kill you."

She looked over at him as they reached the door. "I haven't forgotten. But she's here. That makes her look innocent, don't you think?"

"I'd go with less guilty. But you have no idea what this woman wants. Or why she's shown up now. You have to admit, it's suspicious."

"Which is exactly why I don't think she's involved."

She could tell he didn't agree. "Well, you'll be here to protect me," she said as she reached for the doorknob.

"Yes, I will."

But before she could grab the doorknob, the door swung open, and there was Dana, practically jumping up and down in her excitement.

"Easy," he said behind her. "Let's not get carried away until we find out what is going on."

"I'm glad Beau's with you," Dana said as DJ entered the house. "Hud's on his way," she whispered to Beau loud enough that DJ heard it.

"Really, the two of you…" She stepped into the living room and stopped dead. The woman who rose from the chair by the fire looked more like their mother than even DJ did. DJ stared at her half sister. They looked so much alike it was eerie.

"Bianca?" she asked, although there was little doubt this was the half sister she'd been told about.

"Dee Anna. Or is it DJ? Oh, I'm just so glad you're all right," Bianca said, rushing to her to give her a quick hug. "I have wanted a sister my whole life. I can't believe we were kept apart." She stepped back to take in DJ. "We look so much alike. We could be twins." She let out a nervous laugh.

Out of the corner of her eye, DJ had seen Beau start to move. But he stopped short when Bianca merely threw her arms around DJ.

"I am so glad to see you," Bianca said as she stared at DJ. "I was so worried."

"Worried?" Beau asked only feet away.

Her sister hesitated. An older woman, whom DJ had barely noticed, stood then and moved to her. There was kindness in the woman's eyes. "I'm Ester."

"Ester," DJ repeated as Bianca stepped back to let Ester take DJ's hand.

"I made your doll," Ester said. "Your father kept me informed on how you were doing over the years. I wish I could have done more."

Tears welled in DJ's eyes. "Thank you. I named her—"

"Trixie. That's why I sent you Bianca's, so you would know there were two of them. Two of you. I couldn't let you go on believing you had no family or that no one cared other than your father."

DJ looked to her sister. "And my grandmother?"

Both women hesitated. Bianca looked guilty, which sent a sliver of worry burrowing under her skin.

"Grandmama is not well," Bianca said.

Ester let out a snort.

Just then, Marshal Hud Savage arrived. "What's going on?" he asked after Dana introduced him as her husband.

"That's just what I was about to ask," Beau said. "Where does a hit man fit into this happy reunion?"

ROGER DOUGLAS'S CELL PHONE vibrated in his pocket. It surprised him. All the way to the airport it had been buzzing constantly, but it had finally stopped until now. He'd thought, as he'd waited for his flight, that both Marietta and the accountant had given up.

Now he pulled it out, curious which one had decided to give it one more try. He saw who was calling and hurried to a quieter area before answering.

"You didn't tell me about the private investigator who isn't letting her out of his sight," Andrei Ivankov said.

Roger wasn't sure what to say. He'd taken the call only because he'd thought the hit man had finished the job. "I take it you haven't—"

"You take it right."

"It's just as well. The client wants to call off the—"

"I'm sorry, I must have misunderstood you."

"She doesn't want you to finish the job." Roger knew the man was born in Russia or some such place, but his English was better than Roger's own.

"I have been out here freezing my ass off and now she wants me to forget it? I had my doubts about dealing with you. I get paid no matter what, plus extra for my inconvenience, and if I don't get paid, I will track you down and make you wish you'd never—"

"Don't threaten me. There is nothing you can do to me. I really don't give a damn if you kill her or not." He'd raised his voice, and several people had turned to look in his direction. He disconnected the call, then tossed the phone to the floor and stomped it to death. Now a lot of people were staring at him.

Roger felt heat rise up his neck. He'd always prided himself on never losing his temper. But he wasn't that man anymore, he reminded himself. He wasn't the meek lawyer who had to kiss Marietta Pisani's feet.

He'd picked up what he could of the cell phone, tossed it in the trash and started back to his seat when he heard his flight called. Clutching the bag full of Marietta's money, he smiled as he got in line.

It wasn't until he was sitting down in first class, drinking a vodka tonic and dreaming of his new life, the bag shoved under the seat in front of him, that he relaxed. Just a few more minutes.

Glancing out the window, he felt his heart drop like a stone. Two security guards were headed for the plane along with several police officers. He downed his drink, figuring it was the last one he'd get for a while.

"It was a misunderstanding," Bianca assured the marshal. They had all gathered in the dining room around the large old oak table. She turned to her sister. She couldn't believe how much they looked alike. They really could have been twins. "You have to forgive Grandmama. It was her attorney, Roger Douglas. When she found out what he'd done…she was beside herself and demanded he put a stop to it."

Hud and Beau exchanged a glance. "I called the power company. They didn't have any men in our area."

"So the man who was seen on the power pole?" Beau asked.

Hud nodded. "It must have been the shooter."

"Shooter?" Bianca asked.

Dana filled them in on what had happened, first someone taking a shot at DJ, then a man found dead near one of the old barns. "He apparently had been hired to kill DJ."

Bianca's eyes welled with tears. "I'm so sorry. I had no idea. My grandmother had no idea. I'm just so thankful that he missed and that he is no longer a problem."

Hud's cell phone rang. He stepped away to take the call. The room went silent. Bianca prayed that it wouldn't be bad news. She was worried about her grandmother and what would happen now.

"That was the police in San Diego," Hud said as he came back to the table. "They've arrested Roger Douglas. Apparently he made a deal and told them everything, including that he had hired a hit man through another man to kill Dee Anna Justice. He was carrying a large sum of money that he admitted had been stolen from your grandmother, Bianca."

Bianca let out a relieved breath. "I never liked Roger."

"Me, either," Ester said. "He certainly pulled the wool over your grandmother's eyes for years."

"Where is your grandmother now?" Hud asked. "The police said they'd tried to reach her..."

Ester saw her alarm and quickly waved it off. "I got a text from my sister a few moments ago. May was looking after Marietta. She said the fool woman packed a bag and took the first flight out, headed this way."

There were surprised looks around the table. Then Dana got to her feet and announced, "I've made brunch. I think we should all have something to eat while we wait for our new arrival."

Hud said, "I'll have someone pick her up at the airport and bring her here. But the police in San Diego will still have a few questions for her."

DJ FELT AS IF she was in shock. She kept wanting to pinch herself. She'd gone from having only her father to having this family that kept getting bigger and bigger.

Dana told Bianca and Ester that they could stay in one of the cabins on the mountain as long as they wanted. "I know you and DJ have a lot to talk about. But first you have to share this brunch I've made."

"Are you sure there is enough?" Bianca asked. "We don't want to intrude."

Dana laughed. "I'm used to cooking for ranch hands. I always make too much. Anyway, you're family. There is always room at my table for family." She motioned DJ into the kitchen. "Are you all right?"

"I don't think I've ever been this all right," DJ said, smiling. She felt exhausted from everything that had happened. The Cardwells. Beau. Her near death. And finally meeting her sister and the woman who'd made her Trixie and had watched out for her from a distance. It felt as if it was all too much. And yet she'd never felt happier.

She hugged her cousin. "Thank you so much."

"It's just a little brunch," Dana said with a laugh.

"That and you, this ranch, everything you've done. Somehow I feel as if it all had to come together here where it began."

"Have you heard how your father is doing?" Dana asked.

"He's going to make it. His sentence is about up. He's getting out of prison soon." DJ wasn't sure how she felt about that. She could understand now why he'd been afraid of her mother's family finding out about her. The fact that he hadn't taken their money made her almost proud of him. Maybe there was more to her father than she'd originally thought. Maybe when he got out they could spend some time together, really get to know each other.

From the window, DJ could see Beau outside talking to Hud. Both looked worried. "They aren't going to arrest my grandmother, are they?" DJ asked as Dana followed her gaze to the two.

"No, I'm sure it is just as your sister said, a mistake, since that man has confessed to everything."

DJ hoped so. The marshal and Beau turned back toward the house. DJ stuck her head out the kitchen door to see Beau and Hud enter the house. Beau caught her eye and smiled reassuringly.

She felt a shaft of heat fall over her like the warm rays of the sun and almost blushed at the memory of their lovemaking. Beau was so tender and yet so strong and virile. Her heart beat a little faster just at the sight of him.

MARIETTA HAD ASSUMED she was being arrested when she landed at the airport and saw the two deputies waiting for her. She was pleasantly surprised to hear that she was being taken to the Cardwell Ranch, where her granddaughters were waiting for her.

On the drive up the canyon, she stared out at the snowy landscape, rough rocky cliffs and glazed-over green river. She'd never seen mountains like these, let alone this much snow, in her life. It kept her mind off what might be waiting for her once she reached the ranch.

Whatever was waiting, she deserved it, she told herself. She'd been a fool. The police had left a message that Roger Douglas had been arrested at the airport carrying a large amount of money on him. Her money. She shook her head. Who knew how much he had squandered? She would deal with that when she got home. If she got home.

Her chest ached. It was as if she could feel her old heart giving out. *Just stay with me a little longer. Let me try to fix this before I die.*

She was relieved when the deputy driving finally turned off the highway, crossed a bridge spanning the iced-over river and pulled down into a ranch yard. She stared at the large two-story house and took a breath.

One of the deputies offered to help her out, but she waved him off.

This was something she had to do herself. It very well might be the last thing she ever did.

Chapter Nineteen

They had just sat down to eat Dana's brunch when they heard a patrol car drive up.

Everyone looked toward the front door expectantly. DJ wasn't sure she was ready to meet her grandmother. This was all happening too fast, and yet she couldn't help being curious. This was the woman who thankfully hadn't put a hit out on her. But she was the woman who'd apparently planned to buy her off.

Standing up, DJ prepared to meet her grandmother. Everyone else rose as well and moved into the living room. Hud went to open the door for the elderly woman who'd just climbed the steps and pounded forcibly on the door. She remembered Bianca saying the woman wasn't well, a bad heart. Now she wondered if that was true or if that was just what her grandmother wanted her to believe.

Like Beau, she hated always being suspicious. Wasn't there a chance that they could change? That love could make them more trusting?

Love? Where had that come from? She glanced over at Beau and felt her heart do that little jump it did when she saw him. She did love him.

The realization surprised her. She'd cared about

some of the men she'd dated, but she'd never felt as if she was in love. Until this moment.

What a moment to realize it, she thought as an elderly woman with salt-and-pepper hair and intense brown eyes stepped into the room.

DJ felt Bianca take her hand. Beau was watching the older woman as if waiting for her to do something that would force him to take her down.

She almost laughed. He was so protective. He shot her a look that said, *You can do this.* She smiled. He had no idea how strange all this was for her. She'd dreamed of family, and now she had all the complications that came with one.

WHEN THE DOOR OPENED, Marietta almost fell in with it. "I want to see my granddaughter before you arrest me!" she said to the man in the marshal's uniform. It was just like them to have someone here to arrest her the moment she arrived at the house. But she wasn't leaving without a fight, she thought as the man stepped back and she barged in, more determined than ever.

What she saw made her stagger to a stop. Bianca standing next to a young woman who could have been her twin. Their resemblance to each other gave her a shock that almost stopped her old heart dead. This was the child Carlotta had given birth to? This beautiful thing?

"What are you doing here?" Ester demanded. The accusation in her housekeeper's tone shocked her. Clearly their relationship had changed.

"You're starting to remind me of your sister," she snapped. "I came to see my granddaughter."

"*Which* granddaughter?" Bianca asked. She was

holding DJ's hand, the two of them looking so formidable, so strong, so defiant. Her heart lodged in her throat as she looked at the two of them. She couldn't have been more proud or filled with shame. If she hadn't been the way she was, these two would have gotten to grow up together.

She could see her daughter in both of the women, but especially in DJ. The woman was more beautiful than even she knew. Marietta thought of that Bible verse about not hiding your light under a bushel basket. DJ was just coming into her own. Marietta wondered what had turned on that light inside her, then noticed the cowboy standing near her, looking just as fierce. Of course it had been a man.

"I came to see *both* granddaughters," she said and had to clear her voice. "But especially you, Dee Anna. I can't tell you how sorry I am that this is the first time we have ever met."

Carlotta was right. All she'd thought about was the family fortune and some ingrate of Walter Justice's trying to steal it. Staring at these two beautiful women, she felt a mountain of regret. She hadn't thought of Dee Anna as anything more than a mistake. She'd simply acted as she'd done all those years ago when she'd had Carlotta's marriage to Walter annulled. Both times she'd listened to Roger.

"DJ," Bianca said. "She goes by DJ."

Marietta smiled at her other granddaughter. She could see that the two women had already bonded. "DJ," she amended, her voice breaking as she held out her wrinkled hands to her granddaughter. "Can you ever forgive me?"

THERE WERE TEARS in her grandmother's eyes as DJ stepped to her and took both her hands in hers. Marietta pulled her into a hug. The older woman felt frail in her arms, and she was truly sorry that she hadn't known her before now.

"We should all sit down and have something to eat," Dana said. "Food and family go together."

"I need to ask Mrs. Pisani some questions," her marshal husband said.

"Not now. We are going to eat this brunch I made," Dana said in a no-nonsense tone as they gathered around the table again. "DJ, sit here by Beau and your grandmother. Ester and Bianca, would you mind sitting across from them? Hud—"

"Yep, I'm sitting down right where you tell me," he said.

A smattering of laughter moved through the room.

"I married a smart man," Dana said and introduced her husband and herself.

DJ didn't think she could eat a bite but was pleasantly surprised to find she could. "This is all so delicious," she told her cousin.

Everyone seemed to relax, commenting on how good the food was. Ester asked for one of the recipes. They talked about Montana, life on the ranch, Christmas and finally how they had come to know about each other. Marietta said little, picking at her food, her gaze on DJ.

Ester informed Marietta that Roger Douglas had been arrested. "He confessed not only to stealing your money but also to being behind hiring a hit man, so it looks like you're off the hook."

Her grandmother shook her head, smiling sadly.

"We both know better than that. So much of this is my fault. Carlotta was right." She teared up again but quickly wiped her eyes. "I'm just so happy that my granddaughters have found each other."

WHEN THE MEAL was over, DJ was sorry to see it end. Dana had offered the cabins on the mountainside to Bianca, Ester and Marietta, but Bianca had declined, saying she was worried about her grandmother.

"She looks too pale," her sister had said confidentially to DJ. "She shouldn't have flown. I think all this might have been too much for her. I want to take her to the hospital to make sure she is all right."

"I'm not sure what good that will do," Ester said, not unkindly. "The doctors have told her there is nothing they can do for her. We've all known she doesn't have much longer."

"I know," Bianca said.

"Do you mind if I come with you to the hospital?" DJ asked.

"No, not at all," her sister said and smiled.

As Hud left to head back to work and they prepared to leave, snow began to fall as another storm came through. The clouds were low. So was the light. "I know you need this time with your family," Beau said as they all headed out onto the porch. "But if you need me..."

That was just it. She needed him too much. He crowded her thoughts and made her ache for the closeness they had shared.

"I'd like to finish helping you decorate the tree," she said.

"I'd like that, too. But we have time. Christmas is still days away."

"Yes," she said. "It's a date, then." She bit her tongue. "You know what I mean."

He nodded. "We kind of skipped that part. Maybe... well, depending on what you have planned after Christmas..."

They left it at that as he started toward his vehicle.

THE CRIME SCENE tape was gone. Everything seemed to be back to normal around Cardwell Ranch, Andrei thought as he watched the goings-on through the crosshairs of his rifle.

There'd been a lot of company today. He'd watched them come and go, the man with Dee Anna Justice giving her a little more space.

Several times he could have taken a shot, but it hadn't been perfect.

Now everyone seemed to be leaving. His birthday was only days away. He had to make his move. His leg was better. Good enough.

He adjusted the high-powered rifle and scope. It didn't take him long to get Dee Anna Justice in the crosshairs. A head shot was the most effective, but at this distance he didn't want to take the chance.

For days he'd been conflicted. But now he felt nothing but calm. His reputation was at stake. He would finish this.

Shooting into a crowd was always risky, but the confusion would give him his chance to make a clean getaway. Now it felt almost too easy. Was this the shot he'd been waiting for?

He aimed for DJ's heart and gently pulled the trigger.

DJ AND HER newfound family stood on the porch, saying their goodbyes to Dana. Her grandmother stood a few feet away. DJ heard Bianca ask her if she was feeling all right.

Beau had stopped near his pickup. She could feel his gaze on her. Something in his expression made her ache to be in this arms. He was dressed in jeans, boots and that red-and-black wool coat. His black Stetson was pulled low, but those blue eyes were on her. Her skin warmed at the thought of his hands on her.

"You're my granddaughter in every sense of the word," Marietta said as she stepped to DJ and took both of her hands again. "If I have any money left—"

"I don't want your money. I never have."

Her grandmother nodded. "I am such a foolish old woman."

DJ shook her head and hugged the woman. Marietta hugged her hard for a woman who looked so frail. As she stepped back, DJ heard Beau let out a curse.

She looked past her grandmother to see him running toward her. He was yelling, "Shooter! Everyone get down!"

DJ couldn't move, the words not making any sense at first. Then she reached for her grandmother. But Marietta pushed away her hand. As she looked up into the older woman's face, she found it filled with love and something else, a plea for forgiveness, in the instant before the woman stepped in front of her as if to shield her.

The next thing she knew, Beau slammed into her, knocking her to the porch floor. "Everyone down!"

In the distance came the roar of an engine. Beau

was pushing her to move toward the door of the house. "Get inside! Hurry! DJ, are you hit?"

She couldn't do more than shake her head. "My grandmother?"

That's when she looked over and saw the woman lying beside her. Blood bloomed from her chest. DJ began to cry as Beau ushered them all inside the house, then carried Marietta in.

"Put her down here," Dana ordered, pointing to the couch near the Christmas tree. She had the phone in her hand. DJ knew she was already calling Hud and an ambulance.

She and her sister rushed to their grandmother's side.

"Stay here! No one leaves until I get back!" With that, Beau was gone.

BEAU DREW HIS own weapon from his shoulder holster. The sound of a vehicle engine turning over filled the icy winter air as he raced to his pickup. He could make out the silhouette of a vehicle roaring down the road toward Highway 191.

He started his engine, fishtailing as he punched the gas and went after it. By the time they reached the highway, he'd gained a little on what appeared to be an SUV.

The driver took off down the icy highway. Beau followed the two red taillights. He quickly got on his cell and called in the direction the man was headed, then tossed his cell aside to put all his attention on driving.

The highway was empty as the driver ahead of him left Big Sky behind and headed deeper into the canyon, going south toward West Yellowstone. But it was also icy. The last thing Beau wanted to do was end up in a ditch—or worse, the river. But he wasn't going to let the man get away.

As he raced after the vehicle, his mind raced, as well. Hud had been so sure that they had the hit man and that a local man had killed him. Was it possible another hit man had been hired when the first failed? Or had there always been two?

THIS WOULD BE how it ended. Andrei could see that now. For so long he'd had trouble envisioning his life after his forty-fifth birthday. Now he knew why.

He'd just killed some old woman. It was worse than he could have imagined. Shame made him burn. He had failed to kill his target and he wasn't going to get away, he thought as he looked back to see the pickup right behind him.

It was that cowboy. What was his story, anyway? The PI had been suspicious and jumpy from the start. Otherwise he wouldn't have spotted him just before he'd fired. The cowboy had probably caught the reflection off the rifle scope. Just Andrei's luck.

Ahead all he could see was snow. He hated snow. He hated cold. He hated this contract. All his instincts had told him to let it go. Stubbornness had made him determined to finish it no matter what. And all because of the coin toss. It had never let him down before. Not that it mattered now.

He felt his tires lose traction on the icy road. He touched his brakes as he felt the back of the car begin to slide and knew immediately that had been a mistake. But it was just another mistake, he thought as he cranked the wheel, trying to get the car to come out of the slide. Instead, it spun the other way. He was going too fast to save himself. He saw the guardrail coming up and closed his eyes.

BEAU'S HEART WAS POUNDING. He still couldn't believe how close DJ had come to being killed. If he hadn't lunged for her. If her grandmother hadn't stepped in front of the bullet. So many *ifs*.

The taillights ahead of him grew brighter as he closed the distance. He knew this road. He suspected the would-be assassin did not. He could see that the vehicle was a white SUV. Probably a rental.

The canyon followed the river, winding through the mountains in tighter turns. He pressed harder, getting closer. His headlights shone into the vehicle, silhouetting the driver. A single male.

Just then, he saw that the driver had taken the curve too fast. He'd lost control. Beau watched the SUV go into a slide. He let up off his gas as best he could. He knew better than to hit his brakes. They would both end up in the river.

The SUV began a slow circle in the middle of the road. He could see that the driver was fighting like hell to keep it on the road, no doubt overcorrecting. The front of the SUV hit the guardrail and spun crazily toward the rock wall on the other side, where it crashed into the rocks, then shot back out, ping-ponging from the guardrail to the cliffs on the slick road until it finally came to rest against the rocks.

Beau managed to get stopped a few yards shy of the SUV. He turned on his flashers and jumped out, glad there wasn't any traffic. Drawing his weapon, he moved to the vehicle.

The driver was slumped to one side, his deflated air bag in his lap and blood smeared on what was left of the side window. Beau tried to open the driver's-side door, but it was too badly dented. He could hear sirens in the distance as he reached through the broken glass to put a finger to the man's throat. He was still breathing, but for how long?

"GRANDMAMA," BIANCA CRIED and fell to her knees beside the couch. DJ, taking the towel Dana handed her, pressed it to the bleeding wound in Marietta's chest.

"An ambulance is on the way," Dana assured her, sounding scared. The towel was quickly soaked with blood.

DJ joined her sister, her heart breaking. "You saved my life," she said to her grandmother. "Why would you do that?"

Marietta smiled through her pain. "It still can't make up for what I've done. If I had time…"

"You have time," Bianca said. "You can't leave us now."

Her grandmother patted her hand weakly. "My old heart was going to play out soon, anyway. I didn't want you to know how bad it was or how little time I had." She looked from Bianca to DJ and back. "Seeing the two of you together… I'm happy for you. You have a sister now."

She looked to DJ, reached for her hand and squeezed it. "Forgive me?" she whispered.

"Of course," DJ said, and her grandmother squeezed her fingers. "Take care of each other." Her gaze shifted to Ester. "Take care of my girls."

Ester nodded, tears in her eyes.

Marietta smiled and mouthed "Thank you" as her eyes slowly closed. Her hands went slack in theirs. She smiled then as if seeing someone she recognized on the other side.

Bianca began to cry. DJ put her arm around her, and the two hugged as the sound of sirens grew louder and louder.

Epilogue

Beau looked out his office window, watching the snowstorm and feeling restless. It was over. DJ was safe. The bad guys were either dead or in jail. It hadn't taken Marshal Hud Savage long to put all the pieces together with Beau's help. The man Roger Douglas had hired was arrested and quickly made a deal, naming not one but two hit men. Andrei Ivankov, a professional hit man, died before reaching the hospital in Bozeman. Jimmy Ryan, a thug for hire, was also dead, killed, according to lab results, by Ivankov.

Mailman Burt Olsen was in the clear. According to Dana, Burt and her sister, Stacy, had a date for New Year's. Dana figured they'd be planning a wedding by Valentine's Day. Apparently Stacy hadn't waited for Burt to ask her out. She'd invited him to the movies and they'd hit it off, making Dana say, "I told you so."

Meanwhile, Dana's best friend, Hilde, went into labor Christmas Eve. She had a beautiful eight-pound, nine-ounce baby boy. Dana had called earlier to ask if Beau had heard from DJ. He'd said he'd been busy and now wished he'd asked how DJ was doing, since he was sure Dana had talked to her.

"You going to spend the whole day looking out that window?" demanded a deep female voice behind him.

Beau turned to look guiltily at his assistant, Marge. She stood, hands on hips, giving him one of those looks. "What do you want me to do?"

"You should never have let her leave in the first place."

"She was going to her grandmother's funeral in Palm Desert."

"You could have gone along."

He shook his head. "She needed time."

Marge scoffed at that and shook her head as if disappointed in him. "You mean *you* needed time. Apparently you haven't had enough time in your life."

"I hardly know the woman."

Marge merely mugged a face at him.

"It was too soon," he said, turning back to the window. "She had too much going on right then." He glanced over his shoulder. Marge was gone, but she'd left the door open.

He walked out into the reception area of the office to find her standing at her desk. "What? You aren't going to keep nagging me?"

"Would it do any good?" She sounded sad. Almost as sad as he felt.

NEW YEAR'S DAY, Dana listened to the racket coming from her living room and smiled to herself. There were children laughing and playing, brothers arguing good-naturedly, sister and sisters-in-law talking food and fabrics, cousins discussing barbecue, since they had a batch of ribs going outside on the large grill. The house smelled of pine, fresh-brewed coffee and cocoa, and gingersnap cookies decorated by the children.

She wished her mother were here. How happy Mary Justice Cardwell would have been to see her family all together—finally. It was what Dana had hoped for all her life. It was one reason she would never leave this old house. Her children would grow up here— just as she had. She hoped that someday it would be her grandchildren she would hear playing in the next room.

"Do you need any help?" her cousin DJ asked from the kitchen doorway.

Dana stepped to her and pulled her into a hug. "Having you here means more than you can ever know." She drew back to look at her cousin. She'd seen how much Beau and DJ had loved each other. But for whatever reason, they'd parted. It broke her heart.

She'd had to twist DJ's arm to get her to fly up for the New Year. "You wouldn't consider staying longer, would you?"

"I have to return to California. My editor has a list of assignments she wants me to consider."

"I have to ask about your grandmother's funeral," Dana said.

"It was quite beautiful. As misguided as she was in the past, she saved my life. I'll never forget that. Also, I've been spending time with my sister and my father, actually. He's trying to figure out what he wants to do with the rest of his life. That was nice of you to offer him a place here on the ranch."

"I hope he takes me up on it," Dana said. "After all, this is where he belongs. Zinnia would love to see him again. You know, she's a widow."

DJ laughed. "You just can't help matchmaking, can you?"

"I have no idea what you're talking about," Dana said, smiling. "Bianca is also always welcome here on the ranch. I spoke with her about coming up and spending a few weeks. She wants to learn to ride horses. So you have to come back. There really is no place like Montana in the summer."

"You sound like Beau." DJ seemed to catch herself. "He mentioned how nice it is up here once the snow melts."

"Yes, Beau," Dana said, unable to hold back a grin. "The night I saw the two of you dancing down at The Corral, I knew you were perfect for each other."

DJ shook her head. "I'm afraid you're wrong about that. I haven't heard from him since I left."

Dana laughed. "Trust me. I'm never wrong."

IT WAS ALMOST midnight when there was a knock at the door. The old ranch house on Cardwell Ranch was full of family. Dana had just passed out the noisemakers. DJ had seen her watching the door as if she was expecting more guests, but everyone was already there, including DJ's cousins—Jordan and his wife, Stacy and Burt, and even Clay and his partner.

Dana ran to the door and threw it open. A gust of cold air rushed in. DJ saw her cousin reach out, grab Beau and pull him in. They shared a few words before both looked in her direction.

She groaned, afraid of what Dana had done to get Beau over here tonight. Her cousin was so certain she wasn't wrong making this match. DJ almost felt sorry for her. As much as she and Beau had enjoyed their time together, as much as DJ felt for him, sometimes things just didn't work out, she told herself as he walked toward her.

If anything, he was more handsome than the first time she'd seen him standing in the airport. His blue eyes were on her, and in them she saw what almost looked like pain. Her heart lodged in her throat. Tears burned her eyes.

"We need to talk," he said as he took her hand. She was reminded of the night at The Corral when he'd said the same words. Only that night, he'd dragged her from the dance floor, out into the snowy night.

Tonight he led her into the kitchen and closed the door. When he turned to her, she looked into his handsome face and felt her pulse pound.

"I'm a damned fool," he said. "I should never have let you go. Or at least, I should have gone with you. Since the day you left, I've thought about nothing but you. I would have called, but I was afraid that once you got back to your life…"

"Are you just going to talk, or are you going to kiss me?" DJ managed to say, her heart in her throat.

He pulled her to him. His mouth dropped to hers. He smelled of snow and pine and male. She breathed him in as he deepened the kiss and held her tighter.

"I never want to let you go," he said when he drew back. "If that means leaving Montana—"

"I would never ask you to leave a place you love so much."

He looked into her eyes. "Then what are we going to do? Because I don't want to spend another day without you."

"With my job, I can work anywhere."

He smiled, his blue eyes sparkling. "You'd move to Montana if I were to...ask you?"

"What are you saying, cowboy?"

He looked down at his boots for a moment, then met her gaze again. "I never saw you coming. This was the last thing I expected, but now that you've come into my life... Come back. Come back to me. I know it probably seems like we haven't known each other that long, but..." His hand went into his pocket. He seemed to hesitate as he studied her face for a moment.

DJ held her breath as he pulled his hand from his pocket and opened it. Sitting in the middle of his large palm, something caught the light.

She felt her eyes widen at the sight of the diamond ring lying there.

"It was my mother's. She left it with her sister so my father didn't pawn it."

DJ couldn't help but smile knowingly. She and Beau. Their connection, as odd as it was, ran deep.

"Would you consider marrying me? Not right away. We could have as long an engagement as you need." He seemed to catch himself and dropped to one knee. "I know this should have been more romantic—"

She shook her head. "It's perfect," she said, seeing his discomfort. She held out her left hand. "And yes, I will marry you. And no, I don't need a long engagement. Leaving here, leaving you, was one of the hardest things I've ever done. It was breaking my heart." Her eyes filled with tears. "Montana feels like the home I've never had. Somehow, I've never felt that I deserved to be happy. But with you..."

He slipped the ring on her finger, rose and pulled

her into his arms. "That's exactly how I feel. As if I deserve this if I'm smart enough not to let you get away."

She smiled as he lowered his mouth to hers. "I love you, DJ," he whispered against her lips. In the next room, a cheer arose. It was a new day, a new year.

* * * * *

PRIVATE BODYGUARD

TYLER ANNE SNELL

This book is for one of my best friends, Rachel Miller. Thank you for listening to everything I had to say about Darling's story, as well as every other story I've ever created! Your enthusiasm, wisdom and friendship have made my life exponentially better. Here's to many, many, many more years of staying up late and talking about books!

Also, the quickest of shout outs to Hunter Hall. Our friendship is also killer!

Chapter One

"It was just a little misunderstanding."

Darling Smith was standing behind the bars of one of two holding cells in Mulligan, Maine, and not at all amused.

Deputy Derrick Arrington, however, was all humor. Maybe that was due to the fact that the two had dated on and off the year before with less than favorable results. They were normally amicable if not downright pleasant, but Darling figured it wasn't every day he was able to arrest his ex. Her thoughts slid back in time for a moment.

Oh yeah, she would have loved to put a certain man from her past in the slammer and throw away the key.

"That should be tattooed across your forehead, Darling. 'It was a little misunderstanding, Officer. I'm too cute to be up to no good.'" He grinned.

"Deputy Arrington, did you just say that I'm cute?" she replied with a big dose of sugar.

He pointed at her and laughed. "See? That right there is what I'm talking about."

"Oh, come on, Derrick." Darling dropped the cuteness from her tone. She was tired. "We both know that George Hanely overreacted." Just saying the gate guard's name made her mad. He'd acted as if he was a Secret Service agent and Darling was an enemy of the state.

"He did his job. George saw a *suspicious person snooping around private property.*" He eyed Darling a moment, waiting for her to confess. He'd keep waiting, too. "What's more, that *suspicious person* was found going up to his employer's garage."

"Not confirmed, just accused," she said.

The deputy shook his head. "I'd take this a little more seriously, Darling. You were caught breaking and entering into Nigel Marks's house. He's a beloved figure in this town. This will be the first time he's been back to stay for a while in years. The last time he came, do you know what he did?"

Darling let out a long breath. She had already researched the millionaire, but that didn't mean she was buying what he was selling. "He donated a new wing to the children's library."

"That's right. He was here for a little over a week, and he brought joy to an entire town's kids. Now he's coming to stay for almost a month. His visits, even if they are work related, usually benefit our community." He paused, making sure he let his words sink in before he tacked on, "We want him to enjoy that stay, not worry about some spunky private eye."

"I preferred 'cute,'" she grumbled.

"Well, I preferred starting my Tuesday morning with a cup of coffee and not picking up a criminal just as the sun rose."

"Accused criminal."

He rolled his eyes and checked his watch. Derrick was tall, had jet-black hair and the bluest eyes she'd ever seen. He was handsome, sure, but he also wasn't anywhere near her type. Though, admittedly, her type had revolved around one man and one man alone throughout the years. She stopped herself before she could picture him, angry for entertaining thoughts of a past best forgotten.

"Okay, I'm going to head back up," he said. "I just wanted to come check on you and see if you wanted that one phone call."

"But Deputy, why would I call you when you're already here?"

"Oh, Darling, how I've missed your sarcasm." They both knew that was a bold-faced lie.

It had been two days since Elizabeth Marks had walked into Acuity Investigations and asked for the twenty-five-year-old's help. Darling could recall with almost perfect precision the way the graceful woman had breezed in. She had shaken Darling's hand with a firm grip but had seemed hesitant to introduce herself. However, Darling hadn't needed to know the woman's name to understand she was important, if only financially so. It had been Elizabeth's shoes—silver-toed, red-soled, python-heeled Louboutin shoes—that had spoken volumes to Darling. Mrs. Marks came from money, and that always made a case more interesting.

"My husband is having an affair," Elizabeth had said after adjusting the Gucci sunglasses that sat atop her crown of bleach-blond hair. "I just need concrete proof now."

Darling had been taken aback. Normally when a spouse sought out a private investigator, it was to confirm a suspicion. The way Elizabeth's back had straightened and her shoulders had squared had suggested there were no doubts in her accusation.

"If you already know he's cheating, why do you need the proof?" Darling had asked.

A surge of energy had seemed to pulse through Elizabeth. Her face had become lively for a moment.

"We married when I was young, my husband, Nigel, and I. His career was just taking off, and we were so in love. He drew up a prenuptial agreement that I should never have signed, but I was foolish and naive and believed he was the man I wanted to spend the rest of my life with." She had stopped herself then, as if trying to pick the right words. "If I divorce him right now, because of the prenup, I'll receive almost nothing. Even the money I personally earned. But if I get proof that he's cheating, it will void the prenup and I can take at least half of what he owns, which will be enough for me."

So that had been the bottom line.

Darling sat on the uncomfortable cell's cot as the memory of their first meeting came to an end and a new wave of determination washed over her. She wasn't the biggest fan of the wealthy—having a past like hers left an unforgettably sour taste in her mouth for them—but she had believed in the woman's pain and anger enough to want to help. Just because Darling had fought her own personal battle against the rich, and lost, didn't mean Elizabeth deserved the same fate.

"You sure you can do this?"

Oliver Quinn looked up from the desk to see his boss leaning in the doorway. Nikki Waters's tone was light, though her demeanor carried unintentional importance. Since she not only founded the Orion Security Group but also ran it, he decided that importance was deserved. He certainly respected it.

"Excuse me?" he asked, half of his mind still going through the travel details in the open folder between his hands. He was twenty minutes away from heading to the airport to start a three-week contract and, since Oliver was the lead agent of Team Delta, he was triple-checking their route. He wanted to avoid as much traffic as possible—a goal made easier by the somewhat remote location.

"Maine," she replied, staying in the doorway. It was almost seven in the morning and she was dressed in her workout clothes, her dark red hair slicked back in a short pony tail. Most likely she was headed to the twenty-four-hour gym across the street. There were several of them spread throughout downtown Dallas. "In April, no less."

Oliver raised an eyebrow at her.

"Oh, come on," she continued with a smile. "Every time I checked in on you during that stint in Montana two years ago, you talked about how crazy you were going from being in the cold."

If he had been a rookie like Thomas, the newest addition to Delta, or even someone who had been around a year like Grant, he would have thought she was serious in questioning whether he could do the job or not. However, if there was one thing he rarely doubted, it was Nikki's faith in his abilities. If she hadn't believed in them, she wouldn't have sought him out when Orion had only been a name.

"What can I say? I'm from California. We tend to love the sun and heat. I don't think Maine will be too bad, though. I'm just glad we aren't going there a month earlier. I can handle April."

She laughed. It was clipped. He knew something was bothering her and waited until she spoke again.

"Listen, I wanted to thank you for not giving me grief about this client," she said. "I know Mark and Jonathan think taking him on is unnecessary." She was referring to the lead agents of the other two teams and Oliver's closest friends. They had worked together before Orion, sharing a past that had been fused together by tragedy.

"They don't like thinking about the big picture," he said, trying to lighten the mood. He knew she had been struggling with her decision to accept millionaire Nigel Marks as a client.

"It's just…" She hesitated. "We've spent the last few years claiming to protect those who need it but can't afford it. That's the Orion Group's bottom line. We provide security and guarantee safety to those who don't have bottomless pockets. And now we're taking on an almost monthlong project with a millionaire?" She sighed. "I feel like I'm selling out."

"But if we don't occasionally pick up an elite client, then we can't continue to be Robin Hoods. Right?"

Nikki snorted. "Robin Hoods, huh?"

"Well, we don't steal from the rich, but you get the idea."

She seemed to like that way of thinking and nodded. "You're right. I need to be firm in this decision. You're heading there soon?"

Oliver pulled out his plane ticket. "Since he insisted on us meeting him there, I want to head up there a little earlier to make sure everything is okay," he said. "The rest of Team Delta will follow but might be a bit late since their flight last night was cancelled."

"Team Delta. It still sounds as corny as it did when Mark suggested the name."

"Says the woman who named her security group

Orion," he replied. Though as he said it, he glanced past her to a picture framed on the wall. The real reason behind the name.

The picture weighed less than an ounce, but it left an unbelievably heavy weight on his heart.

Nikki didn't have to follow his gaze. She knew what he was feeling. Her pain had turned to anger over the years. His had only drowned in guilt.

"Well, be careful," she said after the moment passed. "And, Oliver? Keep this client happy. We need him, as much as I hate to say it."

Oliver needed to ensure everything was on the up and up since Nigel had been clear he didn't want to start the contract until Wednesday morning. He still didn't understand why the man had hired a security group to protect him while he traveled if he didn't want to use them as he traveled *to* Maine. He'd been cautious enough to hire Orion after he'd earned a few nasty anonymous letters at work. He clearly had felt threatened. Oliver didn't think about it too much, though. He'd learned the hard way that most of the upper class was stubborn, and arguing with them did little to change their minds.

Oliver tried not to dwell on the past as he arrived at the airport and then boarded his plane.

Nigel Marks had been transported by way of his private jet; Oliver's long legs were pressed against the back of a snoring man's chair in coach. When he finally landed, stretched and turned on his cell phone, he wasn't in the mood for the voice mail from Nikki.

"Oliver, I received a call from the security guard who watches Nigel's house. I think his name is George? Anyways, he found a woman lurking around early this morning and had the cops come pick her up. They are holding her on trespassing and potentially breaking and entering. George didn't give me all of the details. He seemed too excited. I already talked to Nigel. He's actually at work in the next town over and will be delayed until later this afternoon. He liked the idea of you going to talk to her to see if she's a threat. Call me after you do." She didn't say goodbye. She was in business mode. Nikki the boss, not Nikki the friend.

He hung up, aggravated.

"Great," he grumbled, making his way to baggage claim. "Not even in town and already having problems."

The town of Mulligan—a name that Oliver found humor in—was thirty minutes away from the airport via one dust-covered SUV. Oliver hated rentals. Due to the company's track record, no agent was offered the rental insurance that was an option with each vehicle. In his line of work, there was a high chance they would receive damage in some form. Oliver knew from experience the rental companies were a pain to deal with when that happened, and as team lead, he was the one who dealt with it. The man he'd rented the car from had taken his sweet time passive-aggressively warning Oliver about how it would be unwise to bring it back in anything less than pristine condition. Every pothole he bumped through made him cringe.

Thinking of the uptight man only dampened his darkening mood. He mentally ran through a list of questions he would ask Nigel Marks's intruder as the vehicle's GPS directed him to Mulligan's police department. It wasn't until he was nearing Main Street that his phone blared to life.

"Quinn," he answered, pressing the speaker button.

"It's Nikki." There was no mistaking the annoyance

in her voice. "I wanted to warn you that our intruder is a private investigator."

"A private eye?"

"Yep. I finally got the chief on the phone, and he said she's a local. And she's feisty. Try to figure out why she was snooping around, but don't make her too mad. If she's a local, it might make the next three weeks unpleasant."

"Okay. Don't tick her off. Tread lightly. Yada yada."

"The sheriff also made a point to warn me not to let her name fool you."

Oliver raised an eyebrow to no one in particular. "Her name? What is it? Candy? Bunny?"

Nikki laughed. "No, even better. Darling."

Oliver almost swerved off of the road.

Before he could stop himself, the image of a woman popped into his head. Dirty-blond hair, round green eyes, a button nose and a set of soft, curvy lips.

"Come again?" he asked. He was already certain he'd heard Nikki wrong.

"Her name is Darling. Darling Smith."

A silence followed before Oliver found his voice again. "I hate to say this, but I can almost guarantee she's already pissed at me."

FOOTSTEPS SOUNDED FROM the stairs, bringing Darling out of her haze of absolute annoyance. Derrick had been coming down a few times each hour to talk her ear off. She wished Nigel Marks's lackey would hurry up and question her. Anything was better than staying any longer in the mildew-scented cell. As the steps got closer, she ducked her head and rubbed her eyes. She didn't think she could take another round of Deputy Derrick.

"If you're going to keep bothering me, the least you could do is bring me a coffee," she called when the footsteps stopped outside of the bars.

"Well, I haven't been in town long, but I'm sure I could find some somewhere."

Darling's heart skipped a beat. Slowly she raised her head to look at the new speaker. She could only stare.

Out of all of the town jails in the world, Oliver Quinn had picked hers to make a grand appearance in.

It had been almost eight years since she had seen him, yet she recognized him instantly. Brushing six feet, the twenty-eight-year-old had broad shoulders and a stocky but muscular build, giving him the look of a well-toned soccer player. His blond hair was cut short but not too short, still covering the top of his forehead with a golden swoop. His amber-colored eyes and ridiculously soft-looking lips only added to the attractive angles of his tanned face. Not to mention a jawline that simply begged to be touched. For a moment Darling wondered why she ever had ill feelings toward the man who looked like an angel. But then, all at once, she remembered not only who he was but also what he had done.

No matter how handsome he was, Oliver Quinn had crushed her heart. A fact Darling wouldn't forgive or forget anytime soon.

"Miss Smith, this is the security agent Nigel Marks sent," Deputy Derrick said, coming up behind Oliver. "His name is—" He stopped, noticing Darling's deer-in-headlights stare. "You okay?"

Oliver, with a small smile attached to his lips, was about to interject, but Darling found her voice. Though she had to tamp down several less-than-pleasant responses.

"Deputy Arrington, this is Oliver Quinn," she said, standing. "We used to make out in my father's Ferrari." Derrick raised his eyebrow before looking at Oliver.

"What can I say? Fast cars and pretty girls equal a winning combo in my book," Oliver shot back with an easy laugh. It was not the response she had expected, but Derrick thought it was funny enough. When Darling didn't show signs of joining in on their shared mirth, the deputy sobered.

"Do you want me to stay down here during the questions?" Derrick asked her directly. They might not have had the best romantic relationship, but they did consider each other friends.

"I can handle this one," she answered. It earned another little laugh from Oliver.

"When you're satisfied she isn't a threat, let me know," Derrick said, turning to leave.

"She isn't a threat. You can let her out now." Oliver moved aside and motioned to the lock. Derrick and Darling exchanged a confused glance.

"You don't want to question her?" Derrick asked.

"I do, but unfortunately, I have to get back to work." He looked at her. "I was thinking we could pick this up tonight?"

Alarm bells as loud as the Monday-morning trash pickup rang in her head.

"Like on a date?" she blurted, heat rushing to her cheeks.

Oliver gave off another short laugh. "More like catching up with a few pointed questions concerning my client," he said. Then, when she was about to decline fiercely, he added, "I need to make sure I was correct in saying you aren't a risk. If you are, my client will press charges."

Both men looked at her, waiting for an answer.

If Oliver was the only thing that kept her from receiving the potential wrath of Nigel Marks, she'd have to take up his offer. She sighed, thinking about her bad luck so far on this case.

"Fine, but you're buying."

Oliver produced a business card as Derrick opened the cell door. He handed it to Darling, never dropping his grin.

"Would it be okay to stop by your office around seven?" he asked.

"Do I have a choice?" she replied with one of her sweet, yet not sweet at all, smiles.

"Of course you do, but it might be better if we could have that dinner."

"Then I guess that's what will happen."

The three of them went back upstairs. Oliver the Bodyguard didn't even hesitate to get into his car and leave, while Darling got into her car that had been brought to the station. She sat in the driver's seat, trying to process all of what had happened in the past ten minutes. Fate? Coincidence? A cruel joke? She couldn't decide which category her situation fell into.

She might have kept wondering had her phone not buzzed with a text she had been hoping to receive. Looking at the caller ID, she couldn't help but feel better.

Darling pulled up to the Mulligan Motel a few minutes later with excitement coursing through her. Her caller was Dan Morelli, a transplant from New Jersey and the owner of the less-than-ideal motel. There was a Holiday Inn fifteen minutes south of Mulligan, but those who participated in not-so-legal extracurricular activities often stayed at the Mulligan Motel.

Or people who wanted to meet someone in secret.

"Hey, Dan," Darling greeted him, walking into the lobby with her camera swinging around her neck. Dan had been a valuable contact throughout the past few years, keeping an eye out for certain persons Darling had cases on. Though since she had tried to stay away from the dirty-laundry spectrum of stereotypical private-eye jobs, she hadn't seen him in a good few months. She'd paid him in cookies, movie rentals and the promise of an exciting bust in the past. There wasn't much else to do in Mulligan for a man who hated the cold. Plus, he'd confessed once that Darling reminded him of his little sister, which apparently worked in her favor.

Dan didn't look up from his paper when she stepped inside.

"Room 212," he responded, intent on his crossword. "And you figured that out all on your own."

"Of course I did. You know nothing—everyone knows that, Dan."

He laughed but didn't say anything more. Darling went behind the desk and grabbed the key with the chain marked 212. Some people might have felt guilty for what she was doing, but Darling could justify it easily enough. Nigel Marks had spent a few hours in the Mulligan Motel's room 212 last night. And what's more, he hadn't been alone. The millionaire had left while the sky was still dark, but his mistress hadn't checked out yet. It was time Darling paid a visit.

She walked up the stairs and down the length of the second floor until she came to a stop at the last door. A TV could be heard on the other side, but no voices. Darling, using a method her former boss had applied in the field before, adopted a high-pitched voice and knocked.

"Room service," she sang. There was a Do Not Disturb sign hanging from the doorknob. If she kept nagging, the woman would answer, annoyed yet visible. Then Darling would do what she did best and question or trick her into confessing. Who needed pictures when the mistress would admit publically to the affair? Sure, it was a little brash of her and maybe not what she would have done under normal circumstances, but she felt oddly off-kilter after seeing Oliver. Even though they'd barely had a conversation.

She knocked a few more times and waited.

And waited.

"Room service. I'm coming in," she sang again in a lower voice. She slid the key into the lock and turned, an excuse for her intrusion ready on her tongue.

But no one yelped in surprise or yelled in anger. Aside from the TV, the room was still and spotless. Maybe Dan had gotten it wrong, Darling thought. There was no luggage or bags of any kind, the trashcans were empty and all the lights were off. She walked past the two double beds and peeked into the bathroom, hoping for some kind of clue that would prove Nigel Marks's mistress had been there.

However, the proof she found was more than she had bargained for.

Lying in the bathtub was a woman wrapped up in the shower curtain. Blood was everywhere.

Chapter Two

"And you're sure she won't be a problem?" Nikki asked after Oliver more or less summed up his visit to the police station. He had admitted to knowing Darling, just not *how* he knew her.

"I'm sure. She was just curious, that's all," he said for the third time. Nikki might not have been fond of taking on Nigel Marks as a client, but now that he was under contract, she was going to make sure nothing bad happened. "Listen, I don't blame her. This place is impressive. I'd have done the same thing. If it makes you feel better, I'm catching up with her when Thomas and Grant relieve me tonight. I'll bring it up again and if she lies to me, I'll catch it."

"Well, just try not to tick off the long-winded gate guard, George, while you're there. I'd really like to avoid talking to him again."

Oliver agreed and they ended the call. He looked through the window to the gatehouse down below. George Hanely had been like a kid on Christmas as he recounted the story of how he had saved the Markses' home from the more-than-suspicious private investigator. Oliver had been at Nigel Marks's home for less than ten minutes, and in that time he had watched George re-enact what had happened.

He had led Oliver from his post in the small one-room, half-bathroom house that sat at the front of the drive around to the garage. It, like the house, was large. It could easily fit several cars. Darling had been spotted next to the side door. Her story of just being close to the gate that surrounded the property was hard to believe. The iron gate was a good forty to fifty yards away. If she had been trying to get back over the fence, then why come so close to the garage?

Oliver could guess the answer. She was trying to get *into* the garage. But why?

Ever since he had seen Darling, he had been assuming that she was still the same girl he'd known before. The fact that she was in jail to start off with had proven the opposite. And a private investigator?

He smiled to himself. *That* he could believe. Darling had loved the challenge of a good mystery.

He remembered the first time he'd met her. She had been butt up in a Dumpster behind an office complex, rooting around in discarded papers and files. At the time he'd assumed it was a part of some weird bet. She hadn't looked homeless with her designer clothes and perfectly manicured nails. Then, when she found exactly what she didn't want to find, she had opened up in a burst of emotion to the nineteen-year-old him. Her world wasn't over, but it had changed. Through the next few months the once-spoiled, once-naive teenager transformed into a thoughtful, compassionate young woman. The people around her hadn't appreciated the changed Darling, and slowly she had become isolated. Oliver, however, had formed a bond with her, staying by her side until…

Self-loathing pulsed through him at the memory of the last night he'd seen her. *Time can heal all wounds, but seeing the girl whose heart you shattered only breaks out the salt and pours it into the gashes*, he thought with a frown.

Seeing her after all those years had been a shock to his system. One he wasn't sure was entirely good or entirely bad. As he tried to clear his mind, he marveled at the fact that he still felt so strongly about what had happened almost a decade ago.

Oliver left the guest bedroom Nigel had assigned to him and started to go through each room of the house. He checked windows, catalogued all exits and got his bearings of the Markses' second home. Its large size didn't surprise him in the least.

After finishing his sweep, he made his way back over to the gatehouse. George, a slight man in his thirties with dark hair and a pasty complexion, could barely keep his excitement at bay at having someone to talk to. Oliver didn't blame the man one bit. Even though Nigel Marks hadn't been at his house in years, it was still George's job to watch the gate daily. If it had been Oliver's job, he would have hated it. However, George seemed to take pride in his tasks, and Oliver spied a movie player and several movies under the front desk, which must have made sitting in one room day in and day out a little more bearable.

"So, have you ever met Mr. Marks in person?" George asked when Oliver was satisfied with each part of the property. Aside from the gatehouse, garage and house, there was nothing but open land surrounding the acres the Markses owned.

"No," Oliver admitted. "My boss handles the client

interactions before the contract start date," he explained. "Do you see him often? I was under the impression he didn't come visit much."

George shrugged. "He calls to check in from time to time and ask about things," he said. Oliver noticed the gate guard puffed his chest out a bit. "I keep him informed on what's going on in Mulligan." There was no mistaking that George definitely took pride in working for Nigel. Oliver could respect that, even if he wondered what kind of social life the guard was left with after the hours he worked. Having a good boss was an absolute must for Oliver, especially after the nightmare of what had happened with his last. "That's how I knew that woman was up to no good."

They had just stepped outside the gatehouse and were facing the private drive. It wasn't as cold as the Montana case had been, but there was a chill in the air that moved with the breeze. Oliver tilted his head as another gust pushed against his clean-shaven face, and he thought about his next words carefully before speaking.

"You mean the private investigator? She seemed harmless enough," he said, not believing himself as he said it.

George snorted. "Private investigator. Yeah, that sounds a lot better than what she really does."

Oliver raised his eyebrow. "What does she really do?"

"Sneak around, break the law and ruin lives. Just like the rat of a man she got her office from," he explained with a surge of anger.

"From what I could tell Derrick seemed to like her," Oliver added.

"Deputy Derrick and her are close, if you know what I mean."

A quick burst of jealousy flashed through Oliver. The

idea that Darling was with someone romantically hadn't yet breached his thoughts. Not that it should matter either way.

"And as for the chief, he's one of many people here that have fallen for her charms. If you ask me, she uses her looks to get what she wants. It's repulsive. She should be using her time better, you know? Get married, have some kids."

Oliver's brief jealousy turned to a not-so-brief anger. It was true he couldn't claim to know this new, older version of Darling the same way he had known the younger one, but he seriously doubted she was this repulsive person George was claiming. He was about to set the man straight when his cell phone beeped.

"They're almost here," Oliver said instead. "I want you to call me if anyone other than my team and Nigel comes to this gate. No matter the time. Are we clear?"

George straightened his back and almost looked as if he was ready to salute. "Yes, sir," he barked.

Within minutes a black SUV came up the drive, followed by a sleek silver two-door Audi. Originally, Nigel was supposed to be escorted from his home in California to Mulligan, but a week ago he had changed this detail, much to Nikki's frustration. He had spent two days in the neighboring city, working to put out business-related fires due to his company's newest merger while he stayed at a four-star hotel less than a block from that branch of Charisma Investments. The other two members of Team Delta had been ordered to pick Nigel up that morning, officially starting their contract time frame.

Oliver nodded to Thomas Gage, Orion's newest recruit, as he rolled down the SUV's tinted driver's side window just before the gate. His build was on the lean side, with narrow shoulders and arms toned but not as built as the rest of Team Delta. He had light brown skin, dark hair and bright blue eyes that Nikki had commented on more than once. Thomas never sported facial hair, and that decision often got him mistaken for younger than twenty-five. This was his third job as a Delta agent. Oliver liked his humor and lingering innocence.

"Hey there, Boss," Thomas greeted Oliver with a smile. He motioned to the backseat, where Nigel Marks sat with a laptop on his lap and a phone to his ear. He looked up and gave a quick wave before turning his attention back to his work. "He had an emergency call that couldn't wait," Thomas explained.

Oliver motioned through the gatehouse window for George to open the gate. George didn't hesitate, and Thomas moved the SUV the rest of the way up the drive, parking in front of one of the garage doors. Grant Blakely arrived next, driving Nigel's high-end rental. He was already grinning as he paused next to Oliver.

"This assignment may not completely suck after all, especially if we get to play with his toys," he said as soon as the window was down. He petted the dashboard.

Oliver chuckled. He missed working with his old team of Jonathan and Mark, but he had grown fond of Grant. The thirty-four-year-old was the epitome of intimidating without even trying. Tall, wide and thick with muscles, the dark-skinned bodyguard never looked as if he couldn't win in a fight.

"Just wait until you see the house," Oliver said. "Any problems getting here?"

"No, sir. It's about a thirty-minute commute with no traffic. How about on your end? Did you deal with the private eye?"

"The threat wasn't as threatening as we thought, but just to make sure, I'm going to ask a few more questions after my shift." Grant nodded, and Oliver once again told George to open the gate.

"The man driving Nigel is Thomas, and the one in the Audi is Grant," Oliver explained to George. "You have all our numbers. Don't hesitate to use them if you need to. At all times there will be two of us with Nigel."

George took the three cards with their numbers and put them in his pocket. Although he said he understood, Oliver could tell his attention had moved toward the cars, where his true boss had just exited.

Nigel Marks was over six foot, of average size and dressed in a proper suit. His salt-and-pepper hair was cropped close to his head, with a pair of reading glasses resting on top. The file Oliver had been given said Nigel was fifty-three, though he looked years younger. The file also said he was an avid runner, competing in marathons and triathlons in his spare time. That would account for the toned body his suit did little to hide. As Oliver approached, Nigel ended his call and extended his hand.

"Sorry about that," Nigel said with a smile. "This merger has made everyone forget how to do their jobs. You must be Mr. Quinn."

Oliver shook. "Call me Oliver."

"It's nice to meet you, Oliver. Nikki spoke very highly of you and your team. Hopefully you won't get too bored on this job."

"It's a good sign when a job stays boring," Oliver replied.

Nigel seemed to consider this and laughed. "I suppose you're right. Well..." Nigel waved to his house as Grant and Thomas joined them. "As I told Nikki, feel free to treat this as your home while here. There are no off-limits areas, but I do ask my office be left alone unless I'm with you. I have a feeling that my free time will be spent in there." He paused as his phone rang. His pleasant mood seemed to slide away in an instant. Replacing it was the look of a tired man. "My work is never done."

DARLING FELT AS if she was frozen yet couldn't stop everything around her from moving. It wasn't until her vision started to tunnel that she realized she was about to pass out. With a quick dose of good sense, she backed out of the bathroom and crouched, flinging her head down between her legs. In the moment she couldn't remember why that stopped a person from fainting, but she knew she needed to try it nonetheless.

So there she was, crouched just outside of room 212's bathroom and its body in the tub, trying to calm her stampeding heartbeat and erratic breathing.

This case was nothing but bad, bad luck.

A car door shut in the parking lot some time later. Whether it was seconds or minutes, she wasn't sure. The room hadn't been the only aspect of her reality that had warped when she had seen the body. However, instead of sending her into a bigger fit of worries, the sound of the outside world started to make her focus.

She took two deep breaths and slowly righted herself. The camera around her neck slapped against her chest, reminding her of the reason she had been there in the first place.

Nigel Marks and his mistress had been in this room the night before. He had gone, but his mistress hadn't checked out. It wasn't a stretch of the imagination to guess it was her unfortunate fate that she was the one wrapped up in the tub. Darling knew she had to call the police, just as she knew that once she left the room, she'd never be allowed back in.

At the moment, it was a thought that didn't sit right with her. So, blaming the impulse on her desire to solve mysteries, even ones seemingly cut and dried, she took her camera from her neck and walked back to the bathroom doorway. With hands she let shake, she snapped a few pictures of the bathroom and its deceased guest before she turned back and took a few of the bedroom. Another car door slammed shut in the distance. She glanced once more toward the bathroom.

Darling felt a mixture of anger and sadness pull at her heart. Nigel Marks might be a powerful man in the business world, but by killing this woman, he had unwittingly stepped inside Darling's domain.

Darling hurried to the main office and was thankful that Dan was still alone. He didn't look up when she came in, he just raised his hands.

"I know nothing," he said, still in a bubble of humor. It was a bubble she was about to pop.

"Dan, you need to call the police. There's a dead body in room 212."

Dan laughed, thinking it was a joke until he finally met her eyes. Darling figured she must have looked as serious as the situation was. She watched his face and mood sober.

"Where?" was all he could manage.

"Wrapped up in a shower curtain in the tub."

His lips thinned, and his brows pulled together. "You better give me the key and leave, then," he said after a moment. He pulled the only landline phone the office had from the second shelf of his desk. Darling felt a quick wave of fondness for the man. He was always trying to cover for her.

"I don't want you to lie about how you found the body," Darling said. "I'll tell the deputy the door was already open." She handed the key back to him. "We don't have to tell anyone about the key. Though I don't think they'll care either way." It seemed obvious to her what had happened.

Dan nodded and pocketed the key.

"Then you call them," he said, already shrugging into his coat. "I want to go see it for myself."

Darling sat behind the front desk with a very loud, long sigh and did as she was told. Deputy Derrick wouldn't be happy she had managed to get into this mess, but at least this time she wasn't guilty. Not that she would have admitted she had been guilty that morning. Instead of dialing 9-1-1, she called the man directly. In a small town like Mulligan, where the members of police force could be counted on two hands, Derrick had the dual duty of being their trusty investigator as well as deputy. Instead of puttering around with someone else in the bull pen, Darling went straight to the source.

"Deputy Derrick," he answered on the second ring.

"Derrick, it's Darling. I hope you're not busy right now."

She heard him snort. "Is that your way of trying to ask me out? We both know how well that works," he said, all humor.

"Well, not quite."

"Where are you calling from?" he asked after a pause. She knew him well enough to recognize something close to suspicious concern creeping into his tone.

"The Mulligan Motel," she paused for a moment and

then dove in. "There's a body in room 212, wrapped up in the tub."

"A body?"

She nodded. Then, realizing he couldn't see her, she said, "And Derrick? The last person seen leaving the room was Nigel Marks."

There was silence on the other end.

"Stay there and tell Dan don't let anyone else in that room," he finally said. "And I mean it, Darling. No one else goes in there."

Darling agreed to his no-tampering-with-a-crime-scene rule. Suddenly her morning indiscretion didn't seem as bad. She even bet Oliver's need to question her would disappear when he found out.

Oliver.

She pulled his card out of her back pocket and looked at his number.

If Nigel did kill whoever it was in the tub, where did that leave Oliver?

Chapter Three

Oliver didn't answer when Darling called him.

Somewhere in the back of her mind, she felt she owed it to him to give him a heads-up that the man he had promised to guard was about to need a lot more protection than he could offer. Oliver had said she wasn't a threat, vouching for a woman he no longer knew. Plus, it was no fun to be blindsided. She knew that from experience.

"This is Oliver Quinn. Leave a message and I'll get back to you as soon as possible," his voice mail recording answered. Darling felt her face heat up after the beep to leave a message came and went. She realized then that giving him a heads-up might also give Nigel one before the cops were even able to see the body in the tub. She didn't want to be the one responsible for giving the number one suspect time to lawyer up or possibly run. Although he probably had already done one or the other. It wasn't as if the body could have gone unnoticed for too long.

"Um, hi, it's Darling," she floundered. "I need you to call me as soon as you get this. Something's happened. Thanks." She let out a long sigh as she ended the call. She liked to believe she was a very confident and sure woman, but mix any part of Oliver into her life and she suddenly felt off her game.

Darling went back up to the second floor to find Dan, trying to push thoughts of her ex clear out of her head. She had walked into the crime scene that, most likely, her current client's husband had created. That gave her a new set of problems and concerns without adding the complication of the man from her past.

"I talked to Deputy Derrick," Darling told Dan, who was standing in the doorway to room 212. "He said no one else needs to go in there until they get here."

Dan didn't answer right away. His eyes were stuck on a point somewhere in the main room. She wondered if he had peeked in the bathroom yet. When he met her gaze, she knew he had. He looked haunted.

"Do you think he really did it?" he asked. "Nigel. Do you think he really killed her?"

Darling shrugged. "I can't say for certain, but I can make the leap and say I think there's a pretty good chance he did. You said yourself that he stayed the night here."

Dan nodded, but there was no enthusiasm in it.

"Do you want me to wait in the lobby and send the cops up when they get here?" she asked when it was clear Dan wasn't going to talk. He nodded again and returned to staring into room 212. She patted him on the shoulder and made the walk back, thinking a dead body in your hotel couldn't be good for business.

Darling sat behind the desk again but didn't let her mind wander. Instead she thought about Elizabeth Marks, the only other woman who knew about her husband's affair. Or, at least, she had thought so. If Nigel went to jail for murdering his mistress, she'd be in the clear to take what was hers, and possibly his, and leave without any strings attached.

A coldness seeped into Darling's heart.

She pulled her phone out and went to her email. Searching through discount offers and social media updates, she found the itinerary Elizabeth had sent to her after she had signed on to the case. During the duration of Nigel's work trip, Elizabeth would be with her mother in the Bahamas. She claimed that if she were far away with no chance of accidentally spotting Nigel and his mistress, he might get careless. It would be easier to catch him, she had said with vigor. If the schedule Darling was looking at was correct, the two women would have left for the trip on Sunday, two days ago. That meant Elizabeth wasn't even in the country when the woman had checked in.

Plus, why would you hire a private investigator if you were just going to kill the problem?

All at once, Darling realized there was an easy way to figure out who the mistress was.

Jumping up, she hurried to look out the door to make sure no one was coming. Derrick had been at the police station when she had called, which meant she had very little time left before he arrived. She ran back behind the front desk and pulled a big leather-bound registry book out. Dan hated leaving it on the desktop because he claimed it got in the way of his crosswords. He only pulled it out when a new guest had already handed over the money. It was also the only way he kept tabs on the people who checked in and out. Darling could have slapped herself. She couldn't believe she hadn't thought of looking at the registry as soon as she had come in.

She flipped through a few pages until she found the

entries from the night before. Three people had checked in. All were after 6:00 p.m., and none of them were Nigel Marks. A car door shut in the parking lot, and for the second time that day, Darling took a picture of something she probably shouldn't have. This time it was with her phone, but that reminded her she needed to hide her camera or else Derrick would take it from her. He was always suspicious of her, which, she guessed, was deserved in this case. She grabbed the camera, put it in the bottom drawer of the desk and replaced the registry seconds before Deputy Derrick came into the office.

"Two times in one day, huh?" she greeted him. Derrick didn't think it was funny. She sobered. "Sorry, it's been a weird day."

Whatever he had been about to say, he must have changed his mind. His face softened.

"What room?" he asked.

"Room 212. Dan is waiting outside. I told him not to go back in, like you said."

Derrick nodded. Behind his knitted brows, he was probably running through police procedures.

"You okay?" he asked when she kept staring. "I mean, like emotionally," he tacked on. He had never been that great at talking about feelings, so the question surprised her.

"Yeah, I didn't really see much."

He nodded and turned for the door that led to the stairs outside. He paused long enough to add, "And Darling, don't leave. I have a *lot* of questions for you."

"I know."

"I NEED YOU to call me as soon as you get this. Something's happened. Thanks." Oliver hadn't recognized

the number, but he sure did recognize the voice and the oddness behind it as he listened to Darling's message. He didn't have long to think about it, though, before his phone rang again.

This time it was George.

"Oliver, the police are here," he started. "They want to know if they can come in."

"The police?"

"Yeah, they say they need to talk to Mr. Marks."

Oliver looked up as if he could see his client through the ceiling.

"Let them in," he answered, ending the call.

He left his spot in the kitchen next to the back entrance and walked down the long hallway to the front. Grant, off duty until seven that night, was sitting in the dining room, reading one of the many books he had brought with him. He looked up as Oliver opened the front door.

"Something is up," Oliver said over his shoulder. A police cruiser was parking next to his rental SUV. Two male cops got out. "I need you on duty right now," he added, seeing their facial expressions. This wasn't a courtesy visit.

"Good afternoon, officers," Oliver said when they were a few feet away.

"Afternoon," the first one responded. He was in his upper fifties and had almost no hair left on his head. He was built strong but didn't look intimidating with his short height. "I'm Officer Barker and this is my partner, Officer Clay." He motioned to the much younger black man next to him, whose lack of hair looked more intentional than his partner's. "You must be one of Mr. Marks's bodyguards."

"Yes, sir. How can I help you?"

Officer Barker looked considerably more uncomfortable than Officer Clay. They shared a glance before Barker straightened his back and answered.

"We need to talk to Mr. Marks," he said. "Now."

"Okay," Oliver said. He turned to nod at Grant, who had been hanging back in the dining room to listen. "Can I ask what about?" Oliver ventured as Grant walked out of the room, heading for the stairs.

Again Oliver caught the feeling of unease that passed between the officers.

"Something's happened," Officer Clay answered. Oliver instantly recalled Darling's voice mail. "We shouldn't say anything more until we've talked to Mr. Marks."

Oliver wanted to push for more answers but had to remind himself that he was the bodyguard, not Nigel's personal assistant. He let the officers stand in silence until the man of the hour made his grand appearance.

"Officers," Nigel said, a question already in his tone. "What can I do for you?"

"We'll give you some privacy," Oliver said, falling back into the house with Grant but maintaining a sight line. Nigel didn't seem to notice, and as soon as they were out of earshot, the officers began to talk in lowered voices.

"What's going on?" Thomas asked. He had come down the stairs with Nigel, face filled with curiosity. Not that Oliver could blame him.

"The cops are here," Grant answered. He turned to Oliver. "Do you know what's going on?"

Oliver watched as Nigel's entire body visibly tensed.

"No," he answered. "But I can guess it's probably not good."

Probably not good was an understatement. In less than

five minutes, Nigel Marks was in the back of the cop cruiser and as mad as a hornet. Before they had driven away, the businessman had asked Thomas to call his lawyer.

"About what?" Thomas had asked.

"I'm being accused of murder," Nigel had bit back.

All three bodyguards didn't have time to hide their surprise.

Oliver had had many interesting things happen in his line of work, but he could definitely say a client being accused of murder was a first. No matter the new unique circumstance, he couldn't forget he was team leader. He sent Grant and Thomas—who had followed Nigel's directions and was calling Nikki to get the man's lawyer's information, and also an earful of confusion from her— to the police station. There they would continue to work as his bodyguards until Nigel was officially convicted of the crime or cleared of it.

Oliver made sure George knew he needed to keep an extravigilant eye on the gate and jumped into his rental, already calling Darling. It wasn't a coincidence she had called. She knew something.

She always did.

Minutes later, Oliver pulled into the lot of the Mulligan Motel. The coroner's van along with two police cruisers were parked next to the entrance, while a few guests stood around, but he had eyes only for one woman.

Darling was sitting on a bench next to the lobby's front door, concentration aimed at her phone. She had been brief during their call but had admitted they had found a dead body. Though how it was linked to Nigel, he wasn't sure yet.

"Apparently my questions are going to have to be

asked a little earlier than planned," he said by way of a greeting. It made the woman jump, but she didn't appear angry when she met his eyes. His body tensed at her gaze.

"Believe me, you aren't the only one who has questions." She stood and stretched. He was acutely aware of her five-five height, having to incline his head down slightly to look at her. A memory of how easy it was to pick her up into his embrace flashed across his vision. "Where is Nigel, and why aren't you with him?"

Since Nigel was a client, what went on in the man's private life was confidential. Oliver was under contract, which meant, unless it was public information, he couldn't divulge the fact that the businessman had been taken to the jail. Even if the person asking was Darling.

"Grant and Thomas are with him," was all he gave her. "Now, what's going on here, and how is it connected with Nigel?"

Darling was visibly trying to hide her anger at not being given a full answer, but she reined in the emotion along with any words born from it. She pushed her shoulders back when she was no longer actively trying to hide her displeasure.

"A body was found in the room your boss was staying in last night," she answered. Oliver didn't correct her with the difference between boss and client. His interest level had jumped off the charts instead. He was about to push for more when the Mulligan Motel's front door swung open and the deputy walked out. His mouth was set in a grim line, one that thinned when he saw Oliver.

"I'm surprised you're here," the deputy said, coming over. "I thought you'd be at the station."

"So Nigel was arrested?" Darling cut in before Oliver could comment.

"He was picked up a few minutes ago," Derrick said, relieving Oliver of having to withhold the information. Even though Darling kept her face guarded, he didn't miss the satisfaction that the cop's words brought her. "Which is why I didn't think you'd be here," Derrick said to Oliver.

"The rest of the team is with him," he repeated. "I came here to find out what's going on." Oliver sent a pointed look to Darling. "And how you're involved."

Darling crossed her arms over her chest.

"I was actually about to ask the same thing," Derrick said. The two of them focused on the private investigator. She shifted under their collective gaze. A long exhalation escaped between her lips.

"I was working a case," she admitted. "It led me here and, to my surprise, right up to a dead body. But as soon as I found it, I called you," she said to Derrick.

The cop outdid her earlier sigh and pinched the bridge of his nose.

"What's your case?" Oliver had to ask.

Darling set her jaw. "I'm not at liberty to say."

"Dammit, Darling, a woman is dead. You need to tell me everything you know," Derrick said with tried patience. Oliver guessed murder wasn't a normal occurrence in Mulligan.

"So it is a woman, then?" she asked. Derrick nodded. It was her turn to skate around a direct answer. "I didn't look hard enough. How was she killed?"

"And how is Nigel connected, again?" Oliver tacked on.

The deputy wasn't happy about the questions. "It's my turn to say 'no comment.'" Darling opened her mouth to argue, but he held up his hand. "This is an ongoing murder investigation, Darling. I can't give you anything right now. Not even for old times' sake."

Oliver didn't like the way he said the last part or the way the deputy brought up their shared past. The past that Oliver's past few years didn't even touch. However, a small part of him did feel a sort of odd joy to know that whatever relationship they'd had was now seemingly over.

"Now, please go wait inside so I can take your statement," the deputy said to Darling before focusing on Oliver. "And I suggest you head to the station. We're going to need to talk about that client of yours."

He was gone after that, leaving Oliver and Darling speechless on the sidewalk.

"You said Nigel was the last to see the woman alive?" he asked, voice low and serious.

"He spent the night with her, Oliver."

"Are you sure?" Nigel had said he was in his hotel in the city until the morning. Neither Grant nor Thomas had said otherwise. "It could have been a mistake."

Darling's lips turned down. "It looks like Nigel Marks isn't the saint you thought him to be." There was no mistaking the undercurrent of anger that coursed through her words. He was a step away from a dangerous territory with her.

"This isn't how I pictured running into you after all of these years." Silence stretched between them as neither had a response ready for the topic of their past. Oliver then continued, "I'd still like to catch up, but it looks like tonight might not be good." He had already started a mental list of things he needed to do. "Can I treat you to breakfast tomorrow instead?"

Darling seemed to be thinking it over. Eventually she

nodded before she, too, disappeared back into the building. Oliver retreated to his SUV, pulling his phone out to call Nikki along the way.

The job was officially no longer boring.

Chapter Four

Darling chewed on her bottom lip, not stopping until she tasted lipstick. She was standing in the lobby of Acuity the next morning, staring into a folder, confused beyond belief.

The afternoon before had blurred by after she'd given a statement to Derrick and then been ushered home. He wasn't happy with her investigating, or the fact that she wouldn't say for whom, and had in so many words let her know that she wouldn't keep that secret for long. So instead she had tried to reach Mrs. Marks. The resort manager she had spoken with had taken a message and promised to give it to her when she returned.

It had eaten Darling up as she lay awake in bed, fuming that Oliver knew more about what was going on with Nigel than she did. Here he was, stepping into her town, and he had already managed to be on the inside loop with the infamous Mr. Marks. She could have called Oliver, sure, but her pride had shut that idea down quickly. Admitting she needed the fair-haired man in any capacity was something she refused to do ever again.

After only a few hours of rest, she had opened Acuity to find a folder filled with curious things lying on the hardwood floor, slipped under the door as an unmistakable greeting.

Now between her hands were four eight-by-ten pictures of Nigel Marks with a woman who wasn't his wife. Each picture—printed on glossy card stock and dated—was focused on the businessman and a red-haired woman in four varying shows of affection. The first two had them in an intimate embrace, while the third and fourth were of the two sharing meals. In one of those, Nigel was even holding the woman's hand, a smile splitting his lips. None of the four pictures had a clear shot of the female's face, but there was no denying it was the same woman in each and that the couple was happy. All pictures were dated from the previous December up until March, the month before.

Elizabeth Marks had been looking for proof that her husband had been seeing another woman in secret. From what Darling could tell, she was holding that proof.

But why?

She stood there, cycling through each picture again, when a knock at the door made her jump. The folder fell to the floor. She hurried to pick it up when she noticed there was something still inside it.

"Knock, knock. It's me," called Oliver from the other side of the locked front entrance. "You in there?"

Darling didn't immediately respond. Her eyes were glued to a newspaper clipping that had been stuck to the inside of the folder. It was a picture of her parents that she knew to be almost nine years old. However, it was the words written in red across it that grabbed all her attention.

Do the right thing this time.

"Hold on," Darling said after another knock sounded. She hoped Oliver didn't catch the waver in her voice. She put the pictures, including the clipping, back into the folder and tucked it under her arm to unlock the door.

"You okay?" Oliver asked immediately. Perhaps her poker face wasn't at its best today. He wore a zip-up black jacket over a black shirt that looked good contrasting with his lighter hair. Staying away from the all-black body-guard stereotype, he'd donned beige cargo pants with more pockets than she cared to count. She didn't recognize the brand of tennis shoes, but she bet that he could run fast in them if needed.

"Yeah, just tired," she lied, leading him into the lobby. "Let me just freshen up and I'll be ready to go." She stuffed the folder into her purse and excused herself to the bathroom. There she turned on the faucet and took a deep breath.

What had briefly felt like a gift that could close her case against Nigel now felt tainted and wrong. As far as she knew, no one in Mulligan was aware of her parents' past, especially the quiet part she had played in the background.

Do the right thing.

She didn't need to wonder what that meant.

Whoever had sent her the folder wanted her to turn it in to the cops. But why not just do it themselves? If the red-haired woman was the same one who had been left in the tub, that meant the pictures definitely linked the two before the hotel room. Why would they give them to her?

Darling ran her hands under the cold water but didn't splash her face. For the first time in a long while, she had taken pains to look nice. She wore a pale pink blouse that dipped down into a V—not enough to be seductive, just feminine—a pair of comfortably tight light blue jeans and dark brown boots that folded down at the ankle. Her hair was twisted up into a purposefully messy bun so the yellow daisy earrings she loved so much could be seen with ease. A subtle coral tinted her plump yet small lips. They were downturned at the moment.

She'd convinced herself that Oliver's presence in Mulligan was a good thing. What Oliver had done in the past had broken a big part of who she was, but she liked to think she had come out stronger because of it. As soon as she had turned eighteen, she had left California, her family and all of those bad memories behind. There was no reason to dredge them up now. If she could keep her head up while Oliver was in town, then she could get through anything.

That thought alone pushed a wave of new purpose through her bones until it made her stand taller. Putting away the man behind the murder of the woman in the tub was more important than her failed love life. Nigel Marks's mistress deserved better.

Darling eyed her purse before nodding to herself in the mirror.

She *did* need to do the right thing.

"You ready for some breakfast?" Oliver asked when she emerged. He was talking to her but looking around the office's lobby. Pride swelled in her chest.

Acuity Investigations was housed in an old strip mall that predated half of the other businesses in Mulligan. Acuity was at the tail end of the shops, next to a narrow road that deposited drivers back on Main Street. The reason Jeff Berns, Darling's former boss, had rented the particular space was its proximity to traffic yet its back-door access so clients could be as discreet as they wanted.

Darling remembered the first time she had walked into Acuity. The cream-colored walls, leather and oak furniture, pictures of boats nestled in calm water and slightly musty smell had been a sharp contrast to what she referred to as her former life. Instead of turning her nose up at Jeff and his place of employment like her parents would have, Darling had embraced it with vigor.

Acuity wasn't fancy or elegant, but it was important to her. As Oliver's eyes traveled along the hardwood floors to the heavy oak door that led to her office, in the back of her mind she hoped he felt that truth ring through his bones as she did.

"Actually, would you mind if we swung by the police station really quickly?" Darling asked when his eyes finally moved back to hers. "I need to give something to Deputy Derrick." When he didn't immediately respond, she tacked on, "If you don't have enough time, we could reschedule."

"No, it's fine," he answered. "Just as long as we actually eat afterward."

Darling slipped into her black faux-leather jacket and smiled inwardly at its comfort before ushering Oliver out and locking the door behind her. They walked in silence up to his SUV. She was oddly saddened when he didn't open the door for her. The Oliver from younger years had not only opened the car doors for her but also occasionally put on her seat belt, laughing and mock-admonishing her about the importance of car safety.

The memory tugged at long-forgotten heartstrings. Now as they settled into their seats, the disconnect between the present and the past stretched between them.

"Is this visit for business or pleasure?" Oliver asked as the SUV pulled out of the parking lot.

She gave him a sideways glance. "Business."

He nodded to the road. "Does it have to do with Nigel?"

"It does," she admitted.

"What is it?" he ventured.

"Something very important."

She didn't elaborate and he didn't push.

"I don't think he did it, Darling," Oliver said. "I don't think he killed that woman."

Darling couldn't help the reflex to tense up, her body readying automatically for a verbal spar. It was a response she had picked up out of necessity as a young female investigator. She rolled her shoulders back to ease the new tension and answered with a controlled voice.

"Did he admit to being at the hotel last night?" she asked.

She knew Oliver sensed the mood change. He shifted in his seat and lost his smile.

"I didn't get a chance to ask. As soon as he was released, he locked himself in his study with his lawyer and son. They were still there when I left."

Darling's control cracked. "They *released* him?"

Oliver nodded. "I don't think there was enough evidence to hold him."

"But he was there," Darling exclaimed. "He spent the night with her!"

"Just because he spent the night with her doesn't mean he killed her, Darling." Instant anger filled her veins at how he said her name, as if she was some confused child.

"So, what, it's just a coincidence, then? You can't comprehend that a man like him, an adulterer, could ever do something like kill his mistress?"

She watched as his jaw hardened. "We don't know for

sure he was having an affair," he said. "The visit could have been business-related for all we know."

Darling laughed. "Oh, you're right. They probably just sat around and talked business all night."

"It's possible," he tried, but Darling wasn't having it. Defending men like Nigel, bending to their wills, was unforgivable in her book. Heat rose from the pit of her stomach, but it wasn't embarrassment. It was the force of an old wound breaking open. She yanked the pictures from her purse right as they turned into the station's parking lot.

"He seems to like to talk to women in secret," she said, barely able to keep her voice level. Oliver took the pictures from her hand and cycled through them just as she remembered the clipping was on the bottom. Operating on the assumption that Oliver knew he was dealing with an angry Darling, she snatched the pictures back and threw open the door. "I'll be right back."

She marched into the weathered, blue-painted building without looking back. Her head was almost spinning with the range of emotions she had experienced in such a short amount of time. It amazed her how Oliver brought out the worst in her, no matter what attitude she wanted to convey. Instead of seeming put together, she had come off as truly childish in the end. Her cheeks heated; this time it was all shame.

The Mulligan Police Department was poorly insulated. Derrick had liked to joke that was one of the reasons the town's crime rate was so low. No one wanted to spend the night in the cells. She hadn't even liked spending the morning in one. Darling wondered how Nigel Marks's act would shake the community's relative peace and quiet. She made a mental note to grab a newspaper after her breakfast date was finished to see how the media had handled it.

"Hey, Trudy," Darling greeted the bundled-up secretary. She was the first and only barrier between the front doors and the bullpen.

"Darlin' Smith, I hope you're not in trouble again," she said. Her tone was laced with disapproval. Trudy had more grandchildren than most people had fingers. She was proud of this and often acted as Mulligan's mother hen, believing she had earned that right even more with every relation that had come from her and her children.

"Not today," she said with a small smile. "But I do need to see Derrick. Is he in?"

"No, ma'am. He should be in soon, though. Do you want to wait?"

"Um, no, but can I just leave something on his desk?" Darling flashed the woman the folder, though the pictures were in her other hand. Trudy nodded and let Darling around her to the rows of desks. Another cop sat focused on his computer and didn't seem to notice or care as she went to Derrick's space in the corner. Glancing at a picture of Derrick's niece and nephew positioned next to his keyboard, Darling felt as if she was making a good decision by turning the evidence in. Derrick wasn't her Mr. Right, but he was a good, just man.

However, in true Darling fashion, she quickly snapped pictures of each individual image and their corresponding dates before slipping them into the folder, minus the newspaper clipping. She stuffed that into her back pocket.

A source dropped these off at my office today.
Darling.

She scribbled down the lie and was suddenly glad that Derrick and his questions weren't there yet. He'd call her, no doubt, but not until after he had investigated the evidence. If he caught her now, it would be the other way around, a thought that made her hightail it out of the station.

Dodging one ex only to get into the car with another.

The Red Leaf was one of two local coffee shops in Mulligan. Like the town, it was quaint, yet endearing in its own right. They also made a mean coffee, Darling said after she had returned from the station. She hadn't apologized for her outburst, but he hadn't expected her to, either.

Bailing Darling Smith out of jail had never been on Oliver's list of scenarios for when, and if, they ever met again. Sure, he'd thought of the possibility of crossing paths when he went home to California to visit family. Maybe even a random encounter in an airport as he traveled for work. But never like this.

Occasionally, he'd wonder what he would say to her during a chance encounter. *How have you been? Isn't the weather nice? Have you cut your hair?* They weren't good greetings, but how else could he skate around the topic of their past? Now, as they sat across from each other in a worn leather booth, he doubted such a thing could be accomplished. Darling hadn't forgotten or forgiven what he'd done, and he couldn't blame her for that.

He hadn't forgiven himself yet, either.

"Expecting a call?" he asked as she took care to adjust the volume on her cell.

"Expecting? No. Hoping? Still no, but I can't ignore it." He raised his eyebrow so she explained, "Work-related."

"Ah, I know the feeling." He pulled his phone from his pocket and placed it on the table, as well. With the recent changes in the job, Nikki had made it clear she wanted all guards to have their phones on at all times, even when they were off the clock.

"So, I have to ask. You didn't seem at all surprised to see me yesterday... Why?" she asked, getting the conversational ball rolling. Darling had never been a fan of silence.

Unlike the seventeen-year-old he had left behind, this Darling was all grown and all woman. Oliver couldn't deny she was beautiful—she always had been—but now there was something more as he really looked at her. The way her dark green eyes bore into his, trying to figure him out, was so fierce it almost shook his resolve to leave the past just where it was.

"My boss told me the name and I couldn't imagine it being a coincidence," he said honestly. "Though I wasn't a hundred percent given the circumstances."

"Ah...circumstances. You mean the trespassing accusation."

Oliver made a gun with his hand. "Bingo."

"Well," she said, "given recent developments, I'd say that *accusation* is the least of everyone's worries. Wouldn't you agree?" she finished, crossing her arms over her chest. That movement meant Oliver needed to tread softly.

"We wouldn't have taken on this case if he was a bad man, Darling. I stand by what I said earlier. Just because he was there doesn't mean he did it, and I'd like to ask you to drop whatever case you might still have that involves him," he said. And, apparently, it was the wrong thing to say. Almost instantly the color in her cheeks rose, her brows lifted and her lips thinned. Knowing a storm was brewing, Oliver made a second conversational mistake, hoping to pacify her. "For old times' sake, Darling."

He might as well have kicked her beneath the table.

"I can't believe you're still simply rolling over for the big dogs," she bit out, angry. "Nigel Marks is a millionaire, so that makes whatever he does justifiable? Is that why you do what you do, Oliver? Do you get some kind of thrill from protecting the rich? Did you ever stop and wonder why that's even necessary? No, you probably don't, because all you care about is pleasing the elite, just waiting for them to yell 'jump.'"

She stood so abruptly that the booth's seat pushed back and scraped the tile. The waitress and few patrons looked over, but Darling seemed oblivious. Like them, Oliver looked at her, but in a state of awe.

"You know what?" she said. "I'm not going to sit here and be talked to like I'm still the girl you used to know." She grabbed her purse and started to leave, pausing for a second to finish her tirade. "And Oliver, if I still had a case, I certainly wouldn't drop it 'for old times' sake.'"

And just like that Darling Smith became the one who left.

Chapter Five

There was a reason Darling had picked the café as a place to talk with Oliver—it was only a block away from her office. He watched her through the café's front windows as she walked in an angry huff down the street, turning into the strip mall's parking lot and disappearing around back. Each step had been rigged with tension, each movement forced.

The waitress waited until Darling was out of view before coming to the table. She also didn't look so pleased with him.

He let out a long breath.

"Can I place a to-go order?" he asked, glancing back out the window.

For the first time in years, Oliver let the past wash over him, bringing in the flood of memories that pieced together the last conversation he had had with the younger Darling.

She had been wearing a white dress with daisies printed across it, a stark contrast to the tears that had streaked her cheeks.

"They're horrible, Oliver," she had yelled. "They'll never change! They of all people have no right to tell me what I do and don't deserve. So, please, let's just leave. Let's run away together and never look back!"

"We can't."

"Oliver, I love you," she had said, taking his hands in hers. They had been soft and warm. "And if you love me as much as you say, we *can* make it." There had been so much hope in her eyes, despite the tears she had shed because of her parents. Despite everything she had gone through in the past year. So much hope that Oliver could still see it clearly today.

"But, Darling," he had whispered. "I don't want to."

Just like that, the hope had died, and the memory of breaking Darling Smith's heart had burned itself into his mind, becoming another moment he could never forget.

It still amazed him that such a brief conversation had made such a big impact.

"Order's ready," called the waitress, holding up a paper bag and a cardboard cup holder. Oliver pulled himself out of the hardest conversation he'd ever had and paid for the food.

Instead of climbing into his rental, he followed the same path Darling had taken until he was, yet again, at Acuity's front door. He didn't knock this time. She wouldn't have let him in if he had.

The private investigator was standing behind the lone desk in the front room, a scowl still attached to her face, when he pushed into the lobby. Her hair billowed around her head, a crown of dark blond that seemed to crackle to life as the rest of her grew angry at the sight of him. Before she could get on a verbal roll again, he held up his café spoils in surrender.

"I'm sorry," he said, smile wiped from his face. He let his hands fall and took a step closer. "After all this time, I shouldn't have asked, and certainly shouldn't have expected, you to listen to me. It wasn't fair." Her lips parted to talk, though he wasn't sure which emotion was trying to push through. He continued before he could find out. "Although you weren't fair, either. It's clear you've made a few assumptions about me—some I'd like to correct—and, again, I can't quite blame you for that. But the fact remains that it's been eight years since we last saw each other. Our lives have changed—we've changed with them." He took one last step forward, testing her waters. "Give me the chance to set a few things straight, Darling."

"You don't have to answer to me," she replied. Her voice was low.

"You're right," he agreed. "I don't have to, but I need to."

Darling's expression—brows drawn together, lips thin, jaw set—slowly changed to a more pleasant mask. For the first time since he had walked in, she looked at his peace offering. She didn't smile, though he knew she could smell the delicious chocolate-covered confections, but she didn't continue to frown. If he wanted to find a safe ground with Present-Day Darling, he was going to have to come to terms with the fact that she might not warm up to him again. He would have to settle for whatever she gave him and ignore how the idea of never being in her good opinion hurt deeper than he'd like to admit.

"I'm surprised Carla still served you after the scene I caused," she finally said. "You must have done some quick sweet talking."

Oliver smiled. Dangerous Darling was gone. He'd get a chance to explain everything now. Well, at least the real reason behind his love and respect for the Orion

Group. That explanation meant more to him than she could fathom. The desire to tell her what had happened three years ago had been replaced by the need to explain the past the moment she had stormed out of the café.

"I told her I needed to score some points with you." He motioned to the bag in his hand. "Hopefully freshly baked chocolate donuts and a coffee with two creams and three sugars will do just that."

Joy flashed through him as the corner of Darling's lip quirked up.

"You're lucky that my breakfast preferences aren't one of the things that have changed over the years."

Darling walked forward, grabbed the bag and led him into her office. It was a much smaller room, but Oliver instantly liked it. Exposed brick walls, once painted white and now chipping, were decorated with certification plaques, black-and-white pictures of Mulligan scenery and a rusted sign that said Acuity across it.

"So you actually own Acuity, then?"

"I sure do. Expenses and all." Even as she said it sarcastically, he saw the pride in it. She was comfortable behind her desk. He was sure her ease was subconscious. Darling Smith had found her place in the world after all. He wondered how her parents felt about it but knew he'd never ask her that. If he was a gaping wound, they were bottomless caverns. "I interned here when I was eighteen. Jeff didn't tell me then, but he was ready to retire. So, he started to groom me as his replacement. When I was done with all my certifications and schooling, he split. Now it's just me." She bit into her donut and her eyes fluttered closed. "And more than occasionally the sweet, sweet Red Leaf pastry."

"Sounds like a good setup. I'm happy for you."

Darling flashed a small smile. "Thanks," she said. "Now, what about you? What assumptions do you need to clear up?"

"I feel like you have the wrong impression of me."

"I still stand by the fact that you don't need to explain yourself to me. You could be married with kids and living in the suburbs of Canada for all I know. Not that it would be bad if you did. I just want you to know that you don't owe me anything, Oliver."

This made him laugh. He lifted his left hand to show ringless fingers.

"No marriages, children or suburban Canadian living. Just an apartment in Dallas, where Orion's located." It might have been his imagination, but he thought she looked pleased at this information. He had already done his research on her. She wasn't and hadn't been married. Although he wasn't sure if she was attached currently. He decided against asking her that, too. "I know you aren't forcing me to explain, but I'd still like to do it."

"All right, then, I'm listening." She set her pastry down and laced her fingers together on the desktop. Oliver took a deep breath and began.

"I know you think I've sold out by working for a company that caters to the rich and privileged, but that's only partially true. Before I worked for Orion, I was hired as an agent at another security agency called Redstone Solutions out in California. I was excited—thrilled—with the offer because, one, I needed the money, and two, I was good at what I did. A lot of people think bodyguards just stand around and occasionally have to tackle someone, but the truth is there's a lot more to it. Strategies and problem solving, for instance. Redstone let me lead an exciting life of travel and leisure while also challenging me at every turn." Oliver felt pride and nostalgia surge through him. Though it didn't last long. It never did. He felt his smile sag and his face harden. Darling leaned in closer. "But then Morgan Avery was killed, and everything changed."

Darling's eyebrows rose in question, but she didn't interrupt.

"Redstone is a large company with more connections and funding than you can imagine. Its reach isn't limited to the US, either. I was based in the California branch as a part of a three-man team when Morgan Avery first came in and asked for our help. She was twenty-one and an astronomy student, utterly brilliant. She'd been competing for a spot in an elite university program in the UK that, if she made it in, would make her career. But when she was invited to the final round of the competition in England, she started getting these really nasty letters. Anonymous letters that threatened her life. So, she came to Redstone Solutions asking for a team to escort her while she traveled there. The only problem was, she didn't have enough money to come up with the minimum payment. My boss turned her away after she practically begged us to reconsider." Oliver's jaw tightened and his fists balled. "For a week straight, she tried to convince us, and for a week we had to turn her away. The day before she was scheduled to fly out, she was found dead in a ditch near the airport—beaten and almost unrecognizable. The police were able to find the killer—a competitor—and send him to prison for life, but it didn't matter. The damage was done." Oliver took a long pull from his coffee before continuing, finding a better place in his mind. "Morgan's death was an eye-opener for us."

"Us?"

"Nikki, the secretary, was the person who talked to Morgan the most. After Morgan's death, she became furious and left Redstone to start her own security agency. She asked me and my then-team to join her." He smiled. "We did, and that's Orion's origin story."

"Secretary to boss, huh?" Darling sipped her coffee. "I like the sound of her."

"Nikki was and is a beast in the business world. When she left, she already had a few connections willing to fund Orion. Since then, she's kept it going *and* growing with no issues."

"She sounds like my kind of woman," Darling replied with a smirk. Oliver laughed.

"She's something, all right." He sobered. "We've spent the last three years offering our services to those who can't afford it but need it, specifically when traveling. Without her connections and the occasional sponsor, we'd never be able to take on our clients for basically free."

He watched as Darling's ears seemed to perk right up.

"Basically free?"

Oliver smiled, but he was sad. "We'll never turn away another Morgan."

"Wow," Darling breathed. "And Nigel Marks is one of those sponsors you have to take on occasionally?" she guessed.

"Bingo. Team Delta was assigned and now, here I am."

"Team Delta?" She snorted. "What are you, five?"

Oliver held his hands up and grinned. "Hey, don't look at me! My bud took the Orion Belt theme and went with it. He got a kick out of Orion Belt's three stars also being referenced as Delta, Epsilon and Zeta. "

Darling's eyes widened as she understood the meaning behind the name. Her voice softened. "Morgan was in astronomy. The name Orion was chosen to honor her memory," she said.

Oliver nodded. "It was her favorite constellation." A warmth that was equal parts fondness and sadness pooled in his chest as he remembered Morgan. "Darling, I know I have no right to come into your life and start trying to call the shots, but I have to state this again. I don't think Nigel killed that woman, and unless he's convicted or decides he doesn't need us, he's my number-one priority while in Mulligan." Oliver wanted to put his hand out to touch hers, to show her that she should trust him. To show that even though Nigel was his top priority, he still cared for her. Even though he shouldn't.

Darling, to his surprise, seemed to choose her next words carefully.

"I understand," she said in almost a whisper. "But, tell me, why are you so sure that he's innocent?"

"The surprise on his face when he found out about the body," he answered.

Darling huffed. "Surprise can be faked, Oliver. I do it every Christmas when Trudy gives me a can of peanut brittle wrapped in reindeer-decorated paper."

"True, he could have faked the surprise," he conceded. "But not the pain." Oliver replayed the moment when he'd watched as the cops had told the wealthy man about the body. He didn't need to hear the man's response to know it had caught him completely by surprise...and hurt him.

Darling hesitated, brows pulling together, but she didn't have time to respond. Her phone blared to life, a cute jingle that felt out of place within the conversation. She let out a long sigh as she read the ID.

"Excuse me a second," she said, standing.

"No problem."

Oliver was able to drink the rest of his neglected coffee, pairing it with one of Darling's chocolate-covered circles of delicious sin, before the private investigator came back. The look on her face made him stand.

"What's wrong?"

Darling bit her lip. "Do you want a list or a long-winded sentence?" It was a less-than-halfhearted attempt to lighten whatever mood had erupted around her. Oliver answered with an equal lack of mirth.

"List."

"One, the medical examiner believes our Jane Doe was killed yesterday morning," she ticked off. "Two, that puts Nigel in the clear since he was apparently eating breakfast with your team while you were bailing me out." Oliver wanted to feel relief at her words—that he had been right about Nigel's innocence—but Darling's grim expression had every part of him on guard. "Three, they haven't been able to identify the woman yet." There was a hesitation after the words left her mouth.

"Couldn't Nigel identify her? If he met with her he had to *know* her."

She held up four fingers. "Four, Nigel is denying that he was ever even at the hotel, let alone in Mulligan, last night. No one has stepped forward to prove otherwise, and it's Nigel's word against Dan's. There are no security cameras at the hotel, either. None that work properly, at least."

Oliver's instinct was to question Dan's claim of seeing Nigel in the first place, but he felt an irrational loyalty to him, because it was obvious that was how Darling felt about him.

"I don't think prints take that long to process," he said

instead. "Surely they'll figure out who she is within the week and go from there."

Darling's face darkened. She held up her hand. "Five," she said, voice shaking despite her calm exterior, "all of her fingers and teeth are missing. Someone removed them."

Chapter Six

Any chance of normal conversation disappeared at the grim news.

"Removed?" Oliver repeated.

Darling let her hand drop to her side and settled back behind her desk. Her half-eaten donut wasn't as appealing as it had been minutes before.

"Postmortem, but yes," she confirmed.

Oliver also sat back down, though he didn't relax.

"Who told you all this?"

"Derrick," she admitted.

"You two must be close if he'll disclose information about an ongoing murder investigation."

"We used to date, but now we don't," she said matter-of-factly. "I think he told me to warn me."

Oliver's eyebrow rose at that. "Warn you? Of what?"

"That my case against Nigel isn't safe anymore," she said. "Considering the murder."

"So he thinks Nigel is still connected even though he's denied being in town?"

"I'm not the only one who trusts Dan. Just because Nigel has an alibi for where he physically was at the time of the murder doesn't mean he isn't connected." Darling recalled the pictures of the millionaire and the red-haired woman. Derrick had confirmed their Jane Doe also had red hair. If they could prove it was the same woman, Nigel would have no choice but to offer her identity up.

"You think he's denying knowing her because he had someone else kill her," Oliver summarized. Darling didn't nod or shake her head. She was trying indifference. "Why would he go through all of that trouble?" he asked.

"Something tells me he can't afford an affair right now."

Darling froze. She was being too candid with Oliver, though she wondered if it even mattered anymore. Soon the town of Mulligan would hear the rumor that Nigel had been at the hotel and the woman who had been with him was dead. With or without denials, the idea that Nigel was an adulterer would cross each resident's mind at least once. The beloved Nigel Marks was about to have his image tested with or without her saying a word.

"Ah," Oliver said with a slight nod. "The prenup loophole. If he cheats, the wife can take at least half of everything Nigel owns."

"What?" She feigned ignorance but barely concealed her surprise. Oliver wasn't buying it.

"You aren't the only person with connections," he said. "If working for Redstone Solutions taught us anything, it was to be thorough in knowing the clients we take on. That includes the threats to them. Orion may be small and less well funded, but that doesn't mean our analysts are anything to laugh at." That piqued Darling's interest, but she didn't interrupt to follow up. "If Elizabeth Marks wasn't in the Bahamas right now, she would be the first person I would suspect. Although, like you said about Nigel, she could still be connected even though she wasn't physically there."

"But, even if what you say is true about this prenup

thing," she said, "why kill the mistress when you can expose her?"

"Why expose the mistress when you can kill her?"

"Ah, casting blame on the jilted wife. An overplayed card, don't you think?" Darling quirked her lip up into a grin.

He laughed. "I'm assuming the case you have against Nigel is about infidelity. Why else would you be snooping around his house and then the hotel he was at?"

"Nigel Marks is almost a legend in Mulligan. Who's to say I'm not his number-one fan?" Darling had her eyebrow raised high, a smirk across her lips to match. She knew Oliver wasn't dumb, but she wasn't going to admit to her deal with Elizabeth yet. There were a few questions she needed to ask the millionaire's wife first.

"Last time I checked, you weren't the biggest fan of the upper class," Oliver said. She couldn't deny that. "That's why I assume you asked the hotel owner to keep an eye out for Nigel, just in case."

Darling held up her hands. "Okay, you got me," she said. "I am Nigel's number-one fan. I have a poster of him over my bed and everything."

Oliver laughed, and the mood around them softened. They lapsed into small talk while picking up and finishing their food, avoiding the topics of murder and blame. They were delving into their individual pasts, while the one they shared wasn't brought up. Darling silently marveled at how the Oliver that sat across from her was so similar to the one all those years ago, and yet completely different. She couldn't quite put her finger on it, though she didn't want to, either. Trying to define Oliver Quinn would be a slippery slope—if she found she liked the new one, then what? It was better for everyone if she just played nice and treated the man as an old friend, nothing more and nothing less.

"Speaking of the job," Oliver said, "I need to go relieve Thomas. He worked well past his hours last night."

"Not to pry into your work, but where does the whole murder accusation leave you with Marks?" she asked, standing with him and ignoring the small part of her that wanted him to stay.

"Innocent until proven guilty." He shrugged. "The fact that he was with my team during the woman's death is an ironclad alibi, in my mind. The only way we'll stop working for him now is if Nigel terminates the contract or Nikki calls us off. Considering he already signed a contract, it'll cost him more to get out of it than to stay in it, and last time I talked to Nikki, she said we continue to do our job. She's a good person, Darling. There's a reason we all trust her to make the right call."

Darling nodded, not wanting to point out that everyone at some point was wrong. If this was Nikki's time, it meant Oliver and his team were protecting the man behind a woman's murder. But she let that thought slide. She wasn't Oliver's mother or wife or even his girlfriend. Darling couldn't dictate his choices just as he couldn't dictate hers.

"It *was* nice catching up with you, though," he added, meeting her eyes and holding her gaze. "Even the bumpy parts."

Darling couldn't help but smile back. "It certainly has been interesting."

Oliver picked up his coffee and slid his phone back into his pocket. Darling didn't know if she was supposed to hug him or shake his hand as a goodbye. It wasn't as if they had done either in greeting the day before when he had strolled into the town jail to get her out. As she struggled with trying to figure out what to say to the man who had broken her heart, Oliver saved her the trouble.

"I would say goodbye, but I have a feeling you'll pop back up in the middle of wherever you aren't supposed to be. So I'll just see you then." She returned his smile with a mischievous one of her own and watched as he walked out of her office.

He was absolutely right.

An hour passed without any new leads, evidence or answers. Darling was feeling unbelievably restless. She half expected Derrick to call or stop by with a no-nonsense attitude about her case, but Acuity's door remained closed and her phone remained quiet.

So Darling, unable to cope with the fact she wasn't making progress, made a list of all the evidence and facts she had. It reminded her that her camera was still beneath Dan's desk at the hotel.

"Better than sitting here and doing nothing," she said to the office.

Despite yesterday's discovery, the Mulligan Motel looked as normal as it ever did. No one was in the office, but Darling preferred that. She hurried to grab her camera, hoping to avoid explaining to Dan why she was back.

It took a few seconds to register that there was no camera to grab.

"What the?" she asked herself, squatting to make sure it hadn't been pushed out of view.

Darling's blood ran cold.

There was a piece of paper where her camera had been. Written across it in red ink was a message.

You already did the right thing, Darling. Now stop.

Chapter Seven

He wasn't tall, he wasn't big and he wasn't intimidating. His shoulders weren't wide, either, but he still held himself up straight and proud. With dark hair, muddy-green eyes and a surprisingly hard jaw, Jace Marks was sculpted with equal parts his father and the most average of people.

Oliver shook the twenty-six-year-old's hand and couldn't help but compare him with Nigel.

While his father dressed to impress, Jace wore a blue flannel button-up, jeans and tennis shoes. Instead of having a cropped haircut like Nigel's, Jace slicked back his short hair with a pair of sunglasses resting on top. Despite the past forty-eight hours, he looked rested enough.

However, one detail that matched his father to a tee was the trademark smile he wore easily. It spoke of wealth, privilege and many, many secrets.

"It's good to properly meet you," Jace said. He shook Oliver's hand. He had a firm grip, which also surprised Oliver. "A passing hello at the police station isn't the same thing, if you ask me."

"No problem. I didn't realize you would be in Mulligan during our stay," Oliver admitted. All clients were asked to disclose pertinent information. That included their travel companions.

"When the merger got complicated, Nigel called me in," he answered. "I hadn't planned on staying, but given recent events, I feel I should be here to support him."

They were standing in the kitchen, Oliver next to the back door with a clear sight line to the front. Nigel was still upstairs in his study with his lawyer, Stan, while Grant was stationed outside the door. Oliver had sent Thomas to rest as soon as he had come through the door, considering the new recruit hadn't slept yet.

"Nigel," Oliver repeated the name. Had he been informed wrong? Was Jace a stepson and not the millionaire's blood relation?

"He doesn't like when he's referred to as Father in a work setting," Jace answered with an apologetic smile. "He doesn't want anyone to think he's partaking in favoritism. So we keep to a first-name basis when working, but I guess it's become a general habit."

Oliver supposed that made sense. He didn't call Nikki by her first name in front of the new recruits or clients, but that was more of a show of respect. Members of Orion earned the right to be familiar with the head honcho by doing a good job and remaining humble. Nigel having his son call him by his first name might make sense, but Oliver couldn't deny he didn't like the informality of it. If he'd ever called his dad by his name, Jacob Quinn would have been fast to correct him.

"So you work at Charisma?" Oliver asked when it was apparent Jace wasn't leaving the kitchen anytime soon.

He sat down at the island and faced Oliver. "It's the only place I've ever worked," he said with notable pride. "I oversee the company's support specialists and deal directly with the more complicated clients, walking them through every part of the investment process. With this merger going through, however, I'm hoping to make the move up in the ranks. But now, with this..." He looked up at the ceiling and shook his head. "I just hope it all gets taken care of before it does any damage to the company."

Oliver couldn't help the raise of his eyebrow or, he was sure, the look of slight disgust that contorted his face. If Darling had been in the room, she would have flown right off the handle at how crass the millionaire's son was being. She would have pointed out in no uncertain terms that he was referring to a human being who had been murdered and that finding justice for her was much more important.

But Darling wasn't there.

"Hopefully it will be sorted out," Oliver offered.

Jace nodded, oblivious to Oliver's thoughts. "You know, I told Nigel he shouldn't have even come back to Mulligan for the merger. I could have handled it and stayed in the city, but he's getting stubborn in his old age." He frowned, and his brow creased. "If he had listened to me, this whole ordeal could have been avoided. But he loves this place, the small town he came from and the people who love him. I wonder, though, if they'll love him after all of this."

Oliver didn't have an answer to that.

"I should get going now. This merger won't happen by itself." Jace grabbed a water from the refrigerator and started to leave. "In case Nigel didn't tell you or your boss, my mother will be here by the end of the week."

"No, I haven't been told that yet," Oliver said, already cursing in his head.

"This family is all about supporting one another," Jace

said. "You accuse one of us of murder, you accuse all of us of murder." He said it with sarcasm, meant to be an offhand joke, but Oliver saw the irony in it. Jace's parents were, in fact, the top two suspects.

For the next three hours, Oliver did the more boring parts of bodyguard work while his mind kept running. If a thought wasn't about his current client, it was undoubtedly about a petite, sandy-haired woman with more attitude than even she probably knew what to do with. Darling Smith was incapable of ignoring what was wrong in the world. It was an infuriating and endearing quality that he hadn't realized he missed.

He moved through the first floor, scanning his surroundings with tried interest. Oliver liked to memorize each piece as if he hadn't done it the previous day. That way, if something was off—if something had changed—he'd be more likely to notice.

The smaller details often ended up making the most impact.

THE LONGER DARLING stared at the note, the harder she willed it to explain itself.

"Who wrote you?" she asked it for the tenth time. "And why?"

Like the nine times before, the note didn't answer. Instead, it stayed frustratingly still against the top of her desk, its red ink blaring across the surface.

You already did the right thing, Darling. Now stop.

There was no denying the message had been intended for her.

So, Darling had gone back to her car with the hairs on the back of her neck standing at salute, also confused.

She had driven back to Acuity and pulled the newspaper clipping with the first note out to compare the two.

The handwriting and color had matched perfectly.

Whoever wanted Nigel's affair out in the open was not only was watching Darling but also had taken her camera. Why? The cops had seen everything in that room plus more once they had gotten there.

Darling growled to her office.

It felt like a threat.

Had Nigel caught wind of her case against him, or had he figured it out like Oliver had? But then why give her the pictures of Nigel and the red-haired woman, and urge her to turn them in to the police? And why tell her to stop?

Stop what?

Darling cast a long look at her empty coffee cup. It was nearly five, and she had put off calling Derrick for hours. Just as her resolve to disclose everything began to dissolve, her phone chirped to life with the name Liz across the screen.

"You're very hard to get a hold of," Darling greeted her, no humor in her voice.

Elizabeth didn't waste an excuse.

"We both know I'm a suspect in this murder. I'm having to cut my vacation short while recording my recent movements to send over to my lawyer. All under the ever-watchful eye of my mother. Be thankful I was finally able to step away from her."

"Does she not know about your case with me?"

"No. I love my mother, but I don't love her tendency to run her mouth. Give her enough wine and she'll tell you every secret she's ever been told." Elizabeth was tired, that much Darling could tell. She pictured the woman's impeccable posture slightly bent, makeup pulling double duty to hide the stress in her face. "Have you told anyone about our case yet?"

"No, ma'am. I wanted to at least talk to you first." There was a silence, and Darling used it to her advantage. "Did you hire another private investigator to trail Nigel before me or after me?"

"No," Elizabeth responded. "Truthfully, hiring you was a last-minute decision. The less people know about my plans to leave Nigel, the better. That being said, I want you to go to the police and tell them everything."

Darling had to take a beat to process that. "About the case?"

"About the case, the reason why I hired you, what you've found, everything." There was a change in her tone. Elizabeth had moved from tired to determined in a breath. She brooked no argument with her words. "Give them total disclosure. I don't want them looking at me as a suspect. I didn't hire anyone to kill that woman, and I don't want anyone to think I did. I will ask, though, if you think the police could keep my desire for a divorce on the private side of the investigation?"

Darling thought this over. "I can't promise anything, but I think they would. Nigel has denied knowing the woman or even seeing her, so right now, I think they are just trying to figure out who she is. I don't think they would take the time to publicize your marital problems."

"Good. Then, please, could you tell them everything while still trying to keep it from Nigel?"

"Yes, I can do that." Darling wanted to exhale in relief. Elizabeth didn't know it, but if she hadn't called before six, Darling would have told Derrick everything anyway.

"Great. Now, one last thing," Elizabeth said before her

voice dropped to almost a whisper. "I don't care how you do it, but I want you to find out who that woman is. My husband may be a cheat, but he's no killer. Something isn't right, and now my family is suffering for it. I will not stand for that."

Darling didn't doubt for a second that anyone who crossed Elizabeth Marks would regret it. She just hoped Jane Doe hadn't been one of those people.

Darling accepted the job, though she didn't tell Elizabeth she had already decided to pursue the woman's identity. She marveled at how straightforward Elizabeth had been. It was refreshing in a way. She wasn't sugarcoating anything, and she wasn't trying to get Darling to lie about their involvement. No, she knew she was in a compromising position and was trying to get out of it. Full disclosure to the police. That hadn't been what Darling had expected, but she was happy to comply. Grabbing her coat and cell phone, she began dialing Derrick's number as she closed up Acuity for the night.

The sun was setting, leaving a light glow hanging around the parking lot. It was serene and almost calming. A feeling Darling tried to hold on to as she approached her car and saw the door was cracked open. On the driver's seat was a paper bag.

In it was her camera.

Chapter Eight

Darling's body went on high alert. She turned her head from side to side, scanning the parking lot for her mystery figure. Her hair slapped her cheeks at the movement, and a chill found its way into her bones.

She was alone.

"Hello?"

Darling was so startled she nearly threw her phone. She had forgotten she had called the deputy.

"Hey," she exclaimed into the phone. Her nerves pushed her voice into a high octave. She tried to tamp down her fear. "We need to talk again." She checked the back for any unwanted passengers, then climbed into the driver's seat. Her grip on the phone had gone tight, as if talking to a police officer made her instantly safe. She knew this was not the case.

Derrick said some not-so-nice words before answering.

"More evidence, I'm guessing."

"Something like that," she hedged. "I'm coming to the station now."

"Unless you know for certain the identity of either the deceased or her killer, can we meet at Carter's? I'm just now going off duty and haven't had a lick of food since this morning."

At the mention of food, Darling's stomach let out a loud growl.

"That actually sounds good, but you think you could pick me up from my place? I'd like to change. It's getting cold." Even as she asked, Darling started her car and backed out of her spot. What had been a cute outfit that morning was now feeling like a poor choice. April in Maine might have warmer days, but its nights could get nasty quickly. It helped that her apartment was midway between the station and Carter's. The return trip would also have them passing by her place on the way to his work.

Plus, she was hoping he'd be chatty when boxed inside a car.

Derrick agreed, and within fifteen minutes Darling was dressed in a long-sleeved royal blue sweater and a heavier coat. Her ankle boots were swapped out with a pair of black boots that laced up her shins, keeping her calves warm. She didn't bother with refreshing her makeup or checking her hair. Impressing Derrick was nowhere on her list of things to do.

Darling lived in a large house built in the 1900s that had since been converted into four apartments. Hers was apartment number three and tucked away on the left side of the second floor. In her years of living in Mulligan, she had found she loved the two-bedroom, one-bathroom dwelling. She jogged down the community stairs and wondered if Oliver would like her home.

It amazed her how complicated life could become within two days.

"Whatever you're about to say or ask, I'd like you to hit your pause button until we've sat down and at least have drinks in front of us," Derrick said when Darling had situated herself in his Jeep. So much for Chatty Cathy. "A man can only take so much on an empty stomach."

OLIVER PULLED ON his beer, looked around Carter's Bar and Grill, and wondered what it was like to live in Mulligan. It was such a small town compared with most places he had visited through the years. A giant leap different compared with Dallas, especially. The fact that Darling had settled in Mulligan made him question the town even more. Was it that great a place, or had Darling's need to distance herself from her old life driven her to settle for the exact opposite?

Now off the clock, Oliver took his time finishing his beer. The noise level in the restaurant had risen considerably. He turned to survey the new crowd. Should he get a table or stay at the bar?

"Evening, Deputy," he heard one of the waitresses call. He cast a quick glance toward the door and was surprised to see Deputy Derrick holding the door open for none other than Mulligan's private investigator. The couple didn't see him as they were seated.

Couple.

Darling had already told him—of her own accord— that she and the deputy were no longer an item. Either way, it wasn't Oliver's business. He had been in town for only two days and had spent no more than an hour or two with her during that time. Feeling a connection that wasn't there was a distraction he didn't need and one he was sure Darling didn't want.

When he'd left home—and Darling—eight years ago, he had been firm in his decision. What Darling didn't know wouldn't hurt her...at least, he had hoped it wouldn't, not forever. He had watched the younger Darling change into an independent, clever young woman within the year they had spent together. She'd had so much potential at such a young age. He had never doubted her future would be bright. His, however, had always been in question. When he left Darling behind, he hadn't ever planned on returning to her.

He laughed to himself.

Now he was in Maine, sitting a few feet away from the same woman and her ex, the deputy.

In a way, Oliver was glad she had dated Derrick. He hoped that, even though it hadn't lasted, she had been happy. He hoped she had opened up to Derrick—or to some other man—letting him in to her carefully guarded world. Because even though he had purposely broken her heart, Oliver had hoped it would one day mend.

He watched as Derrick pulled out her chair, and the two settled into their seats. Darling had changed clothes but kept her yellow daisy earrings in. She had always loved daisies.

"Want another?" the bartender asked, pulling Oliver's attention away. He was thankful for it. He needed to give Darling and her life the privacy they deserved.

"Yeah. Can I also get a menu?"

The bartender tossed a laminated menu over and slid him a replacement beer.

"Our steak dinner is a favorite," he said, pointing out the item listed under Entrees before going to tend another patron. Oliver didn't keep looking. George had said the same. If a Mainer praised it, then that had to mean it was good, right?

"It's a lie."

Oliver sloshed his beer in surprise at the new voice to his left.

Darling was amused.

"A lie?" he questioned, regaining his composure.

Darling took the menu from his hands and set it on the bar. "The steak dinner is good but not amazing," she continued. "You'd be disappointed."

"Your friend George the Gate Guard would beg to differ."

Darling snorted. "Well, George is a liar. Didn't we already establish that yesterday?"

It was Oliver's turn to laugh. "We didn't, actually."

Darling waved her hand through the air as if to shoo off such trivial thoughts.

The bartender made his way back over, but before Oliver could put a word in edgewise, Darling had caught his attention.

"Hey, Benny, Oliver here will take one of your fantastic lobster rolls," she said. "And can you send it over to our table?" She pointed back to where Derrick was seated, talking on his phone. Bartender Benny nodded.

"Well, looks like I'm eating some lobster, then. And not alone."

"You can't just come to Maine and not have one of its best dishes. Plus, if I remember correctly, you're a fan of fresh seafood." Oliver nodded, conceding that. "And as for the whole eating-alone thing, that's just sad." There was a teasing tone in her voice, but when she spoke again the humor was gone. "I need to tell Derrick something about the case. I have a feeling I'll cross your client's path again before this is all over. I'd rather keep you in the loop." She held up her hand to silence any questions Oliver was about to ask. "But first, I also *really* need a drink."

Chapter Nine

Derrick greeted Oliver with a nod that picked up enthusiasm only when he saw the beer Oliver had gotten for him. The past two days had been long for Darling, but she knew they were nothing compared to what Derrick was having to deal with.

"I hope you don't mind dining with an out-of-towner," Oliver said. He took the outside seat next to Darling. It wasn't a long booth, and their thighs touched as he got settled.

"Listen, as long you don't go on a killing rampage before we get our food, I'll be fine."

"I'll see what I can do," Oliver responded.

Derrick had stayed true to his plea to keep shoptalk out of the picture until he at least had a drink. He and Darling had done almost no talking on the ride over to Carter's. Then she'd seen Oliver sitting alone at the bar after they were seated. The act of including him had been impulsive.

Why? she wondered.

She waited as each got his fill of his respective drink. Darling found that her lips wanted to remain shut, also, until her drink arrived.

"So, how are you enjoying Mulligan so far?" Derrick asked.

"Well, aside from the Marks residence, I've only had the pleasure of visiting a few places." He tipped his beer toward Derrick. "The police station was my favorite, by the way. I'm a sucker for being colder inside a building than I am outside it." Derrick let out a laugh. It seemed genuine. "But Mulligan has its charms. I don't know if I'd be singing the same tune year-round once the snow comes in, but for now I can see the appeal."

"The appeal. You've traveled around the world and you think Mulligan is appealing?" The deputy held up his beer. "That's mighty generous of you." They clinked their bottles together, and Darling rolled her eyes.

She listened to them talk a bit longer before her drink arrived. She had readjusted her attention to the small glass between her hands.

"Is that milk?" Oliver asked, peering at the cream-colored drink.

"This, my friend, is another part of Maine you should partake in." She took a long sip. The creamy goodness of Allen's Coffee Flavored Brandy mixed with milk created one of Darling's favorite after-hours drinks.

"It's cheap and delicious," Derrick supplied. "This one here can only take so much before she turns into a puddle of giggles."

"A puddle of giggles?" Darling said. "Is that even a thing?"

"I think I get what he means," Oliver defended the deputy. He turned his attention to Derrick. "Right before her eighteenth birthday, Darling got ahold of the key to her father's liquor cabinet and called me after she did a few taste testings. She laughed for almost the entire conversation. I caught maybe one or two words the whole time."

The two men laughed, and even Darling found herself smiling. In the time that she had met and fallen for Oliver, a lot of bad had happened in her life. However, when she was able to step back from her pity party, she could remember the good times, too.

"Okay, so I may turn into 'a puddle of giggles' when I drink a little too much, but at least I don't cry or yell!" As if they had planned it, the two men shrugged. "But, just in case, I think I better go ahead and talk shop." Darling took a large gulp of her drink and dove in.

"Elizabeth Marks hired me last week to get proof—pictures—of Nigel with another woman while he stayed in Mulligan. She believes he's been having an affair for quite a while." None of this information fazed either man, so she continued right along. "She planned her trip to the Bahamas with her mother for the duration of his stay because she thought the fact that there was no way she could accidentally catch him might entice him to philander."

"That's a different spin on reverse psychology if I ever did hear one," Oliver observed.

"The Markses have a prenup that—in the foolish throes of young love—Elizabeth signed without question. If she divorces him now, she forfeits money she thinks she deserves, including the funds she actually made herself."

"But if he cheats and she can prove it…" Oliver started.

"Then that prenup is void, and she's free to take, at minimum, half of everything he owns," Darling finished.

Derrick leaned forward. "Which gives her one hell of a motive to hurt both her husband and his mistress. This is the kind of thing you tell the police who are investigating a murder," the deputy bit out.

"We both know you already checked her alibi, and it's as clean as Nigel's. I knew from the start where she was and that she couldn't physically do it."

"Did you see her in the Bahamas?" Derrick pushed her. "Do you know for a fact that she actually went?"

Darling sighed. "Derrick, I had Dan keep an eye out at the hotel just in case Nigel stopped by, and that's exactly what happened. Nigel spent the night with Jane Doe. Dan saw him. We both know that now Nigel's lying about even being there. We also both know that Elizabeth Marks was checked in to her resort at the time of Jane Doe's death."

"Then why are you telling me this now? Why not keep it to yourself if you think it's not a big deal?" Darling knew Derrick was angry with her for withholding information. She didn't blame him for it, either. If she had been a cop, she would have been angry, too.

"Elizabeth wanted me to disclose everything to you because she realizes she's a top suspect. She wants me to tell you everything we've talked about and everything I've found," Darling explained.

"Just like that?" Oliver asked, clearly impressed.

"Just like that. Sure, she wants discretion—if Nigel finds out she's wanting to divorce him, he could do it first and leave her with nothing—but she isn't stupid. Hiring a private eye to follow your cheating husband and then running off to the Bahamas for an airtight alibi? Yeah, she's smart enough to know how that looks."

The men thought that over, and Darling used the silence to take a few more sips of her drink.

"Have you had any luck with figuring out who Jane

Doe is?" she ventured when they appeared too involved in their own drinks. "Any new leads?"

The deputy rested his bottle on the table. He began to thumb the label off as he answered. He seemed to be considering each word he spoke.

"We have hit a few…snags."

"Snags?" Darling and Oliver asked in unison.

"We're still searching several avenues in an attempt to identify her, but as of right now, we're no further than we were when you found her." Derrick wasn't much for sighing, but his body sagged with the weight of frustration. "As far as we can tell, no one has reported her missing. We've sent her picture and description out to other departments to see if anything catches, but so far it's been one dead end after another. We even checked with cab companies and car rental agencies since we still can't locate the car she went to the hotel in. If we don't find something soon, we'll have to take this to the media."

Darling shifted in her seat, as if she could move away from the bad information.

"Has anyone reported on the death yet?" Oliver asked. It was a question that Darling hadn't answered, either. Meaning to buy a newspaper wasn't the same as actually buying one.

Derrick shook his head and pulled a long strip of the beer label off. "Nigel's name might be in the clear because of his alibi, but word has already started to spread that he was possibly at the hotel with Jane Doe. Covering a story, even without his name directly in it, is still getting too close to insulting Mulligan's golden child," he said. "I don't expect that to last much longer, though. The chief has a meeting with a local reporter first thing tomorrow morning." He shot a look at Darling. "Rebel Nash."

Darling let out a whistle. Rebel Nash was a Mulligan transplant who was the embodiment of unwavering determination and absolute stubbornness. If anyone was going to break the story *with* Nigel's name in it, Rebel would be the one to do it.

"From the little I know about her," Darling explained to the out-of-towner Oliver, "Rebel values the truth more than the consequences of losing Mulligan's hero. Which, I have to say, I like about her right now."

Oliver smiled. "Just what everyone needs, another you in a different profession."

Derrick laughed and Darling picked up her glass. "I'm going to take that as a compliment, thank you."

"I knew you would," Oliver replied with a smirk.

The food arrived shortly after, and their conversation all but died. Well, the one in which Darling was included. Derrick and Oliver went back and forth, sharing their war stories about law enforcement and personal protection before switching gears to sports. Darling watched her exes with interest as she sipped away her drink.

When Derrick was tense, it was hard for him to ease up. Finding the humor in a case, if only for a brief stretch, was a task in itself. Darling knew that emotionally, it was hard for him to get out of his head long enough to enjoy his surroundings.

Oliver, on the other hand, knew when to laugh and did it with no issues. He was lighthearted but could slip into a more serious tone when needed. She watched as he laughed and slowly began to remember all of the sweet moments they'd had together. Sure, age had changed Oliver—he was more confident and there was no denying he had more muscles beneath his shirt—but Darling still could see the boy she'd once loved.

Darling let out a laugh at the thought. Both men paused their conversation but didn't comment. She ordered another drink and thought back on the case.

"What about the ledger?" she asked suddenly. She'd interrupted the men, but Derrick knew what she was talking about.

"We didn't think about looking until this morning," he said with obvious disapproval. Whether it was of himself or the other deputies, she didn't know. "When we went back, someone had torn out the last three pages. We grabbed it for prints, but nothing so far."

Darling brought up the pictures on her phone and slid it over to Derrick. "I took these yesterday, after I found the body." Derrick's eyes went wide. "I swear I would already have given it to you had I remembered," she hurried on. "But with everything that has happened, it slipped my mind." The real reason being the mysterious letters. It had knocked her off her game, along with the amber-eyed man sitting next to her.

"You took a picture of the check-ins from the night Jane Doe checked in?" Derrick wanted clarification, but with his free hand he was already waving over the waitress.

"Yes. I wanted to use it as evidence against Nigel that he was having an affair. At the time, I didn't realize Jane Doe would stay a Jane Doe."

"Check, please," Derrick called to the waitress. "And you haven't searched these names yet?"

Darling shook her head. "I didn't even think about them until just now."

"Send me this picture. I'm going to go back to the station and run them."

Darling took her phone and did as the deputy said.

"I'll take care of the food," Oliver chimed in. "You go ahead and get outta here."

Derrick might have reconsidered had he not been given a new lead, but instead he just left.

"Looks like my snooping comes in handy sometimes, huh?" Darling said after she'd sent the picture. Oliver laughed and gave the waitress his card when she came back. "You don't have to pay for me," Darling added.

"Consider it a reward for your snooping."

"I'll finish my drink to that."

And she did just that.

Oliver not only paid for dinner but also extended his gallantry to offering Darling a ride home. They settled into his rental, each pushing through the cold of outside, before Oliver started the engine and its heater.

"I have to say, Mulligan keeps on surprising me," Oliver said.

"Do you mean Mulligan or its murder mystery?"

"Both," he admitted.

"I still can't believe that no one can tell us who Jane Doe is," Darling dove in. Her lips were a little loose and her body was a little warm, and not from the heater.

"Yeah, you would have thought that the cops would have found a witness by now. Even someone who had seen her at least driving through town." Oliver clapped his hands together. It made Darling jump. "On the way in from the airport, I only passed one gas station," he said, eyes bright. "I'm assuming that on the other side of town there's a gas station leading into Mulligan?"

Darling thought for a moment, then nodded.

"So there's a chance she might have stopped at either one of these gas stations, depending on which direction she was coming in from? We even checked with cab companies and car rental agencies since we still can't locate the car she went to the hotel in."

"That's a slim chance, but yes."

"Why don't we go check it out, then?" He started the car, suddenly energized. "A slight chance is better than anything you have right now."

He was right about that. Even if Derrick was able to identify her, getting video of Jane Doe could make all the difference in the case.

"Okay, so let's assume she did drive in but not from the city side."

"Why not?" Oliver asked. He had his hand on the gearshift, ready for direction.

"If she was already in the city, why would Nigel *and* Jane Doe drive out here to Mulligan to meet? I'm sure there are plenty of places they could have done it there," she reasoned.

That was all Oliver needed. He backed out of his parking spot.

Once again, they were a team.

Chapter Ten

The clock read nine fifteen when Oliver cut the engine in the parking lot of Zippy's Pump & Pour. Its two pumps were positioned in what they hoped was the front security camera's range.

"Okay, that's Connor-something," Darling said, pointing through the windshield to the clerk inside.

"Looks young. How do you know him?"

"Just from getting my gas here on occasion." She gave him a quick wink that made him wonder if she was feeling her two drinks yet. "They're the only place in town that carries the candy bars I really like."

"Do you think he'll let us see the security footage?"

Darling bit her lip as she thought. Oliver couldn't deny it stirred up some feeling within him. He readjusted in his seat.

"Maybe," she answered. "I don't know enough about him to make that call yet. We're going to have to find out."

Oliver nodded and they entered the station. It was small, and Connor was undeniably bored. When they walked to the counter, he stood from his stool and smiled.

"Hey, hey," he greeted them. His eyes slid over them, stalling on Darling. "Whoa! You're the private eye."

Darling's cheeks tinted red, but Oliver didn't know if that was another aftereffect of brandy or surprise at Connor's obvious admiration.

"Private investigator, but yes," she said with a smile. "That's me."

"Awesome! I was telling my buddy the other day I wouldn't mind doing what you do," Connor said, excitement only mounting. "You wouldn't happen to be hiring right now, would you?" He lowered his voice and leaned closer. Oliver and Darling leaned in, too. "Because working here kind of sucks."

Oliver couldn't help but chuckle.

"We aren't actually hiring at the moment," Darling said. Connor looked supremely disappointed. "But you might be able to help us now if you're not too busy."

Connor's disappointment was short-lived. He smiled, and it was downright mischievous.

"I'll do anything you want!"

Darling cut a quick smile to Oliver. "Well, great!"

Oliver wondered how the private investigator was going to approach the topic at hand. If he was a betting man he would have put his money on the honeypotting approach. Being sweet to lower the boy's defenses, getting information with a nice tone and even nicer words. Or would she try to trick him into giving up what they needed to know? He leaned against the counter and watched with interest.

"Were you working here two nights ago, by chance?" Darling asked.

"Oh, yeah, I've worked night shift for the last week and a half." Connor lowered his voice. "My boss is out of town 'on business,' but I think that's a load of crap." He made finger quotes to show what he must have thought was a lie.

The private investigator took a beat before responding, no doubt noting the employee had some obvious disdain for his employer. "That's gotta be a drag." She let her body droop a bit as she said it. Oliver realized it was because she wanted Connor to feel as if they were on the same page as him. It was an approach somewhere between honey-potting and straightforward. She wanted to be relatable.

"I told him I'll quit if he keeps me closing every single night. I mean, I can do it once and a while, but I have a life, you know?" Oliver nodded in unison with Darling. A different thrill than the one he'd felt in the car filled him as he realized they were in secret cahoots, working together toward the same goal without any friction from their past breaking in. He wondered if she felt it, too. They had always made a good team.

"I don't blame you," he said to show his empathy further. Conner nodded again, giving them both a look that clearly said he liked them. Darling must have realized it, too. She straightened slightly. She was going in for the kill.

"Well, the thing is, two nights ago, a woman might have stopped here." She paused and pulled out her phone. She scrolled to one of the pictures she'd been given of Jane Doe and Nigel. "This woman. Do you remember her, by chance?"

Connor squinted at the phone's screen for a few seconds before snapping his fingers.

"The redhead, yeah! She was here." Oliver and Darling shared a look. They had gotten supremely lucky. "She didn't come in, but I remember her getting gas."

He winked at Darling. "I don't forget a pretty face, especially a new one in town."

"Do you remember if anyone was with her? In the car?"

"No, she was alone," he answered, brow wrinkled as he thought. "Why? Is she in some kind of trouble? Is she a criminal?"

Darling raised her hands and laughed. "No, no, she's—" Oliver could tell she was looking for the right thing to say.

"We're worried about her, is all," he interjected. "She came to town for a visit but hasn't checked in for a few days, and we thought she might have stopped by here."

"She isn't from around here, so we're really worried," Darling added. "You said she didn't come in, but that camera outside would have seen her, right?"

Connor was emphatic as he answered. "Oh yeah! You two want to see it? We still have tapes from a week ago." He lowered his voice again. "I may have fallen behind on changing them out, but, hey, it's not like I get paid out the yin yang to keep up with it all." Oliver raised his eyebrow at Darling as Connor ushered the two of them to the back room. Oliver couldn't tell if he was being so lax with security because he seemed to dislike his current boss or if he was trying to show off for the woman he wanted to be his new boss. Either way, after throwing around several VHS tapes, the clerk popped in the right one and hit Play.

"You can fast-forward as much as you want," he said as a ding sounded from the front door. "There's no sound—the boss is too cheap, ya know—but everything else works okay. I'll be back!"

"We seriously lucked out that the boss isn't around,"

Darling whispered, already hitting the fast-forward button. She kept her eye on the time stamp in the corner of the screen. "I think we also lucked out that our Jane Doe stopped here.

"Good call, by the way. I hadn't even thought about the possibility of her coming here." Darling turned to give him a quick smile. It made his breath hitch for a split second. When they were younger, sometimes Darling would look at him and the world around him would slow. A candid moment from the woman that reminded him how beautiful she was in every way. It caught him off guard as he realized that all the time that had passed hadn't changed that feeling.

Her lips turned up, her cheeks rosy, her eyes unrelenting as they searched for the truth. Darling Smith was determined, and Oliver knew nothing would get in her way.

"Just trying to get the town PI on my side," he ribbed her.

She turned her attention back to the television monitor with a laugh.

They quieted as the footage's time ticked by, leaned in and focused. The footage wasn't in color and, at best, only a step up from unrecognizably grainy.

Oliver pointed to the pump farthest from the security camera. Partially hidden by the pumps was a young woman exiting the driver's side of a car. She disappeared behind the pump before reappearing to put the nozzle in her gas tank. Her hair was shoulder-length and wavy. Wearing dark pants and a light button-up blouse, she rubbed her hands together before walking to the trash can between her car and a van closer to the building. An older woman stood against it as she waited for her vehicle to fill up.

"Is that her?" Oliver asked, still uncertain. Darling's eyebrows drew together, her eyes squinting at the screen.

The woman in question was all smiles as she caught the older woman's eye. Her mouth began to move, but without sound, they couldn't hope to decipher what the two were saying.

"Yes," Darling answered. "That's our Jane Doe. Her smile is identical to the one in the pictures. Working on the assumption that the woman in those pictures *is* our Jane Doe. Which is what I'm doing."

Oliver continued to watch as Jane Doe held a conversation with the older woman at the neighboring pump. There was no denying she was happy about something, almost bouncing as she talked. The conversation didn't last long. Both women finished their pumping and paused to say goodbye to each other before getting back into their respective vehicles. Jane Doe drove off first. Darling paused the tape as soon as the car was out of view.

Oliver kept silent as she rewound the tape and they watched it for a second time. The van at the next pump and the angle of the security camera made the scene difficult to decipher. Only the driver's side door and seat, and the back end of the car where the gas tank was could be seen around the van and pump. The color of Jane Doe's car was dark, but aside from that, the black-and-white footage didn't give anything away.

"It's clearly a four-door, and a smaller one at that. I'd say it's an older model, too." He scooted closer as if that could help him figure out what the model was. The new proximity didn't help. "I'm not a car guy, so I can't make this call. Pause it as she drives off."

Darling did as he said, but the picture was blurred.

"They may have a security camera, but it sure isn't that high-tech," she muttered.

"The boss is a lot of things, including cheap," Connor said from the doorway. Darling jumped.

"Sorry, we just need to figure out what kind of car this is." She put her finger up to the blurred spot that was Jane Doe's car. If Zippy's had had a camera at the pumps, they would have been able to see the make and the license plate. But that wasn't the case.

"Ew, yeah, sorry about that." He, too, squinted at the footage, as if that could suddenly make it clearer. "The farther away from the camera you are, the worse it comes across on the tapes."

"Do you remember anything about the car she was in?" Oliver asked.

The question turned Connor's cheeks red. "No," he said with the shake of the head. "I wasn't really focusing on anything else after I saw her." There were no perverted or salacious undertones in his statement, just honest appreciation for the woman's beauty. It earned a sincere smile from the private investigator.

"Connor, would you mind if we borrowed this?" she asked. "I'd like to take a closer look at it."

The clerk shrugged but nodded. "You can keep it for all I care," he said. "The boss man doesn't ever look at them unless we've been robbed."

"Great! Well, if he does happen to find out and isn't happy about it, tell him to give me a call. I'll set him straight."

"Yes, ma'am."

"This was surprisingly productive," Darling said when they were back in the car.

Oliver gave her a questioning look at her new level of excitement. He was betting she was definitely tipsy.

"Because we know where she was the night before she was killed?" he asked.

Darling laughed. "No," she exclaimed with a grin. "Because for the first time, we have a witness who talked to Jane Doe."

THREE OF THE FOUR names from the hotel ledger checked out. Derrick guessed the fourth was a fake. Darling could hear the stress in his voice as he said he would be tracking down the other three people to see if they saw anything at the time of check-in. Even though he was sure he had already questioned each the day the body was found. Darling had been hesitant to give their new information over to the deputy, but Oliver had urged her on. Plus, she supposed she owed it to the main investigator on the case.

"And you're sure it's her?" Derrick asked.

"Yes, but we can't figure out the make of her car," she said. "But, if you let me, I can track down the woman she spoke to and ask her tomorrow if she saw anything…"

She waited for the backlash from suggesting she help in the murder investigation, but it never came. With an exhalation so loud that Oliver chuckled in the seat next to her, Derrick relented.

"I'm only saying yes because we're swamped…and I know how crafty you can get." Darling smiled at the windshield. Being called crafty was a much nicer descriptor than what private investigators were usually given. "Call me if you get something, and try not to do anything illegal."

"He acts like I do illegal things all the time," Darling said once the call was over. Oliver raised his eyebrow.

They were still seated in his rental, parked at the curb outside her apartment. "I don't, I should add."

"Of course not." A wisp of a smile trailed across his lips, suddenly bringing her attention to his mouth. His lips were thick, yet entirely masculine. And, when pressed against hers, made the world feel whole. Darling cleared her throat and reached for the door handle at the thought. Fantasizing about the bodyguard in any way was dangerous. Considering there was a murderer on the loose, there was enough danger for all of them without reigniting old feelings. A monumental distraction that could cause either one of them to slip up at their jobs.

"Well, I guess I should turn in for the night," she said, hoping her heated cheeks weren't visible in the darkness of the SUV. "I have a feeling tomorrow's going to be a long day."

Oliver nodded and started to get out, too.

More heat ran up her neck. Did Oliver want to come up to her apartment? There wasn't much they could do other than watch television, talk or get *reacquainted*. However, Oliver didn't seem to care about any of that.

"I'm going to walk you to your door, if you don't mind," he said, coming around to her side. "Mulligan is a little too surprising for my liking at the moment."

"And it's appealing, too, right?" she teased.

He cast her a sideways look as they walked up the sidewalk and to the front door. "It has its perks."

If she hadn't been blushing already, she would have blushed then. Or maybe it wasn't a blush at all. Maybe it was the alcohol. Either way, she led him into the foyer and up the stairs to the left. When they stopped in front of her door, she turned with every intention in the world to say good-night, but he had stopped much closer to her than she had realized. Having to tilt her head up to meet his eyes, Darling's thoughts scrambled.

The world became quiet. It didn't make a peep as she held Oliver's gaze. She imagined the feel of his lips against hers—soft yet rough, full of desire and passion—and almost rocked up onto the pads of her feet to close the space between them. The rest of her body tingled in anticipation of such a bold move.

The bodyguard had been in town for two whole days. Almost a decade spanned between now and their past. Even though they had gotten to catch up on the major life changes they had gone through, they were still swimming in a sea of unknowns.

Yet at the same time, Darling felt as if they had picked up right where their old lives had ended. Fitting together without resistance like two pieces in a large, complicated puzzle. Could it be that easy? And if it was, did that mean they *should*?

Darling felt weight settle in her feet, declaring they weren't going to support her pushing up to make an impulsive decision. It was time to break the news to her brain that kissing Oliver—although almost every part of her wanted to—wasn't going to happen.

"Thanks for coming with me tonight," she said, almost whispering. She took a step backward and grabbed the doorknob. "I should probably get some sleep now." She unlocked the door and opened it wide, breaking eye contact for a moment so she could cool slightly. "Thank you for dinner, too. Next time is on me."

Oliver blinked a few times before simply nodding. He didn't hesitate as he turned and headed for the stairs.

"Let me know if you need anything," he called over his shoulder. But he didn't stop, and he certainly didn't turn around.

Chapter Eleven

Harriet Mendon lived in a tiny yellow cottage surrounded by one hundred or so other tiny, brightly colored cottages. Darling parked at the curb and waved to a mother and her young girl who were walking past. They smiled and waved back, their minds already returning to the beautiful day.

Darling wished she could follow suit. Not have to worry about talking to a stranger about another stranger who had been murdered. She could—get back into her car, drive to the coast and relax next to the water—but she was too invested in Jane Doe's case to stop now. Finding her body had somehow given Darling a sense of protectiveness over the case, deeply investing her into the pursuit of truth in what had happened. Sure, getting into the car and leaving would have been easy, but it wasn't an option her heart could reason was good.

The cottage's front door was baby blue and sounded thin as Darling rapped her knuckles against it. After taking the security tape from Zippy's to Acuity—and watching it a few more times—Darling had plugged Jane Doe's pump mate's license plate number into her computer. Using a private investigator database she paid for monthly—a tool that often came in handy when searching for a name—Harriet Mendon had been the result. In a town as small as Mulligan, it wasn't hard to find her address thanks to a stack of old telephone books Darling's former boss had left behind. Now, waiting for Harriet to open the door, Darling wondered if she should come up with an alternate story for how she'd tracked the woman down. One that sounded less calculating.

As far as broaching the topic of Jane Doe, Darling wasn't going to dance around the reason for her visit. She was going to ask Harriet to tell her about her conversation with the young woman and hope it was enough to identify her. Or damn her killer.

However, Harriet didn't come to the door. Darling knocked again and listened for any noise from inside the house. It remained quiet.

"Great," she muttered. She took out one of her cards and quickly wrote a note across the back before placing it into the jamb next to the doorknob. Hopefully Harriet Mendon's interest would be piqued enough to call.

Darling drove back to Acuity with her mind somewhere else entirely. The day might have been beautiful, but the temperature was already dropping. She wondered how Oliver was faring with the chill but then decided it wasn't safe to think about the man. Thinking of him in any capacity—no matter how innocent—pushed thoughts of his lips and their almost-kiss right between her eyes. Would it be a familiar feeling or some new sensation since the last time their lips had touched? Her parents would get a kick out of how, after everything they had said and tried, Oliver Quinn had found his way back into their daughter's life after all.

The thought of her parents brought on another set

of memories she needed to stay away from, but it also helped her trail back to what was important.

Jane Doe had tangoed with the wealthy, too.

She just hadn't survived the dance.

Darling recalled her silent laugh and jovial attitude when talking to Harriet at the gas station. "I need to find you, Harriet," she said aloud. "I will find you."

A handful of cars were parked in the lot behind Acuity, all of which Darling recognized as belonging to the strip mall's tenants. Still, she kept alert. It was best to not forget about her mystery note writer and the fact he or she had been watching her. With caution, Darling swept her eyes all around her as she went to Acuity's door. Her mind dropped to the next task on her mental list. She wasn't the most patient person. Waiting for Harriet to see her calling card was beyond Darling's current capabilities. She was going to have to find her at work and go from there.

All she needed was to search a little longer on the internet until—

"Whoa."

Acuity's front door was cracked open, the top window pane broken out. Through the hole, Darling could see shards of glass littering the lobby floor. Her hand went to the doorknob on reflex, but fear caught up to her. What if the culprit was still inside? She pictured Jane Doe wrapped up in the tub.

Maybe she needed to call in some backup.

NIGEL WAS ACTING STRANGE. There was no doubt about it.

"Are you okay?" Oliver asked when the businessman came down from his office. He was visibly shaken. Eyes too wide. Face taut. Oliver glanced up the stairs where he knew Thomas stood guard next to the office door. Grant wasn't on the clock for another few hours. Oliver had rotated between perimeter checks and standing guard at the two entrances to the house's main floor. He'd looked out at the gatehouse each time he made an outdoor pass but kept his distance from it. He appreciated the loyalty George had for his job, but he didn't want to get caught up in a conversation with the man. Aside from the three bodyguards and their client, Oliver knew they were alone. The lawyer and Jace were at the new Charisma branch's office. Which was why his concern was so acute. There was no reason Nigel should look as off-kilter as he did.

Nigel blinked several times, clearing his throat when the words still didn't come.

"Yes. I just got off of the phone with Deputy Arrington." His voice wavered as he answered. It put Oliver on even higher alert. Why would Derrick call Nigel if Nigel alibied out? What was the point? "He told me how the young woman was killed. I don't think he believes I had nothing to do with her death." He gave Oliver a weak smile and went to the refrigerator. Unlike his son, instead of a water, he went for a beer. "I didn't kill her, but that doesn't mean I don't feel sympathy for her…" He dropped eye contact for an instant. "Bludgeoned to death with a hammer seems barbaric."

"A hammer?" It was the first Oliver had heard about it.

"Yes."

"Seems cowardly."

Nigel gave Oliver a look that questioned him and agreed simultaneously. The older man wanted to say something—Oliver could feel it—but he didn't. Instead he nodded and made his trek back up the stairs.

A few minutes went by before Oliver decided to check

in on their client. Thomas was standing in the hallway next to the door. When he saw Oliver, he shook his head.

"What?"

Thomas lowered his voice to a whisper. "I don't know what you said to him down there, but he's really upset." Oliver raised his eyebrow and the younger bodyguard shrugged. "I heard a weird noise and looked in and he was crying."

"Crying?"

Thomas nodded. "He stopped when he got a call but, man, I hope he doesn't do it again. I wasn't trained to handle all of that."

Oliver didn't know what to say to that, so he left the bodyguard to go back downstairs. He didn't know if he should feel sympathy for the man. Had he been crying for the loss of Jane Doe? The woman he claimed to not know?

His phone started to vibrate in his pocket. When he saw it was Darling, he knew she'd find the information interesting.

"Quinn," he answered.

"Oliver, can you come to the office right now?" she asked in a rush.

"Why? What's wrong?"

There was worry in her voice. "I—well—the thing is…" She sucked in a deep breath before another gushed out with her words. "I think someone broke in to Acuity and might still be here but I don't want to call the cops just yet."

"Wait, where are you now? You aren't *in* there, are you?" He could imagine the spunky private investigator hiding in the office bathroom as the culprit went through her things a few feet away.

"Of course I'm not in there! I'm sitting in my car, watching the door from the parking lot," she defended herself. "If they are still inside and decide to leave, I'm going to catch them on film." Again, it wasn't hard to imagine Darling sitting in her car, looking through the lens of her camera at her office.

"You need to call the police, Darling. This isn't some kind of game." As he said it, he was walking upstairs to Grant's temporary room.

"I know it isn't a game, but the police have a lot on their plates already. I'm not going to call them until I've personally assessed the damage. If you can't come, though, I'll wait a few more minutes before going in myself." Every word held a stubborn edge.

"No. Don't go in." He knocked on Grant's door. "I'm headed that way now."

If Grant minded stepping in for Oliver while he "attended to a personal matter," he didn't show it. Oliver didn't like up and leaving during his shift, but he took solace in the fact that Nigel planned on working from home for the rest of the day. Just in case, though, he paused at the gatehouse as he was leaving.

George took his time coming out. He looked ruffled, as if he had been caught napping. Oliver didn't have time to admonish the guard for sleeping on the job. Not when he was leaving in the middle of his own shift.

"Hey, George, I'm running out for a bit," Oliver said. "Until I get back, call Thomas if anyone shows up here. Okay?"

George nodded, and Oliver left before the man could get a conversation going. He had a private investigator to worry about.

Minutes later, he pulled into the strip mall's parking

lot, next to Darling's car. He was relieved to see her face bob into view when he walked up. True to form, her camera was in her hands.

"No one has come out," she said in lieu of a hello. "I didn't hear anything when I first was at the door, either. I just wanted to be on the safe side."

"Caution isn't a bad thing," he pointed out. "You stay here and let me go check it out. If you hear anything, take off and call the cops." He could see an internal battle wage across her face. Why had she called if she was going to argue about him going inside without her? She must have been really nervous.

"Okay," she agreed after a moment.

Oliver adjusted his shirt to keep his gun covered as he walked to Acuity's entrance. He didn't often carry it—Orion's bodyguards used nonlethal weapons as much as they could—but it was never too far away from him, either. If someone had broken into Darling's office—in his opinion—that showed malicious intent for her. Oliver wasn't about to go easy on someone who had shown that level of disregard for the investigator. Especially when she was in the parking lot, yards away.

The door was cracked open. Whoever had broken the glass had snaked a hand through the window to unlock the door. He wondered if anyone else in the strip mall had heard the break. Pulling his gun out, he quietly pushed the door open enough to get a good look at the lobby. No one was inside. He moved into the room, gun raised and ready. Whoever had broken in was either being really quiet or wasn't inside anymore. Oliver moved slowly to Darling's personal office. The wood was splintered; the door was ajar. He paused to listen again for any movement.

Nothing.

Using his foot, he nudged the door open. Anger flared within him. He stood alone in the office.

It had been tossed.

Desk drawers were on the floor, the filing cabinets had been toppled over and pried open, papers were scattered around and—the detail that made Oliver's blood run hot—every framed picture on the wall had been smashed.

He went back out into the lobby and made sure to check the small bathroom before going outside to wave Darling in. She was more than ready and hurried over. Oliver returned his gun back to the back of his jeans and frowned.

"I hate to say it, but someone trashed your office," he told her before she could move through the lobby to her personal space. Oliver didn't like watching her face fall at the news.

"Is it bad?"

"It's not pretty."

He followed her back into the small, disheveled room. She stood in the doorway for a few seconds, eyes roaming over the mess. Then, like a switch had been flipped, she hurried to the other side of the desk and started to move through drawers on the floor and their spilled contents.

"It's gone, Oliver!"

"What's gone?" But before she could answer, it dawned on him. "The security tape."

Darling nodded, clearly upset and stood straight again. An overpowering urge to comfort her pushed him forward. He put his hands on her shoulders, making her look up into his eyes. The moment from the night before played back into his mind.

She was close enough to kiss.

"Oliver, there's something I need to tell you."

"Yes?" his voice dropped low. Her green-eyed stare could stir up a drove of feelings in mere seconds.

"I think I know who did this," she whispered. "And you aren't going to like it."

"YOU SHOULD HAVE told someone—told me—about this note writer, Darling," Oliver fumed. He hadn't liked her story about the warnings—plus the mention of her parents and the news article—she'd received from her anonymous stalker one bit. He'd already called the station and talked to Derrick directly, recounting everything she had told him.

The doubt she had harbored that the note writer was trying to help had left the moment she'd seen her office and found the security tape gone. She wasn't dealing with a third-party player anymore.

Darling believed they were dealing with Jane Doe's killer.

Oliver paced back and forth in the lobby, face reddened with emotion. His words were angry, but she knew he was worried. However, that didn't mean she liked being scolded by Oliver, of all people.

"You can't keep making these decisions," he continued. "It's reckless and stupid."

"Stupid?" Darling asked, voice pitching high.

"Yes, stupid." He put his hands out wide, exasperated. "How am I supposed to protect you if you don't give me all the facts?"

In the back of her mind, Darling knew it was concern that made his tact disappear, but it triggered the deep-rooted pain Oliver Quinn had left all those years ago in her heart. Their camaraderie from the night before vanished.

"Protect me?" She laughed. "News flash—I don't need you to protect me, Oliver. I've taken care of myself for the last eight years just fine. Thank you for coming over here, but I realize now that it was a mistake." Once she said it, she felt a twinge of regret, but her pride wouldn't let her back down. "So, if you don't mind, go back to work and protect the person who actually wants it."

She walked to the broken door and held it open for him. The sound of a car door shutting derailed whatever he was about to say. They both looked out to see Derrick walking toward them.

"Darling, I—" Oliver started.

"Please, just leave."

"But I wanted—"

Darling heard the strain in her voice as she pleaded one last time with him. "Oliver, you owe me that much."

The bodyguard's brow creased, but he didn't have time to answer.

"I have some words for you," Derrick called, coming closer. He looked exhausted.

"Oh, I know," Darling said, trying to sound annoyed rather than wounded. "Mr. Quinn was just leaving. He has to go back to work now."

"Yeah, I guess I was," the bodyguard said, not meeting Darling's gaze. Instead he looked to the deputy. "But first, can I grab a quick word with you?"

Derrick must have liked Oliver, because he didn't give him any snark about the request, but Darling was done with the fair-haired man. She excused herself to the bathroom and took a long look at herself in the mirror.

How could one man make her feel so crazy?

THE SKY WAS dark by the time Oliver decided he couldn't take it anymore. His shift had ended an hour earlier, but he had stayed on the house grounds, going over Elizabeth Marks's itinerary. She was set to be in town in two days, which meant Oliver and his team would have to scout out routes and try to foresee any vulnerabilities that their trip to pick her up might cause.

Vulnerable.

What Darling had looked like when she had told him to leave.

He balled his fist.

He didn't want to leave her side, but she had been right. It wasn't his job to keep her safe. He had given up that privilege eight years ago when he'd left her without so much as a backward glance.

The idea that someone had been watching, following and threatening Darling put fire through his veins. Despite their past and her present wants, Oliver wouldn't have left her side had Derrick not convinced him she'd be safe.

"Listen, we're at a point in this case where we're waiting on results and information to come in," Derrick had said when Oliver had pulled him to the side at Acuity. "Whoever is messing with Darling won't get away with it. I'll make sure of it."

Derrick had promised he'd keep an escort outside her house that afternoon and through the night. Until they caught the culprit, he wasn't going to let her be alone. Oliver might have been wary of the deputy when he'd first come to Mulligan, but now he was grateful for his presence. It was true they weren't currently dating, but that didn't stop Derrick from being zealous about keeping his friend safe.

Still, Oliver couldn't ignore the worry that ate at him.

He would at least check in with Derrick, even if Darling didn't want his concern.

The temperature had dropped considerably since the sun had gone down. He wondered how he would handle Mulligan's true winter. Just the thought of the massive amount of snow made him turn the heat on high. By the time he pulled up outside of the old house, he was downright toasty.

It was a feeling that didn't last long.

All lights were off in Darling's apartment, from what he could tell. In fact, the entire building was dark save for the foyer light, which could be seen through the front windows of the common area. It was there on the front steps, in the faint glow of that light, that Oliver saw the outline of a body.

He swung his car into the parking lot between a police cruiser and Darling's car, all feeling of warmth gone from his body. For the second time that day, he grabbed his gun from his console. This time, though he didn't pretend to not have it.

No one sprung from the cruiser as Oliver hurried from his rental, gun in clear view. But he wasn't expecting anyone to. If they hadn't seen the body from this close, chances were no one was in the car.

The body belonged to a man lying on the top step and porch. He was on his side, face away from the parking lot. Oliver pulled out his phone and used the flashlight to see that the man was Derrick.

Blood was caked on the back of his head, and his left leg was bent at a weird angle. Oliver checked for a pulse. It was weak.

Adrenaline began to pump through him. Dialing 9-1-1,

he ran through the entryway and took the steps two at a time to Darling's door. It was shut but not locked.

"Darling?" Oliver called into the apartment. He didn't bother knocking, and he didn't worry about her privacy when no one responded. He quickly searched each room, gun raised. There was no sign of struggle inside.

Oliver ran a hand through his hair and went back to the front door.

"What's the nature of your emergency?" the operator finally answered.

"Deputy Derrick Arrington was attacked and needs immediate medical attention," Oliver bit out. He was angry at himself. "And private investigator Darling Smith has been kidnapped."

"What is your location?"

Oliver repeated the address as he checked the door. It wasn't broken, and there were no scratch marks to suggest someone had tried to pick the lock. He kicked the bottom of the door. Pain exploded in his foot, but he didn't care. He shouldn't have left Darling in the first place. He pulled his fist back this time, ready to let the door know the anger and regret flowing through his blood when he noticed a piece of paper sticking out from under the doormat.

He moved it out of the way, careful not to touch the actual paper. Its neat red writing made Oliver growl in absolute anger.

One more strike and you're out, Darling.

Chapter Twelve

Cold.

Seeping, slithering, unrelenting cold.

It didn't just push against her body. It invaded. Twisting and turning around every inch of her skin. Darling repeated her first waking thought.

"Oh, my God."

She was sitting outside in what was a clearing, as best she could tell. Whether it was night or early morning didn't matter. She couldn't see a thing. Darkness and the freezing air had combined and were currently conquering her. In the back of her mind, she calculated the normal temperature after the sun went down. It could drop to anywhere between forty to fifteen degrees. She certainly felt as if it was more like fifteen.

And that's when she realized why she felt the chill so acutely.

She was naked.

Fear, panic and slight hysteria rose up into a small scream that bubbled from her lips. With shaking hands, she clamped her mouth shut, afraid that whoever had put her here was still around. That's when the pain around her neck registered. Between deep breaths, she recalled her last memory of walking out of her apartment.

And then strong hands wrapping around her neck and squeezing until darkness came.

Before she could even replay the memory again, she had to entertain a new, terrifying one first. Tenderly she got to her feet and focused on the lower parts of her body. She nearly cried with relief when she found there was no pain or soreness south of her waistline. Whoever had tossed her into the freezing unknown without a stitch on had at least not taken advantage of her in such a horrible way.

It was enough of a silver lining to put a little light back into her dark situation.

A breeze picked up, and Darling wrapped her arms around her chest. Closing her eyes, she listened.

Deafening silence.

No noise from the town. No cars. Nothing.

A picture of a territorial moose or bear happening upon her made Darling's eyelids flutter back open. She prayed right then and there that her demise wouldn't be by some hungry animal. Though dying of exposure also wasn't fun. Before her mind could fill up with images and stories of lost hikers and stranded civilians who couldn't outlast the cold, Darling put one foot forward.

Standing still wasn't going to save her.

She walked in small strides, feeling dead grass and dirt between her toes before putting her weight down. Mulligan was a small town surrounded by enough rural land that she could have been anywhere within the town's limits. That included a stretch of land south of the town center that was reserved for hunting. Just as Darling didn't want to be eaten, she didn't want to stumble across an old hunting trap.

What if she was no longer even in Mulligan?

Minutes crept by and nothing seemed to change. Just grass and dirt—no trees or asphalt—pressing against feet she was slowly losing feeling in at each new step. Worry and panic, which Darling had decided to push clear out of her head when she took her first step forward, were using a battering ram to get back in.

Someone had knocked on her door. Thinking it was Oliver, she had flung it open, ready to fight. Yet no one had been there. Curious, she had moved down the stairs and out to the front porch. That's when she had seen Derrick.

Darling's heart squeezed as she remembered him sprawled on the steps. Had there been blood or any obvious wounds? She hadn't found out before someone had decided to choke her out.

Darling let out a humorless chuckle.

With its battering ram taking another charge, panic got one step closer to getting in.

What felt like ages later—though realistically she bet it had been only an hour at best since she had awoken—Darling's steps faltered. Her body ached and shook from the cold. Her mind had become blank. Slowly she angled her gaze down to question the change in her walking. A cloud must have finally passed by, because the blessed moonlight broke through and created a hazy glow around her. For the first time since she had opened her eyes, she could see. Pale skin stretched downward—too pale—and a dark spot that looked suspiciously like blood covered the grass next to her left foot.

Panic hadn't given up. She felt it hoist its battering ram back up for one last attempt to break down her emotional barrier.

Darling bent to investigate but lost her balance and

toppled over. She repositioned herself into a better position and felt a thrill of happiness that she could still feel anything in her almost-numb limbs. Pain meant she was still alive. The moment she couldn't feel at all was the moment she would lose it.

The blood—because it was blood and not her imagination—was coming from her foot. Her left one, to be exact. She wiped at the cut on her sole, but more blood replaced what was now smeared across her hand. There was nothing in the cut and nothing in her immediate area that looked sharp. Yet as she wiped another layer of blood off, the wound kept bleeding at a good clip.

How could she not feel the large gash in her foot?

The answer didn't matter. Panic took three steps back before rushing the door that was made to keep her sane and rammed it clear off its hinges.

Darling Smith finally hung her head and let out a sob. It shook her body more than the cold.

"WE'LL FIND HER. I promise you that," the chief said.

Chief Sanderson was a tall, thin man in his fifties with cropped gray-white hair and a clean-shaven face. His badge and gun were visible on his belt, but it was his demeanor that spoke of authority. He and Oliver stood outside Acuity's office, retracing Darling's steps for the second time. Looking for anything that might lead them to who was behind her disappearance.

Her phone was off—all calls going straight to her voicemail—and no one from her building or the strip mall claimed to have heard or seen anything out of the ordinary.

Oliver wanted to believe the chief was right—needed to believe him—but it had been hours since he'd found the empty apartment and the injured officer. Derrick had been alive but hadn't woken up before his surgery. Chief Sanderson had said that even though he temporarily was out of the woods, they wouldn't know the extent of the damage from his head injury until he was conscious. They didn't know if the same hammer that had killed Jane Doe had been used, but they did know the same method had been.

Hit from behind to knock them out of commission.

Though it looked as if Derrick hadn't gone down without a fight. His leg had been broken in two places, and his knuckles had been bloodied.

Oliver hoped Darling was putting up a better fight.

"This case...it's all theory and no conclusive, hard evidence. This note writer, a possible affair and now our own kidnapped private investigator," the chief ground out. "We're missing something big here."

"Whatever it is, I think Darling must have gotten close to it."

"It's time we get closer. Excuse me." The chief stepped away to answer his phone.

Oliver had been surprised when the chief had personally accompanied him in an attempt to find out what had happened. He could have sent other deputies but hadn't hesitated in getting his hands dirty. Oliver was finding he liked Sanderson just as he liked Derrick. Both men were fond of Darling and, instead of seeing her as a nuisance because of her profession, seemed to respect her. Sanderson wanted her to be found. It helped that the popular opinion had changed about the connection between Derrick's attacker and Darling's note writer.

Which also meant the chances were high that the mystery person was directly connected to Jane Doe's murder.

Oliver's stomach dropped as his mind jumped to the worst possible outcome for Darling. He needed to find her. Whoever was behind this couldn't have been this careful. There had to be a trail he could follow somewhere.

Like water to the face, Oliver knew for certain there *was* one person who knew more than they did.

Nigel.

Pulling out his phone, he scrolled through his contacts and went straight to the number of Orion's senior technical analyst, Rachel Delvough. Although he'd brought Grant and Thomas up to speed on the situation, he hadn't yet made a call to Nikki. As far as he was concerned, they were still doing their job correctly with the other two members still protecting the client.

The client he was about to target.

"Hello?" Rachel answered after a few rings. It was almost ten in Dallas, but she didn't sound as if he had woken her. Though he wouldn't have cared if he had. Darling's life was more important than being polite.

"Rachel, it's Oliver."

"What's wrong?" Orion operated with a handful of people. Everyone knew everyone else. Rachel was more connected at times than the rest, considering she handled all the behind-the-scenes affairs of each agent.

"I need a favor," he said, turning his back on the chief. "And I really need you to do it, Rachel." He wasn't as close to the quiet analyst as he was to Nikki, but he liked to think she'd help him out. Even if what he wanted was illegal.

"Okay...what is it?"

"Can you remotely look through someone's phone?" Nikki had hinted that Rachel's technical background might not have been wholly on the up-and-up. She hadn't used the word *hacker*, but he was taking a shot in the dark.

"Look through? Anything specific?"

"The incoming and outgoing call logs."

Nigel was lying about not knowing Jane Doe. If Oliver could see the numbers he had called or been called from, maybe he could find out who Jane Doe was. And if Nigel *had* hired someone to kill her and take Darling.

"Yeah, I can do that. But Oliver, it's illegal."

Oliver's fist balled. He wasn't angry at Rachel but at himself.

"Listen, I wouldn't ask unless it was absolutely important," he said.

There was hesitation. "Do you need it tracked, too?"

"No." He knew Nigel was still at his house.

"Whose phone?"

"Nigel Marks's."

More hesitation. Rachel knew exactly who Nigel was. She knew he was Orion's ticket to keeping afloat.

"Does Nikki know about it?"

"No," he admitted. "Listen, I wouldn't ask unless it was necessary. Please, Rachel."

He could hear movement on the other end of the phone.

"I'll have to head back to the office. I'm assuming you need this now?"

He let out a breath of relief. "As soon as humanly possible."

"I can do it. And Oliver? I won't lie to Nikki." Her voice was resolute. He didn't blame her. Everyone at Orion respected their boss. "But I won't bring it up to her unless you do."

"Deal."

The called ended, and Oliver was left feeling helpless. His job was to protect people, and yet he was invading the privacy of the client he had been hired to guard and had let down the only woman he had ever loved.

Oliver blinked.

Was that true?

And did he love her still?

Chapter Thirteen

Debrah and Andrew Smith had both come from money, but that didn't stop them from wanting more. They took to the business world, becoming a force many respected. Debrah and Andrew were inspiring. The perfect role models for a child with a growing mind like Darling.

So when Darling's childhood friend Annmarie Moreno's father accused the tycoons of running a string of Ponzi schemes, everyone including Darling couldn't help but not believe him. It was absurd, she had thought, but Annmarie's father didn't back down.

So Debrah and Andrew made sure to prove him wrong, in a very public way. A newspaper article and a televised interview painted a picture of their innocence, and their accuser's jealousy and greed.

It ruined his career and social standing in the community. He left the city with Annmarie and life returned to normal.

Until Darling received an anonymous email claiming the evidence that her parents were lying was about to be thrown out. She was given an address and told what to look for, and less than thirty minutes later, Darling's entire world had changed.

That was also the first time she had ever met Oliver—

standing in a Dumpster, holding the first clue in a series that would prove her parents had lied.

And destroyed a man's life because of it.

Since then she'd gone down the rabbit hole and found nothing but corruption. Bold-faced lies that built up until the moment she realized they would travel great lengths to ensure their fame and fortune were never threatened. That was the moment she asked Oliver to run away with her. Little did she know as she stood there watching him walk away, tears blurring her vision, that within the month, she would be on a plane to Maine, to a small town named Mulligan.

Now, as Darling pressed her hands to her cheeks, unable to feel her tears, she mused how her end felt intrinsically connected to the beginning of her adulthood.

Corruption.

Despair.

Oliver.

The last point—the man with golden hair—didn't hold the same dark weight as the first two points. Even if he had denied her all those years ago, she couldn't find the heat behind her anger for it. In fact, she realized the anger wasn't there at all anymore. She liked the life she had made since. She liked to think she had made a difference and left a mark in the lives of those she had met and helped through the years.

All Darling felt now was a needling of regret.

She should have kissed Oliver when she had the chance.

Thinking of kissing him replaced an ounce of cold with an ounce of warmth. She hoped she could hold on to it for a long while.

Darling closed her eyes, took a deep breath and stood.

It wasn't the most graceful of movements, and she did struggle, but in the end she was back on her feet.

The moonlight hadn't waned while she had reveled in her breakdown. She let her eyes adjust and started to turn in a circle to see if she could make out anything else. She stopped halfway through the cycle.

She was in a field of short, dead grass. A tree line darkened the distance, giving her no bearings for where she actually was. However, it was the hunk of black metal to her direct right that made her heart flutter. Without the moonlight, she might not ever have seen the car.

With an extreme amount of caution, she dragged her heavy feet and closed the space between her and her possible savior. Darling wasn't sure if she wanted someone to be in the car or not. Her rising grief and fear had kept the idea of her attacker being nearby from her mind. What if this was her attacker's car? But why would the attacker still be here? If her body hadn't been numb, she would have felt the hairs on the back of her neck stand as the idea of someone staying behind to watch her crept in.

No one jumped out from behind the car to grab her as she neared it. She circled it anyway. Better to see the attacker now than drop her guard and be surprised later. It wasn't as if she had much of a chance to defend herself either time, though. When she was satisfied she was alone, she peered into the car to find it was empty save for some clutter in the front seat floorboards. She tried the driver's door handle and let out a shaky breath. It was locked.

The other doors also wouldn't open. Scouting the immediate area, she found a rock that fitted in the palm of her hand. Squaring her shoulder, she approached the backseat's right window.

She threw the rock and watched as the window only cracked.

"Co-come on!"

She scooped the rock back up and threw it again. This time it missed the window completely. Trying to aim when you couldn't feel your throwing arm or hand was definitely difficult. The third time she was able to widen the crack. At this rate she would freeze where she stood.

I can't feel my face, she thought with a new sense of determination. *I need to get into this car.*

This time she gripped the rock and took a deep, shuddering breath.

Go through the window.

The sound of glass shattering cut through the silence.

She dropped the rock, ignoring how the new cut across her hand dripped blood, and unlocked the back door. Reaching around the front seats, she hit the unlock button for the rest of the doors. It felt like so much work, but she finally managed to sit behind the wheel with a slight feeling of accomplishment.

There were no keys in the ignition or anywhere else in the car, as far as she could tell. Her inner optimist hung her head. The center console had CDs in it, and the glove compartment was filled with napkins. Food wrappers littered the floorboard. A silver watch stuck out from under one. but Darling had little use for that. The small hope that she would be able to drive away or, at the very least, turn the heater on, withered away as the rest of her search turned up empty.

She would have to wait it out until the sun came up. The car was a few degrees warmer than outside. If the wind was kept at bay, she might survive the night. In a last-ditch effort to find something to save her, she hit the button that popped the trunk. Once more she pushed back out into the cold.

The trunk contents didn't give her any relief. A bag of tools and a greasy, balled-up hand towel. Darling cursed but grabbed the towel and, after a quick thought, the yellow-handled hammer. She settled back into the driver's seat and locked the doors. She pulled her knees to her chest and rested her head on top, draping the hand towel over her shins. It didn't warm her, but at least it was something.

A few minutes went by. Exhaustion was trying to drag her into sleep.

Leaving her naked in the cold Maine darkness sent a pretty clear message. Someone wanted her to die but didn't want to get their hands dirty.

Darling just hoped she could make whoever that was regret it. She might have been naked, hurt and as cold as a Popsicle, but she wasn't dead. Debrah and Andrew Smith had passed on the drive that kept Darling from cracking again.

With a small smile, Darling formed a thought so clear she wondered if she had actually said it out loud.

You should have killed me when you had the chance.

OLIVER WAS SECONDS from calling Rachel for the third time when the chief jogged over to him. There was no mistaking he was excited.

"We tracked her phone!"

"What?" Oliver followed him to the cars when he didn't stop. "I thought you couldn't if the phone was off."

"We can't. It just came back on." Oliver's mouth opened in surprise.

"I'll follow you."

He left no room for the chief to mistake his statement as a request. For the first time since he had met the man hours before, the older man laughed.

"I knew you would."

Chapter Fourteen

Oliver drove, white-knuckled, in a convoy to the point where Darling Smith's phone was located. The sun was starting to rise, creating a crisp blue landscape without a cloud to blemish it. Under different circumstances, he would have called it serene and even beautiful. However, his heart was in his throat, terrified of the possible outcomes when they found Darling's phone.

In front of him was Chief Sanderson in his four-door pickup. Bringing up the rear was a deputy named Casey Heath in her patrol truck. Oliver raced along the asphalt between them with no worry about what the cracked road might do to his rental. Finding Darling had become his top—no, his only—priority the second he'd found Derrick unconscious. Everything else was on the back burner.

The chief braked for a second. The action bit into Oliver's nerves. They didn't need to stop. They needed to keep going until they found her. After a few beats, Sanderson flipped on his left turn signal and drove off-road. Without hesitation, Oliver and Heath followed.

He made a left onto the new road, and they whizzed down it, away from town. He didn't slow until they had gone past trees on either side. He braked, and Oliver followed suit. They were on a dirt road, dense tree lines surrounding them.

"It's coming from around here," Sanderson called after he swung out of his truck. His hand rested on the top of his piece, a silent gesture that Oliver didn't miss.

His security experience had already tensed up his body but not enough to hinder the fluidity of his movement. He didn't have his gun out, but he didn't think he needed it, either. His adrenaline was too high. He would use his strength to overcome whatever obstacles the unknown was about to throw at them.

"Spread out," Sanderson barked. They all fanned out. "Darling?" he called.

Silence.

Less than a minute later, Deputy Heath yelled.

"Over here!"

The phone was on the ground just inside the tree line a few feet from their cars. It was on but unattended. Deputy Heath shooed Oliver's hands away when he went to grab it and instead threw on a pair of latex gloves.

"We don't know who has been touching this," she said.

"Check the recent calls and texts," Sanderson ordered. Oliver looked over her shoulder.

"The last call she made was to me yesterday when she found someone had broken in," he confirmed.

"And the last text…was from a week ago." Heath quickly browsed the last few pictures. They were of the photographs she'd received at the start of the case.

Heath pulled a plastic Baggie from her pocket and dropped the phone in.

"The phone was placed here," Chief Sanderson said when the bag had been returned to the patrol truck. Oliver agreed.

"It wasn't thrown from a car when they realized she had it. It wouldn't have landed like that," he said. The phone had been on the other side of a tree. "It was purposely placed here."

"But why was it turned back on?" asked Heath.

"For us to find," the chief said at the same time Oliver said, "So we'd find it."

Silence didn't have time to fall around them. Oliver bet that the same sick feeling had exploded within the chief.

"We need to find her," Oliver said, voice hard. "Now."

"Agreed. Heath you go through there," the chief said, pointing to the trees behind them. "Just in case." Heath went back to her truck and pulled her rifle out and did as she was told. "Oliver, follow the road in your car until you are on the outer perimeter of these trees." He held up his hand before Oliver could complain. "We know we won't find her in the direction we just came from. If she was on foot, there's a chance she came out on the other side. Darling doesn't seem like the kind of woman who would hide. Follow the tree line. If you see anything, call my cell." He reached in his pocket and produced his card.

"But if she's in there—" Oliver started. He didn't get far.

"Deputy Heath and I know these woods. You come, you'll slow us down." There was no more discussion as Chief Sanderson began his trek. Oliver saw the reasoning, but he didn't have to like it.

The road extended south for another mile before the trees thinned and open fields replaced them. A quick scan showed no sign of people. Oliver cut the wheel and took his rental off-road. He followed the outside of the woods as the ground sloped uphill and down, but he did so at a slow clip.

An emotion he couldn't quite place clung to his mind and body like a second skin. Fear and longing. Regret and anger. They were mixed in with the unfamiliar feeling, causing a calm before the storm. It was the only way for him to stay focused.

Oliver slammed his hand against the steering wheel.

He had hoped beyond hope that Darling would be with her phone. Being the stubborn woman she was, he'd hoped she had taken down the bad guy and would be waiting for the cops to come. She'd make some wisecrack about Oliver being a day late and a dollar short, and then life would become simple again.

Finding Darling's phone—one that had most likely been purposely placed there—without the private eye at its side brought on a flood of thoughts Oliver didn't want to entertain.

He focused on the trees that he drove past, occasionally scanning the land to the left. He was so intent on the woods he almost missed the spot in the passenger's side mirror. Slamming the brakes, he turned and looked through the SUV's back window. A black car sat a few yards from the woods, its hood angled away from view.

Oliver threw the SUV in Reverse and sped toward the car. He put the SUV in Park and dialed the chief's number. The chief picked up on the first ring.

"I followed the tree line and found a car in the middle of nowhere. Going to check it out. Hold on," he said, not giving the chief room to respond. Oliver's body was even more tense than before. If caution was a tangible material, it would have been dripping off him by the bucketload. He slipped the phone, still on, in his back pocket and approached the car from the rear.

The car was an old Mazda and seemed to be in good

condition minus a dent in the fender and a broken back window. The tires, as far as he could tell, weren't deflated, either. So why was it out there?

Oliver snatched his phone out and yelled into the receiver.

"It's Darling!"

He didn't hear if the chief responded. He had come around the passenger side of the car and had seen her through the windshield.

She was curled up in the driver's seat with a small towel around her feet. Blood was streaked across her face and, he realized with anger and concern so poignant he almost stumbled, she was completely naked.

Oliver pulled on the door but it didn't budge. It was locked. Darling didn't stir. He ran back to the open window and unlocked it before opening the door and unlocking all doors from the passenger side. Then he was back at Darling's side.

She was leaning against the back of the seat but slumped over toward the center console. Her knees were pulled against her chest, her arms slack at either side. Her cheek was pressed against the top of her knee. She was pale.

So pale.

"Darling?" Oliver's voice came out in a whisper. A harsh yet faltering sound. He placed his hand on her blood-stained cheek. He felt the cold all the way in his heart.

A feeling he would never forget.

"Darling, please…"

With his free hand he pressed his fingers to check her pulse. For one horrible moment there was nothing. Then, like a storm in the distance, Oliver felt a soft beat.

He backed up and tore off his jacket. It wasn't thick or long, but it fit around her front easily enough. Oliver put one hand around her shoulders and the other under her knees. There had been a time where an entirely naked Darling in his arms would have made him happy in every way possible, but as he pulled her limp body against his chest, Oliver felt no glee.

"Keep beating," he whispered, as if her heart could hear him.

"Okay."

Oliver looked down, wide-eyed, at the woman in his arms. She tilted her head back and gave him the smallest of smiles.

"God, you're beautiful," he said.

Her smile didn't disappear.

"You found me," she whispered.

"You bet I did."

She made a noise that almost sounded like a laugh, but she didn't speak. Oliver cast a quick glance back into the car. There was no blood on the beige seat, he was happy to see.

"Are you hurt?" he asked anyway. He turned, trying not to jostle her too much, and walked toward his rental.

"No," she answered, voice still low. "I'm cold."

Oliver held her tighter.

"How long have you been—" He was cut off by the sound of a vehicle approaching. Darling tensed so quickly that Oliver had to look down to make sure she was okay.

"Who?"

"Chief Sanderson," he answered as the four-door raced toward them. Deputy Heath wasn't far behind.

"Keep me covered," was all she said.

Oliver angled his body to the side so the chief couldn't see Darling's skin that wasn't covered by the jacket. It was an absurd thing to worry about in the moment, but she sounded so weak. The protective side of him needed to do this for her. It was his fault he hadn't kept her safe in the first place.

The chief kept his truck running and jumped out. He waved Oliver over and flung open the back door.

"It's quicker to drive to the hospital than to wait for an ambulance," he said. Oliver nodded and realized there wasn't a way to shield Darling's body from the older man.

"Could you step aside for a sec?" Oliver asked, a few feet from him. Sanderson sent him a confused look.

"We don't have time to waste," he shot back.

"I'm naked," Darling spoke up. The chief's eyes went skyward at the news. Oliver hurried to get her into the backseat, repositioning the jacket after setting her down. He was thrilled to see she was able to sit up on her own.

"I found her in that car—driver's side—unconscious," Oliver said. "I need to go with her."

The chief nodded his approval, and Oliver slid in next to Darling, shutting the door behind him.

Deputy Heath ran up to the truck and was given quick instructions. Sanderson was inside the cab seconds later, already reversing and heading back to the road.

"Any serious injuries?" the chief asked, eyes not moving to the rearview mirror.

"She says no, but there's blood on her face."

"My foot," she replied. "I cut it."

"And your hand." He caught her wrist and followed the dried blood to her palm. Her skin was still so cold.

"Were you outside all night?" the chief asked.

"Yes," Oliver answered for her when she nodded. His

anger almost boiled over at the realization. In one fluid movement, Oliver took off his shirt.

"Let's put this on you," he said, already moving her to face him.

"No," the chief cut in. "Put her against you."

Oliver raised his eyebrow. "What?"

The chief was all business when he answered. "She'll warm up faster from your body heat. Just putting your shirt over her—although it's a kind gesture—won't work fast enough. Sit her on your lap and let her hug your bare chest. Your warmth will become her warmth."

Never did Oliver think he would see the day that a cop told him to hug a naked Darling, but it wasn't time to marvel. Darling didn't argue. She must have been a lot colder than he'd thought. She didn't resist as he pulled her onto his lap. She slowly moved her legs around him while he helped guide her arms into his jacket to cover her back.

Oliver made sure to keep eye contact with her as he wrapped his arms around her torso and pulled her down until her bare skin was pressed against his.

Darling's eyes fluttered closed for a moment before she returned the embrace. He waited as she settled her cheek against his shoulder. There was no denying she needed the warmth. Her skin was as cold as ice.

"How long to the hospital?" Oliver asked when Darling relaxed against him. Absently he began to rub her back beneath the jacket.

"Ten minutes. You still with us, Darling?"

Oliver felt her nod against his shoulder.

"What happened to you?" Oliver didn't want to push her, but he also needed to know. Whoever had done this was still out there. "I went to your place and saw Derrick on the ground and you nowhere to be found."

"Derrick okay?"

"Just a nasty bump on the head is all," the chief supplied. "He'll be back to it in no time."

Darling nodded into his shoulder again. As her cheek moved across his bare skin, he had to repress a shiver.

"Someone knocked. I thought it was you," she said, voice a bit louder than before. "No one was there. I went downstairs and then—" She let out a shuddering breath. Oliver looked down to see tears shining in her eyes. She tilted her head to the side, and Oliver cursed.

"What?" Chief asked.

Oliver let out another string of obscenities before he answered.

"Someone choked her," he bit out. "There are marks on her neck. I don't know how I missed the bruising before."

"I didn't see a face," she said after the chief also voiced his anger. "Flat chest. Male. Then woke up outside."

Oliver returned his hand to her back, satisfied she hadn't been hit over the head like Derrick.

The cab of the truck became silent as their individual thoughts formed faster than their mouths would let them. Oliver was trying to keep his growing anger under control. To put hands around Darling's neck until she had passed out, and then to strip her and leave her in the cold to die were two acts that painted an unsettling picture of a man with nothing but bad intentions. The idea that he had been watching Darling and waiting for her to leave her apartment was one that crawled under Oliver's skin and simmered. But at the same time, a thin yet strong layer of guilt covered it.

He shouldn't have left her alone after someone had ransacked her office. Even if Derrick had consoled him with promises of her staying safe.

Darling sighed, and Oliver felt the movement go from her chest to his. Despite the fact that she was completely naked—and pressed against him—Oliver noted that the overriding emotion he felt was protectiveness.

Sure, he could admit that what he had seen of her today was all woman and all beautiful. Her curves, her breasts, her hips, her legs. But instead of overpowering feelings of lust and desire, he had instantly felt the need to keep that body safe.

To guard it with his own body.

In that moment, Oliver realized the only person he wanted to be a bodyguard for was wrapped up and shivering in his arms.

Chapter Fifteen

The chief took charge of the entire hospital when they came in. He barked orders no one questioned. That included giving Darling privacy until she was placed in a room with a nurse, a doctor and a gown.

"We need you to step out of the room for now," the nurse told Oliver after he'd made sure she was situated on a bed. He started to argue, but Darling silenced him.

"It's okay," she tried to assure him. "I'm safe."

He didn't want to point out that she'd thought that before. Instead he kept his mouth shut. She'd been through enough.

"Heath found something," Chief Sanderson said, bustling over. "Call me if you learn anything new or she remembers anything. Give me your keys and we'll have someone bring your car over."

"Thanks." In truth, he hadn't even thought about the rental.

"And tell Darling we'll get the bastard who did this."

"You bet your ass we will," Oliver responded. The chief gave him a quick nod and was gone.

Now that Darling was safe, Oliver was able to think about the rest of the world. Grant and Thomas were having to stretch themselves thin to cover Oliver's day shift, but he couldn't see a way around leaving Darling.

He let out a long exhalation and slumped against the wall. There wasn't enough time to rest.

"You look tired."

Standing next to him in a black pantsuit and matching heels, Nikki Waters was the last person he had expected to see. At least, not this soon.

"It's been a long twenty-four hours," he said. Nikki didn't smile.

"How is Miss Smith doing?"

He glanced back at the shut door.

"Cold," he said. "Scared, but won't admit it. I don't think there's any permanent or life-threatening damage."

"I'm glad to hear that."

"How do you even know about all of this?" He motioned around them.

"Thomas told me about the break-in when I called for a status update." She shrugged. "With all these unknown variables continuing to come into play, I thought it best to jump on a flight and come out here." She was waiting for Oliver to say something, but he didn't want to start a conversation he knew wouldn't end well. Nikki must have realized this. She turned her body toward the empty room across from them. "Can we talk in private a moment?"

Oliver followed without complaint. He moved himself so he could see over Nikki's shoulder to Darling's room. If anyone who wasn't hospital staff tried to get to her, they'd soon find out they would have to go through him.

"I don't know where to begin, really," she started. Her posture was stick straight, her arms across her chest. "But I suppose I'll start with this. What were you thinking,

Oliver? You asked Orion's senior analyst to *hack into an active client's phone to take information*." Disbelief and blatant disappointment blanketed each word. "Do you have any idea how much trouble we would be in had I not stopped Rachel when I called to tell her I'd landed?"

Oliver was taken aback.

"It was necessary—it still *is* necessary—to find out what Nigel's hiding," he said, frustration pouring out. "Nigel is connected to all of this. We have to know how, and that call log could be the key."

"Then let the police get a warrant for it," Nikki snapped back. Her cool composure cracked. "Did it ever occur to you that getting evidence illegally would hurt your case more than it would help it? Courts would dismiss whatever evidence you found. Plus, what makes you so sure he's involved with that woman's death or Darling's abduction? You told me yourself that in your gut, you didn't believe he killed the unidentified woman. What changed?"

That gave Oliver pause. She was right. Oliver knew in his gut Nigel hadn't had anything to do with the death. When he didn't come up with a good answer, she continued.

"Just because there isn't another obvious suspect doesn't mean you should jump on one of the only suspects you *do* have. This is one bad judgment call I can't overlook, Oliver. You didn't just jeopardize Rachel. You jeopardized us all. Every agent—their families—and every person we ever would protect in the future. You put us all—including yourself—in danger."

Oliver was about to protest. Finding a kidnapped Darling didn't compare to the remote possibility that Orion could be held accountable for the breach in security. He had already decided that if it came down to it, he would shoulder all of the blame. However, Nikki didn't give him a breath to say any of that.

"All of it—all of this—could have been avoided had you just come to me directly," she said, voice cooling. "Instead you went behind my back, asked an analyst to go against her ethical code and broke the law. You should have come to me, Oliver."

"You'd already made it clear I wasn't supposed to get close to Darling," he reasoned, thinking back to his first day in Mulligan. "I thought you would have shut me down and then out. I didn't want to take that chance."

"That chance? Oliver, I started Orion because I believe that every life deserves the basic right of safety, no matter that person's financial situation. For three years I have busted all of our collective asses to make sure we offer virtually free services and every client who comes to us can rest a little easier. What makes you, Oliver Quinn, think that I wouldn't have done everything in my power to help when I knew a woman's life depended on it?"

Oliver's mouth slid open, but no words came out. Like a fish out of water, he stared at her. She had him there.

"I—I wasn't thinking straight," he admitted. "I'm sorry, but I couldn't take the chance."

"And _that_ is why I'm taking you off this case and sending you home." Whatever anger had been within her was seeping out. Her resolve, however, was absolute. There was no reprieve to be had. As he responded, he hoped she could see his level of intensity, as well.

"She's more than just a friend. I can't leave her, Nikki. Not until this is all put to rest," he said, voice low, unyielding. "I won't leave her again."

For an instant Oliver thought he saw Nikki's body sag. She let out a low breath and shook her head slowly.

"Then I'm afraid I'm going to have to ask for your resignation."

"He took my earrings."

Darling rubbed at the smoothness of her ear lobes. They were warming up, as were her fingers, but she didn't feel any yellow daisy earrings beneath them. "Doesn't that seem oddly personal?"

"Excuse me?" Nurse Jones looked up from the end of Darling's hospital bed. Her glasses slipped to the tip of her nose.

Darling shifted her weight. The readjustment moved her foot, which earned her a glare from the nurse. She put her hands around the top Darling's foot to hold it still.

"Never mind," Darling said.

Nurse Jones finished her evaluation in silence. Considering she was inspecting the stitches on the bottom of her foot, Darling didn't want to annoy the woman. Even though she had been one of the handful of people who had seen Oliver carry her in wrapped around him naked, she hadn't questioned Darling about the situation when they were alone.

Not that she felt the need to talk to the older woman about it. Darling still had to sort her through her own thoughts.

"Okay, looks like your little stunt didn't tear open your stitches," Nurse Jones said, standing with her hands on her hips. She was a stern woman in her fifties and didn't care for any excuses. So Darling didn't give her one.

"Next time I need to get to the bathroom, I'll hit the

call button," Darling promised. "And not try to get there without my crutches."

Nurse Jones nodded and turned her attention to the rest of her patient. "And how do you feel now?"

It had been almost an hour since she had been passed off to the doctor. Hot water bottles and blankets had been applied to her body in an attempt to make her warm as the cut across her foot had been stitched. The doctor had confirmed she was suffering from hypothermia but, lucky for her, taking shelter from the wind had helped her more than anything. Also, Oliver's body temperature had begun to put warmth back into hers on the ride to the hospital. It was a great starting point, the doctor had exclaimed.

Some of the warm water bottles were still placed across her stomach and thighs while Darling kept buried beneath three thick blankets.

"I wouldn't say cozy, but I'm not cold anymore," she answered. Darling held up her bandaged hand. "This doesn't hurt anymore, either."

"And your throat?"

On reflex, Darling's hands flitted to her neck. She could still imagine the strong grip that had brought her to unconsciousness wrapped around her.

"It doesn't hurt as much when I talk," she admitted.

Nurse Jones wrote on the clipboard in her hand without commenting. The woman showed no signs of sympathy. The nurse had obviously seen a lot working in a hospital. Darling wasn't going to hold it against her that her bedside manner was lacking.

"Okay, I'll have to get the doctor to sign off on it, but I think you're good to leave just as soon as that young man brings you your clothes. You still need to take it easy, though." The nurse tapped Darling's big toe. "No pressure on this for four or five days. We'll set up a time for you to come back and get the stitches removed." She pointed to the set of crutches leaning against the bed. "Use those. Understand?"

"Yes, ma'am."

"Good."

The nurse left without another word. Darling let out a long, deep sigh and pulled the top blanket up to her chin. She imagined the cloth was a nice, hot bath. Her body submerged in water that would stave off any cold the night could bring. Scented candles along the lip of the tub, all combining in the epitome of a relaxing atmosphere.

"Should I come back later?"

Darling jumped and turned to see Oliver standing in the doorway. A duffel bag thrown over his shoulder, a smirk attached to his lips.

"Sorry. You looked like you were enjoying your thoughts."

Darling laughed. "I was actually dreaming of a bath," she said. "Cheesy, right?"

He walked over and put the bag next to her. "After what you've been through, I'd say you have every right to a bath. Heck, I'd even go so far as to say a bubble bath."

She followed that with another laugh but cut it short. Something seemed off about the bodyguard. He was smiling, but the expression didn't reach his eyes.

"What's wrong?" Darling asked with such intense concern it almost moved her. Oliver looked surprised.

"What do you mean?"

"Your smile doesn't reach—" She stopped herself and then amended, "Your smile seems off. Fake."

He crossed his arms over his chest. His eyebrow rose. "My smile seems fake," he repeated with obvious mockery.

Darling felt a flare of frustration lick to life inside her. When would Oliver realize that she could read him as easily as he could read her?

As if on cue, Oliver's face softened, and his voice lost all contempt. "I'm tired. I haven't gotten much sleep recently."

It was Darling's turn to soften. She reached out and took his hand. She had thought her skin had warmed considerably since she had been brought in, but where Oliver's hand touched hers, there was nothing but brilliant heat. Instead of pulling away, she squeezed.

"Thank you for finding me. I didn't get a chance to say it earlier."

Oliver squeezed back.

"Thank you for not freezing to death," he replied with a new tilt to his lips. Together they laughed and dropped hands. The moment passed, and Darling opened the duffel.

"Now, the question is, are you as good at finding a decent outfit?"

"If your idea of a good outfit is a white tank top, skin-tight jeans, and a red thong…" Darling's face heated before she could stop it. "Then that's not a good outfit. And on that note, I'll leave you to change." He started to leave but paused to add, "Unless you need help?"

"No, thanks. I think I can do it."

He shrugged and closed the door behind him. It wasn't as if he hadn't seen *and* felt her naked body only a few hours before. Heat flared up her neck and into her cheeks.

Oliver had picked out a sweatshirt, jeans and tennis

shoes. It meant he had grabbed the first thing he'd seen in her closet and chest of drawers. As for undergarments, thankfully he had gone sensible and picked a no-lace beige bra and a pair of black cotton bikini-cut panties. Darling spent the time putting on each item trying to recall what all he had seen when going through her underwear drawer. He had to have seen every type of underwear she owned. From the see-through special occasion lace to the long, unattractive pieces meant for a Maine winter. Within the past few hours, she had lost a lot of privacy points with the bodyguard.

Nurse Jones came back in just after Darling had wrangled on her pants, taking care not to disrupt the stitches on the bottom of her foot. Dr. Williams had signed off, and she was officially being discharged.

"Will the young man outside be taking you home, or do you need a ride?" the nurse asked after she had put some ointment on Darling's foot and wrapped it up. "It's the end of my shift, so I could drop you off." She shrugged to show indifference, but Darling smiled. Apparently the nurse wasn't completely apathetic.

"Thank you for the offer, but I suppose I'm with him."

Nurse Jones mimicked her smile for the first time. "That's not a bad lot to have."

"I suppose not."

Darling turned down a wheelchair to help her to the car and instead put a crutch beneath each arm and began an awkward gait down the hallway. Oliver carried her bag and kept close. He still seemed off somehow, but she was going to believe it was because he was tired. She couldn't deny she was in the same boat. The sleep that she had gotten in the car hadn't been sound or comfortable.

And she hadn't been too sure it wasn't the beginnings of death by exposure.

"Should I go see Derrick before we leave?" Darling asked. "The nurse said he should be waking up soon."

"It might be a better idea to let him rest for now," he answered. "I checked in on him before I went to your apartment, and he was still sound asleep. I think it's his pain meds."

Darling nodded. Guilt outlined with a sad edge cut inside her. If Derrick had not been watching out for her, he never would have been attacked. If she had only listened to Oliver and taken his offer to help protect her... Darling paused in her thinking. Whoever had taken her was determined. Hospitalizing an officer was a great testament to that fact. If Derrick hadn't been there but Oliver had, then it would have been Oliver hurt. Or worse.

Her guilt ebbed away.

Another feeling tore through her at the thought of a horrific fate befalling the bodyguard. She glanced sideways at him. When the chaos around her died down, she would have to think about why her heart and mind always seemed to clash when the topic of Oliver Quinn was put on the table.

Chapter Sixteen

The bathwater stopped running, and a few seconds later, a splash sounded.

"You okay?" Oliver couldn't help but call out.

They were back in Darling's apartment. To celebrate, Darling had indeed drawn herself a bubble bath.

"I'm fine," she answered through the door. "You can stop hovering now!"

Oliver fell into the couch when he was finished with another security sweep. He settled his back against the armrest so his sight line to the front door wasn't obstructed, a habit. The conversation with Nikki started to replay in his head.

He was no longer a bodyguard.

All to save Darling.

He hadn't fought Nikki after she had asked for his resignation. It was a choice he didn't resent. Funny, he thought, how once upon a time he had left Darling to protect her, and now he was staying to do the same.

Why was it so easy to sacrifice everything for a woman who would never trust him again?

"Oliver!"

In a flash he was off of the couch and standing at the bathroom door. "Are you okay? What's wrong?"

"I'm fine! I was just going to see if you were hungry?"

"Hungry?" he repeated, his adrenaline on the brink of spiking.

"Yeah, I haven't eaten in—" She stopped. Oliver almost opened the door all the way to make sure she was okay. "Breakfast yesterday, I suppose. So, I thought we could maybe order something? There's a pizzeria on Main Street that delivers. Unless you need to go back to work?" She had hesitated before her last question had slipped out. It made Oliver wonder if she knew about his conversation with Nikki. He pushed that thought away.

"No, I can stay," he answered. That was a conversation he didn't want to broach through a partially opened bathroom door. "And pizza sounds good."

"Wonderful," she almost sang. "I don't have anything here to eat. There's a magnet on the fridge with the number. Order whatever you want. Just make sure there's a lot of whatever it is."

Oliver shut the door and did as he was told.

Instead of sitting back down to swim in his deepest thoughts, he looked around the living room. Like the rest of the small apartment, it was filled with character. He found he liked it more than his apartment.

The bathroom door opened.

"Need any help?"

"No," she replied, frustrated. "But I sure do hate crutches." They clinked against the hardwood floors as she started to go for her bedroom. That gave Oliver an idea.

"Wait, are you dressed?" he asked, though he was already moving.

"Yeah, why?"

He held up his finger to get her to wait and walked

past her into the bedroom. Going straight for her mini-office in the corner, he grabbed the chair and rolled it back into the hall.

"It's no wheelchair but, really, isn't it a chair with wheels?" He cracked a smile and Darling laughed. She wore a long-sleeved white robe that fell to her ankles and tied around the middle. Her hair was wet and wound up into a bun atop her head. It was the first time in eight years he had seen her without a lick of makeup on, and he had to admit she was still as beautiful as ever.

He helped her angle herself into the chair and placed her crutches against the wall.

"Where to, madam?" he asked with little bow. She laughed again. He liked the sound.

"I heard the couch is all the rage this time of the year," she said playfully. "A five-star destination second only to the kitchen bar."

"Then that's where we'll go." He did another quick bow and began to roll the chair toward the living room. He kept an eye on her foot, careful not to jostle it. They reached the living room, and without letting her stop him, he lifted her from the chair and placed her on the couch, her back against the armrest and legs stretched out. He sat on the edge of the coffee table right in front of her.

"Are you comfortable?" he asked.

"My foot is sore, but I guess that's normal for having it split open and stitched back up. I didn't get it wet in the bath. I was too afraid," she admitted, rotating her ankle. As she spoke, Oliver's gaze went to the bruises on her neck. "It doesn't hurt that much," she whispered, tone changing with her mood.

Oliver couldn't help it. He reached out and traced

the skin around the bruise on her right. It made Darling shiver. He stopped but didn't pull away.

"I thought you were dead," he breathed. "When I found you in that car...for a moment I thought you were—"

"But I wasn't," she interrupted, voice soft. Her hand covered his. They sat still, both caught in a moment that couldn't be summed up in words.

Oliver leaned in. "I'm glad," he whispered.

Darling searched his face, but he only had eyes for those lips. Careful not to spook her, he slowly closed the space between them, giving her plenty of time to move away. His heartbeat sped up when he realized she wasn't going to.

The kiss was soft and warm. A ribbon drenched in sunlight. He wanted it to continue—to get lost in a moment that could be so much more—but he let it end.

After everything that had happened, Darling was vulnerable, whether she wanted to admit it or not. And he couldn't deny he wasn't in the best spot, either. He didn't want to take advantage of her. He was finding that she still meant too much to him.

He pulled back and smiled. The private investigator's cheeks were tinted red, her lips a shade of dark pink.

"Better than I remember." As the words left his mouth, Oliver feared he had overstepped their relationship by bringing up the past. However, Darling didn't seem to mind it. She mimicked his smile and opened her mouth to speak. Her response was cut off by a knock at the door.

"If that's not at least a large pizza, I'm going to be so upset," she said instead.

"I did you one better. I ordered two." Darling thrust her fist in the air in victory, and just like that, they returned to normal.

Ten minutes later, they were seated at the kitchen bar, plates covered in pizza slices and minds set to work. The question about who they were together was put aside for a time when one of their lives wasn't in danger.

"You know what I don't get?" Darling asked after putting down another large bite. "Why take me in the first place? I mean, I realize that stripping me down and dumping me in the cold is a pretty clear way to kill me without having to actually kill me, but why *take* me?"

"You must have gotten too close."

"But why not warn me instead?" It must have been a question she had been wondering about for a while. She put down her food and angled her body to face him. The top of her robe opened a fraction, giving him an uninhibited view of the top of her bare chest. She didn't notice his glance downward. He tried to refocus. "I get a folder of pictures of Nigel and Jane Doe with a note telling me to do the right thing—plus the article with my parents—and I follow those instructions. Then I go to get my camera with pictures of the hotel crime scene and there's another note, warning me to stop snooping. The camera is returned before I go to the police, but this time with no note."

"Then we take a trip to the gas station, confirm Jane Doe was there and get the security footage. You find out the woman Jane Doe talked to was Harriet Mendon. The next day Acuity is ransacked and the security tape is gone," he continued.

"But *with no note*." Darling said this with a punch, as if it held more importance than all of the rest.

"Yes, but then you come back here and get taken. There's a new note with a threat saying you have one more strike left. Though you didn't see that note." Anger began to build within him once more. He pictured her sitting in that car again, motionless.

She kept on, not noticing the tension. "Right! One more strike. Implying that I hadn't yet crossed whatever line had been drawn." Darling lowered her voice. "So, I ask again—why take me less than two hours later, and why not leave the note at Acuity?"

"Whoever it was, they got sloppy."

"You're right," she exclaimed. "*They* did!"

"Wait, what?" Oliver tried to follow the train of thought she was already on but came up short.

"Oliver, I think we're dealing with two killers. Hear me out," Darling began. "Two people are trying to frame Nigel. Note Writer enlists my help to make the case seem more valid. He—or she—is observant, smart. He knows what to say and when to say it. He's careful. But then he trashes my office without a note? Then *kidnaps* me? What's the point in leaving a threat on my door and then taking me after I clearly hadn't left the apartment or done anything else on the case?"

"You think that like all the good crime-fighting and crime-committing teams, one of them is the brains and the other one is the hothead," he finished for her.

"What's more, I don't think they're communicating all that well, either. I think the brains wrote the last-strike threat without knowing about Acuity being ransacked or vice versa. The note writer wanted to scare me. The other one wanted to hurt me."

"If this is all true, then our problems just doubled. What's worse than one killer? Two."

Chapter Seventeen

Darling was trying to put all the clues back together but couldn't help but see them now as two separate lines, running sloppily parallel next to each other.

"Two people would make killing and cleaning up after Jane Doe easier," she said aloud. "A rich man like Nigel wouldn't have a problem finding a killer for hire with his wealth."

Oliver didn't skip a beat. "I know you are keen on thinking Nigel is behind this, but I'm telling you, it's not him. Thomas caught him crying yesterday, just after Derrick called to tell him about how Jane Doe was killed." He knew now that had been an attempt to shake whatever truth Nigel had about the woman free. "Do you really think Nigel Marks would cry over a mistress he'd killed? If it's anyone in that family, I'd bet it's the wife. They share the wealth. She just as easily could have fronted the money for a contract killer."

Darling held in her rebuttal. Her desire for Nigel Marks to pay for all of his indiscretions was great, but she was finding the idea of him being behind Jane Doe's murder didn't quite sit right with her anymore. Although she wasn't ready to point the finger at Elizabeth, either. She still believed the older woman was too smart to do something so stupid. And if she really thought about it, if Elizabeth was going to kill anyone, it would probably be her husband.

"We need to figure out who our Jane Doe is," Darling said instead.

A booming knock sounded at the front door. It was so unexpected that Darling almost fell off her stool. Oliver's reflexes were a lot more productive. He was off his stool and standing in front of Darling, using his body as a human shield. He had even reached back to help steady her.

"I'm not expecting anyone," Darling whispered. "If you were wondering."

Oliver nodded and reached over the bar to the kitchen counter. He pulled two of the steak knives out of their wooden holder next to the toaster. He passed one to Darling and brandished the other. She grabbed the handle of her knife and watched wide-eyed as the bodyguard silently crossed the room and sidled up to the front door.

The knock sounded again. Oliver waited for it to stop before calling out.

"Who's there?"

Darling marveled at how controlled he was. He looked like a man about to go to war. Calm, calculating and also ready for whatever what was about to happen.

"Chief Sanderson!"

Darling relaxed, but when Oliver didn't, she tightened her grip on the knife handle. Slowly the bodyguard cracked open the door. He must have been okay with what he saw. He straightened his back and opened the door wide. The knife in his hand remained there, but the chief didn't seem to mind it as he looked between them.

"Sorry to intrude, but I have some new information

I'd like to talk to you about," Chief Sanderson said. Darling hadn't been too focused on the chief when she had ridden in his truck that morning, but now she could see as clear as day that he hadn't been getting much sleep, if any. Dark circles hung beneath each eye, and there was a droop to his shoulders as he moved to the chair next to the couch. Darling swiveled her stool around to face him while Oliver took point, standing between the two.

"Is it about Derrick? Is he okay?" Darling asked out of the gate. If anything happened to Derrick, it would be her fault. Derrick was one of the few friends she could claim as her own. She might not have been in love with him, but that didn't mean she wasn't loyal to him.

"No, he's fine. Sleeping last time I checked in," he assured her. "You two expecting company?" The chief looked at the knife in Darling's hand. Heat rose in her neck, and she put the weapon back on the counter. Oliver relaxed his hand but didn't put his knife down.

"We weren't, and that was the problem," he said with a nonapologetic smile.

The chief let out a chuckle. "Better safe than sorry," he said.

"So what's the news, Chief?" Darling asked. For him to personally visit was out of character.

"Well, we finally found what we believe to be Jane Doe's car."

"That's wonderful," Darling exclaimed. Surely they could find out who she was now. That was a break they all needed. The chief, however, didn't seem as enthused. She shared a look with Oliver. He didn't understand the chief's current emotion, either.

"The car was stripped. No plates. No insurance."

"Then how do you know it belongs to Jane Doe?" Oliver asked.

Chief Sanderson's face was absolutely stony when he responded. "We found the murder weapon on the front seat. A blunt object that fits the indention in Jane Doe's skull with trace amounts of blood on it."

"So—if you can get her prints—you should be able to ID her now. At least faster, I hope, than sending her blood off?" Oliver supplied.

The chief shook his head. "She isn't in the criminal database, so unless she's been printed at some point in her life, it'll still be difficult to see who she is. The system isn't perfect and sometimes, no matter how hard we try, it doesn't work." He cracked a smile. It wasn't happy. It was downright malicious. "So we're going to get Nigel Marks to tell us who she is."

That surprised Darling.

"Why?" Oliver asked.

"We found evidence that suggests Nigel was in that car recently, which means he knew our victim. Not even his fancy lawyer will be able to deny it. He's now physically connected to her."

Darling couldn't believe it. "What is the evidence?" she asked.

"I can't disclose that information." Before Darling could complain, he held up his hand. "But I'm sure if you think really hard about it, you'll remember."

"What do you mean, I'll remember?"

"You were in the same car, too."

Darling felt her eyebrows slam together.

"Wait a second." Oliver held up his hands. "You mean the car we found her in this morning belongs to Jane Doe?"

The chief nodded.

"Oh, my God," she said, drawing both men's attention her way. "The watch! It was Nigel's watch? It *did* look expensive. I didn't really think too much about it, given the situation."

"Well, some people should think twice before they get their names inscribed into their accessories."

"And the hammer," Darling exclaimed, realizing what the blunt object the chief was referring to was. "It's the murder weapon." Darling's raised her eyebrows when the chief nodded. She looked down at her hands and cringed. "I picked that up. It was in the trunk and I—I wanted a weapon! Did I mess up the evidence?"

The chief gave her a sympathetic smile. "No," he said. "We were able to tell the older blood versus the blood left from your hand. As for her prints, I'm betting the hammer will be wiped down like the car, save for yours. But I'm trying to remain optimistic."

"What about Nigel's alibi?" Darling asked.

"It still holds. We're just accusing him of hindering a murder investigation now. He's lied to us, and now we have physical evidence that ties him to the victim. It's enough to hold him until we get some answers. I'm sure his lawyer is already earning his keep right now." The chief stood to signal the conversation was over. "I also came by to make sure you were okay." He didn't smile, but she could hear the concern in his voice.

"I'm much better, thanks," she replied. "I would have been worse had you two not found me."

"Don't look at me," Chief Sanderson said. "Blame this guy. If he hadn't been so concerned about you, we wouldn't have gotten to you when we did."

Darling turned to Oliver. He shrugged, trying to look indifferent.

"Well, I need to get back to it. I'm going to have an officer stop by later to take down your official statement and also take your prints so we can know which are yours in that car." The chief turned to Oliver and put out his hand to shake. "Thanks for not giving up. Not everyone can keep their cool in these situations. I suppose I'll see you and your boss around the station since we have Nigel in custody now."

Oliver shook back. An emotion that Darling couldn't place flared to life across his face.

"Actually, I'm no longer on the case," he said, surprising Darling. "I might have said and done some things I shouldn't have when I couldn't locate Darling. I personally don't regret it, but professionally it wasn't the best call to make. Though I can't complain at the moment." Oliver looked pointedly at Darling.

"I can't, either," the chief agreed.

The chief said another quick goodbye and left. Darling waited until she thought the older man was out of the building before she turned on Oliver.

"You were taken off the case?" she asked with concern. "What does that mean? Does Orion lose the money now?"

"No, my team is still working with Nigel. Only I was taken off." He sat back down at the counter. Darling held her hands wide in question. "Though I don't know if even they will be working on it now that Nigel has actually been linked to Jane Doe. He might not be guilty of killing her, but this new evidence will make Nikki take a long second look. Do you think he'll admit to the affair now?"

Darling decided to put a pin in the issue of him getting dropped from the case and instead went along with this thoughts. Because, truth be told, the new information hadn't made the case any easier. Every clue was another layer of confusion. It was as if they were looking over a map and everything was a fraction off. They needed a key that would show them the correct way to decipher it all.

"I would imagine Nigel will either come clean about everything or give an alternate version. Something that covers him," she answered. "Elizabeth should be in town soon, right? To admit to the affair now would ruin everything for him. He's a smart man. He has to know he's got his back up against the proverbial wall."

"Nigel *is* a smart man." Oliver was looking at the wall, but she doubted he was seeing it. Concentration mixed with confusion were two expressions she could pick out with ease. Darling knew the feeling well. "So, why would he leave a watch with his name in his mistress's car?"

Darling had already picked up on that thread of thought.

"It could have been an accident." She didn't feel the certainty in it as she said it.

Oliver cast her a questioning look. "But…"

"But, I can't get over the fact that I was the one who found the car. Me being taken and then left to find it couldn't have been a coincidence, could it?" Like with the car, Darling tried to recall with new attention the moment after waking up in the darkness until her trek to the car. "If I hadn't had walked that way, it's true I might not have found it, but now that I think about it, there was no other place for me to go."

"What do you mean? You could have walked off in any direction. You just lucked out and happened to go the direction the car was already in." Darling knew Oliver was playing devil's advocate now. She knew the idea of her finding the car being a coincidence wasn't sitting well with him. However, he wanted her to work for her side of the argument. He was challenging her as he always had. Normally it would have made her angry, but she realized it was helping her work her own thoughts out, as well. Oliver Quinn, annoying her into being a better person.

"No, I think that was the only place to go," she said. "I heard the chief tell the doctor at the hospital that he guessed I had to have been left a few yards away from the Pinketts' property line." She envisioned the aerial shot of the land she had once seen framed in the police-department lounge. It, along with other land reserved for hunting, was showcased in the room. "If that's true, then if I had decided to walk in the opposite direction, I would have run into their woods." Without meaning to, she shivered.

"Okay, so you could have walked into the woods."

"But I wouldn't have. Not with its hunting traps and animals galore," she rebutted. "Plus, it somehow felt creepier to be trapped among the trees instead of out in the open."

Oliver's frown deepened. He made to grab her hand but then changed tactics and put his own around his cup instead. Darling felt a twinge of sadness. Whatever moment they had had earlier seemed to have been lost in the muck of all the questions regarding Jane Doe's fate.

"You wouldn't go into the woods, but that doesn't mean whoever took you knew that. What about the road that cut through it all? If you had found that, you could easily have missed the car."

She didn't have a response for that. If she had found the dirt road Chief Sanderson and Oliver had come in on, she *would* have followed it one way or the other. She never would have seen the car. Maybe it *was* a coincidence. "Then why turn my phone *back* on?" she asked with a tilt of her head. "Why take my phone, turn it off, then turn it back on later so the car and I could be found?" Oliver didn't have an answer to that, either. She let out a frustrated sigh. "We need fewer theories and more facts," Darling muttered. "I'm so tired of guessing. What if we're just grasping at straws?"

"Well, let's look at the facts, then." Oliver got up from his stool and disappeared into her bedroom. Moments later he was back with a pen and one of her notebooks. He flipped it open to a blank sheet and started a numbered list. "Nigel Marks spent the late night and early morning at Mulligan Motel with Jane Doe."

"Which he denies having done."

"Jane Doe was killed while Nigel was eating with Orion agents. Giving him a valid alibi."

"Elizabeth Marks also has a confirmed alibi," she added. He quickly wrote that down.

"Jane Doe's fingers and teeth were removed, meaning the killer didn't want her to be identified, or maybe the killer wanted some trophies." Oliver hesitated before writing the last part down. Darling tried not to picture the body in the tub. "Then a mysterious person gives you pictures of Nigel and Jane Doe over the course of several months this year. Nigel's lawyer reasons it could be anyone or the images could be doctored. Without the original files to be tested, the cops can't keep him or get him to reveal her identity. You get another note saying to stop investigating, and they take your camera only to return it. Acuity gets ransacked, you get another note and then you're taken. You find Jane Doe's car stripped car with Nigel Marks's watch in it."

When he was done, she looked down at the short-hand list.

"I feel like we're just talking in circles now," she breathed out. "We're missing something."

They lapsed into a thoughtful silence. Maybe it was time to leave the case alone. Maybe they were hurting it instead of helping. It was already her fault that Derrick, the lead investigator, had been hospitalized. If she hadn't kept digging...

"Oh, my God, that's it," Darling exclaimed. Oliver met her wild stare with skepticism.

"What?"

"Let's stick with the theory that there *are* two people involved in the killing of Jane Doe. So far they've shown up whenever I discovered something new. The office was tossed looking for the security tape. They got it, so that should be it, right? But then they grab me two hours later? Why?" Before Oliver could answer, she beat him to it. "Because I found Harriet Mendon."

"Wait, what do you mean you found her?"

"Before you and I had it out at Acuity, I looked up where she worked."

Oliver's features seemed to reanimate.

"Oliver," she continued with new enthusiasm. "I think Harriet Mendon is our key."

Just as quickly as excitement at a new lead flashed across his face, a darker emotion replaced it. When he spoke, it made the hair on the back of Darling's neck stand up.

"Then we'd better find her before they do."

Chapter Eighteen

Darling found the number of the boutique where Harriet Mendon worked and left an urgent message with the owner, a friendly woman named Barb. She also left a new message on Harriet's home machine. One way or the other, she wanted to cover all her bases.

"Okay, it's time I change out of this robe," Darling said when she was done. "Make yourself at home."

Oliver looked around the living room with a new perspective after she went to her bedroom. He imagined his recliner in the corner, the picture of his parents next to the one of Darling and friends on top of the bookcase, his shoes tossed off next to the front door and the fight that would always come from him leaving them there.

Holiday get-togethers, quiet nights spent in, loud meaningless arguments that would never last long and makeups that would certainly last longer. There they were, moving around the small space without an ounce of regret or anger or guilt.

He pictured the two of them finishing something they had started when they were basically kids.

And loving every moment of it.

"It just isn't my week," Darling said a few minutes later, interrupting his thoughts.

"What happened?"

"Do you want a list or a long-winded sentence?"

He gave her his full attention. "Let's go long-winded sentence this time."

She took a deep breath.

"Elizabeth called because she's at the police station with Nigel—who apparently finally realized it was a good idea to tell the truth about knowing Jane Doe. But Elizabeth wouldn't say the name—and because of everything that happened, she terminated my contract," she said in a rush. "Finding Jane Doe's killer isn't her top priority anymore."

"Or she wants the police to handle it since you were *kidnapped* and left for dead by the same person or people," Oliver pointed out. Darling frowned and sent him a pointed stare. He held up his hands in defense. "It's guilt, Darling. She doesn't want to deal with it if something happens to you while under her orders." His thoughts turned to Nikki. "It has nothing to do with your job performance."

"I know," she admitted. "But the way she spoke…" Darling's brow furrowed and she sucked on her bottom lip, thinking of the right words. "She didn't sound upset at all. I guess I just assumed that finding out the identity of her husband's mistress might hit a nerve, even if she already knew about the affair." She shrugged. "Either way, I've been fired, so the case doesn't matter anymore."

The private investigator tried to look nonchalant. She leaned on her crutches in the doorway of her bedroom, gaze going through him as she focused on some thought in the distance. Oliver didn't point out that neither of them was ready to let the case go without getting justice for those who had determined Jane Doe's fate *and* hurt Darling. He crossed his arms over his chest and waited. It didn't take long.

"Who am I kidding?" Darling exclaimed. "Like being fired is going to stop me."

Oliver clapped. "That's my girl!"

Darling smiled. He could see how tired she felt.

"But first, coffee?" he suggested.

That earned a bigger smile. "That sounds wonderful, Mr. Quinn."

"DEPUTY HEATH, I never got a chance to thank you for helping to find me."

They had already gone through an entire pot of coffee waiting for the deputy to show up to take Darling's statement.

"It's no problem," she replied, wasting no time in getting down to business. She pulled out her printing kit, and Darling offered her hand. The older woman looked as if she also needed some coffee. "I can't wait until we catch those sons of b—"

"Those?" Darling interrupted. A wild kind of excitement crossed her face. Oliver bet she was ready to call out every clue she had that connected to two killers rather than one. "As in more than one?"

Oliver watched as the deputy's cheeks tinted pink. "I *meant*," Heath said, "whoever is responsible. We have a very promising lead and I—personally—am confident we'll have this case closed up soon."

The private investigator held her comments back while Deputy Heath finished the prints. Her gears were turning. That much Oliver could tell from his seat at the kitchen counter. With a bit of distance between them, he tried to look at her from an objective viewpoint.

Tired yet determined. Hurt yet unperturbed. Curious yet cautious.

"I can't disclose that information right now," Heath said after everything was done. "Give us tonight, Darling. Everything will make much more sense in the morning."

Oliver was ready to point out that after what Darling had been through, she deserved at least the name of Jane Doe, but the investigator shot him a silencing look. Neither pressed the issue as the deputy left.

"A sane person would probably take all of this—" Darling waved her arms around "—as a sign to change professions, huh?"

Oliver came around and took a seat next to her. "I don't know if you've noticed, but you aren't like most people." He patted her knee on reflex. She didn't pull away.

"I guess you really dodged a bullet back in the day."

Oliver tensed. Whether it was an off-the-cuff remark or a pointed comment about him rejecting her, he didn't know. What he was sure of was that he didn't like that she seemed to be blaming herself for what had happened. He cleared his throat.

"Darling," he started, but he was cut off when she touched his hand with hers.

"I don't want to talk about it," she said, voice resolute. "What you've done in the last week is more than most would have done for me. You saved me and it cost you. I'm sorry for that, Oliver." She meant to pull her hand away, but he held it fast. Darling's green eyes were calm as they searched his.

"Don't you dare apologize to me after what I've done," he said, voice filled with grit. "And I'll never regret what

I did trying to find you. Never." Unlike their kiss earlier that day, the atmosphere darkened. There was lust—he was certainly feeling it—but there was also pain. Had he gone too far when he left her? Had he changed her life for the worse instead of for the better? These thoughts pushed Oliver off the couch as if he had been burned. Darling let go of his hand, eyes wide. He didn't miss the flush across her cheeks, either.

"Well, thank you," she said in a rush, also standing. "I—uh—think I'm going to dry my hair." She reached back and took her crutches leaning against the couch. Oliver didn't respond. Guilt and regret were slamming against his rib cage. He shouldn't want her—shouldn't imagine a life with her—after deciding to cut ties with no explanation. She had a life. She deserved better than him. Always had, always would.

He watched as she awkwardly began her walk back to the bedroom. The crutches clinked in the silence. However, she didn't make it far. Oliver was in front of her in an instant.

Her eyes were red, tears waiting on each rim. His last image of the younger Darling had been with tears in her eyes, but his mind didn't connect that vulnerability or memory to the woman standing in front of him. He didn't connect it the day she found out what her parents had done, and he didn't even think to compare it to the cold, naked woman he had held in his arms that morning.

Bringing his hands up, he cradled her face and moved closer.

There was the difference. Between his fingers and the heat of her skin was an electricity he couldn't ignore. It coursed through each of them before crashing together. Rapid, shocking, sensational.

And it was begging him to not let go.

Before the world could catch up to them, his mouth covered hers.

Chapter Nineteen

Hunger. Passion.

Pain. Lust. Desire.

Everything exploded in the kiss. Darling didn't know which thought to rest on as Oliver's lips pushed and pulled at more than just her body. There were a million reasons they shouldn't be intertwining and yet she couldn't recall a single one.

Darling's eyelids fluttered closed, and she let herself enjoy the moment. Oliver's lips pressed against her with an undeniable hunger that ate its way right into hers. Her crutches clattered to the ground as she wrapped her arms around his neck, seeking a new anchor. A new lifeline. His tongue found hers, and they tasted each other for the first time in eight years.

Their painful past melted away. They were finding their way back to each other. Back to the home they had made all those years ago. Darling moaned against his lips. She had missed this.

Oliver deepened the kiss, moving his arms around her and pulling her flush against him. It forced a new proximity that woke up every part of her body. She arched against him and he grabbed her hips. She felt him push against her and a new thrill began to pool below her waist. Another moan escaped against him. Oliver silenced it with his own. Instead of raw hunger, Darling could feel the control in it. He deepened the kiss only to break it off a moment later.

Darling looked up at him, confused and breathless.

His face was flushed. His lips red and swollen. Those amber eyes searched her face in the quiet. For once, Darling dared not speak.

There weren't a lot of things in life she felt she absolutely needed.

But right then, she knew she needed Oliver Quinn.

"Darling," he whispered, voice husky. Another shock of pleasure pulsed through her at the sound. He closed the space between their lips again. It was a soft kiss that burned slowly.

He didn't speak again.

With one quick movement, he picked her up and put her legs around his waist. Darling gladly hugged his body back, not breaking their connection. Then they were moving down the familiar path to the bedroom.

Though as she began to unbutton his shirt, she realized that where they were going was a place neither had visited before.

THE SOFT CARESS of cotton against her bare skin.

The mattress that molded against her every curve.

The warmth of a man around her heart.

A wisp of a smile trailed across Darling's lips.

She stretched out, feeling for her bodyguard beneath the sheets. Her hand found the edge of the bed instead. Slowly her eyelids opened.

Fear made her heart beat against her chest. For one awful moment, Darling thought she was back in the clearing, naked and in the dark. However, as panic tried to claw its way through her, common sense blocked its path.

She could feel the bed beneath her, the sheets around her. She smelled the citrus that had attached to her skin after her bath. The scent of Oliver's body wash that mingled with it.

No, she wasn't in danger here.

She waited as her vision adjusted to the low light of the room. From where she was, she could see out into the hallway and to the stools at the kitchen counter. Light filtered across the floor from the TV. She closed her eyes again, still tired. She couldn't lie there and think about what had happened between them *and* keep her eyes open. There wasn't enough energy to sustain both acts.

So she burrowed back beneath the covers and let her smile widen. When she was younger, she would often imagine what it was like to be with Oliver. Would he be gentle? Would he be rough? Or would he be a man who walked the line in between?

It was as if she had been holding her breath for years, waiting for Oliver. Now that she had let him back into her life, into her home and her bed, she felt she could let that breath out.

She drifted back to sleep, thinking of the bodyguard, only to wake up a while later, looking at him.

"Hey there," he said.

Darling stretched and smiled. "Hey back." She glanced to her alarm clock to see it was still late. Before she could ask what was going on, Oliver answered her.

"They're running a news story about the murder. I wanted to make sure you saw it, too."

That made her sit up.

"Yeah, I really do want to see it."

Much like before, Oliver carried her across the apartment. The heat of his bare chest against her was a welcome reminder of that afternoon. However, this time, once they reached their destination, he set her down and let go. She marveled at how badly she wanted to stay in his arms—to be wrapped up in his touch—but told her brain to focus.

Which wasn't hard when she looked at the television. On its screen was a local news reporter standing in front of the Mulligan police station. A spotlight from her camera crew was positioned on her face, trying to keep viewers' attention on her and not the crowd behind. Even in the dark, Darling could make out reporter Rebel Nash and a handful of others in a semicircle around Chief Sanderson and a few of his deputies behind her. The woman who filled the screen, however, looked excited about whatever story she was reporting on. Oliver turned up the volume on the TV.

"—a corporate conspiracy that is connected to the death of a Jean Watford, found dead in a bathtub at the Mulligan Motel. One of Charisma Investment's board members and its interim CEO, resident Nigel Marks, has refused an interview at this time. His attorney issued the following statement—'My client cannot confirm or deny at this point in time that Ms. Watford was guaranteed a top managerial position within the company, but she was being seriously considered. The fact that this could have been the cause of her death is abhorrent, and the Marks family wants nothing more than to see those responsible brought to justice.'"

A picture of a red-haired woman—apparently their Jane Doe—popped up in the corner next to the reporter's head.

"Jean Watford, age twenty-three, resided in Miami, Florida. She was visiting Mulligan on business."

Her picture was replaced by an image of two men talking to each other by the side of a building. They stood in the shadows and didn't seem to be aware someone had been taking their pictures. Darling didn't recognize either of the older men but knew by their outfits alone they were high-level businessmen.

"CFO Lamar Bennington and executive assistant Robert Jensen are being held for questioning after an anonymous tip led to the discovery of controversial emails about Ms. Watford, including one that contained information pertaining to what police believe to be the murder weapon. Both men are currently denying these charges."

The reporter changed gears and gave viewers some background on Charisma Investments and their merger, which was almost complete. Darling already knew this information. She muted the television and gave Oliver a questioning look.

"So, Jean Watford wasn't a mistress?" she asked. Her entire investigation had been based on that one assumption.

"I suppose he—" Oliver's phone began to ring, cutting him off. "I don't know who this is," he muttered before answering. "Oliver Quinn here," he answered. Darling watched as his face hardened. He held up his finger to ask her to wait and headed to the bedroom for some privacy.

Darling sighed. She wished the police would give her phone back soon. Surely there would be no reason for forensics to keep it now that they had men in custody. She didn't like being without it.

The local news cut to a weather segment, so Darling turned it off. She reached for her office chair and hopped into it. Pushing herself with her good foot, she went to the kitchen counter for a pen and paper. Before she could forget the two men's names, she wrote them down. There was no need to pen Jean Watford. Now that she could put a name to the body in the tub, she knew she'd never forget either for the rest of her life.

"Well, looks like we have more of a story to go with," Oliver said when he came back into the room a few minutes later. "That was actually our friend Deputy Derrick. He's fine, by the way. Should be discharged in a few days." He grabbed the arms of the chair and rolled Darling over to the couch, sitting in front of her. He placed his hands on her thighs as he continued. "He was brought up to speed right before the news segment aired. He figured we were watching or, at the very least, deserved a bit more than what they had to offer."

Darling knew that the only reason they were getting the special treatment from Derrick was that the case had become personal for the three of them. Once he had been attacked, Darling had been taken and Oliver had helped save them both, Derrick had mentally put them on the same page. A task he wouldn't have done otherwise.

"Tell me," was all Darling could manage. Something akin to hesitant excitement had started to flow through her. The case felt as if it was almost over, even if it had taken a turn she didn't expect.

"Nigel admitted that he had been seeing Jean in secret for the past year. He met her at a business conference when he was in Miami and was impressed. Apparently Jean was a very smart cookie. Nigel was beginning to finalize the merger but wasn't happy with the people who were going to be in charge. He wanted some new blood and decided to start grooming Jean in secret."

"Why in secret?"

"He was afraid that if he publicly acknowledged he was about to restructure the new business, stocks would suffer and he'd have to deal with unnecessary backlash. No one was supposed to find out until the end of the month, but apparently word got out somehow."

"To the CFO and the assistant?"

Oliver nodded. "Nigel told the chief that the CFO had formed not-so-beneficial friendships with those who worked for him. He didn't care that they weren't doing their jobs anymore."

"And Jean was going to take one of their jobs at the new company?"

"Bingo. Nigel wasn't sure why the executive assistant was involved. He only guessed Bennington offered something in exchange for his help. They had emails about the rumor that Jean was going to replace someone, and the CFO was furious about it. They flew in the day before Nigel, and neither of their alibis can be confirmed for the time of death."

Darling leaned back, trying to take it all in.

"Robert, the assistant, also can't provide an alibi for the time Derrick was attacked and you were taken," he added, voice dropping to a whisper. "But they found a long blond hair on his jacket that the chief thinks might be yours."

The excitement she had been feeling at shutting down a case left in an instant. She recalled the picture of the two men, trying to place a face with the body that had choked her. Oliver took her hands in his and rested them against her legs again. It was enough to ground her emotions and make her able to ask another nagging question.

"What about the murder weapon? Surely they weren't stupid enough to *email* about it?"

"Bennington asked the assistant if he had some tools they could use for a secret project."

"The hammer!"

"He didn't ask for one specifically, but he did mention they needed to make sure they had pliers."

Darling's mouth dropped open. "To pull out her teeth," she said, horrified. "They put all of that in emails?"

Oliver shrugged. "Derrick said the chief thought Bennington was under the influence of some narcotics when they picked him up, so that definitely could have made him sloppy. Plus, I think this is a man who usually gets what he wants. Having a loyal follower—like Robert Jensen, who had access to Nigel's entire schedule, emails and probably calls—helped him pull off the murder without leaving anything behind."

"If all of this was business related, then why didn't Nigel just tell the cops about it all when Jean was found?" Darling didn't understand why the man had preferred to look guilty rather than coming clean in the first place, especially if the link would be easy to make when everything was out in the open.

Oliver's eyes lit up. "Get this," he almost sang. "He thought his wife was the one behind it. That she had hired someone to take care of a woman she thought was his mistress."

Darling didn't speak for a moment. "Wow. If they stay married, they definitely are going to need some counseling about trust."

Oliver agreed. "That's all Derrick knew. They were getting search warrants to go through each man's hotel room and belongings, but the way it sounds, both men are in trouble."

Darling nodded. "So, it's over, then?"

"It looks that way. The killers are in custody, and Jane Doe now has a name." Oliver squeezed Darling's hands. "No more looking over your shoulder. Unless I'm walking behind you and you just want to see all of this." He motioned to his chest and abs. A smile had stretched his lips, changing the mood from dark to playful. He felt relieved, and she knew it. But did she feel it, too? The motive, means and suspects made sense even though she had never even known about them until now. Logically, everything had fallen into place. However, her gut felt as if something was off.

Oliver brought his hand up to her chin and pulled her face forward.

"I know that look," he whispered, an inch from her lips. "You took the entire day off, remember? That means the night, too." He brushed his lips across hers, sending a wonderful thrill from her stomach downward. "That means no overthinking."

"But that's what I'm good at," she defended herself with no real weight behind the words.

He passed his lips across hers again, pausing only to speak. "Not tonight, my Darling."

Chapter Twenty

Everything felt so right.

Darling opened her eyes and didn't want to move. She could feel Oliver's even breathing against her back. His arm was thrown over her, pressing the warmth of their naked bodies together.

It was perfect.

She didn't want to leave the bed, but her mouth felt dry and she desperately needed to use the bathroom.

So, as carefully as she could, Darling slipped out from underneath his arm and grabbed her crutches discarded on the floor. Oliver didn't move once. It made her wonder how much sleep he'd skipped the past few days.

Once she was up and moving, Darling decided to go ahead and start the day. It was almost ten in the morning and she felt wildly energized. She knew that was greatly due to the naked bodyguard in her bed. With each step she took, her body reminded her just how close they had become the night before. Though in the light of day, she wondered what that meant for their future. Did they have one, or had it been a one-day event?

The bodyguard had promised to stay by her side as long as the threat of her kidnappers was still out there. Now that they had been caught, she didn't need protection. Why would he stay in Mulligan when his life—his home—was two thousand miles away?

She tried to push the troubling thoughts from her mind as she took a quick shower, awkwardly hopping around to avoid putting too much pressure on her foot. It took the attention from the potential heartbreak she might have to endure again from her fair-haired bodyguard.

Darling managed to dress herself without falling over. She chose a red, long-sleeve top that plunged low to show some cleavage, and a pair of dark jeans that hugged her nicely. It was a more flirty outfit than she usually wore but, as she looked at Oliver's still-sleeping form, she had the urge to break out of her boring wardrobe habits. Not that he seemed to mind when she was and wasn't dressed up.

Oliver stayed asleep throughout the next half hour as she got ready and made breakfast, confirming her suspicion that he had been seriously lacking sleep. She tried to be as quiet as possible but found that when her food was gone, a restlessness was beginning to replace her feelings of contentment. Her gut was back to telling her something was off about Jean Watford's death. But what was it?

"Do you really think Nigel Marks would cry over a mistress?"

Darling snapped her fingers as Oliver's words replayed in her head. That was it.

She went back to the bedroom and grabbed her laptop, putting it in a bag so she could avoid dropping it while using her crutches. Moving to the living room, she powered it on with new vigor. Working on a hunch, she opened an internet browser and searched Jean Watford's name. After some digging, she found the young woman's public social media profile. It had all the information Darling needed.

She did some quick math and typed in a new search.

A few minutes later she found a picture that nearly confirmed her hunch. The picture was from the early '90s and showed a young Nigel Marks at a Christmas party. He stood tall—and rather handsome—amid a large group of people. The quality wasn't the greatest, but Darling got the break she needed when she saw the name of each person printed across the bottom. It didn't take long to find the last piece of the puzzle.

Standing next to Nigel was a red-haired woman with a giant smile.

Her name was Regina Watford.

Darling's mind began turning at such a fast pace she almost felt dizzy. This was why Nigel hadn't admitted to knowing Jean. He *did* have an affair. It was just twenty-three years and nine months earlier.

If Darling was right, she was looking at the night the businessman had strayed from his wife of twenty-six years with the red-haired woman at his side and produced a child—Jean.

Darling thought about the pictures she had been given of Nigel and Jean from the past year. Everyone had thought the two happy people were having an affair, but that was because the daughter angle had never entered their minds. Now, the pictures of the two laughing, hugging and dining in public fit the scenario of a father and daughter meeting. Had they been seeing each other in secret for years or had they just reunited?

Before she could talk herself out of it, Darling went back to the bedroom and grabbed Oliver's phone. She went into the bathroom and shut the door. Scrolling through his contacts, she found Nigel's personal cell phone number.

For some reason she couldn't quite place, she needed to confirm the truth. She hit Call and waited with bated breath.

What was she going to say?

"Nigel Marks's phone," a man answered after two rings. "This is Jace Marks."

That put a kink in Darling's plan. Did Jace even know about his half-sister?

"Um, hi," Darling stuttered out. "This is Darling Smith. I, uh, just had some information for Nigel I thought he might like to know."

"Darling Smith? The woman who was kidnapped?"

"Yeah," she responded, uncomfortable.

"How are you?"

Surprised at the concern, she answered on reflex. "I'm okay. My foot is sore, but I'm alive."

"That's good. It would have been another senseless tragedy had that bodyguard not found you."

"I'd have to agree there." She cleared her throat. "Is there any way I can speak with Nigel, though? It won't take long."

"I'm sorry but no. He's currently unavailable. The best I can do is pass along a message."

"No," she said a little too quickly. She tried to sound calm as she continued. "It's personal. I'd really like to talk to him myself." She wasn't about to announce the real reason behind the call.

"Hold on, then," he said. She didn't hear anything on the other end of the line and looked at the phone to make sure the call hadn't dropped. "We're about to leave the police station and head home. You can meet us at the house, but we have to ask that you keep this meeting and whatever information you have private until Nigel has talked to you. This family has had enough false accusations and rumors started lately."

"Sure thing. I completely understand."

"Thank you. We'll see you soon."

Darling ended the call, shocked at how easy it was to get a meeting. She supposed it made sense that the Markses wanted to go ahead and squash any remaining gossip within the town or general public. Charisma Investments was going to suffer thanks to the actions of Lamar Bennington and Robert Jensen. They didn't need any more bad press.

She returned Oliver's phone to the nightstand and watched as the bodyguard continued to sleep. He looked so peaceful, she decided not to wake him. She wasn't a child. The danger was gone. She could go tie up this loose end without him. Her kidnappers weren't out there to get her. She could be back within the hour.

Bending low, she pressed her lips to his temple. He didn't stir.

She wrote a quick note and left.

Laughing at the fact that the last time she had been at Nigel Marks's home she'd been arrested, she thrummed her fingers against the steering wheel as she drove. It was amazing how a week could change everything.

The gate to the Markses' house was shut, but Darling could see a car parked in the driveway beyond it. She pulled up to wait at the gate and rolled down the window. George Hanely had never been one of her favorite people. He might not even let her in.

However, he never came.

She sat up straighter to see into the gatehouse. No one was inside.

"Getting lazy, George?"

She put the car in Park and opened the door. Pulling her crutches from the backseat, she made her way to the window. George was probably lounging, watching one of his daytime soap operas or whatever it was the man did all day. She looked inside, ready to scold the gate guard but stopped short.

George was sprawled out on the floor, facedown.

Darling tried the doorknob and let out a breath of relief when it opened with no resistance. She knelt beside the unconscious man, almost falling in the process.

"George?" She felt for a pulse and was happy to feel the beat against her fingers. "Hold on. I'll call for help."

She got back up and looked to the phone on the desk. Oliver was going to be upset that she had yet again found herself connected with the police in such a short span.

"Don't move."

Darling froze, hand hovering above the phone.

Turning slowly, she felt her stomach bottom out.

George Hanley was not only coherent but also sitting up and smiling. A gun was in his right hand, pointed at her, but that wasn't what put ice in her blood.

In the palm of his left hand were her two daisy earrings.

"Just so you know how serious I am."

AN ANGRY CHIRPING pecked at the haze of sleep around Oliver until, finally, he had to make it stop. Rolling over, he grabbed his cell phone and gave it a stare that could kill before turning off the everyday alarm. It was meant to make sure he was wide-awake by noon, which, to him, was a time that no man should sleep past. Even on his days off. Although, given recent events, he had meant to deactivate it the night before. But then a beautiful private investigator had let him into her bed, twice.

All thoughts of the alarm and pretty much anything else had gone out the proverbial window the moment their lips and bodies met.

Afraid he had woken her, Oliver rolled back over, ready to laugh that they had slept in. He was disappointed her side of the bed was empty. The rest of the room was, too. In fact, he couldn't hear any movement in the apartment.

"Darling?" he called, swinging his legs over the edge of the bed. He stretched wide and noticed a note on the nightstand.

"'Tying up a loose end with Nigel. Didn't want to wake you. Be back by lunch,'" he read aloud.

He read it again as if it would make more sense. It didn't. Of course the maddening woman wouldn't give him more information than that. What loose ends were left?

Oliver picked his phone back up and went to his recent call list. He sighed and made a mental note to take her by the police station to get her phone back. Now there wasn't a way to reach her directly. He was about to put the phone down when he noticed the most recent call was placed earlier that morning. Darling had used to his phone to call Nigel.

It was a bold move. One she wouldn't have made unless she had a solid lead on something.

Suddenly Oliver's calm wasn't as resolute. A sinking feeling of apprehension slunk in.

He dialed the number again and put it to his ear.

It went straight to voice mail.

"Okay," he said to the empty apartment. "Time to get dressed."

Five minutes later Oliver was in his rental and driving toward Nigel's vacation home. He could have called Thomas, Grant or Nikki to let him talk to Darling if she was with Nigel, but after his talk with Nikki the previous day, it didn't feel right. Darling wasn't in trouble. He was just being overprotective. Jane Doe's, or rather Jean Watford's, killers had been caught. The men who had taken Darling were being held...or were they?

He rolled his shoulders back. The seed of doubt that had sprouted in his mind was growing, but there was no need for it, he tried to reason with himself. Yet it was a pill he couldn't seem to swallow. The closer he got to the vacation home, the more his nerves pricked. Why, he wasn't sure, but he knew he wouldn't shed the sudden restlessness until he set his eyes on a certain sneaky private investigator.

Oliver was sorely disappointed that no one seemed to be home when he arrived outside the gatehouse. No cars were in the driveway minus one he believed to belong to George. His aversion to calling Nikki was starting to ebb. He pulled his phone out just as it buzzed against his palm. It was a Maine number but not one he recognized.

"Oliver Quinn," he answered, getting out of his SUV to look into the gatehouse for its guard. He mentally snorted at its emptiness. He was probably goofing off somewhere, not doing his job.

"Hello. I think this is the number I was supposed to call. Barb said some people were looking for me?" a female responded, uncertainty clear. There was a blanket of noise in the background.

"Harriet Mendon?" Oliver guessed.

"Yeah, that's me! Now what's this about?" She didn't sound mad or scared. Only curious. An older Darling, he quickly mused.

"The woman at the gas station you stopped at on the way out of Mulligan the other night—the one with the red hair—was—" Oliver paused and changed where the statement had been headed "—she died the next morning." There was a tiny gasp, but she didn't interrupt. "There was a guy—a bad guy—who thought whatever it was you two talked about might have been something that could have hurt him. We just wanted to make sure if you saw him to call the police, but you shouldn't have to worry about that anymore. He's with the police now."

"Oh, wow, I leave Mulligan for the first time in ten years and suddenly it gets exciting," she answered after a beat. "I am sorry about that young woman, though. She was so happy and vibrant. Made me feel young again just talking to her. How did she die?"

"I'm not sure," he lied. Jean's death was probably already splashed across the local paper. Harriet would be able to read about it all when she got back. Oliver didn't want to rehash the details.

"What a tragedy. I can't imagine what the man thought she told me. We only talked for maybe a minute. Nothing out of the ordinary. She was just excited to meet up with her dad and relax for a few days."

Oliver stopped, his hand against the SUV door.

"Her dad? I thought she was in Mulligan on business," he said, recalling the reporter's words from the previous night's news.

"I don't think so. I remember her specifically saying she was going to spend time with her dad and enjoy some downtime," Harriet said. "She was smiling ear to ear. Does that sound like she was about to work to you?"

"No," Oliver answered. "It doesn't sound like work had anything to do with her visit to Mulligan after all."

Oliver didn't extend his conversation with Harriet Mendon past the new information. He also didn't question the validity of what the woman had gleaned from her chat with Jean. The security footage had shown a happy young woman, not someone about to dive into a stressful, secretive business world.

No, Jean Watford was about to go to meet up with her father.

She had been on the way to meet Nigel Marks at the Mulligan Motel.

All at once, the clues and lies made sense. The pictures of Nigel and Jean over the past year—meeting in secret—with the two of them enjoying each other's company without any sexual or provocative contact. The pain and surprise Oliver had picked up on when Nigel had been told about Jean's death.

In Orion's research on the Marks family, Oliver couldn't recall a single detail about a daughter. Half, step or otherwise. Jean Watford must have been one of the best kept secrets of Nigel's life.

That's what Darling was referring to as her loose end, Oliver realized. That's why she had called Nigel. She had figured it out, and the always curious Darling needed confirmation.

But where was she now?

Oliver took another look at the house. His feeling of unease had grown so strong, he felt as if it was a tangible object he could wield to cut open the gate. Had the entire story of Jean Watford joining Charisma Investments been a lie? If so, where did that leave the motive for her two supposed killers?

A new puzzle was coming together just as the old one was falling apart.

Oliver flew through his contacts until he found Grant's number. He hesitated and passed the name, going straight for another. He pressed Call next to Nikki's name, not willing to make the same mistake twice. Knowing her, she was still in town and would remain there for the duration of the contract. "Yes?" she cut right to the chase. Oliver could hear several voices in the background.

"Are you still with Nigel?"

"Oliver, you know I can't divulge information like that on a current—"

"Is Darling with him?" Oliver's voice had dropped to an almost icy plane of existence. Nikki picked up on it immediately.

"No. We've been at the new Charisma building since this morning." He could hear her moving away from the group of people next to her. She spoke louder. "Why?"

"She called him while I was asleep and then left a note saying she was coming here to talk to him. I'm at the vacation house now."

"Unless she called him before five this morning, she didn't talk to him," Nikki said with certainty. "He's been in board meetings all day, trying to clean up this mess. He literally hasn't left the room in hours. The room has a glass wall and everything. We've been able to see him at all times, and not once has he made or picked up a call."

"Could he have done that when you looked away?" Oliver reasoned.

"Here, he's coming out now. Let me just ask." He could

hear her annoyance at not being taken at her word, but Oliver needed to know what had been said during that call.

It could be nothing.

It could be everything.

Muffled voices filled his ear. It was a white noise that did nothing to break the silence of the outside world around him. He stood back from the gate and wondered if Darling had come here at all. If George hadn't been at the gate, she would have had to leave. Why wasn't George there to begin with? It was paramount he be at his station when the house was empty. To make sure it stayed that way.

Oliver went to the gatehouse and tried the door. It was locked. He cupped his hand and looked inside. Everything seemed normal.

"Oliver," Nikki said, bringing his focus back. "Nigel said he never talked to Darling. He can't even find his phone."

"He's lying, then," Oliver responded with grit. "My phone said the call was made." He didn't need to look again to know that was true. It not only was received but also lasted almost a minute.

"Well, Nigel didn't speak with her." Nikki kept talking, but Oliver didn't hear it.

"I need you to get Rachel to track George Hanley's cell phone," he ground out. Oliver tried the doorknob again, and when it didn't budge, he took a step back.

"What? Why?"

Oliver didn't answer as he threw his shoulder into the door. It splintered at the lock and swung open.

"Oliver?" Nikki's confusion was turning into anger.

"Because I'm pretty sure George Hanely took her."

"How do you know?"

Oliver had scanned and rescanned the gatehouse each time he had made a sweep while on duty. George was a neat person. Every item in the small room had always been in a specific spot and order. His DVDs all were stacked nicely next to his television, his books were ordered next to his security tapes, and even his chair had always been pushed beneath the desk when he was occupying it. Now Oliver saw a room out of order. A few of the books were strewn across the desktop, the chair was on the other side of the room and one of the DVD cases lay in the corner, cracked open. However, it wasn't the unusual state of the space that caught his eye. It was the set of crutches poking out from beneath the desk that coaxed a concerned Oliver into the gatehouse. The blood on one of the pads only threw fuel onto the burning fire within him.

"Her crutches are here. Nikki, I need you to track him now," Oliver repeated, more urgent than before. "Please."

This time Nikki didn't hesitate.

"Give me five minutes," she answered. Her voice had taken on the calm of the determined woman he knew her to be.

"Let me talk to Nigel," he added. Again she didn't even pause.

"What's going on?" Nigel asked a few seconds later.

"George Hanley took Darling," Oliver said. "I need you to tell me why."

"What? He took her?"

"Yes. Now, what the hell would he want with her?" Oliver was moving around the room, looking for something that might clue him in to where the gate guard had gone.

"I have no idea!"

"Come on, Nigel. I talked to the man. He seemed to worship you, said you two were great pals. Think!"

"You're mistaken," Nigel said hurriedly. "Mr. Hanley is close with my son, Jace, not me."

Everything stopped for a moment.

"Hello?" Nigel asked, bringing Oliver out of his icy thoughts. He only had one question left.

"Did Jace know that Jean Watford was your daughter?"

As if he was standing in front of the millionaire, Oliver could see the older man had reached the same conclusion as he just had.

"Oh, my God."

Chapter Twenty-One

It was a three-story building with cracked gray siding and a crumbling roofline. There was a workshop in the back, attached by a makeshift walkway that hadn't fared well against the weather. The several acres around each were untouched and gave clear sight lines to the road in the distance.

Darling took in all of these details as George drove up the long dirt drive. She had been to this abandoned house hidden near the heart of town before with Derrick who had said knowing its location might help with future cases considering the amount of criminal activity that happened there from time to time. It was dubbed the Slate House and hadn't been occupied in almost twenty years. The local teens really liked it as a location to drink in private, considering its next neighbor wasn't even in shouting distance.

A shiver ran up Darling's spine.

Perhaps that's why George was taking her there, as well.

"Why?" Darling asked the gate guard for the third time. Her chin was throbbing, but with her hands bound behind her back, she couldn't touch her face to assess the damage. She took solace in the fact that before George had managed to wrestle the plastic zip ties around her wrists, she had been able to do some damage of her own. Her crutch had made an excellent bat. The bleeding gash on his forehead was a testament to that.

George didn't slow the car until they were next to the workshop's outside door at the back of the house. He cut the ignition without answering her yet again. Never had she hated the silence more.

"George, why are we here?" she asked, expanding her earlier question in hopes he would answer. Instead he opened his door and got out.

For one wonderful moment, Darling thought he'd leave. That he would just walk off and give her enough time to figure out an escape route. But George didn't do that. He turned to the back door and opened it, and for the first time since he'd yelled at her to get into the car while simultaneously shoving her, he spoke.

"Someone wants to talk to you."

He reached into the car and grabbed for her. Darling tried to shrink away, but George was faster than he looked. He caught her jacket sleeve and tugged hard.

"Don't fight it, private eye," he snarled as he struggled to pull her out and up. "You brought this on yourself."

"What are you talking about?" Darling yelled. He shut the car door and held her by the tie on her wrists, bending her slightly so she couldn't stand at full height. Without her crutches, the weight she put on her foot made her wince.

"Have you ever heard of the story where curiosity killed the cat?" He started to walk to the door, pushing her in front of him. She stumbled and considered making a run for it, but no sooner had the idea popped into her head than she felt the gun poke into her back. If anyone would shoot her without warning, it would be George. Whatever anger he was harboring for her, it was malicious. He stopped in front of the door. "In this story, you're the cat."

George let go of her wrists long enough to open the workshop's door, then pushed her inside. Darling wasn't sure what she had expected to find in the tiny room, but she hadn't foreseen the lone two chairs and freestanding electric lights in the least. The chairs faced each other between the white peeling walls and the concrete floors. It felt cold and sterile.

And terrifying.

Whatever was about to happen, Darling was positive she didn't need to be a part of it.

George shoved her into one of the chairs and stepped back while she righted herself. He didn't take the seat opposite.

"You don't even remember me, do you?" he asked, voice pitching higher than normal.

Darling was confused by the question. Surely he wasn't referring to the trespassing incident that had just happened. Apart from that, she had seen the man only in passing. Nothing that would earn her the death stare he was giving her now.

"What do you mean?" she asked instead.

George laughed.

"Of course you wouldn't bother remembering what you did."

"Just tell me," Darling snapped. She was afraid, but she didn't want George to see it.

"Wow, you ruin a family's life and you don't even remember it," he said, surprising her. The gun in his hand stayed trained on her as he spoke. Darling glanced at the door they had just come through. If she managed to escape she would be out in the open. She hoped he wasn't a good shot, because he could hit her easily. But if she could somehow make it into the house, there was a chance she could find something to defend herself with or, at the very least, hide until Oliver found her.

Because he would.

He had done it before.

"Then tell me about it," Darling said. She wanted him to talk, get distracted and waste time.

The gate guard kept the gun pointed at her. Standing behind the chair opposite, he would not miss if he wanted to shoot her.

"You know, when you first came to Mulligan, I thought you were cute. Young, new, interesting." Darling searched her memory for George when she was new to Mulligan but was drawing a blank. Whatever memory he was in, she wasn't sharing it. "Even when I heard the rumor you were working for Jeff as an intern, I still thought that made you more interesting than the women I had grown up around. But then you stuck your nose where it didn't belong, and I realized you were no better than your scum of a boss." He waved his gun at her in a sudden burst of anger. Without meaning to, she yelped.

"My father skipped out on my family when I was a kid," he said. "My mother worked her fingers to the bone trying to give us a good life. When I graduated, she hurt her back on the job at the woolen factory. For the first time in years, she was able to take a break, and she deserved it." Recognition started to prick against Darling's memory. "So, I encouraged her to tell a little white lie and say she was still hurt. Have herself a little vacation."

Darling could almost feel the color drain from her face. George must have seen the change.

"Ah, you do remember me," he said.

"Workers' compensation fraud," Darling responded as if she was reading the file Jeff had handed her years ago. She hadn't put together that George had been Carmen's son. Their last names were different, if she recalled correctly.

"That's it."

"It was more than just a little white lie," she said with an even tone. "She was collecting it for a year and a half."

George grabbed the chair and hurled it into the wall. The echo it made rocketed Darling's fear skyward, but it was nothing compared to what she felt when she realized where the gun was. George held it level with her face. His hand was calm. His eyes were filled with rage.

"You watched and followed her like she was some kind of criminal when all she was, was a woman who worked herself into the ground to provide for her family," he roared. "She had to spend a year in jail and pay almost fifty thousand dollars! It broke her, it bankrupted us and it was all because you and your boss wanted to make a little cash!"

Darling wanted to say that, although she could sympathize with his mother, her actions had been illegal. Darling had done her job the correct way, observing an energetic woman with no issues and reporting back to the insurance company that had hired Acuity. But she didn't say anything. George was enraged. He had already cast the first stone and didn't seem to regret that one bit. Anything she said now would only fan the fire. She didn't want to give him any more reason to use his gun.

"All out of questions?" he spat when Darling still

didn't speak. Her back was ramrod straight. Her heart was racing.

"I wouldn't talk to you right now if I was her, either."

Darling gasped as a voice spoke from the doorway. She hadn't heard or noticed the door open, and she hadn't expected that particular man.

"You're too passionate, George. It's terrifying." Jace Marks smiled a perfect smile at the gate guard. His eyes slid to Darling's look of surprise, and he laughed. "After all of his obsessing over how bothersome you can be, I'm kind of shocked you didn't put the dots together much sooner."

He grabbed the discarded chair and set it up across from her. In the process of sitting down, he took the gun from George's hand and pushed the man gently aside. Darling watched the interaction with new attention. George was being obedient and took the spot behind Jace with obvious pride. She had never known the two even knew each other, yet the loyalty George was exuding for the younger Marks was concrete.

"The dots," was all Darling could manage at first.

"Yes, the dots." He crossed his legs and leaned back in his chair. As if they were in a meeting making small talk. "About Nigel's little secret. His tryst from younger years."

"You mean Jean," she said, finding her voice. "Your sister."

"Half-sister," he corrected. "*Secret* half-sister."

"But you knew?" Darling was going back over all the events that had taken place. This time she was inserting the two men before her. Finally what felt off about the arrest of Lamar Bennington and Robert Jensen made sense. "Nigel told you?"

"Of course he didn't tell me," he said. "Perhaps that

would have been the right thing to do, but Nigel doesn't always operate with the best morality."

"Then how did you find out?" Darling didn't know why he was opening up to her, but if it bought Oliver more time to find her—which she prayed he was already trying to do—then she'd keep the conversation going. Although she couldn't pretend that Jace confessing to everything was good for her health. Trying to tie up the loose end with Jean Watford's identity had turned Darling into Jace's loose end.

"A very inebriated family lawyer let it slip that Nigel wanted to make some changes to his will. At first I thought it was to give Mother and me what he had set aside for leaving this pathetic community after his death, but then Mother made an odd comment about Nigel's extracurricular activities. So I followed him, and there she was." Every time he referred to Jean, he acted as if it left a bad taste in his mouth. Darling didn't wonder which of the men had actually killed her. She would bet everything she owned Jace had been the one to do it.

"At first I thought it was an affair," he said, "but after watching them, I realized the affection wasn't sexual. That's when I really did some digging. I even went so far as to steal her hairbrush for a DNA sample to make sure, but when I went to get something of Nigel's, he caught me." He rolled his eyes. "He didn't deny it but had the audacity to ask me to keep it a secret until he could figure out how to tell Mother."

"And you did, didn't you?" Elizabeth hadn't known about Jean. Darling was sure of that. If she had, it would have been more than enough to get out of the prenup.

Jace shrugged as if keeping his father's illegitimate child a secret hadn't been a big deal. "It was just another job in a long list of jobs he had already given me. I really didn't mind the new development."

"But?" Darling wanted to know what had changed.

Jace smiled wide. It didn't last long. His words became low, dangerous. "But then he tried to give her money, and when she wouldn't take it, he promised her a job at the new branch of Charisma." He paused and uncrossed his legs. Moving his head side to side, he cracked his neck. The calm exterior of control he had been trying to exude was beginning to flake off. When he was ready to speak again, however, George put his hand on Jace's shoulder.

"He'll be looking for her soon, Boss," the gate guard said.

Jace didn't look as if he enjoyed being interrupted, but he shrugged the irritation off with a nod.

"Go," he commanded. "And don't waste any time. Shoot to kill, as they say."

It was George's turn to nod. He took the gun from his demented friend and began to leave.

"Shoot to kill? Who?" Even as Darling asked, she knew the answer. George left without a word. She turned her wide eyes to the man in front of her. "Who is he going to shoot?" she almost yelled.

Jace's smile came back. "Your bodyguard, of course."

Darling's breath went shallow. She felt her nostrils flare, and her eyes became slits. Every fiber of her being was warring between anger and fear.

"Why? He doesn't know anything," she ground out. "I didn't tell anyone. There was no need to, since the murderers were already thought to be in custody."

"Oh, Darling, we both know that Mr. Quinn won't stop until he saves you or avenges your death." A shiver shot up her spine at that, but she tried to hide it. "Either way, he's a problem, and I don't need any more of those."

Darling heard her car drive away, picturing it going around the side of the house.

"If we were such problems, then why even involve me in the first place?"

"You mean the pictures," he guessed.

"And the notes."

"When I realized my mother hired you to prove Nigel's infidelity, I checked up on you. With all that happened with your parents, I assumed you had some guilt I could use to my advantage. Plus, considering your relationship with the police here, I figured you'd want to do the right thing and turn in any evidence. The hope was that you being so adamantly against Nigel would help put a nail in his coffin." He made a *tsk* noise. "By the way, I must ask. After you got all of that evidence on your parents and their extracurricular activities, why didn't you turn it in to the authorities?"

Anger was starting to win against the fear she felt at being so vulnerable in front of a killer. She lifted her chin a fraction.

"I would think someone like you would understand," she answered. His eyebrow went up in question, so she explained. "Being the children of powerful people isn't easy, especially when you see how far they will go to protect themselves. Like you, I was afraid." It was the first time she had ever admitted that to anyone. In a small way, she felt a sense of relief at finally saying it out loud. It was a shame the admission was wasted on Jace Marks.

"I'm not afraid of my father," he spat.

"Then why do all of this?"

Jace cracked his knuckles. More of his calm fell away.

"I wanted to be a painter, once upon a time. Travel the world, find beauty in everything, set up shop in Europe and start a family with a woman with dark hair and an accent." His voice trailed off for a moment before clear anger started to shine through. "But Nigel already had plans for me. He had high expectations, and I wanted to meet them all. I graduated at the top of my class in high school and college—where I pursued a degree he picked out—and when it was all done, I went straight into Charisma. I didn't even take a break.

"I rose up through the ranks the right way. No special treatment from Nigel…and no appreciation or approval, either. I gave up the life I wanted to live for the only one I thought would make him happy. Not once has he ever given me a 'good job, son' or 'I'm proud of you.'" His fists balled. Darling readied herself for whatever outburst she was sure was coming. "Then Jean shows up after all of these years, and suddenly Nigel is laughing and smiling? Changing his will to include her even though she didn't want a dime? Giving her a job in the company without her having a college degree? All of it finally helped me come to the most important realization of my life."

Darling gave him a questioning look when he didn't continue. He opened his fists and rubbed his palms against his pants. A small smile lifted up the corner of his lips. He looked as if he had mentally checked out.

"I realized that I could never please my father. So, I found a way to hurt him instead."

Darling swallowed. The bravado she had started to feel stalled at the callousness in his words. "But she was your sister," Darling started.

Whatever thread of calm he had was severed at her statement. He stood so fast that his chair toppled over.

Less than second later he was in her face, hands on the arms of her chair.

"She was a stranger," he roared. Any facade of a sane man vanished as his anger reverberated off the walls, making its way around the small room. He was seething, chest heaving. It wasn't until that moment that Darling felt absolute fear. Jace managed to calm himself enough to keep talking. But when he spoke, his tone was nothing but ice. "And you're about to find out how little sympathy I have for strangers."

Darling didn't try to hide her new fear. Instead, she let it show clearly across her features. There was no hope for Jace. There was no turning back. He had chosen his path, and there was no doubt in her mind that he would kill her when his story finished. Though Darling didn't want the end of it to be the end of her. She also refused to let an angry gate guard be the end of Oliver.

Darling gave the man in front of her a quick once-over. She met his gaze when she spoke.

"You don't have a gun."

And then Darling threw her entire weight against the man who dared threaten her happiness.

Chapter Twenty-Two

Jace was taller and heavier than Darling, but she had the element of surprise on her side. He let go of her chair, and together they fell to the ground.

He let out a moan as his back met the concrete. With her hands still tied behind her back, Darling fell against his chest. She didn't want to lose her momentum, so she brought her knee up hard against his groin. He cursed loudly and swung up, his fist meeting her jaw. The blow was hard enough to make her see stars but also had enough power to push her off him.

Trying her hardest not to pass out, she managed to rock up into a crouching position and, using the wall, eventually stand. Jace wasn't fast to respond, still writhing in pain. It gave Darling all the time she needed to get to the door. She backed against the door and was thankful she could still move her wrists enough to grab and turn the doorknob.

"There's nowhere to go," she heard Jace yell out as she ran through the poorly made hallway to the next door that led into the house. With adrenaline pumping through her body, she opened the door and immediately backtracked to shut it. The task of throwing the deadbolt took precious seconds, but she managed it by getting on tiptoe to lift her hands up. She heard Jace laughing from the workshop but didn't let it slow her down.

The Slate House had three stories. The basement was dark and damp, and had one half bathroom in it. Its stairs were located next to the kitchen—the room she was currently in—but Darling refused to enter a room with only one exit. Without any lights on, the natural light that filtered in through the upper stories' windows wouldn't touch the lower level. The main floor, if she remembered right, had four rooms and no real place to hide since there was no longer any furniture. That left the top floor and its three bedrooms and attic space.

Darling had started to move through the kitchen when a shot rang out behind her. Unable to stop the scream that tore from her throat, she looked, terrified, at the bullet hole in the door she had just locked. Jace had a gun after all.

With more urgency than before, Darling hobbled down the hallway and turned at the stairs. Quickly yet quietly, she took the steps two at a time until she was at the landing. The pain in her foot was incredible, even though she was trying her best to only put pressure on the very edge of her foot, but she knew she had to keep going, If she could find a place to hide, maybe it would buy Oliver enough time to get to her.

She just hoped Oliver would see George Hanley coming.

OLIVER RACED DOWN the road, determination pushing him. The pleas from Nikki to wait for the police replayed in his mind, but he paid them no heed. This time he wasn't going to count on them to guide him to Darling. She had been gone too long. Every second counted now.

He glanced at the gun on the passenger seat. Rarely

did he find a good excuse to bring it out, but he couldn't think of a better reason.

Rachel had traced Jace's cell phone to a piece of land in the middle of Mulligan. George's phone had last been used at the gatehouse, so that had been a quick dead end. Oliver was betting that Jace believed no one else had figured out his connection to the murder or the kidnapping. He had the confidence of his father. Though when Nigel had come to the realization that his son was one of the two behind everything that had happened, Oliver could hear the man crumple.

He had no time to sympathize.

If Darling had been hurt or worse…

He crushed that thought. The private investigator was strong and clever. She wouldn't let someone like George or Jace end her life.

Oliver pictured the two men trying to hurt her, and anger instantly filled him. It took him a few seconds to realize his phone was ringing on his lap. Not recognizing the number, he answered on the second ring.

"Darling?" he asked, hopeful.

"It's Derrick," the deputy replied. "I heard you're going after her by yourself."

"If you're going to tell me to wait, you can—"

"I'm not," Derrick interrupted. "You're driving up to a house that's three stories. There's a front door, a side door that leads to the attached workshop from the kitchen, and a back door that leads off of a second sitting room." Oliver didn't stop the man as he continued to give him a quick layout summary. After detailing the rooms on the main and top floor, he said, "There's also no cover driving up to the house. Whoever is in there will see you coming a mile away. So I suggest you go in fast and hot."

"No problem there," he assured the cop.

"Good luck, Oliver. Backup should be there a few minutes after you."

They hung up without any more comments. Oliver visualized the house from the deputy's description, already forming a plan for entry.

Crash.

A car from the opposite direction slammed into the side of the SUV.

Oliver tried to keep the vehicle from going into the ditch, but the impact was too great. The SUV went to the left just as the airbags deployed, and the SUV flipped before he could do anything to stop it. The windshield blew out and an awful metal crunching sounded before the world stilled.

Oliver gasped, trying to suck in some air while getting his bearings. His seat belt kept him upside down but still in his seat. Below him he could see the ground where the windshield should have been. He tried to look out the driver's side window, but the door was too damaged. When he could catch his breath, he undid his belt. The fall to the car's roof wasn't graceful, but he was glad when he didn't feel any broken bones. Though his left shoulder didn't feel the best.

He tried to open the door, but it wasn't budging. As quickly as he could, Oliver crawled to the passenger's side door, grabbing his gun as he went. He wouldn't have left the vehicle without it. Whoever had hit him had done it on purpose. That he was sure of, at least.

He had been hit about five minutes from his destination, which meant that on either side of the road there was nothing but open fields with trees in the distance. That meant no cover. Oliver kept that in mind as he exited the flipped SUV and moved around its side to the back to get a view of the road he had just been on.

The car that had hit him was in the middle of the road, the front right side dented but mostly intact. Oliver checked his gun, wincing at the pain in his arm. It was Darling's car he was looking at, but it was empty.

"You're harder to kill than I thought."

Oliver spun around, gun raised.

George Hanley met him with his own raised gun.

"Where's Darling?" Oliver yelled. The gate guard was bleeding from his forehead and shoulder.

"Does it really matter?" he said with a smirk.

Oliver pulled the trigger and jumped to the side before George could do the same. The bullet hit the gate guard in the shoulder, and he dropped his gun in surprise. He hadn't expected Oliver to act that quickly.

George tried to bend down to get the gun, but Oliver wasn't through with him. He closed the space between them and punched the sleazy man for all he was worth. George crumpled to the ground.

It was an instant knockout.

"I don't have time for you," Oliver said to the unconscious man. He didn't give him any more thought before jogging back up to the road. The keys were still in the ignition of Darling's car. He hopped into the driver's seat and sighed in relief when the car started. Although the door didn't shut all the way and the window was gone, it did the job of turning around and speeding down the road.

George had been dispatched to take care of him, which meant that Darling was alone with Jace. It was a thought that kept his adrenaline running high.

Derrick had been right about the house being in the middle of nothing but open space. Minutes later, Oliver was speeding up its drive. Darling's car was quiet, but anyone looking out of the windows would see him. Pain went through his shoulder as he cut the engine and opened the dented door. He knew he'd feel more of the crash's damage as his adrenaline wore off and he was able to rest, but for now he needed to find Darling. Thinking of losing her tightened his chest. He pushed the feeling away. He needed to focus.

He hurried to the back door and moved beside it. It was locked. Derrick had said there were two more ways to get into the house. As much as he wanted to burst through the door, he didn't want to give up his location until he had a better handle on what was going on. If he went in, guns blazing, he might spook Jace into doing something he would seriously regret.

Oliver would make sure of that.

Following the wall closely, Oliver crept along its length until he turned the corner to see the workshop extension. He held the gun firm and listened for a beat. Nothing. He turned the knob. It opened with ease. With gun raised, he went inside.

There had been a struggle but thankfully no blood. Two chairs were knocked over and Oliver could see through the open door, down the walkway and into the kitchen. He imagined Darling running into the house and hoped his mind wasn't inventing a wishful scenario instead of a plausible one. He moved quickly through the windowless pathway and into the kitchen. The house wasn't as well-lit as he would have liked—shadows stuck to the corners—but Oliver was thankful the house was devoid of furniture. Only a random assortment of bottles and trash was scattered around. He sidestepped a glass bottle and moved into the adjoining room.

It was empty, and so was the room opposite.

"Here, here, little Darling," Oliver heard Jace taunt.

Oliver pushed himself against the living room wall, looking out through the double-framed archway to the base of the stairs.

"Come out so we can get this over with," Jace called in a singsong voice. "You can't hide forever."

Sweet relief swept through him. Darling was alive.

But where was she?

Oliver looped around the archway, and instead of going for the stairs, he went to the front door. He threw it open, making as much noise as he could, before retreating to the living room again. This time he positioned himself with his gun held high and steady.

Footsteps sounded against the landing and then the stairs as Jace ran down them. Oliver waited until the man was in his sights before he spoke.

"Don't move or I'll—"

Just as Oliver had done to George, Jace raised his gun and shot before Oliver could finish talking. The bullet hit the wall beside him, and he returned fire.

But nothing happened.

His gun jammed.

Oliver pulled back deeper into the room as another bullet struck the wall. He could hear Jace move back up the stairs in a hurry. Oliver cursed under his breath and ejected the jammed bullet from the chamber. Now that Jace knew he was in the house, he might get more desperate to find Darling. Oliver couldn't have that.

Readying his gun, he swung around into the hallway and started to run up the stairs. He didn't expect Jace to keep shooting blindly. Oliver had already made the judgment call that the younger Marks lacked courage unless he was confident everything was on his side. Less confidence, less control. Stepping out to gun Oliver down on the stairs would mean that he would have to put himself in a compromising position. No, Jace was probably already setting himself up in one of the hallway's corners, waiting for Oliver to step onto the landing. The question was, was Jace to the left or the right?

Taking a deep breath, Oliver stepped past the last stair and pointed his gun to the right. It was the wrong way. A bullet whizzed by his ear and shattered the top portion of an already broken window at the right end of the hallway. Another noise filled the air, but he didn't have time to register it before turning and shooting to the left. Jace ducked into one of the bedrooms to avoid the hit. That's when he realized the noise he had heard had been Darling's scream.

He turned his head back to the now fully broken window. Standing on the outside of the house—on what must have been the workshop walkway's roof—was his private investigator. She was bleeding across her chin and her hair was wild, but she didn't seem to be in any major physical distress. She watched him with wide eyes as he ran over to her. Had the bullet hit her?

"I'm okay," she answered his unasked question. "It scared me."

Oliver looked over his shoulder, expecting Jace to pop back out. He needed to get Darling out of the way. She must have been reading his mind again. She ducked to avoid a low-hanging shard of glass. Her hands were bound, so he helped guide her through the window until she was standing inside.

"Oliver!" she yelled before he could usher her to safety. He spun around, gun raised, but it was too late.

Oliver put his body in front of Darling's and felt an explosion of hot pain searing into his stomach. Only on reflex was he able to return fire. It put Jace back into the bedroom, giving Darling enough time to drag Oliver to the left.

"No, no, no," Darling chanted, putting her body under his arm to help him walk. The pain was excruciating. It took all he had not to fall to the floor. The bedroom was empty save for a dark oak bed frame in the middle. Darling guided him to the side farthest from the door. They all but fell to the ground next to it. "Oh, my God, Oliver."

He looked down at the bullet wound and winced at the sight. A bullet in the stomach wasn't good—though most bullets anywhere weren't—and he knew he was in a bad situation.

"You need to put pressure on it," she whispered. "I can't. My hands are tied."

Oliver put down the gun and reached into one of his pockets. The movement made him see stars.

"Lucky you," he said, pulling out his pocket knife. Darling turned and scooted toward him. He cut through the ties easily enough. As soon as her hands were free, she surprised him by taking off her jacket and putting it against his wound. He couldn't stop the yell of pain at the pressure.

"We need to get you help," she said, not apologizing.

"The police—" he said between his teeth "—will—will be here soon."

"You need them now."

Her voice shook as she said it. Oliver wanted to let her know everything was going to be okay, but the truth was, it wasn't. He looked down at his wound again.

He was losing too much blood, too fast.

He was going to pass out soon.

He dropped the knife and picked up the gun again. "There are ten shots left," he said, handing it to her. "Just pull the trigger if you see him."

If Jace thought Oliver was down for the count, he wouldn't hesitate in underestimating Darling and trying to finish her.

Oliver watched as a myriad of emotions crossed the woman's face.

"You shouldn't have jumped in front of me," she said, matching his tone.

"It's part of my job description."

"It's not," she whispered, "but thank you." Oliver didn't miss the red in her eyes. The pain in his stomach intensified. He was sure his own eyes were starting to tear, too. He reached out and took her free hand.

She was beautiful.

"I wanted to, Darling," he started, pausing once again to make sure he didn't hear Jace moving around. Maybe his bullet had also found its mark. Darling raised her eyebrow. He was happy to see she kept control of the gun in her right hand. She could defend herself if push came to shove.

"You wanted to what?" she asked.

"I wanted to run away with you," he continued. "When you asked me, there was nothing I wanted to do more, but—" Oliver sucked in a breath. Darling squeezed his hand.

"Don't."

The pain tripled from his wound. He couldn't hide it. Darling's face softened in acute concern. He needed to finally tell someone—finally tell *her*—the reason he had left the girl in the daisy dress all those years ago.

"I didn't want to hold you back," he whispered. "You would have given up everything for me, and I didn't want you to have to do that. I'm no good for you, Darling, but —" he took his hand from hers and placed it against her cheek "—I'm no good without you, either." His vision started to tunnel. He was on the cusp of unconsciousness. Before Darling could respond, Oliver let his hand drop. "Now focus. I can hear him coming."

Without much furniture in the house, Jace's attempt at stealth echoed off the walls and down to their room. Oliver half hoped he would leave them and make a run for it, but he knew the millionaire's son had too much to lose. In his mind, Oliver and Darling were the only two people who knew about his connection to Jean. Their deaths could ensure his continued freedom, especially since two men were already in custody for it. Although if Jace really stopped to think about it, he'd realize running was his best option.

However, he didn't.

DARLING FELT AS if she was having an out-of-body experience, watching the horrible scene unfold from somewhere else entirely. Jace was almost to the door—all caution apparently abandoned—and the life was visibly draining from Oliver. His revelation had touched a deep part of her, but it had also been terrifying. The bodyguard's breathing had shallowed. She knew he was giving it his all just to stay conscious.

Darling could feel the urge to distance herself and wait for the inevitable to happen. Wait for Jace to make it to them and finish the job while Oliver bled out. To give up and give in. She bit down hard on her lip. She didn't need to distance herself. Oliver needed her now.

She tightened her grip on the gun and took two deep breaths. Jace was nearly at the door.

"I love you, Oliver Quinn," she whispered.

And then she was up and shooting.

Chapter Twenty-Three

Darling was uncomfortable but trying her best not to show it. She was sitting in the hospital hallway with her foot propped in the chair next to her, waiting for Nurse Jones to come back out.

The older woman, along with the doctor on duty, hadn't seemed surprised when Oliver was rushed through the ER doors with Darling limping by his side hours earlier. The chief or Derrick must have given them a heads-up, which was fine by her. It had meant Oliver had gone into surgery almost immediately.

An ache had crossed her heart at seeing him go limp in the Slate House's bedroom. His state hadn't changed in the ambulance, either. There had been so much blood...

"I thought you might need this."

A woman with dark red hair, wearing a smart burgundy pantsuit, took the seat to Darling's left. She held out one of two coffee cups. Darling's eyelids fluttered closed for a moment. The coffee smelled like heaven.

"You must be Nikki," Darling responded once her coffee euphoria was over. The woman nodded and handed the second cup over. It warmed Darling's hands. "You came into town to fire Oliver."

Nikki let out a chuckle. "I've been warned you say

what's on your mind." She smiled. "I have to tell you, I like that in a person. But yes, that's why I came. I won't apologize for it, though. I have an obligation to protect all of my agents, even if it's from themselves from time to time."

Darling nodded. Oliver still hadn't told her what he'd done that was so bad when he was trying to find her, and she didn't care. He had saved her. Twice. She wasn't going to nitpick him about it.

"Which brings me to this point," Nikki continued, leveling her gaze with Darling's. Her expression softened as she spoke. "Thank you for protecting him when no one else could." It was an admission Darling hadn't expected. She bet it was a rare show of emotion for the founder of Orion. Especially with a stranger. "Starting Orion and trying to keep it afloat have left me little time to do much else. I have few friends, and Oliver is one of them. So, thank you."

It was Darling's turn to smile. "I don't know if I did the best job at protecting him. He did still get shot."

"Don't sell what you did short. You shot and then disarmed a man hell-bent on killing you both before the cops even got to you," Nikki pointed out. "If that's not protecting someone, then I don't know what is."

Darling replayed the moment after she had told Oliver she loved him. Jace had been right outside the door, and she hadn't taken any chances on him getting past it. Shooting through the wall, she had hit her target. She rushed him when she heard his gun clatter to the ground. Like Oliver, Jace had passed out from his injury. Unlike Oliver, Jace's wound hadn't been serious. He was currently handcuffed to a hospital bed on a different floor, surrounded by cops.

"I suppose I should listen to the owner of a bodyguard service," Darling said with a smile.

"You've got that right."

They lapsed into a mutual silence as they appreciated their coffees. Darling took the moment to marvel at the past week. It would be a while before Mulligan returned to normal. The gossip alone would carry them into the new year.

"You should let Oliver come back to Orion," Darling blurted after a minute had passed. "I can tell he really loves working there." She expected some kind of pushback, but Nikki kept smiling.

"I'm going to offer him his old job," she said. It made Darling happy and sad at the same time. She wanted to be greedy. She wanted to keep Oliver in Mulligan, to stay with him and live out the rest of their lives together. But she also wanted him to be happy. Orion was a big part of that. "However, I have a feeling he won't take it."

Darling raised her eyebrow. "Why wouldn't he?"

"Have you tasted this coffee?" Nikki shook her cup. "I wouldn't want to leave this place, either."

"The coffee is good but not *that* good."

"Something tells me Oliver feels differently." She paused, letting her double meaning sink in. Darling didn't want to smile, but she couldn't stop it. "On a completely unrelated note, since there is no issue with Nigel paying Orion for its services, we now have enough money to start expanding."

"That's great!" Darling was glad something good had come from everything that had happened.

"I'm thinking of creating a new analyst division. One that would cover finding and assessing threats, and building strategies for the more complicated cases. I wouldn't start it right away, but I do think creating a freelance position now would only help Orion in the long run. So whoever took the job could work from home. Wherever that might be." She winked at Darling. "It would only make sense that that someone would need to have a thorough knowledge of the group as well as an unwavering loyalty…"

"You know, I think I might know someone who fits that description," Darling said, already picturing a certain bodyguard wrapped up in winter clothes, grumpy at the Maine temperature. The thought warmed her heart. "But don't get your hopes up," she said more to herself than Nikki. "This person might be fine staying with his old job."

Nikki took a long pull from her coffee and smirked.

"I think we both know that isn't true."

"I CAN'T BELIEVE you crashed your rental."

Orion Zeta team lead Jonathan Carmichael, Oliver's closest friend, was shaking his head at Oliver. It had been a week since his surgery, and he was finally being okayed to leave the hospital. Oliver had been surprised when Jonathan had shown up instead of a certain private investigator to give him a ride. Though he wasn't going to question his friend. He knew the man had been worried.

They all had, including Oliver.

"I'm telling you, it wasn't my fault," he said. "There should be a clause in those contracts that says if a crazed idiot is trying to kill you by using a stolen car, then the rental place can't get mad at the renter."

Jonathan laughed and helped Oliver into the car. Although no long-lasting damage had been done by Jace's bullet, Oliver was still mighty sore.

"Nikki said the cops thought you had killed that idiot and left him on the side of the road," Jonathan said as he got behind the wheel.

Oliver smiled. It wasn't sweet.

"After what he had done to Darling, I would rather he rot in jail for years and years to come." George had been released two days before with a straight shot to jail. Jace Marks was right behind him. After Jace had awoken in the hospital, he had cracked under Chief Sanderson and Deputy Derrick's unrelenting questioning. Jace had admitted to murdering his half-sister as punishment for his father after convincing his old friend George to help. The two of them had tried to pin the murder on Nigel but hadn't expected the millionaire to have such a great alibi. Then, when Darling started to figure out Jean Watford's connection—which would have shown Jace had a great motive to kill her—they had panicked. George had jumped the gun and, instead of dropping Darling off next to Jean's car with evidence showing Nigel was lying, he had tried to kill her through exposure. It had just been a happy accident the private investigator had found the car. Another accident that ended up benefiting them was Jace's knowledge of CFO Lamar Bennington's and executive assistant Robert Jensen's drug addictions. Framing them was easy, especially when both businessmen were picked up under the influence of narcotics.

Now Jace and George were going away for a long, long time.

Nothing made Oliver happier.

Well, almost nothing.

"I still can't believe that girl of yours tackled a killer to keep him from getting to you *after* she shot him,"

Jonathan observed. "Sounds like you got a good partner in crime there."

"I can't complain," Oliver responded with a smile. Right before passing out in the Slate House, what he thought would be the last thing he ever heard had been Darling saying she loved him. He had been ready to die happy at those three little words.

However, now that he wasn't on his death bed, he was ready to make those words into something much more.

FOR THE FIRST time since Elizabeth had hired her, Darling had no trouble walking up to the front door of the Markses' Mulligan home. Since George was no longer on the payroll, and Grant and Thomas were still doing their Orion bodyguard duty until the end of the month, the front gate was left open, and the gatehouse was kept dark. All it took was one knock on the heavy front door and a smile to be welcomed inside the mansion.

"Which Marks invited you?" Thomas greeted her. He had met Darling while Oliver slept in the hospital. Both he and Grant had made sure to check that their former partner was okay.

"Elizabeth, but I'd like to talk to Nigel for a quick second if that's okay."

Thomas and Grant hadn't hidden their new respect and appreciation for Darling keeping their friend alive when she'd talked with them in the hospital. Thomas wasn't hiding it here, either. Without a question he led her to the second-floor office and through its open door.

"Sir, Darling Smith would like a moment," he said to the millionaire. His tone had gone almost stern, as if warning Nigel that declining her presence wasn't a good idea.

Nigel looked up from the papers on his desk and nodded. Darling bet the man hadn't slept well in days. Everything about him sagged. Only his eyes remained strong, no doubt holding the confidence he had garnered over a lifetime of experience.

"Thank you, Thomas," he said. The bodyguard left but didn't go far, standing on the other side of the open door. Darling wasn't afraid of any more attacks, but she was grateful for the watchful eye. "I'm sorry it's taken so long for us to meet, Ms. Smith. Life has been…" He ran his hand through his hair and let out a long sigh.

"I hadn't expected you to want to meet with me in the first place," she said honestly. From the brief phone conversation she had had with Elizabeth earlier that day, she knew the millionaire's wife had admitted to her husband that she had hired Darling to prove his infidelity. Beyond that, Darling didn't know where that left the couple. What was more, if Darling hadn't kept digging, his son wouldn't be in jail.

"I admit, at first I was angry, but then I realized it was at myself," he said, guilt ringing clear in his words. "I could list the things I should have done differently in my life, but there's no point now. My son killed my daughter, and the simple truth of it all is that it was because of me."

"When did you find out about Jean, if you don't mind my asking?"

"A year ago she approached me at a business convention in Miami. Her mother was a good friend of mine in college. Our paths crossed one night while she was on business. It was only a one-time thing, though I know that doesn't make it right—I was with Elizabeth—but I didn't see her again after that. She passed away a few years ago, and Jean decided to start looking for me. Her mother never told her who I was, and she certainly never told me who Jean was." His brow furrowed. "I would have been there for her growing up if she had." Darling had just met the man, but she felt in her heart he was telling the truth. Finding out he had a daughter had seemed to soften a big part of him. "When we met, I thought maybe she only wanted money, but the more time I spent with her, I realized she just wanted family."

"You tried to set her up with a job in Charisma?"

He nodded. "Her mother was sick for a while, and that drained almost all the money they had. Jean dropped out of school to take care of her but couldn't afford to go back. She was smart—very smart—and I told her that if she did well at her job, after a year the company would pay for her to get a degree. It was the only way she'd let me help. A lot of good it did in the end." Nigel averted his gaze, and Darling pretended not to notice his eyes rimmed with red. He was a strong man but, like everyone else, had a breaking point.

Darling cleared her throat. "I should go talk to Elizabeth now, but I wanted to stop by and give you this." She handed him the folder she had been carrying and stood. "I did a little more digging the past few days and found something that you should know about." Confused, Nigel held up the picture of a little girl that was attached to the file. "Her name is Isabella, she's five and I've been told she is a ball of energy." Darling smiled. "She's your granddaughter."

Nigel's mouth opened to say something but words never formed. He looked back at the picture of the red-haired girl.

"But Jean never said…"

"According to Jean's best friend—who is taking care

of Isabella right now—Jean was going to use this trip to tell you about her. She wanted to get to know you a bit before she included her. Just in case."

"She looks just like Jean," he whispered. Nigel's reddened eyes were now shining.

"I can't stand here and tell you that everything is going to be okay. That the little girl's existence is going to help make everything that has happened better," Darling said. "But maybe someday it will help."

Darling left Nigel with his new revelation without another word. There wasn't anything more to say.

LESS THAN AN hour later, Darling walked into Acuity in a much better mood. It only intensified when she saw Oliver lounging on the lobby's couch. She hadn't seen him since the night before, having visited him every day since he had been admitted. Though they had talked, neither had brought up the topic of their future.

"Well, don't you look better," Darling said as she sat down next to him. "I'm sorry I wasn't the one to pick you up, but Jonathan insisted he could handle you."

Oliver laughed. "That's funny, because he insisted that I couldn't handle you," he said. "He told me any woman with that much fire would just burn me up."

Darling smirked. "That doesn't sound too unpleasant, if you ask me."

Oliver's eyes widened. His smile grew.

"So, how did your meeting with Elizabeth go?" he asked, slightly defusing an escalating moment. A part of her didn't want to answer. Telling him about the last interaction she'd had with Elizabeth in a professional capacity, officially ending her case with the woman, cut the last thread that had in some way attached them while

Oliver was in Mulligan. She wouldn't need his help any-more. There would be no shoptalk left to hide behind to avoid talking about their future.

"Surprisingly well," she said almost reluctantly. "She started by telling me she didn't blame me for what happened to Jace. She understood he needed to be punished for what he'd done. Though you could tell she was hurt by it all. Who wouldn't be? She also paid me because, in the end, I proved that Nigel had an affair *and* I discovered the identity of Jane Doe." Darling left out the part where she had refused Elizabeth's money the first two times it had been offered.

"Is she going to file for divorce?"

Darling shrugged. "She wasn't too clear about that, and I certainly didn't push it. If she does decide to do it, I don't think it'll be for a while. They have a lot to talk about." Elizabeth had been upset—obviously—at what had happened but, as with her husband, there was strength holding her up. Darling was confident that no matter what happened in the future, Elizabeth Marks would be fine.

"So, it's all done, then?"

Darling didn't want to, but she nodded. Fear that she had misjudged their reconnection filled her. But it was only fear that he didn't feel the same.

Darling knew without a doubt that she loved Oliver. She hadn't *stopped* loving him, no matter how many years had gone by.

"Well, I guess it's time to get to work, then." He got up from the couch and walked to the lobby's lone desk.

Darling looked on, confused. "Work?"

Oliver grinned. "You're looking at Orion's first free-lance strategy-and-threat analyst," he paused. "Well, I don't know if that's my official title, and technically it won't be live for a few weeks, but I figured I'd go ahead and check out the available office." He made a show of inspecting the desk.

Darling's heart filled with happiness.

"You're staying?" She stood, unable to contain the mounting joy.

Oliver's grin widened.

"Why would I leave?" He closed the space between them. Taking her chin in his hand, he tilted her head up so their eyes met. "Unless that's a problem."

"Not on my end," she whispered.

"Good, because there's nowhere else I'd rather be than by your side."

Before Oliver had a chance to say any more, Darling pressed her lips against his.

In that one moment, all of the pain from their past turned into beautiful hope for their future.

* * * * *

LET'S TALK
Romance

For exclusive extracts, competitions
and special offers, find us online:

MILLS & BOON

THE HEART OF ROMANCE

A ROMANCE FOR EVERY READER

MODERN

Prepare to be swept off your feet by sophisticated, sexy and seductive heroes, in some of the world's most glamourous and romantic locations, where power and passion collide.

HISTORICAL

Escape with historical heroes from time gone by. Whether your passion is for wicked Regency Rakes, muscled Vikings or rugged Highlanders, awaken the romance of the past.

MEDICAL

Set your pulse racing with dedicated, delectable doctors in the high-pressure world of medicine, where emotions run high and passion, comfort and love are the best medicine.

True Love

Celebrate true love with tender stories of heartfelt romance, from the rush of falling in love to the joy a new baby can bring, and a focus on the emotional heart of a relationship.

Desire

Indulge in secrets and scandal, intense drama and plenty of sizzling hot action with powerful and passionate heroes who have it all: wealth, status, good looks…everything but the right woman.

HEROES

Experience all the excitement of a gripping thriller, with an intense romance at its heart. Resourceful, true-to-life women and strong, fearless men face danger and desire - a killer combination!

To see which titles are coming soon, please visit

millsandboon.co.uk/nextmonth

MILLS & BOON
True Love
Romance from the Heart

Celebrate true love with tender stories of heartfelt romance, from the rush of falling in love to the joy a new baby can bring, and a focus on the emotional heart of a relationship.